"ARE YOU ALIVE?"

They clung beneath the wind and the lightning, against the battering of dead leaves.

She kissed him again, gently, and when she laid her head tenderly on his chest, he realized she was singing, very quietly, as the wind brought the first rain. Then a connection was made, and he remembered Lilla's night songs . . .

"Are you alive?" she whispered.

There was more than nightcold working down his back. He pushed her away, but she held onto his arms as he tried to pry loose her grasp.

She smiled, and in a sudden blue-white flare he saw her eyes, the death there, and would not believe it. Nor could he believe the power in her hands . . .

Books by Charles L. Grant

The Nestling
Night Songs

Published by POCKET BOOKS

CHARLES L. GRANT

NIGHT SONGS

PUBLISHED BY POCKET BOOKS NEW YORK

Another *Original* publication of POCKET BOOKS

POCKET BOOKS, a division of Simon & Schuster, Inc.
1230 Avenue of the Americas, New York, N.Y. 10020

Copyright © 1984 by Charles L. Grant
Cover Artwork Copyright © 1984 by Rowena Morrill

ISBN: 0-671-45249-5

First Pocket Books printing June, 1984

10 9 8 7 6 5 4 3 2 1

POCKET and colophon are registered trademarks
of Simon & Schuster, Inc.

Printed in the U.S.A.

For Kathy—who knows the words to the songs,
sees the dark in the full moon,
and listens to midnight no matter the tune

PROLOGUE

December: After

Dawn.

Silent.

The narrow country road had a wet, ebony sheen, giving it depth, like water under ice, unmoving and cold. It was worn, in small patches, to the graveled bed beneath, and was shouldered by a faintly orange mixture of earth, sand, and smooth round pebbles. Shallow drainage ditches flanked it, seeming higher than the road because of brittle brown weeds that rose above the surface like clusters of huddled old men waiting to be toppled.

On both sides was a state-preserved woodland— stunted cedars and homely scrub pines, bare-limbed oaks with thick rough boles gone gray as the weather, an occasional red maple, ghostly white birches solitary and in cages. The ground was littered in tan and sable, dead leaves and dead needles thoroughly sodden from two days' rain, more mud than mulch and unruffled by the wind. Red-thorn thickets wound darkly through the gloom. Nests in high branches sat deserted and bedraggled.

The rising wind passed from a hissing to a keening, a transformation more a warning than a pause as the rain stopped and the puddles shivered and the temperature accelerated to a sharp, downward plunge.

By noon, icicle buds glinted from power lines and twigs. The road was sheathed. The cloud cover grew sharp edges that turned black and shifted.

A car, its copper-colored hood and white vinyl roof streaked with weeks of dust-turned-mud, the whitewalls scraped nearly to black, made its way down the road. The left taillight was shattered, exposing a tiny bulb.

The driver wore a tan overcoat a half size too large, giving added breadth to his shoulders, added weight to his chest. The buttons were undone, and beneath was a heavy rust sweater and a faded pair of jeans. His feet were snug in blunt-toed boots into which the jeans had been tucked, boots that rose blackly to the middle of his calves. His face was in shadow, but the green of his eyes paid no heed to the darkness.

Four miles from the nearest town he stopped, gripping the wheel tightly. Across the road was a barrier, sawhorses in orange and white stripes with amber reflecting glass strung along the top. A large sign in the center warned of a dead end. He sat for several minutes, listening to the car's heater, watching the branches tremble against the wind pushing in from the sea six miles away. He wiped his palms over his chest. He glanced in the rearview mirror and felt suddenly, unpleasantly, wearily alone.

The thing to do, he thought, was to turn around and head back. He could tell the others he didn't want to risk the law's anger again. They wouldn't believe him, but they'd listen and accept; they had permitted themselves no other choice, and were too frightened to argue.

He inhaled sharply and gnawed his lower lip.

Two months before, they had scattered. Less than two weeks ago they'd returned, one by one, finding Colin where they'd left him—in a motel room overlooking the Garden State Parkway. He'd greeted them

4

somberly, his pleasure at seeing them tempered by the demons that had driven them away . . . that had lured them back. As he had been lured when he learned he could not run.

So they hugged and they kissed, and finally he decided he would have to go back. Just once. Just to see.

He'd driven into Flocks before and tried to rent a boat. But the excuses were the same: too late, too choppy, all the boats in dry dock. Sensible enough, but he hadn't believed it. They'd looked at him—sideways, suspicious—and asked him about the reasons for his visit.

Then he had tried the police, but they informed him the road was closed, and no permits were being issued to wander the state land. Besides, they added, the island was unhealthy.

He avoided Flocks after that, using the back roads until he reached the forest. Once a day, every day. But this, he promised himself, was going to be the last time. Today he had decided there was no sense reliving a nightmare, once you were convinced it was only a bad dream. It had to be that way, or he'd drive himself insane.

His hand dropped to the door latch and lifted. The cold swept in, negating the heater's work, and he climbed out quickly, his hands deep in his pockets until he reached the barrier and shifted the near section to give the car room. Once on the other side, he reset the roadblock and began driving again.

The road changed, covered now with wet leaves grown crisp from the cold, sounding like thin broken glass when the tires passed over them, whispering like sighs. The stones, pebbles, and ribbons of mud reminded him oddly of aerial maps of rivers.

The car didn't move much faster than a walk.

He coughed, and realized it was much too quiet. He switched on the radio to a Philadelphia station, and grimaced at the tinny music that broke from the speakers—an upbeat version of an English Christmas carol, though the holiday itself was already four days in its grave.

The trees no longer closed to form a close horizon. They had parted like gates at some unheard command, and the slate of the clouds merged with the ocean.

For the second time he stopped and cut the ignition. The engine sputtered, raced, sputtered again and died. He shuddered at a surge of bile in his stomach, swallowed hard and closed his eyes tightly until the burning passed. A sniff, and he cleared his throat. A cough as he told himself to stop his damned stalling. Then he reached for the scuffed tan binoculars' case on the seat beside him and looped the strap over his shoulder.

The key case he left on the dashboard.

He could think of nothing else to do.

He stepped into the cold.

The wind slapped at him in desultory gusts, making him squint and hunch his shoulders, driving the pale brown hair away from his widow's peak. He checked the road behind him to be sure he hadn't been followed, then fastened the coat's top button and pulled up the high collar. With a nervous reassuring pat to the car's copper fender he walked toward the sea to the beat of his footsteps, the race of his heart.

And now that he had arrived, all nervousness ended. There was left only a compelling curiosity—bird for a snake—and the first realization that finally there was hope.

He walked slowly, capturing the scent of the sea air's bite, thinking how much he had once loved it and had pitied the poor inlanders because they never knew it except when the wind shifted strongly. A scent. And more. A promise. Of space, of power, of adventure, of dreams. A peaceable confrontation between the wistful and unconquered.

As he walked, the sea spoke to him in a language no man has ever understood well enough to set into words.

He felt almost joyful, almost serene.

6

And finally the road ended its uncurving drive, sliding into a gentle slope that dropped below the level of the forest floor. At the bottom was a wide apron of tire-crushed gravel, out of which extended an equally wide pier anchored in place by fat concrete pilings. To the left was a small shed, its door canted open on one rusted hinge, the windows on either side smashed inward and gaping. A dead gull lay muddied on a curl of roping. A pair of oars was propped against the leeward wall, fan tips jammed under the tin-roof eaves. A sign had been bolted to what looked like a harpoon half buried in the ground. In pale blue lettering was a single word: *Ferry*. There was no price mentioned; Colin knew it was one dollar.

He stood calmly at the top of the slope, pulling on leather-palmed, black woolen gloves. He did not look at the dock yet or at the water, much darker than the sky lowering above it. The waves, because of the bottom's configuration and the obstacles farther out, were low and unbroken save for occasional whitecaps raised by the wind. It was more a bay here than an ocean, a masque for the horizon. When he was ready, he looked steadily across the two miles of open water.

To the island.

To Haven's End.

Then he fumbled with the clasp of the binoculars' case, pulled out the instrument, and with a deep breath heedless of the damp and knifing cold, placed it to his eyes.

Focusing each lens in turn, he saw trees virtually the same as those at his back, a narrow break for the road at the other end of the ferry line, and the trees once again, thicker and shadowed as they climbed the sloping island to the cliffs at the southern tip. A quick scan from one end of the four-mile island to the other and he lowered his arms. Nodded once to himself. Looked up to the sky and decided there were three hours of decent daylight remaining for his vigil. In a move more characteristic than the lines on his face, he tucked his chin toward his neck and considered: three hours, perhaps less. It would be sufficient. Since the day before Christmas it had always been sufficient. And each time he returned, he was slightly more confident, slightly more calmed. Tonight he would signal his gathering strength by turning off the light and sleeping in the dark. The dreams might not vanish, but they would be fought, not just endured.

Three short hours . . . across two miles of water.

He lifted the binoculars back to his eyes and began the slow searching.

Suddenly he caught his breath, blinked and staggered backward several paces. He nearly bolted for the car before realizing that the movement he had seen had not been on the island, the racing streak had not been someone running.

It was snowing.

Snowing: large, wet, spiraling flakes.

Marvelous, he thought with a self-mocking laugh. The Great White Hunter has to squat in a snowstorm.

From his right-hand pocket he yanked a gaudy yellow wool cap to pull down over his ears, over his forehead to his eyebrows.

Slowly, testing the road for snares of unseen ice, he moved down the slope to the landing dock, and sat on an overturned nail keg he'd taken from the shed when the watching had first begun. The water slapped at the pilings. Freakishly, the wind soared over his head, barely touching him. He patted a hand across his chest to be sure his cigarettes were there, drew back his feet to grip the keg's sides, and made his first check: a glance at the water beyond the edge of the dock, to the thin poles that rose there above the agitated surface, outlining a rectangle. There were eight, and the rope threaded through the iron eyes at the top of each, binding them together, was thick with new ice. He strained, and thought he could see the remains of the ferry now settled at the bottom. Charred and splintered and crumbling in the sand.

He nodded, pleased.

Then, with a sigh, he lifted the binoculars again.

Watching.
for the blood
For shapes in the water, for shapes on land.
for the blood
He was certain there were none.
for all that goddamned blood
But he had to be sure.

PART ONE

October: Thursday

ONE

The seashell hummed low over the beach. Indistinguishable from its shadow it blurred through the amber-cast air before lifting abruptly into a graceful sweeping arc. Like a glittering pearl shield it seemed to pause over the jumbled ramparts of a sprawling sand castle, then flipped, fell, and landed on its back. Spinning. Slowing only when nudged by a fan of winking foam.

"Wow!" said Matt Fletcher softly, his large eyes blinking rapidly in disbelief. "Wow, how'd you do that, Mr. Ross?"

Colin held up his right hand, turned it over, turned it back. The hell with physics, he thought; that throw was pure magic.

"C'mon, Mr. Ross, how'd you do it? It's a trick, right? Can you show me? Can you show me how to do it?"

Colin glanced at the young boy beside him, at the elaborate castle, at the shell now corralled by an incoming wave. He raised a thin eyebrow in a parody of nonchalance. "Well, it's all in the wrist, actually. And in eyeballing the fine line of the intended trajectory, testing the prevailing winds, watching your—"

Matt giggled into a palm.

"Mr. Fletcher, I detect doubt in your attitude."

13

"You were lucky," the boy accused.

Colin shrugged again. "So there's a law against lucky?"

"My mother says luck ain't nothing but dumb skill."

"Even assuming you knew what she meant, don't say ain't."

Matt sighed loudly in melodramatic exasperation and shoved a hand slowly through his tangled black hair. "There's no school today," he muttered. "Besides, you teach art, not English."

Colin grunted a quick laugh and jammed his hands into the pockets of his hooded blue windbreaker. The inescapable and definitely refutable logic of a kid out of school, he thought, and no safe way out except to ignore it.

"Luck," the boy repeated as he sidled away. "It was luck, that's all." He grinned mischievously, ready to run.

The laugh broke this time, and Colin shook his head in confession. "I could never do that again in a zillion years."

They stood a dozen yards from the castle, the only interruption along the dark wet apron of the two-mile beach. In swimtrunks and sneakers, light jackets and dried sand, they listened as the tide prepared to turn over. The breeze off the diamond-backed water was cool, but they gave it no credence. It was Indian summer and the sky was nearly cobalt, the beach close to bronze, the few gulls overhead like lazy kites above a park. Soft air, softer light, while at the tips of the dark, slick jetties that flanked the public beach—and quartered it as well—the seaspray fanned wider, lasted longer, flared through with gold as the ocean found its thunder.

It was time to leave, but Colin shifted only slightly, his green eyes squinting comfortably, broad shoulders at ease. His thinning brown hair, still streaked by summer's sun, was just long enough to curl inward at the edges, and stirred as the breeze moved to brush across his cheek. His forehead was high, his nose a

14

measure too large, and his chin not quite squared at the end of a lean jaw. He pulled thoughtfully for a moment at the side of his neck, turned his wrist just far enough to see the face of his watch.

Damn; it had already been a long day, and it would probably get longer. He wished with passing guilt he could stay until tomorrow.

He'd come to the beach shortly after lunch, hoping for solitude and finding instead a half dozen boys working on the castle. As soon as he'd stepped from the woodland separating shore from town he was spotted, and the ensuing invitation to join them was boisterous and laughing. It felt wonderful. Their teacher in school, yet no ogre to be avoided after the last bell had rung. And the two hours had fled in less than an eyeblink before the others had wandered off in search of adventure, leaving him behind to share the castle's finishing touches with Matt, and test all the snacks Peg Fletcher had prepared for the occasion.

He glanced at the small wicker hamper, and his stomach instantly contracted. A beautiful woman Matt's mother was, but cooking was something she should leave to the elves. And if he wasn't going to embarrass himself at the funeral tonight, he'd best stop at the Inn for a giant sandwich or two.

"We gonna leave it?" Matt asked. He was tow-headed and thin, with skin a natural shade darker than most of the others on the island. With a shirt on he looked frail, but without it one could see the young muscles filling into cords. "Maybe I'll build a wall in front. You know, to keep the waves off?" He hugged himself and zipped his jacket halfway closed.

"Better yet," Colin said, "you ought to head on home. Your mother'll have a cat fit if you miss supper tonight."

Matt kicked at the sand. "Oh, she won't care." He looked up defiantly. "I'll be ten at Christmas, y'know. I can take care of myself."

Colin coughed and looked to the sky. "I'm sure you can, pal, but you know mothers."

15

"I said she wouldn't care."

"Really? Are we talking about the same woman here?"

"Sure we are."

"You mean the woman who runs that tacky little drug store on Neptune Avenue? The woman who says I draw like John Nagy? The—"

"Who's John Nagy?"

"Never mind. You're too young." He turned the boy back toward the hamper with a slap to his buttocks. "And the very same woman who single-handedly, as it were, arm wrestled Ed Raines at the Inn and beat him three falls out of four? That woman?" His voice rose as he walked. "Are we talking about the lady who condescends to feed starving teachers now and then? The woman who—"

"What does condescend mean?"

Colin put his hands on his hips. "Matthew, will you please stop changing the subject?"

"Well, jeez, I just wanted to know. Mom's always telling me to ask if I want to know something. So I'm asking." He scowled and shoved his fingers under his waistband. "Gee. Nuts. Goddamn."

"Matthew," he cautioned, "watch your mouth. I've seen your mother turn into a raving, bananas monster when she hears you talk like that."

Matt looked up at him, wide-eyed and innocent. "Mr. Ross, are we talking about the same woman here?"

At irregular intervals through the woods, narrow, gray-planked boardwalks had been laid to guide swimmers to the beach. After snatching up the hamper, Matt jumped to the nearest pathway and began walking briskly, almost marching, whistling at the birds hidden high in the thick autumn foliage. Colin trailed more slowly, taking an extra-deep breath every few paces to see if he could capture a scent of the pastel air—the lazy slants of sunlight touched through with bronze and gold, the shadows more crimson than black, the underbrush still clinging to blotches of stubborn green. For the few minutes the walk would last he could easily still be back in New England, yet the muted grumbling of the surf behind him never let him forget he was riding the ocean on the back of a rock.

A flash of red on the ground.

He swerved toward it, stepping off the boardwalk to the base of a stunted pine. He took a deep breath, then expelled it with a soft grunt as he kicked loose dirt and leaves over what he had seen. When he returned to the boardwalk, Matt was staring with a frown. "A beer can," he said, waving the boy on.

Matt was clearly doubtful, but he made no move to argue. Colin shoved his hands into his pockets to ward off a chill.

He had found a gull, wings and legs torn from their sockets, feathers matted with grime and dried blood, its head eyeless and crawling with busy ants and silent flies. He had found two others like it over the past week, all in the woodland facing the ocean. Still more, a dozen in all, had been discovered on other parts of the island. Street-corner conversation lay the blame on dogs; night whispers said it had to be Gran D'Grou.

Colin had no answers of his own. If it had been dogs, the mutilations were all the more vicious because none of the birds had been even partially eaten. And he didn't believe a dead man would return to stalk the island just to wring the necks of a few raucous birds.

"You going to the funeral?" Matt asked without looking back.

He shuddered once to banish the gull's image. "Yup."

"We're not," Matt said as if he regretted it and at the same time wasn't sure it was safe to be relieved.

"I know."

Matt shrugged, and tilted his head. "Mrs. Wooster is with her sister in Philadelphia. She's sick or something. She won't be back until Tuesday. She's not really my babysitter, y'know. She's the housekeeper. I'm too big for a babysitter."

"Right," Colin said quickly, laughing silently without showing a smile.

"Mrs. Wooster," the boy said a shade louder, "she thinks it's silly anyway. She says people oughta be buried in the ground, not in the water."

"She isn't island, Matt. She thinks we're strange."

"She eats pits. Peach pits and plum pits and orange pits." He giggled. "That's weirder than burying people in the water."

Colin admitted the boy might be right, though it was easy to understand the housekeeper's attitude. There were no provisions for the dead on Haven's End. The nearest town was ten miles inland and had the only cemetery within easy driving distance. None of the island locals bothered to use it. They had lived here for too long, for too many generations, and those who'd first settled here during the Revolution had chosen the Atlantic to be their graveyard. It was illegal, but even those who'd left for the rumored excitement of the mainland were able to find a certain indefinable comfort in the slow trail of boats that would slip through the twilight, form a tight ring from bow to stern, raise high the torches, and break into a deep-throated jubilant hymn as the enshrouded corpse was eased into the current. There were rumors, of course, among the busybodies who sat in the park in Flocks: that the island's inhabitants were obviously immortal since none of them seemed to take sick and die; that rites of foul cannabalism and satanism were performed during the hours of the darkest full moon; that vampirism flourished; that they were nothing more than a colony of ghouls.

Haven's End didn't care. The balm for its grief was stronger than gossip.

Matt paused to shift the hamper from right hand to left, and hitched mightily at his trunks to keep them

18

high on his hips. Then he looked up into the trees, off to one side, a quick check to be sure Colin was still there.

"Pits. Ugh."

Colin smiled.

"Did . . . did you know Gran D'Grou?"

"Sure did. He was one of the first people I met when I came here." A short laugh for the memory. "He said I didn't draw so hot but I had good hands."

"Did you like him?"

He frowned and pulled thoughtfully at a vagrant curl tucked around the back of his left ear. Gran was a black pipe cleaner twisted into the vague shape of a man, with an afterthought lump of black clay for a head—eyes gouged, mouth gouged, cheeks thumbed in, and a surprisingly aquiline nose. Only the old man's hands seemed carefully planned, long-fingered and dexterous, more expressive than his eyes. When he spoke, he whispered as if from the back of a sea cave, and when he wasn't working at the family luncheonette, when he wasn't doing his carving on the bench out front and laughing with the children, he was walking the cliffs and the woods with dark rum snug around him.

But had Colin liked him?

Gran, as more than one person had been eager to tell him, had arrived penniless and frightened from the West Indies with his infant daughter, saying little except to let them all know he was determined to take advantage of what he called America's vast pot of gold. He wasted no time establishing the luncheonette. He charmed the ladies with his French-Caribbean accent, and fascinated the men with stories of the islands he had visited as a young man. In time, his daughter found a husband who had no objection to taking Gran's name; in time, there was a granddaughter who worshipped the old man and became his constant shadow.

And in time Gran knew he would never be rich.

Why he had believed money would fall into his

19

hands no one knew; why he refused to visit the mainland was a mystery as well. But he did, and he did, and eventually he turned to drinking, to the children, and to his carving.

In time his younger self was totally forgotten.

It was tought that Warren Harcourt had tried to get Gran to bring back his dead wife, that it was Gran who had murdered a beachcomber eight years ago as a sacrifice to his gods. A lot of things were thought about the shriveled old man, but in the full light of the sun Colin knew most people felt foolish about these ideas.

"Well?" Matt said.

He blinked and scratched at his chest. "I guess so. He was a hard man to know."

"Well, I think he was spooky." Matt sniffed and wiped a hasty sleeve under his nose. "Y'know, just before he got sick like that he used to stand outside the school and watch the kids come out."

Colin frowned. "He did?"

"Sure! I thought sometimes he wanted to take me to his shack on the beach and cook me or something." He shuddered and scratched his head. "Y'know, he told me last summer I was his favorite because I never laughed at him." A pause for confession. "I never laughed at him because I thought he was spooky and would cook me or something. I mean, he was okay and we had a good time, but he got spooky, y'know? Like those statues he made."

Nearly every family on the island had at least one of Gran's carvings, the school a large collection, and Colin a half dozen. They were fashioned from driftwood and fallen boughs, graceful and disturbing renditions of what Gran called his island dreams. From the Caribbean, not Haven's End. But that's all he would ever say. Several times over the years, Colin had attempted to discover if the carvings represented gods or real people, and the old man told him they were only notions, nothing more.

One day he had shown up at the studio behind Colin's cottage, boldly walking in as if on standing invitation, placing something he called *The Screaming Woman* on the workbench. Colin had been finishing an oil of the fishing fleet as it struggled back to the marina—a difficult piece because the only heroism or romance he wanted was in the faces of the men working the nets. He'd not relished the intrusion, but Gran had never cared; when he was sober he moved about the small island as if it belonged to him, and the people—year-round or seasonal—his loyal, loving subjects. Most called him good-natured because of his time spent with the children, and blithely excused the sometimes haughty attitude he displayed. But Colin and a few others detected behind the crooked, yellow-toothed smile a rippling of disdain whenever he laughed with anyone other than the kids. A suspicion never proved, however, and for that all the more disturbing.

He had examined the offering impatiently (feeling guilty for the impatience), and when he complained that he didn't really much care for wood sculptures of obscure monsters, the old man's hands had almost curved into fists, straightened as he took a deep breath and touched the smooth wood with the tip of one finger.

"See?" Gran had said, eyes squinting, head bobbing. "This not be snake here, it is tail. She is sea woman. Eye cut out? No, no, Colin, it is shadow. You put a light here, the eye come back. You want a big monster, you stick it in the closet; you want a beautiful woman, put it on the television." A laugh like a crackle. "Jesus damn, Colin, you got no imagination."

Colin had apologized, Gran had accepted with a shaking of hands, and left as he always did—without bothering to look at or comment on Colin's latest work.

"Mr. Ross?"

He waited.

"When Gran's gone, do you think Lilla will stop her singing?"

"I don't know," he said. "I would imagine so."

21

"She didn't used to be that way, y'know. She was really neat. She used to give me extra scoops on my cones and stuff. She called me Little Matt, but that was okay because she was fun. But she really got spooky, y'know? Just like Gran."

Colin felt he should say something in Lilla's defense, but the boy was right. When her grandfather fell ill at summer's end, Lilla had begun a withdrawal so gradual no one had noticed until it was too late to reach her. Her eyes dulled, her tongue fell silent, she moved very much as if she were walking in her sleep. Yet there were occasional days when the old Lilla was back without warning—laughing, smiling, walking down the street with the verve of an eighteen-year-old out to conquer the world.

The old Lilla, as she crept into adolescence, took Peg as a friend, since her own mother was reluctant to talk of things beyond the store. Peg loved her as a daughter, tried to show her what she could, and teach her the difference between listening to an adult and experiencing things herself.

And when she was sixteen she latched onto Colin. He knew it was a crush because Peg laughingly told him so, knew he had to be careful because Lilla wanted to know the man's side of men. She would find him walking on the beach, join him, ask him how to deal with the boys she thought were flirting. When he told her to ask Peg, she only laughed and grabbed his hand, dropped it with a giggle and made him feel like blushing.

Despite the potential problem, however, he was taken by her energy, her wit, by the way she took each day as if it were created just for her. So he walked with her, and talked, and when Gran began souring, Colin comforted her whenever Peg could not.

Like the day on the beach when she wept because Gran had started ranting about the whites, how they conspired to steal his work and cheat him of his money. He was old, Colin told her, and the dreams he'd brought with him simply hadn't happened, and when she wept ever harder he slipped an arm around her shoulder and held her. For ten minutes they stood there, until Peg stepped out from among the trees and saw them, and left.

Lilla, lovely, and bright, and little different from any other child who faced growing up.

But then she was . . . gone.

And now the nights were filled with the sound of her singing; words no one could catch, words almost like chanting, all over the island as she followed the shoreline. Each night. Every night. As though erecting a barrier against death with her singing.

Grieving before the dying was the excuse people gave her, and the excuse they gave themselves for wishing Gran quickly buried. With him at last under the water, Lilla once again would be the young woman they loved.

Suddenly, Matt dropped the hamper and began rumaging through it furiously. "Nuts, the shovel! Aw, Mom's gonna *kill* me if I forget it again."

The plea was almost comical in the puppylike look the boy gave him, and Colin granted him a knowing lift of his eyebrow. "All right, you wait right here. I'll be back in a minute."

"You sure it's okay?"

"I'm sure," he said, with a surge of affection that startled him to blinking. "Yeah, it's okay. I won't be long."

He trotted along the boardwalk until he reached the beach, muttering an abrupt oath under his breath when he saw a man by the castle, hands clasped before him as if he were praying. He was tall and heavyset, most of his weight settled in a paunch; he was clean-shaven, with a classic lantern jaw and leonine sweep of white hair, and his eyes were so bloodshot they seemed almost red. He wore a charcoal-gray suit, matching light topcoat and felt hat, and in one hand he held a pair of gleaming black shoes.

"A magnificent edifice here, Colin," he said in a slightly quavering voice.

Colin circled the castle and its moat, frowning until he remembered Matt's threat to bury the shovel in the walls. He knelt with a weary sigh, averting his face when he smelled the lawyer's stale, liquored breath.

"A palace, yes?" said Warren Harcourt.

"A castle, as a matter of fact." His hands plunged.

"Ah. Yes, A castle."

Damn, he thought; where the hell is it? "Some of my students did it. Half day today. I sort of helped out. You know how it is."

"Indeed." Harcourt swiveled ponderously to face south, toward the faint line of the last jetty and the private beach that lay beyond, stretching to the cliffs. "I imagine you'll be at the funeral this evening." A languid, dismissing wave; no need to reply. "I have not been invited. I was not Gran's attorney of record, of course, but I did do some small work for the child's parents before they passed on. He, the old man, never wanted me. There was one, small matter"—a careful belch—"but I didn't go through with it, actually." He frowned nervously. "I don't think Lilla likes me very much."

Colin stifled an obscenity when his palm caught the blade's jagged edge. He yanked the toy shovel free, noting as he did that the man wore no socks.

"Never did like me," the lawyer repeated, and he placed a manicured hand at his waist to cushion another belch. Then he pulled a scarlet handkerchief from his jacket pocket and blew his nose loudly. A deft flick of his wrist and the handkerchief was gone. An eyebrow arched. "I note that you and Peg Fletcher are seeing quite a lot of each other lately. A stunning woman. Stunning and smart."

Colin couldn't help a smile. "Now how the hell do you know that, Warren?"

"I perambulate, Colin, I perambulate." A palm smoothed his waistcoat meticulously. "I may be a drunk, but I'm not blind. Ah, the stories I could tell you. . . ."

Colin believed it. Harcourt was everywhere, but no

one thought him a snoop. Four years ago he and his estranged wife were returning from a mainland party. Both had been drinking, though neither was completely drunk. According to Warren, there was an argument, and his eyes left the road. Too late he discovered his car plunging down the ramp toward the ferry's dock—and the ferry was on the other side. Harcourt survived; his wife did not. And he had confessed one evening when he was very nearly sober that it wasn't guilt at her dying that kept liquor his company; it was guilt that he didn't miss her as much as he thought he should.

So he drank, and wandered, and once a year told Colin he could bring the woman back if only he had the nerve.

A gull shrieked, and Harcourt looked up, startled. "Damned things. Damned . . . things." Suddenly he seemed deflated. "Lilla is an odd child, actually," he said, sniffing, hiccuping. "Not like she used to be, not at all. I do like her singing, though. I gather it's grated on some people's nerves, but I rather like it." He turned his head, his eyes hidden by the hat's sagging brim. "If you should find an opportunity at the ceremonies, please tell her I enjoy her singing."

Colin could think of nothing else to do but nod; Warren was gone, the drunk had returned. Then: "Hey, look, I got poor Matt waiting for me back there. See you around, okay? Take care."

He trotted off without waiting for a response, stopping only once, at the foot of the boardwalk. The lawyer was already strolling down the beach, oblivious to the waves soaking his trousers. At one point he turned, held his shoes close to his eyes and stared at them. He shrugged vaguely before lowering them and moved on, topcoat flapping about his shins, hat trembling in the sea breeze riding in with the tide.

Colin shook his head slowly with a faint, sad smile, then remembered the mutilated gull, and spun around and raced back to Matt.

*   *   *

They came out of the trees onto a small blacktop parking lot sandwiched between the extended log cabin of the Anchor Inn and a battered deserted cottage. Matt headed directly for the street; Colin, however, slowed as he was struck by an unbidden memory of his first visit to Haven's End:

Had he arrived by air he knew he would have seen a heavily forested island four miles long and slightly less than half that wide, rocks and trees on the west and north shores, beautiful sand on the east, a clearing just off center where the town had been settled.

But he had driven, and came out of the mainland woods to the Sterling Brothers Ferry, a pair of huge, high-floating boats like ungainly rafts that carried eight to ten cars and as many passengers as could be squeezed between them. No overhead canopy, a tiny shingled cabin jutting out amidships. The surprisingly smooth ride across the two miles of deep, choppy water to the terminus at Bridge Road, the slow drive for three-quarters of a mile before the trees fell away on the left for the Sunset Motel. Another quarter mile and suddenly there were sidestreets, four of them until Bridge Road met the T-intersection with Neptune Avenue.

He remembered grinning his relief at the sight of the town: clapboards and cedar shakes, Colonials and Federals, all riding high on thick brown pilings or five-foot foundations designed to provide passage for the sea whenever it rose above the tide and tried to sweep the island clean. Thriving lawns and lovely trees. The trees. Save for the town and the beaches, the entire island was tree covered, right up to the point where the cave-pocked southshore cliffs heaved out of the sea.

The sea.

Wherever he turned, the mark of the sea. Air salt-sharp and softly damp, the ground round-pebbled and sandy; the fishermen who made the island famous and kept it from starving when the tourist trade faltered; the motifs of the motels, the Anchor Inn, the Clipper

26

Run; the ghosts of smugglers and gunrunners who'd used it during the previous century; the whispers of pirates who might have used it before; the occasional gold coin, a rusted cannon, a hint of bones found in a cave . . . and the ocean itself, its voice louder at night when a lullaby was needed, muted in daylight when there was living to be done. There was power in that gentle land, power that reminded when the winter storms screamed, cutting off the ferry and eroding the beaches. A power, he thought, that kept the people strong. They fed off it, lived off it, never forgot what it warned might happen if they ever grew careless.

It was perfect. Exactly what he had in mind while he tried to figure out why he could talk well to kids like Matthew and not to adults like Pegeen.

He inhaled deeply, and saw Matt staring at him from the curb. "Something the matter, kid?"

"You all right?"

"Fine. Just fine."

He glanced at the Anchor Inn and decided he'd rather eat at home, caught up with Matt, and they crossed the street together. On the corner was the small, fieldstone police station, behind it on the next corner the hedge-enclosed parking lot of Robert Cameron's Clipper Run restaurant. Several cars were parked near the entrance; diners from the mainland, he guessed as he and the boy continued walking west. Most of the islanders wouldn't be eating until after the funeral.

From one of the yards farther down the street came a sudden gust of laughter; boys playing baseball, he thought, or a fast game of soccer. That Matt wasn't with them wasn't surprising. He preferred studying history or the way colors worked than studying how to steal second base from a fast pitcher. It set him apart, but the boy didn't seem to mind.

"Mr. Ross?"

He sighed loudly. "Good Lord, Matt, don't you ever stop asking questions?"

"But my mother—"

27

"I know, I know. Your mother says you have to ask if you want to learn anything."

Matt squinted up at him. "How'd you know that?"

"It's a great secret you learn when you get to be grown-up."

Matt considered that for a moment while he kicked at a stone and toed it into the gutter. Then he gestured with his free hand back toward the restaurant. "You think you're gonna win the election?"

"You going to vote for me?"

"I'm too young."

"Well, I'll just have to win anyway. It'll be close without your vote, though. Mighty close."

"My mother says she's gonna vote for you. She says she doesn't want to see Mr. Cameron running things and putting in all the gambling and stuff. She says it isn't fitting . . . whatever that means." Almost a half block in silence before he spoke again. "If they build those hotels and things like Mr. Cameron wants, they'll cut down all the trees, right?"

"That's right."

"Then the squirrels won't have any place to live!"

"Right again."

The boy shook his head. "That isn't fair, Mr. Ross." Nope, it sure isn't."

"I wish I could vote for you," he said softly.

Colin placed a hand gently on his shoulder and looked up just as they reached Atlantic Terrace, the town's last cross-street. Three houses down—a small, white, clapboard saltbox—a woman stood on the high narrow porch. She waved, and Colin waved back.

"Hey," Matt said, "you coming to dinner? Mom says she'd like it if you came to dinner."

Colin looked again, and relunctantly backed off. "Can't, pal. I have to get ready for Gran's funeral. I promised Lilla I'd be there. Maybe I'll see you when it's over."

Matt dashed away immediately, hair whipping at his shoulders, the hamper slamming into his leg to give

28

him a curiously lopsided gait. Colin watched with a faint smile until he reached the front yard, then waved at Peg and hurried to his right across Bridge Road. There was no pavement here as the trees closed in and the road aimed straight for the ferry, so he walked on the verge for nearly a hundred yards before cutting into a stand of pine. The underbrush had been cleared away, giving him a clear walk, and a clear view, to his graystone cottage and the small studio behind.

He had no neighbors except for the Sunset Motel two hundred yards farther west, and if it hadn't been for the cars sweeping past on occasion he could easily have been living in the middle of a forest. That was precisely the way he wanted it.

The telephone was ringing as he came through the front door, but just as he reached it the caller gave up. He scowled at the mute receiver, replaced it, and stripped off his windbreaker. A groan as he stretched him arms high over his head, another as he dropped onto the sofa and crossed his legs at the ankles.

"Hello, place," he said, a greeting repeated since the first time he'd walked through the front door and had grinned.

The room he was in was just twenty feet long, the width of the cottage. The walls were pine-paneled and covered with bookcases and framed prints, the pegged floor bare except for a few braided throws, the furniture overstuffed and unmatching—as long as it was comfortable he didn't much care about period or style. Nor did he care that the rooms behind this one were only a modernized kitchen, a gray-tiled bath, and a bedroom just large enough for a chest of drawers and his bed. For some it would be claustrophobic; for him it was no bigger or smaller than it absolutely had to be.

His eyes closed, his fingers laced together and he stretched again, palms pushing outward. He grunted, opened his eyes and found himself staring at the thin scars on his wrists.

I don't get it, Peg had said to him just the summer before; *how can you think about it and not get . . . I don't know, chills.*

It was a long time ago, he'd answered. *It happened to a different man.*

"Sure," he whispered to the empty room. "Sure it did. And next year it'll snow on the Fourth of July."

He grimaced at the show of bitterness no one saw but himself.

At twenty-one he hd married his hometown Maine sweetheart because that was the way life was supposed to be: a college degree, a job teaching art, and a wife to begin a family. But three years later he'd had it with teaching, had decided perhaps it wasn't too farfetched to think about making it on his own as an artist. And why not? He was confident in his talent and his willingness to continue learning, was filled with his vision of what art should be, and ready to take on the toughest critics in the world. His wife was nervous, but supportive because his dream-talk was so vivid. A year later she was nervous and carping because the talk was the same. The year after that she refused to listen and was gone.

He left his hometown, moved down into Massachusetts, rented a loft and worked even harder. There were sales, small ones, but more than enough to keep luring him on. A gallery showing in Boston was followed by one in Chicago. He permitted himself no close friends to distract him from his painting, and the women he sometimes found all finally complained of the same thing—he was cold, he was uncaring, all he should have given them he gave to his canvas.

They were right, but change was too hard, there was work to be done. The one thing he wanted was reasonable success, and definitely before he was too old to enjoy it; basking in fame during his dotage was not his idea of living.

Four years after leaving Maine, he married a woman who was just making it as a novelist. She said she

30

understood him, and he believed it; she said she loved him, and he believed it. His work took on color, his days took on sunlight, and two years after his first New York showing, her heart twisted and stopped, and he never felt more alone in his life.

He despaired, moped, took long walks in the rain; he stared at his paints and could see nothing but black; he stood in front of the bathroom mirror and hacked at his wrists. But when he saw the blood running and felt the pain burning, instead of panicking he grew angry. Angry at himself for not having the maturity to deal with himself as well as other people, and at the world for not handing him people who really *knew*.

He bound himself, and thought he was healed. He had sworn off women until he met Peg Fletcher.

Peg Fletcher, who said she understood, and he wanted to believe it; Peg Fletcher, who refused to allow him self-pity, and he wanted to prove he didn't need it anymore.

He stared again at the scars and stuck his tongue out at them and broke into laughter that had his side almost aching.

The telephone rang.

He shook himself vigorously, reached to the cobbler's bench he used as a coffee table and snatched up the receiver. The first word on the other end told him it was Bob Cameron, owner of the Clipper Run and the incumbent president of the island's Board of Governors. Colin was running against him in next month's election.

Cameron also made no bones about being in love with Peg as well.

"Colin, how's it going?"

He propped his feet on the bench's high end and stared at the curtained window to the left of the door. "I'm not rich yet, if that's what you're asking."

Cameron laughed, a series of seal-like barks that never failed to sandpaper his nerves.

"Or maybe," he said, "you want me to make a

speech at the bash on Saturday. You know, give the folks a little excitement in case the party gets too dull."

The laughter again, though this time he sensed strain and immediately stretched an arm over his head, fist toward the ceiling, a silent celebration for scoring a point.

"Hey, you're welcome to come, you know that," Cameron said once he had sobered. "The party's open even to the opposition. Besides, it isn't a political thing anyway, for crying out loud. It's a celebration for shucking the tourists."

Colin nodded to himself. Sure, and I just know you have some swampland in Georgia you're eager for me to see.

"But that's not why I called," Cameron continued when he heard no response. "I, uh, I was wondering if you had plans for after the funeral tonight."

"Why?" Colin asked warily.

"Well, it's like this—I got a couple of friends over today from Trenton, and I think you ought to meet them. They might change your mind about the casinos and what they'll do for the island."

"What they'll do is ruin it," he said flatly.

"So *you* say."

"So I say, so the Chief of Police says, so says half the island, if not more."

"You're making this awfully hard on yourself, Col. And it isn't doing the island any good, either."

He sat up, his left hand a fist on his thigh, his right strangling the receiver. "Don't," he said quietly. "Don't you dare blame me for what's happening here, Bob. I'm not the one who's promising pie-in-the-sky riches if the casinos come in. I'm not the one promising bigger houses and bigger cars and fancier clothes and all that other nonsense."

"Colin," the man said, his voice straining to hold back anger, "all I want is what's best for Haven's End."

"Jesus," he said in disgust. "Jesus H. Christ, Bob,

this is me you're talking to, not some goddamned fisherman who can barely make ends meet."

"My friends from the mainland—"

"Yeah," he interrupted, "I know all about your so-called friends."

The year before Colin moved south, Peg's husband, Jim, had decided to investigate Cameron's somewhat dubious mainland connections. For months he had worked alone, and for months had held his silence, but it was inevitable that word of his preliminary findings would finally leak to the grapevine. Cameron grew increasingly defensive, the islanders increasingly hostile, and late in April Fletcher's car had blown up while waiting for the ferry on the island-side platform. Jim had been in it. Five and a half years later there were still no arrests.

Cameron had instantly disclaimed responsibility, his rapid backpedaling so skillful that people believed he'd only gotten in over his head. Nevertheless, when he tried once again to bring in the casinos, to make the small sheltered island a refuge for the high rollers discouraged from visiting Atlantic City to the north, Colin didn't trust him, didn't like him, and in a brief moment of weakness agreed to oppose him for the Board of Governors' top position.

"Listen, Ross," Cameron said, civility abandoned, "you've no call bringing up stuff that's dead and buried."

"Poor choice of words, Bob," he said lightly.

"Faggot painter," Cameron snapped. "I'm giving you a chance to get the truth, and all you can do is throw mud. And if you think I'm going to stand by and watch this island go to hell in a handbasket because some goddamned jackass who wasn't even born here thinks he knows better than me what's good for this place, you've got another think coming."

"Bob, you really are a shit, you know that?"

"Ross, I'm warning you . . ."

He had had enough. "Warn me all you want, Bob," he said, "but if you so much as look cross-eyed at me

33

between now and the election, I'll knock your fucking teeth in."

"Peg," the man said righteously, "doesn't approve of violence."

"And you leave her out of this!"

He slammed the receiver onto its cradle and glared at his fists. He knew there were still a few who would never think of him as being really "island"; but there were also enough who had sufficient faith in his judgement—and in the future of Haven's End without the casinos—to back him all the way. There was no denying the fact that Jim Fletcher's murder bothered him. There was also no denying the fact that coming to Haven's End, working with the schoolchildren, meeting Peg and the others, all served to heal him inside as nothing else had.

To his mind that meant he had an obligation.

And if he was ever going to be able to call this place a home, he would have to discharge that obligation before the temptation to flee grew too strong to resist.

He rose suddenly and crossed the room to the narrow, white-curtained window on the lefthand wall. Below it was a chipped cherrywood table. On a strip of white linen in the center was one of Gran D'Grou's carvings.

The Screaming Woman.

Abruptly, the election, Bob Cameron, and the nastiness were gone. In its place a reminder of the funeral, and he hugged himself absently as he realized it was almost twilight.

A car horn blared in the distance. Another answered. A third buried them both.

He backed away from the table.

The figure was carved out of gray-and-black driftwood. It was fifteen inches high, a naked woman standing with her hands at her sides, her head tilted back slightly. At a distance she seemed to be singing; closer, and she could be screaming as her neck was encircled by what appeared to be a headless serpent growing up and out of the base of her spine. Her eyes were blank. Her legs merged at the knees into the body of a second, larger serpent that formed the statue's base.

This not be snake here, it is tail. She is sea woman. Eye cut out? No, no, Colin, it is shadow. You put a light here, the eye come back. You want a big monster, you stick it in the closet; you want a beautiful woman, put it on the television.

Jesus damn, Colin, you got no imagination.

He switched on the lamp standing beside the table and hurried into the bedroom to get dressed.

He didn't blame the island a bit for wanting Gran buried right away. During the last year he had changed, and for the worse. His role of benevolent despot had darkened, and no one had thought it amusing anymore. He snarled, except at the children and Lilla. He spent more time in the woods, more time at his shack, less time at the luncheonette unless he wanted to talk with the young ones. When he looked at passersby it was from the corner of his eye. When he spoke, his voice took on indecipherable insinuation.

And he demonstrated suddenly an uncanny ability to make himself appear to be something he wasn't— instead of an embittered failure, an exile from his home, he was a mysterious figure from an exotic foreign land known for its cultivation of supernatural shadows; instead of a man who steadfastly refused the polishing of his raw artistic talents, he was a worker of dark miracles so convincing even Warren Harcourt thought his dead wife could be brought back.

The dead birds hadn't helped at all.

Lilla's singing was even worse.

And tomorrow, Colin thought, they would look up at the sun and really feel silly about letting themselves be spooked—spooked by a drunk who didn't make sense even with his carvings.

But that was tomorrow.

There was still tonight to get through.

TWO

The beach continued on for a half mile below the last jetty, to the sharp slope where the land rose and the sand gave way to boulders, barnacled and slick, providing throats for the breakers that shattered against them. Down by the beach there were gaps, for tide pools, children, the occasional lovers. Fifty yards more and the gaps closed, the boulders becoming jagged and massive. And at the southern tip they rose to hundred-foot cliffs fringed with wind-twisted trees and tenacious straggly shrubs.

There were sand dunes as well. Two parallel rows spiked with sharp-edged sawgrass, broken and nearly leveled at several narrow places by wind or stormtide or the persistence of walkers.

And there was Dunecrest Estates, the only homes outside town—larger, newer, bespeaking wealth and position in fieldstone and brick. There were fewer than two dozen, half of them facing the ocean, the rest fronting a woodland arm between them and Neptune Avenue, which itself ended where they did, at a street called Surf Court. The development was twelve years old, long enough for the townspeople to call it simply the Estates.

And there was Gran D'Grou's shack.

It stood on a raised spit of land where the dunes met the slope, hidden by dying shrubs, scrub pine, and a colony of weeds. There was no litter, but the ground seemed cluttered just the same, and the roof that pitched away from the ocean was tarpaper-patched, breached at its peak by a rusted stovepipe chimney.

Lilla D'Grou, ignoring the dampness that seeped through the cracks in panes and thin walls, stood at the front room's sand-pitted window and stared at the beach. A wave rose, crested, hissed toward the pines at the end of the front yard. She ignored it. A stiff-legged tern raced the bubbling foam, head bobbing, legs reaching, its tracks in the wet sand fast disappearing, and she ignored it.

She realized with a start that she was staring at her ghost in the window. A lean face, and soft, high cheekbones, and a rounded chin made for a palm to cup it; deep brown eyes slightly raised at the corners, half-closed now in a look that might have been seductive in another time and place, the whole framed by luxuriant black hair parted in the center and settling on her slender shoulders in tangled natural curls. Not beautiful, but arresting, a face and lithe figure that turned men around ten minutes after she'd passed. But the black dress she now wore rendered her sexless.

She signed, her gaze shifted, and the ghost vanished.

To her left she could see the small fishing fleet moving ponderously homeward. Just over a half dozen boats, but they would work until November to drag the last of the harvest into their holds. Patiently. Confidently. Once each day drawing into a large circle for a laughing mealtime rendezvous if all was well, somberly trading well-worn and well-known gripes if their nets remained empty. Most had lived on the island since birth and could, if they'd a mind, trace their lineage back to the original inhabitants—brigands and smugglers and a few honest settlers, who lived on the island in an uneasy truce.

They fished, gossiped, and few ate what they carried

back to Fox's Marina. Most of the catch was swiftly unloaded and packed into refrigerated crates, the crates labeled and thrown onto a truckbed for the mainland. What remained was sold to Naughton's Market or the Clipper Run. And if it were not worth the selling, it was thrown to the gulls.

The gulls that stalked them like winged hyenas.

Lilla watched them without a glimmer of caring, while the shadows of the trees behind the crumbling shack lanced toward the water, jabbed at the darkening sand. Shadows that would last until the night fog rolled it, riding low on the waves like a massive prowling beast, silently pacing the island in furtive spurts of roiling grey. It was treacherous even for the landed—blotting out the stars, defying the bright moon, sifting through the woodland to curl low in the streets, scrape noiselessly at chilled panes, fade the streetlamps one by one to slow sifting spots of diffused white haze.

Suddenly, there was a man walking along the beach. His topcoat was open, his hat back on his head, and his shoes were carried in one listless hand. He walked all the way to the first boulder without looking at the shack, turned and started back, to the snow fence that ran from the last jetty to the woods, the division between private and public bathing. He passed a hand wearily over his forehead, walking with a peculiar gait not caused by the sand—rigid, deliberate, difficult to watch without wanting to help him. He stopped and lifted his left foot, tried to slip on a shoe and fell on his rump. He shook his head and looked skyward, then looked at his shoes and tossed them away. Rising slowly with hands outstretched for balance, he dusted sand from his trousers and moved on, swaying slightly.

She watched him without blinking. Her arms were braced at her sides, her knees pressed against the unpainted wall beneath the canted window. Hearing the rising high tide without listening to it; listening instead to the calm rhythm of her heart. And when it

38

was clear there was no panic to ruin what she'd done, she closed her eyes tightly and hugged herself snugly.

It would be so easy, she thought, to find Warren Harcourt and join him in his drinking. And it would be so temptingly easy to believe that belonging to the only black family on Haven's End had denied her grandfather all the care he'd needed. Too easy. Like running away with Harcourt. Like ignoring the fact that nothing could have saved Gran, nothing at all could have kept his lungs from stalling, his heart from failing. Ninety-seven years he had lived, and he had simply and finally worn himself out with his liquor and his smoking and his constant praying for that one little miracle that would bring him his fortune.

Dead now, when she needed him most.

Dead now, while men like Warren Harcourt stumbled on so damned worthless.

Dead. Gran had been her family, and he'd left her alone.

When she was sixteen, she had decided that either law or medicine would fill the rest of her life. No one in her family had ever been to college before, she would be the first, and she was going to do it right. Her parents applauded. Gran grumbled and told her he could teach her all she had to know, and she kissed his knotted brow, and whispered a laugh in his ear. Peg agreed to help wherever she could, and Little Matt promised to help her study very hard. And Colin her Knight (though he didn't know he had her armor) wrote to people he knew in hopes of snaring a scholarship or two.

When she was sixteen, the boys hung around her shyly, knowing her color and wanting her just the same. Instead of Peg, she asked Colin to help sort out her feelings, not because he was smarter but for the way he wouldn't look at her when he talked.

It was grand at sixteen, and with little ego involved she knew she was smart, she was pretty, she was ready for the world.

When she was sixteen, she and Gran had persuaded her parents to take a day off from running the Neptune Luncheonette. She assured them it would not fall apart or burn down or blow away while they were gone. When they hesitated, Gran scolded them lightly in Caribbean patois. They'd laughed and agreed, and rented a small boat from the marina to sail beyond the breakers.

In taking over the store, she had celebrated by treating every child to free ice cream sodas. And it *was* a celebration—the first full day the elder D'Grous had taken off since she could remember. Even during winter, when most shopowners fled for a three-month respite, they stayed. There was always work after the motels closed, and they felt more secure here, where there was no time for bigotry, or the mainland's tacit harassment.

By noon she was exhausted. A pleasant, high-flying weariness had her flirting, laughing, singing Caribbean songs old Gran had taught her when Mother wasn't around to disapprove of the choice.

She wore her grandfather out.

At five past two, Patrolman El Nichols walked in, and ten minutes later she was in the back room weeping in Gran's arms.

One of the fishermen had started back to the marina for repairs on his engine. On the way he found the sailboat, capsized after a noontime squall. There was no sign of the D'Grous.

When she was sixteen, Gran walked her to the house at the end of Atlantic Terrace where they drew the curtains, turned off the lights, refused to answer the telephone's pleading.

For weeks after the dying, the funeral without bodies, he had stayed, cleaning and cooking, promising all would be fine.

"You know, girl," he said one night at the table, "your old mother was the best woman I know, the best daughter there ever be. But she think I'm a little—" And he drew a circle around his temple and laughed quietly. "She don't remember the island, the other one. She was still very small, too small to walk, when . . ."

He stopped, and Lilla watched his eyes as they followed his mind away from Haven's End.

"Much sickness," he said softly. "I tell your Gram we have to leave, go to the Big Place and be rich. But she died, you see. Then I have . . . small trouble and come too, with your mother."

"Gran, why didn't Momma want you to sing me the old songs?"

His look, then, was almost ferocious.

"Because," he said after too long a time, "she don't remember the true island and the things it can do. She likes it here and she wants you to grow up to be just like her."

"I want to, Gran."

"And I, girl. I promise your mother I give you this chance."

But he had promised her, too, her parents would come back, and they never did.

And he had promised he would guard her—and he'd died last week. The last of her family, when she needed him the most. When she needed him to tell her what to do with the store, her life, the lure of the mainland and all that lay beyond.

He had fallen ill just after Labor Day. He lay on the bed in the shack's back room and hadn't risen again. Instead, he spent long hours, the night hours, telling her of his boyhood on the Caicos Islands, north of Haiti. Very little made sense because he rambled on so much, whispered more often than not, broke into songs he demanded she learn. But his hoarse singing entranced her, until she sang with him, seeing him smile, nodding when she was able to complete a song on demand.

And on the day before it was over, it seemed as if he had found a way to slip into her mind. One moment she was kneeling by the bed, watching his breathing slow and stutter, and the next he was in there—in

41

there —whispering to her, easing her slight panic with a cloak of comforting fog.

He would never leave, he said, if she did what he commanded.

He would never leave if she would obey all his instructions.

And she believed him, even though his eyes remained closed, his lips did not move, and the rise and the fall of his chest became increasingly shallow.

She slept that night in the shack, had been standing at the front window just like this when his breathing stopped and he'd left her. Just like this when she'd realized what happened and raced to the back, where the walls were bare and stained an ugly rust-brown from splotches of dead insects and nails from patches where the roof had leaked. A single window at the rear was closed against the night, covered with an uneven blanket faded from green to streaked white. One chest of drawers squatted timidly in the far corner. Beside it, a chipped oak table held a hurricane lamp whose low flame wavered though there was no draft.

And in the center of the uncarpeted floor was the bed—a cheap imitation brass frame and headboard that cradled a thin, linenless mattress at an uncomfortable angle.

The man lying there was extraordinarily slender. Naked. Not a square inch of dark flesh unmarked by lines here deepened into crevices, there laced across withered and flaked skin drawn around sticks that played at being bones. Like a man immersed too long in salt water. Sexless. Rigid. Eyes wide and staring.

She had circled the bed once, not touching, not seeing. Then she'd knelt on the floor and taken Gran's hand. Snakeskin. She had pressed it to her chest, trembled, wept until she could rub her tears into the insensitive palm while she strained and willed the eyelids to blink, the chest to rise, the knees to flex. Just once. Please, just once. That's all she asked. That's all she demanded.

She willed and wept and trembled until the green-chimneyed lamp with its tarnished brass base sputtered, flared, and died. From rents in the blanket came the waxing new moon's gray-white intrusion. From the cracks in the walls, in the ceiling, in the air, the muted thunder of the cresting tide. She wept, rocking on her knees, pressing the hand hard into her flesh and feeling no pain.

"Gran, come back to me," she whimpered between sobs. "Gran, please. Don't leave me alone, not now when I need you."

The floor creaked rhythmically. The moon began to dim as the night fog returned.

"Gran, listen," she whispered earnestly.

A bloated brown spider walked over the old man's shin.

"Gran, listen, please don't go. Please, Gran? Gran?"

She spread the dead man's fingers until the skin between was taut, near to tearing, took the thumb into her mouth and bit down slowly, not too hard—she wouldn't have him screaming. She lifted her head to glare at the night; to curse the dark and the fog and the moon and the stars; to curse the sea and the island and the shack where she knelt.

The faint cry of a gull, the scrabbling of a rat, the rubbing of sawgrass like the husk of a ghost.

And her voice was a woman's ten times her age. "I won't let you go, Gran. You're all I have, and I won't let you go."

For a long moment there was a last bit of fear and a brief troubled wondering if her mind had let go. Then she took a deep breath and held it until her lungs were aching. She released it in slow spurts and in doing so released her hold on the shack, on the beach, on the island in the ocean. There was only Gran now, and the old songs, herself in a universe of slow-stirring shadows.

The Atlantic spoke, and she listened; the fog whispered, and she cocked her head; the lamp hissed, and she nodded.

Carefully, moving as if dealing with cold, fragile black crystal—*do now all I tell you, child, do it all now and it will all come right*—she positioned his hands over his sunken stomach, one above the other, the fingertips angled toward the shoulders. She did not close the blind eyes—she wanted him to see everything so he could correct her mistakes. *If* she made a mistake. But she would not, dared not. Not now. Not now.

The Atlantic; the fog; the eye of the lamp.

The creaking of the shack; the dead silence of the moon.

She moved on her knees to the foot of the bed, her hands in position to mirror Gran's exactly.

A last thought that momentarily brought life to the brown eyes: *is this what they taught you in school, is this what you learned from Colin and the others, is this what you believe in, is this sane . . . is it . . . sane . . . is this . . .*

The sea whispered.

The thought died.

"I will sing you, Gran," was a prayer and a query, and her voice filled the shack though its volume was low, the words swooping like ravens, darting like hawks, waiting like predators on the dead man's heart. Without joy, without promise, but a hard hopeful urging that surged to match the tide and hold, hold, until the words became a humming that lasted until dawn.

The words Gran had taught her to call on his gods.

And when she had finished and had slept for an hour, she started again.

For five days she worked at the luncheonette until seven, then returned to the shack where she ate, slept, and passed the night singing—staring at the cheap decanter she'd bought at Peg Fletcher's. There was gleaming red liquid in the cut-glass container, and each night a little more.

44

Five days later she walked into the police station and told them Gran was dead.

Dead.

And she didn't notice the way people looked at her now—except during those brief moments when the mind fog lifted and she wondered where she was.

A movement. Her eyes shifted. There. There on the water. Seven longboats making their way south just beyond the breakers. Dark against the sea, the figures within black in their slickers. She blinked rapidly to drive off the hazy past, and saw the people on the beach. Only a few yet, but a few more stumbling down the dunes; not one of them looked in her direction.

The boats turned, pitched, and rolled as they crested the waves and made their way toward shore.

She searched for Colin. Of all the people for all this time, only he understood what magic Gran had had in his fingers, in his soul, to bring to life the driftwood and the pine. He'd helped Gran sell, asking nothing in return, had helped deal with the big city galleries that came sniffing around the shack, hands on their wallets and handkerchiefs to their noses. Gran, however, refused most of Colin's assistance. More often than not he gave the sculptures away, then complained bitterly into his bottle about the few dollars he'd saved. And the closer to death he came, the angrier he grew, lashing out at the island without once ever taking any blame for his failures on his own frail shoulders.

She seemed to recall, then, that the songs he had taught her while he lay on the bed were angry as well. But it was only a feeling, one she could not pin down.

She shivered and hugged herself more tightly.

The afternoon before, Colin had visited her when school was over, having heard through the grapevine that she didn't want Gran buried in the sea despite the fact it was Haven's End's way.

She had met him on the sand, away from the shack.

"Lil, it's all right, y'know," he'd said, hands thrust

into his pockets, brown hair caught in the sea breeze. "If you don't want to do this, it's all right."

She shook her head slowly. "You don't understand, Colin."

He managed a smile. "I'm trying." His look said, *why don't you help me?*

She felt a swirling of the mind fog that had blinded her since the night before Gran died. "It's not a matter of want, it's a matter of must." And she hoped she wasn't overplaying the bereaved role, one she sometimes felt wasn't a role at all. Whenever that feeling came she knew Gran was listening, watching, waiting to stop her. Then the feeling would leave and the fog would come again.

"Lilla . . . Lilla, I'm sorry."

"It's all right."

"I'm still sorry."

She found herself smiling.

A gull shrieked, and veered sharply away toward the water.

He'd looked to the sea, down to the sand, raised his eyes without lifting his head. "Lil, are you all right? I know this isn't easy for you, but . . . are you all right?"

She'd wanted to tell him then; the singing, the nights, the fog stalking her dreams. But she couldn't. *Do all I tell you, child, and it will all come right.* She would have to let them do what they wanted without saying a word.

Then she would do what she must.

There were more people on the beach. They took hold of the longboat's gunwales and dragged them from the surf, hauled them around to face the way they'd come. Cigarettes and a thermos jug of coffee were passed around. Faces, small and pale, were checking the sky as if sniffing the wind. There were no children, and only a handful of teenagers.

Lilla's eyes closed slowly, and she wished Peg were here to hold her, to whisper something to make her feel right, and smile.

She wished Gran were here. The real Gran. The grumbling and mumbling and whittling and bitching Gran. Not the Gran who lay so maddeningly still there in the back room.

Her eyes opened, and she sighed.

Any moment now they would come to take him away. Any moment now Colin and someone else, perhaps Chief Garve Tabor, would climb over the last dune, talk a little, see who was down there and who had stayed away, and then do what they had to do. Colin, who didn't know Lilla would have given every one of her eighteen years if he'd taken her to his bed just once before that man . . . that man at the college . . . that man who'd given her all that horrid stuff to drink and had brought her back to his room and had . . . that man . . . who'd made a bet that black women were different where a white man thought it counted.

That man.

At the beginning of last August a full year ago, over Gran's protests, she had gone to the college for a weekend's orientation.

That man—his name and face gone, leaving only his expression when she returned the next day and spat in his eyes before heading for the Registrar to withdraw her name from the rolls.

That man Gran wanted to kill when he found out. She'd cried herself to sleep too many times and he was there, trembling in indignation while she talked and wept, and she held the old man and begged him not to leave her.

That man, who had taken every man from her bed before she'd known, before she'd loved.

She'd fled back to Haven's End, but Gran was never the same Gran again.

"You listen to me," he said last spring, "this place is no good. It took my fortune. It needs a teaching to show them I am . . ." He stumbled, not finding the words. "They took it because I am old and I am this way." He pinched his thin forearm to show her the color. "I will not forget that they took what is mine."

47

"Gran—"

"You are my Lilla. I love you, and you will help me and I will make it all right. I know this is true because I am your Gran."

A few heads turned to a point just to her left, and she knew who had finally arrived. There was no stopping it now. Colin and Garve Tabor were here, and now it was done.

She turned away from the window slowly, in stages, as if she were dazed. With a shuddering sigh she lowered her arms to her sides, her hands slipping into the folds of her black dress.

—*the songs, child, the songs, if you want me back again*—

She moved flat-footed, bare-footed, from the front room to the back, to the bed where Gran lay.

—*they will take me to the water, give me drink to keep me safe*—

Not an hour earlier she had finished the last singing, the words beyond translation giving her comfort nonetheless. They were his promises (though they sometimes seemed like threats), and when she was done she felt the air close around her like a giant's fist. She waited. And the air rushed from the shack like a banshee's furied scream.

—*be patient, child, I will be waiting*—

Then she had wrapped his body in gray canvas, with a round, ten-pound weight settled in the bottom, and had slowly sewn it closed—except for the face.

She started at it now, biting her lower lip, feeling a burr try to rise in her throat while an abrasion of tears made her eyes sting.

The room was silent; not even the sea.

Gran, can you hear me? Oh, Gran, I'm doing my best, believe me. I tell them you're my Gran and I don't want you to leave me, and they just smile and tell me everything's all right, it's all right, don't worry.

Gran, they love me, they truly do. They only want

48

to see me smile again. They just don't know what it is to be so alone. They love me, but they don't know.

And I don't know what to do now. I don't know what to do.

I sing and I sing and I know it's right because you told me.

I sing and I sing, but I don't know if I sing enough.

Oh, Gran, why don't you sing me again?

She picked up the decanter and pulled out the stopper. The mindfog parted, her hand trembled, the fog returned. She poured the sweet-smelling red liquid into Gran's open mouth. All of it. Every drop. Then she reached down to the floor and picked up a long, heavy, curved needle. She held it close to her eyes in the lamp's wavering light. She licked her lips clear of salty tears and leaned over the corpse, brushing her cheeks before taking hold of the canvas. The needle slashed into the shroud, closing it, covering by stages the waxen black face (with a trace of red at the lips) and the wide staring eyes that did not blink when the needle passed over.

And when she was done, she slipped needle and coarse thread through a gap in the canvas, taking care not to prick her grandfather's scalp.

Then she stood at the foot of the bed, hands clasped at her waist, and she waited. Not moving. Scarcely breathing. As still as the body that waited there with her.

THREE

Light slipped from the air rapidly once the sun had dropped below the mainland forest, and what remained was a dark-spotted haze that tired the eye and made shadows lose their sunset definition. Streetlamps switched on with an insect buzzing, the amber traffic signal brightened in monotonous winking, and the Anchor Inn's neon was a harsh, colorless glare. On the corner behind the police station the Clipper Run's spotlights softened the gold frigate on the stucco wall, and the hedging surrounding the parking lot seemed taller, more forbidding.

For a long moment, nothing moved, nothing breathed.

For a moment, Haven's End waited.

On the mainland, Wally Sterling moored the ungainly ferry to its dock after completing his last commuter run and peered down the road toward Flocks. He saw no lights and grunted, wiped a brusque hand under his white-blind eye, and lit a twisted black cigar with a flourish and a loud, relieved sigh. He expected no more business for the rest of the night. After all, it was Thursday. Gran's funeral. And in the very slight breeze he could sense coming rain. A storm tonight, no question about it. The way things were going these days, he wouldn't be surprised if it was followed by a Carolina Screamer before the weekend was over. They were due for one of them late fall storms—high winds, high seas—so why not now, when it was all goin' to hell anyway.

He forced a belch, and pulled a cheap silver flask out of his hip pocket, unscrewed the cap, and took a long pull at the brandy inside. A brief yellow-toothed grimace, and he pulled off his seaman's cap to scratch vigorously at white hair trimmed to a ragged marine cut. A tug at his hawk's nose. A swipe of a hand over his cleft chin to catch a dribble of brandy he licked off his scrawny finger. Another drink, and he was ready.

He stood on the dock and began taking potshots at the gulls wheeling overhead, using an old target pistol and pretending the birds were the men who had killed his brother Stu. He hadn't hit one in five years, but it didn't stop his shooting.

At the funeral—in Flocks, goddamn it, where a man got a decent burial, down there in the solid ground—a gull had landed on the coffin as it was lowered. It had pecked at the flowers, pecked at the lid, and he'd tried to brain it with a shovel. It flew off, squawking, but by then he knew the damn thing was a sign. Stu had hated them birds, and Wally figured he had to stick around until he'd potted one for his brother.

One of these days he was going to get lucky, and when he did he was going to sell the ferry and move down to Florida, or out to Arizona, some place like that. As far away as he could get from the idiots who lived out there on that rock.

Another shot, another miss; he took another touch of brandy.

Or maybe he could catch those men alive, those who'd blown up Jim Fletcher and caused Stu's dying. Then he'd be a hero, sell his story to the papers, get on the TV. Or maybe not. That would mean involving himself with the fools on Haven's End. The fools and their goddamn casinos that killed little Stu. No. He'd let them do it alone. Let Tabor work his ass off trying

51

to prove it was one of Cameron's cronies, like he hinted when he came around asking questions about who used the ferry that day and did Wally see any strange boats on the bay and crap like that.

Another shot, another miss, another lick at the brandy.

Nope. Nice try, Garve, but old Wally knew better. It was pouring that day, the waves too high for anything but the ferry. Nope, the bomb had been placed by someone on the island.

He grinned. With luck, maybe there'd be another one, and this time it would be . . . he grunted, scratched his hair, his chin, a spot just below his belt. The hell with it. He didn't give a damn. Let themselves kill each other off, all of them. And that was something he knew he could drink to.

Out near the horizon the fog began to move.

In serpentine coils it drifted low over the water, riding the swells and bending away from the breeze; pockets formed here and there in the deepest troughs, eddying, expanding, shredding when an explosive gust reached down from the black; and soundlessly rising it masked the light of twilight in a writhing gray cloud.

In the trees, too, it stirred once the temperature had lowered, teasing translucent ribbons around boles and deadfalls, surging over roots thrust up from the ground. It settled in hollows and resembled cauldrons gently simmering; it sought shrubs to weave them shrouds; it found saplings and gave them cloaks; and it reached out from the shadows like specters seeking form.

It was chilled, but not cold; it was hunting, but not hurried; and it sat beyond the low breakers like a veil not yet drawn.

The passing of the light was joined by the slow seeping of warmth from the sand. Fifteen longboats were ranged evenly along the beach, and three shallow pits had been dug in which fires had been built. The flames were not high, but they were sufficient to create shadows, temporary black ghosts that rippled like whispers across footprints and faces and brought an almost phosphorescent glow to the breaker's caps.

Colin stood with his back to the dunes. He was wearing a heavy, gray Irish sweater, his jeans were rolled to midcalf, and his feet were bare. He stood beside Garve Tabor, who was dressed the same, and whose thinning sandy hair was atangle over his brow. Garve poked the unruly forelock back into place every so often as a matter of habit, after which he would pull his belt up over his slight paunch whether it needed the adjustment or not.

To their right the dunes leveled, and Gran's shack was just visible in the gloom.

"She sure has a sense of the dramatic," the chief said, his voice almost too soft and husky for a man his age, nearly fifteen years older than Colin but not looking it at all.

"She's frightened," Colin told him. "She doesn't want to lose all she has left."

Tabor, whose face in the distant firelight glow gave evidence of his Navaho heritage, shrugged and looked at his watch. "She's not the only one who's lost people, you know."

"Yeah."

Tabor raised an eyebrow. "Hey, this is your first funeral."

He nodded.

"Ah, no wonder you've got the jitters." He nodded. "Makes you think we're kind of barbaric and all that, right?"

"Not exactly, no."

"Weird?"

"That, for sure."

Tabor looked to the water, his profile sharp-edged. "It's a comfort, though. My mother's out there, a couple of uncles. It beat all to hell having them dropped into the ground with mud dumped on them. That, to my thinking, is definitely barbaric."

They waited, and Colin wondered what Peg was doing. Probably finishing the supper dishes. He would call her when he got back. He didn't realize he was staring toward town until he saw Garve watching him, smiling. He shrugged, and the chief laughed.

"You shouldn't wait too long, Col. It does a hell of a job on the man's ego when the woman has to do the proposing."

"Really? Is this from the local expert?" From the waiting mourners he picked out a tall woman with blonde hair rippling to her waist. "Does it mean you're going to ask Annalee soon?"

Annalee Covey was Dr. Hugh Montgomery's nurse, a widow whose husband of three years had been killed in Vietnam when his fighter copter had been shot down a month after the pull out. Two years later, and to no one's surprise, she made it known she was tired of living alone, and she also made it clear to those who pursued her that she wanted one man of her own or no man at all. Garve was scared to death of her. She was a head taller than he was, more aggressive, and, he claimed, too damned liberated for her own good. It had taken Colin only a few months to understand that his friend was torn between the comfort and imagined safety of an old-fashioned woman and the relatively exotic allure Annalee posed. The chief also felt guilty because Annalee's husband had been his best boyhood friend, and it seemed to him too much like incest.

"Well?" he said, turning away to hide his smile.

"We weren't talking about me, Rembrandt," Garve told him.

"No, I don't suppose we were." He cleared his throat and scanned the beach, scanned the sky, and shivered.

Garve laughed quietly. "You feel it?"

"Feel what?"

Garve waved vaguely toward the horizon. "Screamer's coming."

Colin looked skeptical. Despite his years here his friends were still testing to see how much he would swallow. "What are you talking about? What's a Screamer? A ghost?"

The chief laughed again. "No. Carolina Screamer. A late fall storm that comes up from the Carolinas so fast you barely have time to get. A lot of wind, the tides run wicked high."

"You mean a hurricane?"

Tabor shook his head. "No. What it does, see, it pushes the water ahead of it, damn near drowns the island. Folks board up their windows and light out for the mainland, most of them. Lasts about a day, you don't even know it's been unless you forgot to put the car in the garage."

"Sounds great," he said sourly.

"It can be fun, if you're careful."

"Oh, that's marvelous." He looked sideways at the policeman. "And you can sense it?"

"Some can."

"You?"

Garve chuckled and shook his head. "Hell, no. Heard on the radio there was a low forming off the coast. We haven't had a Screamer since . . . since you've come on. I figure we're due."

Colin checked the sky again, the water, and said, "I can't tell you how lucky I feel." Then he looked down at the beach, at the people still gathering. "Funny, I thought I saw Cameron."

"He slipped away about fifteen minutes ago."

Colin grunted his surprise.

Garve spat dryly. "Doesn't make any difference. He was here to be seen, that's all. Slap a few backs, whisper in a few ears. I expect his buddies are waiting for him at the restaurant."

"Oh, you know about them?"

Garve glanced at him oddly. "Do you?"

He gave a brief account of Cameron's phone call, letting the tone of his voice provide the commentary needed.

"Well, well," Garve said. He pushed his hat to the back of his head, and slipped the fingers of his left

55

hand into his hip pocket. "Old eagle eye doesn't miss much, m'boy. It's in the genes with us law folk. There are two of them, actually. Came over this morning. One guy doesn't weigh a hundred pounds, I bet. He's Mike Lombard and his specialty is real estate law. He lives in Trenton and drinks cocktails with the governor. The other one, he has a knife scar from his gut to his throat, and his expertise is political persuasion. The way I hear it, they're looking to Bob to provide them with a donation for their retirement fund."

"Interesting. But shouldn't you be after them or something?"

Garve laughed quietly. "Col, this isn't the Old West. I can't give them twenty-four hours to get outta town just because I don't like their faces. As long as they don't get Cameron to do something real stupid, all I can do is make them very unhappy to see me in their shadows."

Colin would have replied but he realized the mourners were staring past him to the shack. He turned slowly. The door was open, and a few second's watching brought Lilla into focus.

Garve sighed relief. "Time, I guess. Listen, maybe you'd—"

He nodded, took his hands from his pockets and trudged across the sand.

Eliot Nichols glared into the tiny office and dared the phone to ring again. Then he locked the door behind him and rushed to the green patrol car. With everybody and their brother wanting to know if a Screamer was coming (and too damned lazy to listen to the radio), he'd have to speed so as not to miss the funeral. And if he was going to be chief one of these days, attendance was a social must.

Midway along Neptune Avenue, far beyond the darkened gas station—the last business on the street— he passed between the Rising Sun Motel and the Seaview, both constructed in the shape of an H, windows boarded now for winter and the parking lots

56

deserted and filled with dead leaves. He glanced at them automatically, though he really wasn't looking. The Rising Sun was a meeting place for the worst of the island's teenagers. Though they'd never been caught, he knew they generally broke into the second floor rooms in back to party, drink themselves stupid on beer, do a little dope, do a little sex. There weren't many of them, a half dozen tops, and it usually happened only four or five times before the owners returned in spring. But it galled him to know they were there at all. Laughing at him. Not giving a damn. Just biding their time until they were legally old enough to get off the island. They were decidedly unlike the rest of the local kids, and he had a hard time understanding how they got that way.

A hundred yards later he saw Warren Harcourt sitting on the pebbled verge, hat in hand, legs splayed, feet bare, head bowed and nodding. With a groan, he pulled over and climbed out. Shaking his head, he slammed the door shut and hitched up his belt. Harcourt didn't move. Nichols stood over him for nearly a full minute, waiting for a reaction. When the man refused to acknowledge him, Nichols groaned again.

"You idiot," he said, grabbing the taller man's shoulders and yanking him effortlessly to his feet. "Don't you know there's a funeral tonight? Don't you have any respect for the dead?" He punched Harcourt's arm sharply, and had to reach out quickly to keep him from falling.

Harcourt belched.

"Damn it, Warren, why don't you get your butt on home?"

The lawyer blinked several times. "Wanna see Gran," he said. "I wanna see Gran."

Nichols didn't know whether to laugh or kick him. "Gran," he said with exaggerated care, "is dead. For God's sake, that's who they're buryin'! Jesus, you know that."

Harcourt swiveled around to face him, his dark eyes brimming with tears. "Dead?"

57

The deputy nodded.

"Burying him?"

"Aw, Warren, come on! You heard what I said."

The attorney reached several times for his topcoat lapels, failed, and let his hand dangle at his side. He swallowed. "They're not . . . are they burying him at sea?"

"Where the hell else, huh?"

For a moment the liquor seemed gone from the man's system, so much so that Nichols took a step back and frowned.

"Does Lilla know this?" Harcourt asked sharply. "Does she know what they're doing?"

Nichols stared, frowning.

"Well, sir, does she know?"

He put a hand to his forehead and rubbed slowly. He'd seen this happen before: One moment the lawyer was so out of it he could barely stand, the next it was as if he hadn't had a drop in his life. It spooked him. It really spooked him.

Harcourt belched again.

"That's it," Nichols muttered. He took the unsteady man's arms and spun him around toward town. Another moment for consideration and he gave him a harsh shove. "Go! Go on, damn it, before I run you in and throw away the key."

Harcourt lurched forward five or six feet, regained his balance, and walked a half dozen feet more. Then, abruptly, he turned and slipped his hands into his topcoat pockets. He was just beyond the reach of the patrol car's headlights, a shadow barely formed, and Nichols could have sworn he looked almost normal.

His voice was deep, and perfectly steady. "He won't like it, you know. He won't like it at all."

Nichols turned away, more spooked than before, and looked up to the stars. Damn, he thought, wouldn't you know it. Gone more than a week and now the damned fog is coming back.

*   *   *

Matt had asked her again: "Mom, why don't you and Mr. Ross get married?"

And again she'd answered truthfully: "Don't know, darlin'. Maybe because there's a time for things like that, and this isn't it."

It had sounded weak when she said it and Matt had finished his chocolate pudding in silence, cleared the table and gone up to his room when she'd pardoned him from doing the dishes. He wanted to finish the picture of the gulls, he'd told her; he wanted it done by Monday so Mr. Ross could tell him what he'd done wrong and what he should practice on. And when she was alone she washed the plates and listened to the radio, humming when she recognized a melody, shutting the music out when she didn't. Afterward, she wandered into the study where she opened the store ledger and stared at the columns, the figures, the black and red ink.

She held a ball-point pen in her right hand and tapped the retractor knob against her teeth.

Ten minutes later nothing had changed—the store was still solvent, no hints of financial disaster, and she might even be able to give one of her two clerks, Frankie Adams, a slight raise for the winter. If, she amended, he kept his nose clean. She smiled. She might as well ask for a million tax-free dollars. Though the boy was ambitious, and a decently hard worker, he was also enthralled by the local godhood, Carter Naughton. As long as Cart suffered the younger boy's presence, Frankie was going to be a problem. Well, maybe the raise would turn him around. Her good deed for the year.

She pushed away from the desk and stretched, groaned with pleasure, and toed off her shoes. Her hair, a rich and sullen auburn, was bunned at the nape for convenience, not preference. Her blouse and skirt were white and unfrilled. She rebelled against smocks, lab coats, and the like. Pharmacist or not, she didn't believe she lost a dime in sales just because she looked like a woman.

A grin pulled at her classic bow lips.

A woman, huh? The only time she ever considered herself something other than someone who owned a business these days was when Matt mentioned Colin. Or when she saw Colin on the street. Or when Colin took her to the movies, or to the mainland for dinner or a drive. Or when Colin took her sailing. Or . . .

The grin turned to a broad smile, and she laughed aloud.

"God," she said, rising and leaving the small room for the front parlor. "God, Pegeen, you've got it bad."

There wasn't much furniture, but what she had was comfortably old, comfortably thick, solidly reassuring. For a while, after Jim had died, she'd wanted to clear the house of everything that reminded her of him—the fireplace armchair where he'd read his paper every night, the oriental carpet his mother had given them as a wedding present, the polished brass andirons he cleaned after every fire, the framed prints of thoroughbreds. The bed upstairs. His armoire.

Then she'd changed her mind.

One morning, no more special than any other, she woke up and decided that all of it was just as much hers as his, as was the house and the land around it, that he was gone and she was still alive. With Matthew.

She'd cried all day.

Matt had cried with her, as if he'd understood.

Then Colin had arrived, and two years later her son's campaign had begun.

She slumped into the armchair and drew her feet up under her. Directly opposite was the picture window, reflecting the floor lamp to her left, and her shadowed face. She could see the street, however, and the Adams' house on the other side. A puff of fog hung over the streetlamp near the corner. Though the house was warm she hugged herself for a moment and wished she'd been able to attend the funeral. Lilla, she suspected, would be angry with her now, but it was a shame just the same.

60

She massaged her feet absently.

"Mom?"

She looked up, around toward the staircase by the front door. "You called?"

"Can I watch TV?"

"I don't know. You finish your homework?"

"Sure."

She shifted, lowering her feet to the carpet. A stupid question, she thought. If he'd had to read *War and Peace* by morning the answer would have been the same. She glanced at her watch and did some rapid subtraction. "All right," she called back. "But just till nine, got it? Nine o'clock and that thing is off."

"Thanks!"

"You're welcome," she said without raising her voice, then looked to the telephone on the table beside her. Talk. She needed talk, and with the funeral going on she might as well let her mother know she was still alive and unmarried. Then, thinking about the advice she didn't need but would get anyway, she rose, walked into the study again, and stared at the bookshelves and the cabinets beneath them where Jim had stored his files. She'd gone through them after he died, thinking she might be able to find his notes on the casinos and gamblers, thinking she'd be able to march into FBI headquarters and dump them on an agent's desk and demand justice be done. But she hadn't found them. No one had. And despite police efforts . . .

Hell, she thought, and looked back to the phone. Maybe Mother wouldn't be so bad, after all. Maybe she wouldn't be up to her lecture on the virtues of having a husband, and a father for poor little Matthew. Like Jim, she would say with undisguised grief in her voice. Or that nice restaurant man, what's his name again? Something Campbell? Cameron?

Peg's sudden smile was mirthless.

What few people knew, and what fewer would have believed if they had known, was that if Jim had lived another year she would have divorced him. Ironic, even bitterly so, but against all accounts and his crusading to save the island, Jim Fletcher had been a goddamned bastard. Miserly, philandering, and ridiculing her attempts to continue running the store she'd inherited from her father. Once, he'd even attempted to force her to choose between the business and him, backing down only when she'd made it absolutely clear what the answer would have been.

By the time of his death she had grown to hate him.

By the time of his death he had lost his son's love.

"Damn," she muttered, and decided to go upstairs and watch television with Matt. If she were lucky, the picture would be new and Matt would have seen it only a dozen or so times. By the end of the last commercial maybe the funeral would be over. Then she could call Colin and maybe he'd come over for a drink, something warm, some talk . . . maybe a little loving, which suddenly she felt she needed very badly.

But when she reached the staircase she changed her mind and went back to the chair, picked a book up from the floor and opened it to the first page. Soon, she told herself; the funeral will be over soon and then I'll call Colin.

Lilla met Colin at the threshold and faced him squarely. Her face was drawn, her hair tangled and damp. The black dress clung provocatively to her figure, and might have seemed blasphemous had it not been for the dirt and dust that faded parts of it to grey.

"It's time," she said when he was close enough.

He nodded.

"I have no choice?"

"Lilla . . . "

She smiled weakly. "I just wanted to try one more time." Then she sagged, and he held her awkwardly, unable to shake the feeling that all her protests had been lies. He was startled, ashamed, stared over her shoulder into the dark of the shack. Gran was in there.

He could sense the corpse and the shroud. And there was something else—perhaps the scent of her grieving—but whatever it was it wrinkled his nose and would have gagged him had she not pulled away and kissed him lightly on the cheek.

He gave her a weak grin. "Easy, lady, people will talk."

"They do anyway."

She was right. And only a handful understood the affinity binding the two, not as lovers but as friends, both of them outcasts in their own way and recognizing each other instantly.

"You'll ride with me, Colin?"

"Of course I will."

She looked to the beach, the boats. "Colin?" She clasped her hands at her waist, scrubbed them dryly. "Colin, Gran wasn't the man people think he was."

"I know."

She frowned briefly. "No. I don't think so. He—"

The indefinable stench from the shack increased, and he imagined it almost as visible as smoke. He held his breath, amazed it didn't bother Lilla. Incense, he decided then, some crap Gran had brought with him from the Caribbean.

"He what?" he prompted gently.

The stench on the wind now.

She shook her head slowly. "It doesn't matter now," she whispered. Then she turned around.

Stronger.

"Lilla, wait. I'll get some of the others—"

"No!" she said, the child-woman gone in the snap of the command. "He is mine, Colin. If this thing has to be done, I will take him myself.

He opened his mouth to protest, but it was too late, and something about the darkness that seemed to shift just over the threshold kept him from following. He felt embarrassed. He wanted to look back at the others and lift his hands to say *I tried*. Lilla spared him the moment; she returned with the body cradled easily in her arms, and he fell in beside her, holding her elbow to prevent her from slipping.

The stench was gone.

Silently, swiftly, the boats were filled and pushed into the surf. They moved directly east toward the fog's boundary, stopping when they reached a point a mile beyond the jetties' tips.

Colin's arms arched as he rowed the heavy craft, Lilla sitting at the stern, Gran lying between them. But he felt no compulsion to be first at the spot; after all, he thought with a barely stifled laugh, they sure as hell couldn't start without him. The levity shamed him, and he refused to meet Lilla's gaze. He ducked his head and pulled around the already circled boats until he could slip stern first into his place at the top.

The oarlocks were silent, though the oars had been left half submerged in the water. No anchors were thrown, no lines were connected, yet each of the craft maintained the same spacing without needing adjustment. And the dark water in the center was calm, low, as if the ocean were a lake, windless at dusk.

Reverend Graham Otter, standing at the circle's base with his back to the shore, glanced around him once before slipping off his jacket, his black cassock and white collar in startling contrast. He folded his hands at his waist in an attitude of waiting. A moment later he nodded. Lilla rose, turned to face him. Colin followed, watching as the rest of the congregation moved to its feet. There was no struggling for balance, no ripples, no splashes; the boats were still, as were the people in them.

Colin was nervous. Though he assumed he had performed his part well thus far, he suddenly decided this wasn't fair at all. It was his first island funeral, and he should be in one of the other boats, observing, learning, trying to feel the solace that obviously affected the others. But somehow, without his knowing it, he'd been chosen pallbearer, Charon, and God only knew what else. It wasn't fair; he didn't like it; suddenly he turned his head away, blinking aside the flaring afterimage of a match the minister had struck against the shaft of a torch he'd taken from his boat. The cleric held up the flame until it nearly scorched his fingers before bringing it to the cloth soaked almost a day in treated oil. Blue fire, red, spiraled upward and twisted about itself as though it could be bound. Then he handed the torch to the man in the boat beside his, who lit his own torch and passed the first on around the circle until it reached Lilla. She held it close to her face, but Colin could only see the flames rising above her head. When her pause lengthened to a full minute, he thought she would douse it and he swallowed his relief when she finally passed it to her neighbor.

Once it had reached full circle, all the torches were placed in gleaming brass brackets bolted to the sterns. They burned low, with an incessant crackling like dry wood, dark smoke in dark curls rising far above the dark surface.

Blue fire, and red, and pale faces reflecting.

The breakers were muted; no lights on the shore.

The fog began crawling between the boats to the still water.

"Gran," Reverend Otter said then. "Gran, it's time."

Colin saw Lilla's back grow rigid, and he braced himself to grab her in case she changed her mind again. But when she only brought her hands up to take hold of her upper arms he relaxed and tried to listen to what the minister was saying. But he couldn't. He couldn't take his gaze away from the shrouded body, from Lilla's back, from the fingers of fog slipping over the sides.

Reverend Otter droned on; there was a hymn softly sung; yet Colin couldn't help feeling that the others were just as uneasy as he. Garve had told him stories—as had Peg and Annalee, and even Bob Cameron—the highlights of which dealt with the joy of the songs that rose above the sea, the genuine belief there was a better world farther on. That feeling was absent now. And he saw signs of impatient shifting—knees bending and locking, arms swinging, heads nodding.

They want to be gone, he thought, and not just because of Gran.

Then he saw Lilla bend her head for a moment, and realized the reverend had stopped his preaching. Colin waited, wondering if there was something he was supposed to do and cursing Garve for not telling him, staring when Lilla suddenly knelt beside her grandfather and kissed the shroud where his mouth would have been. A slight gesture behind her to keep him where he was, and she slipped her hands under the body, her expression set and her mouth slightly parted. She lifted, shifted, held the dead man against her chest and whispered something to him. Colin strained but couldn't hear her. Then she turned to face the cleric and let the gray bundle slide from her hands into the water, effortlessly, soundlessly, as if it were little more than air.

And despite the weight lashed about its feet, the body floated for several long seconds. Turning through the lacing of fog without disturbing it, sweeping in a complete circle like a compass seeking its direction . . . until it stopped in front of Lilla.

Then nothing moved but the fog.

Finally, the shroud began sinking, slipping smoothly into the black ocean without leaving a ripple behind. Instantly, it was over, and beginning with Otter the torches were thrown after the body until only Lilla's remained.

And when she suddenly whirled around, he ducked instinctively as she hurled the torch as far as she could toward the horizon. He had no idea why, but he knew what she'd done was wrong. Yet she only turned around to wait for him to row her back to shore.

Matt knew Mom was restless, and suspected she might come up to join him. She'd like the movie, too—

66

James Bond again in *The Man with the Golden Gun*. It wasn't so much the shooting and the fights he liked in this one, but the co-star, Christopher Lee, who he knew in real life was Count Dracula. It made the dialogue silly, and sometimes had him giggling hard into his pillow.

When it was obvious she wasn't coming, he slipped off the mattress and wandered around the small room for a minute or two before returning to the bed. There were papers scattered over the quilt from his sketch pad, a handful of felt-tip pens, and a notebook he used to keep track of his drawings. On the walls were a number of pastels he'd done this past summer, taped and tacked and pinned to the white plaster; in the far corner next to the curtained window was an easel that straddled a palette and a case of oils he hadn't yet had the nerve to use; on a single shelf over his bed were two wood carvings that were supposed to be seals but he knew they looked like something no seal ever did; and on the desk were his schoolbooks, already belted together for grabbing in the morning.

He pushed the papers aside and sat, ignoring the flickering from the portable television on the desk. His head shook in dismay. All night he'd been trying to capture the sand castle, and every one of his efforts was a dismal, amateurish failure.

"Nuts, goddamn," he said, and swept the papers to the floor. It was something he hadn't learned yet that was keeping him from doing it right, something he would have to ask Colin about the next time he came to class.

He stretched out, cupped his hands beneath his head, and wondered, not for the first time, if there was something wrong with him inside. Colin had said no, and so had his mother, but if that were true why wasn't his room like anyone else's? There were no pennants on the walls, no cowboy guns in the closet, no footballs or baseballs or an outfielder's mitt. Tommy Fox even had pictures of naked women hidden under his mattress, and he was Matt's age.

But nobody, not anybody put the pictures they drew in school on display in their rooms.

And they definitely hated going to museums—except of course, for the one in New York that had all the dinosaur bones in it, and the stuffed elephants and lions.

No matter what his mother said, he knew he was different. He had to be. And he hated it, hated it a lot. Like when Gran had shown him how to carve things with a knife; he'd done it, done okay for someone who didn't know what he was doing, and it was neat to see how Gran smiled at him in a way he knew no one else got—except maybe Lilla. But the other kids thought it was silly, making things from dead wood. Hated it, like today when the other guys kept poking fun at him while they were building the castle. He didn't say anything to Mr. Ross, but they'd been doing it all afternoon, and even though he was nearly ten he'd almost cried—until Mr. Ross came along and made everything okay.

He remembered the day this past summer that he had told Mr. Ross about, the day with Gran at the luncheonette. There was something funny about the old man's breath that made his nose wrinkle, but Gran was telling him how he used to be a great prince in the island country he came from, and how he bossed everyone around and no one dared laugh at him for being different.

"Good times," Gran had said, picking at his nails with the point of his knife. "They the good days, when I was a young man and had all my teeth." He laughed and slapped his knee. "I tell you, boy, you go with me when I go back and we be king together."

Matt's eyes had nearly popped he opened them so wide. "Yeah? Really?"

Gran had smiled, the true smile he saved for Matt and Lilla. "Oh yes, boy, you believe old Gran when he tell you this is true. Some people here, they don't believe old Gran, but they don't know anything, not these people. They don't know nothing at all what it is like when you be king."

A bunch of sunburned people in shorts had walked by then, had looked at them, and Matt had heard one of them say "nigger."

Gran heard it too. The knife was jabbed deep into the bench.

"They're stupid, Gran," he'd said quickly, wanting to chase them and give them a karate chop, just like James Bond.

But Gran had put a hard hand on his leg to hold him down, and it was a long time before he spoke again.

"Stupid, yes. But they"—and he waved a hand to include the whole island—" hurt *you* too. I know. They got no imagination, but I know what you got in here." A bony finger thumped the side of his head, keeping Matt from asking *how* he knew when no one else did. "We be kings together, okay? Okay?"

Matt agreed readily, and they laughed together. He'd wished he really were a king so he could do something about people who hurt other people. For real, not like in the movies. He wasn't sure, but he thought he'd even kill someone before they could hurt his mother and his teacher, maybe even before they could hurt Lilla. He wasn't sure. But he thought so. If he were a king like Gran said he could be.

But Gran had turned strange, would talk to no one but Lilla, and he guessed the old man was crazy after all.

He shivered and looked over to the window, and wrinkled his nose when he saw the bottom sash still raised. Too cold for that, for sure. On the other hand, if he closed it he wouldn't hear Lilla's singing—if, that is, she sang again tonight. It had been going on for almost a week, and though it spooked his mother, he kind of liked it. One night it would sound like it was coming from the cliffs, and the next it would be coming from the woods on the north shore by Fox's Marina. The night wind took it all over the place. It was sad and it was fast and sometimes it was so lonely sounding he couldn't stand it and wanted to crawl into bed with his mother. She wouldn't let him, though. So he had to stay by the window and look at the backyard and wait until Lilla was happy again.

Pretty, sometimes, in a way he didn't quite understand, but also very spooky. Yes, he supposed it really was about as spooky as you could get.

Especially when it sounded as if he were listening to Gran telling him what it would be like to be king.

But Gran was dead, and now there were only two who didn't think it was so awful and terrible to be different from the rest.

Two, because you didn't count Lilla; ever since Gran died she was too spooky.

Suddenly he didn't want to hear the singing anymore, so he hurried to the window and slammed the sash down, took off his clothes and squirmed under the sheet and quilt. He got up again with a groan and turned off the TV and the lamp, then listened at the door to see if he could hear his mother moving around down there. It was silent and he got into bed.

When his eyes closed he saw a bundle of gray being dropped into the water. Gran. Gran was being buried right while he lay there. Stuck under the water where all the fish could get at him. And Matt couldn't decide which was worse: being eaten by fish or being eaten by worms. Some fish had teeth, but worms made holes; fish took little bites, but worms made holes; some fish could take you in two or three gulps, but worms . . .

He sat upright, blinked, fumbled for the lamp and squinted away from the light as he checked his hands and arms. No holes. He wasn't dead. And he decided right then that he wouldn't die at all. That way, neither the fish nor the worms would be able to get him.

He relaxed and checked the window; unease returned, and he lay back, pulling the quilt to his chin and turning his face to the door.

There was fog out there.

Vaguely illuminated by the light from the kitchen below, it masked the woods and ran rivulets down the pane, pulsed in the breeze as though it were breathing. That was all Lilla's fault. He didn't think anyone had noticed, but he had: All the time Lilla had been singing those dumb, spooky songs, there'd been no fog at all. But tonight, when she was quiet, out there putting old Gran into the ocean for all the fish to eat him, the fog had come back. As if she'd been calling it, and it had taken all this time to get here.

Nuts, he thought. Goddamn . . . goddamn.

In the raised saltbox house on Atlantic Terrace, three in from Bridge Road, Peg Fletcher saw a car drift grayly past the window and knew the funeral was over. She closed her book and went to the front door, opened it, and couldn't believe what she was hearing—

Lilla singing.

Matt Fletcher tossed and turned in his sleep, fat red worms slithering through his dreams, huge black fish swimming through his nightmares, all of them driven—

By Lilla singing.

Colin accepted a ride back from Garve, got out at the police station and nearly broke into a run in his hurry to get home. Lilla had refused to go to the house two doors down from Peg's, and demanded she be permitted to stay at Gran's shack for one more night. He hadn't argued, no one had. Now all he wanted was to get in bed in order to hurry the dawn.

The wind was strong, and he could feel the spider-touch of mist that preceded the rain. Not the Screamer, Garve had assured him, just a quick storm, nothing more. With shoulders hunched and head down, he began a slow trot, and before he reached the cottage he remembered his promise to call Peg. He smiled ruefully. It would have been nicer to go directly to her place, but he didn't think he'd be good company tonight.

Then he stopped, half turned, and listened.

The wind, he told himself hastily as he hurried up the steps and fumbled for his key; it's only the wind. Gran is dead. She's there in his damned shack.

But as the door swung inward he realized he was listening to Lilla's distant singing.

FOUR

Within an hour after the funeral a wind broke from the mainland forest as if it had been lurking there, waiting for its moment. It rocked the ferry at its mooring and sent Wally into the small hut to the left of the landing. He would have opened the single window overlooking the bay, but there was something about the trees' sighing he didn't like—a subliminal wailing, and a distant acrid odor he usually associated with an abnormally low tide, with dead fish and mudflats and the fresh rot of *things* dredged up from the bottom.

He stoked the wood stove, shrugged into his worn pea coat, and sat in the chipped Boston rocker in the corner. There was a cot and a blanket beside him, but he made no move to lie down, the temptation of sleep long banished by his nerves. Instead, after lighting a bitter pipe he hadn't cleaned in weeks, he flipped through worn magazines whose words blurred before his one good eye, whose photographs of nude women smeared as if the eye were weeping.

The wind skimmed over the water, raising white-caps in its wake, coasting over the island and shredding the fog. There were thick night clouds looming overhead, blotting out the stars. The tidal swells hunched and the breakers grew more insistent, slamming into the jetties to form walls of brief gray. The caves

73

that pocked the cliffs added deep-throated howls to the keening overhead.

The boats at the marina scraped against their docks; branches scraped against windows; the amber light on Neptune Avenue flared once, and went out.

The ocean was cold, nearly as cold as it was dark, and Lilla felt her flesh tightening as if she had been suddenly encased in stiff, cracking leather. She was naked, and she had begun to wish she had worn something to warm her, but there had been very little time to pick and choose among her wardrobe—most of it she kept in the house on Atlantic Terrace, and the few pieces left were in a trunk in the shack.

Besides, she thought, the clothes would be a hindrance, and right now she needed all the freedom she could get.

After Colin had reluctantly left her at the door, clearly not believing her assertion she was fine; after Reverend Otter had paid his condolences and commented on the service; after Garve and the others had drifted silently off the beach, she had sat on the floor, cross-legged and waiting. Patiently at first, until the wind began to blow; then fidgeting, drumming her fingers hard on her thighs, rocking on her buttocks, humming to herself until she thought it was midnight.

Hang on, Gran.
Hang on, hang on.

She sat, humming and rocking, and every few moments blinking her eyes slowly as if vaguely aware of a distant beckoning light just below the horizon. A light that stirred memories, a light that had her frightened.

Once she shook her head violently and leapt to her feet. She stared about her in helpless panic. This is wrong, she thought (the light flaring for a moment). This was all wrong and she was condemning herself to the worst kind of hell if she . . . if she . . . (the light flickered) . . . if . . . (the light died) . . . she sighed,

74

closed her eyes, a spectral smile on her lips. A smile that lasted until she opened the shack's door.

Hang on, Gran,
I'll be singing you soon.
Hang on, hang on,
don't leave me, don't leave.

She stumbled down off the flat and raced up the beach, vaulting the snow fence as if it were only a foot high, landing lightly on hands and knees in a dark spray of sand. A scramble for balance, and she was running again. No attention was paid to the wind now, or to the waves that hissed angrily toward the woods. She was dimly aware the moon and stars were gone, and just as dimly heard the distant blare of a car's horn.

The beach narrowed, became rocky, and the trees stalked the waterline. She slowed and moved into the shadows, picking her way cautiously through dank shallow pools and across long stretches of mossy rocks, dead leaves, and sodden needle carpets. Her hands shoved aside branches, her face ducked away from sharp twigs, and she felt nothing at all when a wide thicket she plunged through tore gaps in her dress. Her hair matted and snarled. Cracks spread across the heels and soles of her bare feet. And finally she bent forward into a partial crouch and slipped past stiff shrubs to the edge of the marina's reach.

To her left, on the other side of a crushed-gravel driveway, was a sturdy, three-story white house topped by a widow's walk and girdled by a closed-in porch. A station wagon and red jeep were parked in its shadow. A wide, well-kept lawn spread down to the water, illuminated in silver by spotlights bolted to tall poles at the end of each dock. All the boats, including the trawler, were there rocking against the nudging of the wind, dull thumps soft in the night air as used-tire buffers caught the hulls and eased them back.

On this side of the drive, in line with her left

shoulder, was a huge, gray, barn-like structure that served as Alex Fox's workhouse, starkly outlined by glaring lights in the eaves.

She waited, squatting on her heels.

Then, on command of a timer Fox kept in his kitchen, the lights snapped out, one by one in rapid sequence, the black vacuum filled by a photo negative afterimage that blinded her for several moments. Once her vision cleared, however, she was out of the trees and running, hitting the nearest dock as quietly as she could and darting out to the end. A rowboat moored at bow and stern rose and fell with the rising wind.

She thought nothing, planned nothing. Her hands untied the ropes, her right foot pushed the boat off, and the oars were slipped expertly into their locks without a sound. She had almost turned the craft around when she realized what she was missing. She maneuvered back to the dock, tied up the bow and ran for the workhouse. The tall double doors were unlocked and slightly ajar. A swift glance at the house, and she ghosted inside. Though she barked her shins several times against obstacles invisible in the dark, it didn't take her fingers long to locate the shelving she knew was there, and to close around a gaff and a waterproof flashlight.

Once outside, she paused and stared up the drive, marking the place where the gravel became blacktop and started Neptune Avenue. The amber light was out. The Anchor's neon was blind. For all the movement she saw then she could have been the island's only inhabitant. Not even a leaf was stirred by the wind.

In half an hour, arms protesting and back dully aching, she reached the burial place. The water was cold, her flesh tight as cracked leather.

Now she was below the surface, and there were creatures of the night sea she had forgotten or had not known. They swarmed about her like blackshadow lightning, taunting, teasing, darting nips and nibbles at her legs while she fought to keep air in her already straining lungs. Four times since she'd arrived she had slipped out of the rowboat, four times using the rough anchor chain to guide her as she pulled her way down; and four times she had failed, embattled, the cold too much and the air bubbling up and out in reluctant spreading streams, preceding her to the top where she clung wearily to the bow and spit, coughed, felt the salt stinging her reddening eyes and the cuts on her feet.

Her teeth chattered uncontrollably, though she no longer felt the water droplets on her face.

Her hair pulled at her scalp, as if trying to work loose.

On the fifth drive she nearly failed to locate the chain again, and the flashlight gained unconscionable weight.

On the sixth dive, as she sobbed silent fear and anger in equal frustration, she was lucky.

The shrouded corpse lay on the uneven bottom between two low ridges of tide-gouged sand; the feet were half buried by the weight inside, the torso and head canted upward and drifting in the slow-moving current. The pale beam darted over it, passed it, returned and held. Shapeless, yet unmistakable, the light giving it a gray aura that shaded out to black.

Lilla grinned and wanted to laugh, tasted salt water instead and returned flailing to the boat, breaking the rolling surface with a sound like a bark. She clambered over the side and lay panting on the boat's bottom, staring at the sky. Resting. Grinning. A dark strand of kelp burrowed into her hair, and pearls of water shivering across the bridge of her nose, in circlets around her breasts.

"I told you, Gran," she whispered. "I told you. I told you."

She hummed snatches of several tunes, all of them Gran's, and her left hand beat time on the planks while her right used the flashlight like a bloated baton. Her thighs quivered. Her stomach pushed out, caved in.

Hummed the old songs she had sung in the shack.

"Told you, Gran. Told you to trust me."

She giggled suddenly, and covered her mouth.

The cold rushed through her in spasms, and she made herself rigid to drive them away.

A cramp uncoiled in her right foot, and she jabbed out her heel until the pain subsided and died.

Then, over the humming, she heard the thunder coming at her from the mainland. Her head shook in outraged dismay; not now, no, not now, not now. She had found him. She had run the length of Haven's End and had stolen a boat and had rowed right to the spot and she had found him. She knew where Gran was, and now she wanted to rest. The thunder gave her answer. She sighed a weak protest, and saw lightning beyond the trees.

"All right," she muttered. "All right, damn it, all right."

She picked up a gaff with thick roping knotted at its looped end and dropped back into the ocean before the storm changed her mind. Unerringly, she swam directly down to the shroud and plunged the rusted hook into the upper end. She tugged at it repeatedly, as hard as she could to be sure it would hold, then retreated once more to the boat and the air. She lay there for a moment, her breath in shallow gulps, before scrambling around to her knees and taking hold of the rope. A shuddering inhalation, a murmured prayer, a mirthless smile . . . and she began to haul Gran in, feeling her palms sting and burn as she pulled slowly, slowly, hand over hand, bracing her knees on the coils building on the bottom, every few moments glancing over her shoulder to the shore to check for lights.

Hand over hand until Gran was beside her and she could sag against the rear seat, gasping and weeping, cooling her hurt palms against her stomach, her breasts.

She paid no heed to the thunder now, felt nothing but the sea swell beneath the keel and tip her gently, side to side.

"It's going to be all right now, Gran," she said five minutes later, taking up the oars and heading for the

78

beach. "You're going to be all right now. I told you not to worry, didn't I? You got to trust your Lilla, Gran. You don't have to worry now. I've got you. I've got you."

In less than two hours the boat was returned, and the gaff, and the flashlight, and the night was still black.

Lilla sang.
(the dimlight flared and she almost screamed, but a darksoft whispering insinuated itself between the scream and the glare, a whispering that became the fog that comforted her again)
Slowly, she backed out of the shack, her nearly blind gaze on the shimmering glow in the other room. She could see the foot of the bed, she could see Gran's feet, and she could still hear the singing that lingered after she was done.
She walked away from Gran's house without once looking back, making her way stiffly over the dunes to Surf Court. She paid no attention to the looming houses and their yellow porch lights, to the cars in the driveways, to the trembling streetlamps. She showed neither haste nor purpose, as she walked down the road to Neptune Avenue, turned right and followed the broken white line past Tess Mayfair's dark-windowed boarding house, past the Rising Sun and the Seaview, and into the mile-long stretch of unbroken woodland. She did not feel the damp tarmac under her feet, nor the wind pushing hard at her hair.
A gray haze in the distance, the streetlights of the town, but she cocked her head to one side and knew she wouldn't have to go quite that far. There was a dark lump on the verge fifty yards ahead, and when a vicious gust passed over it, it squirmed and tried to crawl.
Lightning reached out to drag thunder after.
Lilla smiled, and kept walking.

The figure shifted again, a shifting shadow against shadows, and finally stirred itself to standing.

Lilla stopped, but kept smiling.

"Warren," she said, her voice clear despite the howling wind. "Warren, you weren't at the funeral."

Harcourt passed a weary hand over his eyes and peered into the darkness, his mouth opening slightly when lightning showed him the speaker. "Lilla!" He tried to straighten his spine, his lapels, reached up for his hat and froze when he discovered it wasn't on his head. He stammered and managed an apologetic smile, became suddenly aware that his feet were still bare. "Lilla—"

She faced him. "You weren't at the funeral." Not an accusation; a simple fact.

"I am . . . was as you see me," he told her, wincing as the storm moved from howls to shrieks. He moved closer, to be heard. "I could not disgrace you."

"You wouldn't have."

"But I would," he insisted, wounded dignity in his eyes. "I would." Then he glanced up the road, back the way she had come. "It's over, then."

"It has been, for hours. Warren, we missed you, Gran and I."

He waved away her kindness. "He's in the sea, then?"

She nodded.

"He let you do it?" He was astounded and relieved.

She reached out to touch him, and even through the topcoat he could feel her cold grip. "Gran is dead, Warren. Now he's buried the way they wanted." Closer, almost touching. "I don't think I want to stay in his house tonight."

Harcourt's expression was befuddled as he attempted to sweep aside the alcoholic fog he carried with him. When her hands moved to the back of his neck, when his skin felt her fingers idly twirling the ends of his hair, he tried not to shudder. She was bereft, he reminded himself; now she wants to go

80

home. But he almost wept when he realized he couldn't remember where she lived.

"Atlantic Terrace," she whispered, as if reading his mind. "Just down from Peg Fletcher's, you know that. It's late. I'm a little frightened with all this," and she looked skyward, back to his eyes.

A slow and deep breath to steady himself, and he nodded. "I quite understand, Lilla. If you need someone to accompany you, you only have to say the word. I am always at your service, as you know."

She dropped her hand to his elbow and smiled at him broadly. "You'll be a gentleman?"

Offended, he almost drew away. "Always, Lilla. Surely you know that."

She giggled softly, kissed his cheek, pressed her forehead to his chin. Her voice was muffled. "You and I, Warren, we're alone on this island now. The others, they think they know what we go through, but they don't. Not really. They feel sorry for us, but they don't care." She looked up at him. "Do they care?"

He wanted to say *yes*, and knew instantly it was a lie.

"You see?" she said.

The wind was a hint of winter, and before he knew it he had his arms around her, drawing her into the warmth of his coat. So small, he thought. He hadn't realized how small she was, the girl-woman, the child. So small, and so soft; he startled himself by feeling things he had thought were long dead. One hand slipped down to the slope of her buttocks, the other into her hair.

They kissed.

Soft, he thought while her tongue searched for his. Soft. So soft.

He felt her trembling against him, and wanted to open his coat so he could feel her stomach and breasts and the ridge of her hips. But to open the coat would mean breaking the embrace, and it had been so long, so terribly long . . . so he hugged her instead and

81

closed his eyes at the low groan that warmed the side of his neck.

"Are you shocked, Warren?" she asked softly.

He shook his head once. "It is a trying time for you, Lilla. Solace, comfort, it's what you need, what you deserve."

"Are you sober?" she asked then, and he almost laughed aloud.

"I would say, my dear, that I am about as sober now as I have been for years. That isn't saying much, I grant you, but it's the best you'll get tonight."

They clung beneath the wind and the lightning, against the battering of dead leaves, against the dust devils that leapt from the verge to the road.

She kissed him again, gently, not insisting, and when she lay her head tenderly on his chest he felt a thrumming through his clothes. He frowned for a long moment until he realized she was singing. Very quietly, virtually unheard as the wind brought the first rain. Then a connection was made, and he remembered El Nichols pushing him down the road, remembered turning around, remembered Lilla's night songs.

"Warren," she whispered, "are you alive?"

There was more than the night cold now working down his back. He pushed her away, but she held onto his arms.

"Alive?" she asked again.

"Of course," he snapped, trying to pry loose her grasp.

She smiled, and in a sudden blue-white flare he saw her eyes, the death there, and would not believe it. Nor could he believe the power in her hands.

He could think of nothing else to say but, "That singing . . .

"You know the words?" she said, turning her head to see him sideways.

"I have had French, yes, and I've traveled a bit in my time."

"Warren—"

"And I am just drunk enough to be glad he's in the ocean."

"Oh, Warren," she said, shaking her head slowly. "Oh, Warren, dear Warren, he's not there, he's behind you."

A gnarled black hand from the dark grabbed his shoulder, and as he whirled to look behind, the razor she held measured the length of his exposed neck.

Then she left him upright in the shadows and walked back to the shack.

Hearing nothing but the wind, and her singing, and something behind her, drinking.

PART TWO

October: Friday

ONE

Another warm day, too warm for October, an August day misplaced in the middle of autumn. The rainstorm was gone, sweeping out to the Atlantic and up toward New York. What was left was the sun that turned the shallows turquoise, brightened the pines' green, shifted red leaves to vermilion and brown leaves to tan. The sea scent was strong, the breeze a welcome cooling, and Thursday a memory buried in a back closet.

It should have been perfect.

It should have been a quiet time of remembering, perhaps regretting, and looking forward to winter and the peace that it brings, forgetting for the moment that spring will start it all again.

But there'd been too many dreams spawned after midnight, too many arguments over a sun-bright breakfast, too many doors slammed and engines raced—and an unnerving feeling that an island four miles long and two miles wide was suddenly an island that had grown much too small.

The school on Haven's End was less than twenty years old and took care of the island's children until they were ready for high school across the bay in Flocks. The building was unimposing by any mainland standards: a single-story brick and gray-glass building raised on a high concrete foundation to keep the rooms from flooding when the occasional hurricane shrieked up the coast. Double doors at the entrance, high taxus and laurels to camouflage the concrete, and massive full pines at each of the front corners. The only sign it might be an official structure was the flagpole by the steps—tall, white, with a gleaming brass ball at the top gripped in the brass claws of a spread-wing eagle. Ocean Street ended almost at its front steps, as if the school were a monument facing a pitted tarmac mall, and behind were the woods that thickened toward the cliffs.

The morning blue, the noon sun, were slowly fading behind a haze.

At precisely two-thirty Colin was positioned in the entrance foyer, smiling and nodding as the children swarmed past him toward two days of freedom. Their shouts were infectious, their laughter a potion, and he rolled his shoulders with impatience to get on with the weekend while his left hand drummed a march on the flat of his thigh. Like his students, he felt that today was too beautiful to be spent inside. Heresy, he knew; a teacher's dedication supposedly knew no weather. But after the previous night's funeral he thought it a miracle the storm hadn't lingered to drench the town in stereotypical gloom. As it was, he'd had a difficult time of it from the moment he'd arrived. The kids and his colleagues seemed touched with electricity, a curious sort of tension that made them jump when spoken to, kept their eyes on the windows, had their attention wandering throughout their lessons—the kind of intangible crackling that preceded thunder.

He suspected the mood was caused by the Screamer. In the lounge, a colleague, Rose Adams, had detailed the effects of such a blow in '74. It had swept in before dawn, tides five and six feet above normal, streets flooded, windows shattered, more than a dozen automobiles pushed down Bridge Road straight into the bay. Luckily there'd been a warning, and most of the islanders had taken off for the main-land. Of those who'd remained, one had drowned on his lawn, another had been dashed to death against a wall by the wind and a fallen tree.

"Of course I'm not leaving," she said when he asked. "Do you think I'd miss one just because of a little wind?"

A throat cleared behind him, and he turned as he moved aside, the smile almost fading when he saw three students waiting, a girl and two boys.

"Excuse me, Mr. Ross," Denise Adams said po-litely as she brushed past him through the door.

"Have a good weekend," he said to the curly-haired brunette. "See you Monday."

She paused on the middle of five marble steps and looked back over her shoulder. "Aren't you going to the party tomorrow?"

He shrugged.

"Carter can vote, you know. You ought to talk to him. You always say every vote counts in any elec-tion." Then she smiled broadly. "I was eighteen last week. I can vote too."

Several comments came instantly to mind, all of them salacious and unbefitting his position; he grinned anyway, for the hell of it, to show her what he was thinking. Her large eyes widened, and her lower lip pulled between her teeth as she waved somewhat doubtfully and took the remaining steps at a delib-erately slow march, her blue plaid shirt tight across her slender back, her jeans-encased hips swinging sharply side to side. The two boys with her ignored him completely. But he smiled at them as well, think-ing the effort wouldn't kill him, though he decided not to ask why they weren't bringing home their books.

The smaller of the two, Denise's brother, Frankie, slapped her arm when they reached the sidewalk. She slapped him back, hard, before he could twist away, and muttered something Colin didn't hear as the door hissed closed. He sneered and ducked another blow, ran to the street and tightroped the center line. The second boy shot an arm around her waist and drew her close, leaned toward her ear and whispered with a leer. She slapped him too, but not nearly as hard as she had hit her brother. Then he looked back over his shoulder and gave a cold smile to Colin.

Colin nodded as if the smile were genuine.

"Sweet, isn't he," a deep voice said behind him. He didn't turn. He watched Carter Naughton walk with Denise up the street, his fisted right hand now buried in her hip pocket.

"He'll do."

"No, he won't," said Bill Efron. "None of them will. They come here three times a week for your tutoring, and I'll bet you your salary they still won't graduate high school in June. I tell you, Colin, there are times when I suspect they're not even human."

Colin laughed quietly. The principal had been fighting with Naughton and his friends for as long as they'd been alive, or so it seemed. Cart was nineteen, tall and muscular, his thick black hair greased to a gleaming and combed in a ducktail reminiscent of the fifties. Frankie, three years younger, tried desperately for imitation, but his curled brown hair wouldn't straighten, he was too skinny for a fitted T-shirt, and Colin didn't believe he really had the heart. Peg had agreed, which is why she kept him on as her stockboy and clerk—a chance for salvation, she'd said when he asked her.

Denise, on the other hand, was what he could only describe as saucy, and sassy, and much too old for her age. She also didn't need the extra work; her high school grades were quite adequate for passing. Though she denied it, he knew the only reason she came was because Carter commanded.

Efron sighed loudly, a frequent martyr to his profession, and pushed aside his tan cashmire jacket to tuck his thumbs around his alligator belt. He was white-haired and balding, his face a pink balloon slowly leaking air. His pale eyes were narrowed in a perpetual

90

squint, a refusal to wear glasses when he was outside his office.

"Wouldn't give you two cents for the lot of them," the principal said bitterly. "Damned state insists we have to train 'em, though. Don't know why Flocks doesn't do it; they've got the teachers and facilities. It's that fool at the high school, of course. Carter has him scared out of his wits. But as long as the kid insists on staying in, there's nothing the guy can do." He shook his head in empathetic resignation. "If the draft were still in, that jerk would be in khaki."

Colin listened without comment. In the first place, he really didn't mind the tutoring he'd volunteered for; he thought it a challenge, rather liked the extra money, and once in a while even Cart gave him hope there might be progress. But Efron was leading up to something else besides grousing. After all this time he knew the signs—the man was corralling his courage for something unpleasant he hadn't the finesse to open squarely. The last time it was a mild scolding for showing Gauguin nudes in the classroom; the time before that it was smoking in the schoolyard; and the time before that it was to announce to the faculty there'd be no raise in the fall.

"I, uh, don't see you out shaking hands," Efron said at last, with a jocular tone so false it nearly creaked. His pink face turned pinker. "I suppose you're saving it for the big party at the Run tomorrow night."

Colin trapped an ill-timed comment by wiping his mouth. "I'm not all that political, Bill, though I have to admit it'd be awfully tempting to make a speech. Maybe I will, just to see what Bob says." He laughed with a shake of his head. "Probably toss me out on my ear." He paused. "Are you going to be there?"

"Probably. If the wife is feeling better."

Colin barely managed to withhold a chuckle, arranging his expression artfully into a display of concern. Efron's wife was notorious for her illnesses, primarily contracted from the soap operas she watched; what the heroines suffered she felt bound to share, as long as it didn't seem that the suffering was fatal. Efron indulged her, and ignored the snide comments, and the rest of the island generally played the game—when there was nothing left to talk about, Mrs. Efron's latest provided an easy topic.

"Well, I hope she's well enough. It should be quite a bash."

Efron nodded thoughtfully, slipped a hand into his jacket pocket. "You won't be giving any speeches, then."

"I made the one last month at the town meeting, which proved to me I should stick to my canvases. Anyway, I figure people can ask me if they want to know more."

"And do they?"

He nodded. "Once in a while. You know how it is."

A pause. "Here in school?"

He turned slowly and leaned as casually as he could against the doorframe, trying to decide if the man was kidding or not. The look on the principal's face said he wasn't, and Colin almost lost his temper. "Bill, I'm surprised. You know me better than that. Here, I teach. I don't campaign. Anybody asks me, I tell them to wait until later."

Efron smiled in weak apology. "I know that, Colin. I just want to be sure you understand."

"It's been over a month. Why haven't you said anything before?"

The principal shrugged his wide, sagging shoulders. "Didn't see the need for it."

"And now?"

The question echoed off the empty foyer's beige-tiled walls, and Efron backed to a wall display case behind whose glass face were ranged a few polished trophies and dark-framed citations. He stared at them as if they were whispering in his ear.

"This isn't a big school, Colin, not like they have in Flocks or the city. But it does have a reputation. And a damned good one, I might add. There are more than a dozen kids here from the mainland whose parents are willing to pay extra to have them learn from us. Our students on the average do better in high school and in college than anyone else in the county." He traced a finger across the glass, as if he were trying to write a message. "I don't want people saying there's any undue influence here."

"You don't have to worry about that, Bill," he said, hoping his annoyance didn't show in his tone. "At least I don't hand out pamphlets to my students to take home to their parents." And the moment he said it he wished he'd kept his mouth shut.

Efron half-turned, frowning. "What's that supposed to mean?"

It was too late to retreat, but he didn't want to argue. A gesture, then, to deflect the tension. "Come on, Bill, don't play games, okay? It's a beautiful day and I don't want it spoiled for something silly like this."

"Are you saying Cameron uses his business to garner votes?"

Colin sighed mild disgust and walked toward the intersection of the foyer and the building's single hallway.

"Colin."

He stopped.

The hallway was deserted.

The voice behind him was solemn.

"Bob Cameron has a restaurant, and what he does there is his affair. It's private, and his customers don't have to read his material if they don't want to. On the other hand, this is a public school. We have a trust here, aside from a legal obligation. A word to the wise—don't abuse it."

He nodded without looking back, continued around the corner and headed for the faculty lounge. Once inside, with the door carefully closed behind him, he lashed out with a foot at the nearest chair, wincing when he connected with the aluminum tubing and a shock paralyzed his leg. Idiot, he thought as he hob-

bled to the back window and looked out at the schoolyard. Idiot—though he wasn't sure yet who deserved
the label.

He put his palms on the sill and touched his forehead
to the glass, staring at the swing sets, the seesaws, the
benches and redwood tables. A man was out there—
Denise and Frankie's father—stabbing listlessly at
pieces of lunch paper and wrappings with a pole tipped
with a nail, stuffing the catch into a canvas sack
hanging from his shoulder. Colin watched him for five
minutes without the man looking up.

Finally, after a long escaping sigh that fogged the
pane, he had to admit that what he had heard wasn't
much of a threat. In fact, 'threat' was definitely too
strong a word since Efron never had been very effec-
tive with thunder. Yet the fact it had been tried made
him wonder what, if anything, was next, and if there
had been something else on the man's mind that hadn't
been said. As he turned away from the custodian
cleaning the yard, he wondered what Cameron had
said to make Efron act.

He shook himself like a dog shedding rain, and
decided he was overreacting to a perfectly reasonable
suggestion. After all, it was Efron's job to keep his
school and his teachers clean in more ways than one,
and Colin was actually surprised it hadn't been
brought up before. Surprised because Bill Efron was
one of the casino's staunchest supporters, and if Colin
won the election they'd be co-members on the Board.

Good lord, he thought with a start, wouldn't that be
something else? A hell of a thing, since the Board also
hired and fired all the teachers. He could see it all now:
a smoke-filled room, a dramatic confrontation, Efron
trying to dislodge Colin's tenure, and Colin passion-
ately voting against him. He laughed aloud, once, and
looked to the ceiling. It would have to be a first,
unquestionably. What other teacher in the state had
the power to save his own skin? Not only a first, it was
ludicrous. Unreal.

He laughed again, this time to himself, and while laughing made his way back to his room for his jacket and briefcase. A check to be sure nothing was left behind, and he was out of the silent building before anyone could intercept him. He paused on the last step to allow his eyes to adjust to the sunlight, and turned right to follow the sidewalk past the school; a sharp left with the cracked pavement and he was heading toward Bridge Road. The block easily stretched twice as long as any he'd ever seen, so long in fact that each street was trisected by narrow concrete pathways lined with hurricane fencing and poplars for shade so pedestrians didn't have to walk all the way to the corner or the shops out on Neptune just to visit a friend.

A flock of gulls swept low overhead, slow-riding the currents like black-and-white kites, and he listened for a moment to their cries on the wind. It was the only sound he could hear, and his footsteps the only proof he wasn't caught in a dream. Nice, he thought as he did each day, very nice indeed.

Across the street there were high-mounted houses clustered under tall trees all the way to the corner, on his side the same until he reached Reverend Otter's fieldstone cottage, one of the few not raised for protection. Then the spired New England church with its vast rock garden on the side and a belfry ringed with a narrow widow's walk for sighting the fleet, the brown clapboard library that used to be someone's home (with an attending fat Doberman asleep and whimpering now in the sun), and finally he reached the corner and Cameron's Clipper Run.

Several cars passed him heading east. Folks on their way to Flocks for a Friday night outing, he guessed. He grinned and waved when one of them honked a horn, and an arm poked out a window to give him a wave back.

A group of kids playing ball in the street across the way.

Someone practicing on a tortured saxophone.

Nice, he thought; I should live again and be so lucky.

A fluttering by the restaurant caught his attention, and he peered through the shade under raw-beamed eaves extending over the entrance. There was a white cloth banner tacked above the door, proclaiming the dancing and dinner that would be held tomorrow night, all in the name of a successful season's finish. As if, he thought in mild disgust, every season before this one had been a total disaster. But it was a good way to discover how many votes the man had, and how many he needed to pry away from Colin.

He swung his briefcase out to batter at the hedge, and wondered maliciously where Bob had found the nerve to interfere with his job, but he also remembered those so-called friends he could have met last night, the ones Garve had described to him on the beach at Gran's funeral.

Tomorrow, he thought, should be interesting indeed.

He checked the sky, took a deep breath to smell the ocean, and decided he should go home before dropping in on Peg. He'd been wrestling with the idea all day, and now he felt a chill.

It was time. Perhaps it was too late. When he awoke this morning and watched the dawn shadows slip off the ceiling, he'd realized that not calling her when he'd returned last night was more than breaking an understood promise; it was stalling.

And not done very adroitly at that.

As he reached the police station and turned onto Neptune, he mocked himself for his procrastination. Subtle as a sledgehammer. Ross, you dumb jerk. Thank God you didn't decide to try your hand working for the State Department; World World Three before you even unpack your bags.

"Hey, Mr. Ross."

He blinked and looked to his right, saw El Nichols standing in the station doorway. "Hey, El, how's it going?"

The younger man looked tired, and his uniform was faintly rumpled. "Could be better, could be worse. You know how it is. I think the Screamer's put ants in the town's pants today, though. I've been out on more calls . . ." He shook his head once to mark his exasperation. "Little old ladies seeing prowlers on their back porches, stuff like that. And in the middle of the day, yet."

"Little old ladies know no clock, El. A prowler's a prowler whether the sun's out or not."

The deputy laughed, a rich and smooth sound that effectively smothered the rest of his souring mood.

"So," Colin said, "you catch any?"

"You kidding?" Eliot slumped against the frame and leaned forward, lowering his voice as if conspiring, or guarding against the ire of his friends. "Hattie over at the library had me go up and down between every damned stack while that monster dog of hers barked his damned fool head off the whole time I was there. Then she made me listen to some theory she has about this Greek or Roman guy named Tantalus and why he did what he did. Jesus, who the hell cares? I never even heard of the jerk.

"Then, I had to go out to Tess Mayfair's boarding place. She say's someone's tramping through her garden killing the flowers. Well, hell, those flowers have been dead since the Fourth of July ten years ago come Sunday, but that don't make a difference to her. No sir. I have to go a hundred yards into the woods out back to prove there wasn't anyone there tryin' to rape her."

Colin sighed his commiseration. "You have to admit, though," he said finally, "Tess isn't anyone you'd want to get angry."

"Tell me," Eliot said with a mock shudder. "Three hundred pounds and six feet if she's an inch. I lived there for a couple of years, y'know, but I got out soon as I could swing it. Jesus, I couldn't even bring a date to the living room!"

Colin lowered his head in sympathy.

"And the westerns," El said. "God, the westerns! Even when I did bring someone in, we couldn't do anything. She has six TV sets, and just before I left she got one of those videotape things. My lord in great blue heaven, cowboys shooting up every damned town in the West twenty hours a day, every one of them John for God's sake Wayne." He shook his head with a slight frown. "Do you know that she once took a vacation to Hollywood and spent the whole time sitting in front of some theater or other, just waiting to see him? Can you beat it? Two weeks just waiting to see John Wayne?"

"Big star."

"Dead star," El said, "and I don't think she knows it."

"That bad?"

"I think she lights candles to him every night. It was hell living there, man, believe it."

"Life's rough on the range, pal," Colin said taking a poke at Eliot's arm and receiving a friendly poke in return. He was about to move on when he saw a sudden and somber alteration in Nichols' expression. "You feeling all right, El?"

The man plucked at his shirtfront. "Yeah, I guess so." A deep breath, a loud exhalation. "Well, not really, actually. A little guilty, I think, because I missed the funeral last night. It was that . . . well, I got tied up, you might say."

"Oh."

"Everything go okay?"

Colin remembered the torch, the look on the girl's face, and it took him a moment before he finally nodded.

"Good. Good. I'd hate to think—" His eyes widened, and his right hand clasped hard over his heart. "Oh my God," he whispered loudly, "you'd better run to get Doc Montgomery, Ross. I think I just now died and ended up in heaven."

Colin almost laughed aloud. With his back to the

avenue he was facing the police station's plate glass window; the venetian blinds were down and he could see the other side of the street reflected as clearly as if the glass were a mirror. There was a gray stucco cottage, and a tiny green lawn, and Annalee Covey standing on the stoop. She was in her nurse's whites, a sweater draped over her shoulders, and her dark blonde hair was dancing with the wind. He had to admit she was more than a little stunning.

"Down boy," he said. "Garve will have your heart out with his bare hands for drooling like that on duty."

Eliot curled a lip in well-practiced disgust. "You kiddin'? Garve? Hell, all he ever does is sit in his chair and wait for her to leave, to come home from the doc's office. It's like a religion or something with him. He looks, but that's it. If she ever winked at him, he'd shit in his pants. I keep telling him he oughta have more gumption, like my grandmother used to say, but I don't think he has any more sense than Frankie Adams."

Annalee hurried down to the sidewalk, turned to Colin's right, and when she was in front of the Anchor Inn she angled across the street with a hasty glance at her watch and a waggle-fingered wave to the two men before she vanished.

"A lovely woman," Colin said.

"I can't argue there, but I tell you, Mr. Ross, I don't think he has a prayer."

Colin raised a warning finger. "Mr. Nichols, you must never underestimate the power of a Native American."

"What the hell is that?"

"An Indian," he said solemnly. "Garve has a little Navaho blood in him, remember? They have power we poor whites don't."

"Shit. The only power he's got is to fire my ass if I don't get back to work."

"Point and hint taken," Colin said with a smile, and gave him a two-fingered salute before moving on.

Eliot grinned, returned the salute, and was in the office before Colin had a chance to say good-bye.

A wooded lot separated the police station from a long, low building with a red-tiled roof and white clapboard siding. On one end was a hardware store, on the other a five-and-dime; in the center was Fletcher's Drugs, one of the few local businesses that kept normal hours once the season was over. It was brightly lighted, its aisles wide and uncluttered, and was serviced by a short counter near the door and a longer one in back.

Peg was there, and she waved when he came in. He smiled and moved toward her, a loud greeting at his lips swallowed when he heard giggling and a slap off to his left. Immediately, he veered over, toward a display case of costume jewelry. As he rounded a rack of greeting cards for Halloween, he almost collided with Denise, who was dancing away from Cart Naughton's grasping hand. Without a pause, he said, "There's no one up front, you'll have to pay for that in back," and pointed to the ring box in the boy's his pocket.

"Yeah," Naughton said, "I was gonna." A careful touch to his hair and he swaggered away, Colin slowly following with Denise at his side.

At the register, Peg was ringing up the sale and dropping the box into a white paper bag. She smiled at Cart, at Denise and asked if she'd seen her brother.

"I don't know where he is," she said without interest. "Maybe he tried to walk on water and drowned." Then she giggled, took Cart's arm, and they left hip to hip.

Colin leaned against the counter and watched them, saw them laughing hysterically as they passed by the window, nearly colliding with a woman pushing a shopping cart filled with groceries. "A lovely couple. The salt of the earth."

"She's a bitch," Peg said, "and he's a prick. Rumor has it his father never wanted him and isn't above letting him know it. On the other hand, there's also a rumor that he wasn't born at all, that he was found in a cave by Tess Mayfair, who thought he was the reincarnation of John Wayne. I, myself, of course, do not listen to such nonsense because I am a professional dedicated to alleviating all human misery with two aspirins and a condom."

He laughed and turned to face her, and was taken as always by the sparks in her auburn hair, by the smooth lines of her face, by the green-gray of her wide eyes so much like his own. A frilled white blouse and a simple black skirt, with a thin gold chain looped close about her neck. He felt himself blushing like ten kinds of a fool, his anger at Cameron now completely out of mind.

"You want something, teach?" she asked with a mock frown.

"You want me to answer that?"

"Not now," she said.

He tried to ignore the suggestive tone, and looked around the store as if searching for something. She did that to him, knew it, and loved it—innuendo and leering, former provinces of the male. It had taken him a while to get used to it, longer still to understand she was only partly jesting.

"The party," she said, slamming the register drawer shut.

"Huh?"

She leaned her elbows on the counter, and rapped her knuckles on his head. "Earth to Colin Ross. Hello in there, are you still with me? I said party. Maybe you've heard about it? Robert Cameron? Free booze and food? He's the opposition, in case you've forgotten."

"Believe me, I haven't forgotten."

"Then will you take me?" And suddenly she smiled slyly. "To the party, I mean."

"I didn't think you meant anything else," he protested.

"Sure, okay. But I want to know now, because if we're going, I have to get a sitter for Matt."

He leaned close, and looked anxious. "Will you just die if you don't go? I mean, will you absolutely and positively wither from mortification at missing the social event of the year?"

"Like a magnolia in a blizzard."

"Well . . . "

"And I won't ever be able to show myself in town again. My god, Colin, I'd be another Hester Prynne."

"Since you put it that way, I suppose I'll have to."

She laughed and kissed quickly the tip of his nose. "He'll die! God, Colin, he'll have a class-A fit!"

"Yeah." And he nodded.

He had planned to use the occasion to sound out his strength, but having Peg there on his arm would jab yet another thorn in Cameron's tender side. A small one, but nagging, and there'd be no Androcles around to pull it out and make him grateful. Bob Cameron jealous and being forced to hold it in was something he definitely did not want to miss.

Petty, he supposed, but why the hell not.

Peg rapped him again on the forehead, to show him she knew exactly what he was thinking.

He exaggerated a pained expression and ducked away before she could hit him again. "Where's Muriel?" he said, looking around the store for signs of Peg's regular clerk.

She scowled. "Family trouble, she says. She won't be in for at least another hour.

"Ha. She probably found a hot pinochle game at the boarding house. If you want the truth, I think you pay her too much. She makes enough for both of us with those damned cards of hers."

"Muriel North," she said mock-primly, "is a pillar of the church, a fine and upstanding woman, and I have never heard a foul word spoken from her lips. I trust her implicitly."

"She's still a shark, Peg. I know. I lost fifty bucks to her my first week on the island. Never again. She respects me now because she knows I'm not stupid."

Then his attention wandered as he saw a flyer for a new flavor ice cream being touted by Naughton's Market. It made him think of the luncheonette, closed now and looking old. "Lilla," he said softly.

Peg frowned. "Lilla?"

"I just had a thought," he said, tapping the paper to show her the connection. "I wonder if she'd go tomorrow. I mean, I know it's only a couple days after the funeral, but with that storm coming I don't know if she should be alone. Besides, she's been hiding out there in that shack for so long, it would do her good to get out and see people again."

Peg's smile was small and loving. "Leave it to you to think of something no one else would. Tell you what, we'll—" She snapped her fingers suddenly. "Oh, hell, Col, would you do me a favor?"

"Ask."

She fussed meaninglessly with the register. "You're not going home to work or anything? I mean, you said you were taking some time off, but—"

"Nope. Hadn't planned on it."

She looked at him closely, at his eyes and the set of his mouth, to be sure he wasn't simply being polite. Then she ran a slow dusting finger over the top of the counter. "Well, look, I really could use your help for a while, honest. I've got an appointment in ten minutes and I don't dare leave the place empty. Frankie, the sweetheart, hasn't shown up yet."

"You mean you want me to run the store? Alone?"

Before he could move, she was already around the counter and shrugging into a green jacket he'd given her on her last birthday.

"Nothing to it," she said hurriedly. "You've worked the cash register before, and you know the prices. If someone brings in a prescription, tell them to come back in an hour. I should be back by then."

"But where—"

She kissed his cheek and lay a palm against his chest. "You're a darling, you know that, right?"

103

"I think I'm a sucker."

She agreed with a wink and headed for the door.

He watched her with a baffled smile, then remembered why he had come. "Hey, Peg," he called after her, "will you go for a drive with me later? When Muriel comes in?"

She nodded without turning, gave him a wave over her shoulder and was gone before he knew it. Reprieve, he thought with a guilty sigh of relief; the governor hasn't called, but the power's temporarily gone out.

He took off his jacket and shoved the briefcase behind the counter. Ten minutes of wandering around the store, picking up boxes and bottles and putting them back down, finger-dusting the shelves, rearranging a few books into their proper slots. A number of customers came in and bought the local paper, chatted about leaving before the Screamer hit, asked after Peg and left with amused smiles. He stood at the entrance and watched the trees push back at the breeze, looked to his right at the bench Gran had used.

He blinked: The old man was there, sitting and talking quietly with Matt while both of them whittled on dead branches found in the empty lot. A handful of other kids came by and stopped, and soon Gran was grinning, his thin arms waving about, his eyes wide with laughter, Matt quietly proud he was the only one asked to join the old man on the bench.

Colin blinked again; the memory was gone.

Hands in his pockets, then he returned to the counter and was ready to read a magazine when Denise Adams walked in.

"Forget something?" he said brightly.

She examined the display of candies below the counter, looked at him without raising her head. "Cart thinks you're in love with me."

"He . . . I . . . my God, you can't be serious!"

He started to laugh, choked it off when he saw her hand move idly to the top button on her blouse; it was already undone, and she parted the material slightly

104

while she picked up a chocolate bar and placed it by the register.

"He's crazy," he said.

She cupped her palms around her cheeks and leaned her elbows on the counter. "I guess so."

"I know so, Denise," he said sternly.

Soft brunette curls drifted over her forehead, covered her hands, spiraled his gaze to the flat of her chest and the rise of her breasts. She's only eighteen, he reminded himself as he punched the register keys, had to correct himself twice before he got it right. The drawer snapped open and rapped his knuckles.

She stifled a laugh, and let one hand cover the chocolate.

"He thinks you look at me that way," she said so quietly he frowned until she repeated herself.

"What way?"

She straightened and dug into her pocket, pulled out a dollar bill and held out her hand. He reached for it automatically, and stiffened when her fingers brushed across his skin.

"*That* way," she said. "You know. He thinks you want to paint me . . . " She shrugged slowly, " . . . without my clothes on."

He slid out the change, dropped a dime and fetched it with a curse, at the same time hunting for a way to get her out without screaming. When he stood she was eating the chocolate, nibbling at each section while she met his confusion with a smile.

"You corrected him, of course," he said, handing her the coins.

"Oh sure," she told him, looked pointedly at her chest to be sure he noticed she wasn't wearing a bra. "Oh sure."

"Good."

She didn't move; her smile made him uncomfortable as the candy disappeared, deliberately slowly.

"I have work, Denise."

She licked a smudge of chocolate from the corner of her mouth. "Don't you?"

"Don't I what?"

"Don't you want to paint me so I can be in a museum?"

He recalled with a wince the look he'd given her when she'd left school, regretted it less than he suddenly thought he should. "Sure," he said. "As long as you wear a tent."

"Oh," she said, and he could have sworn her pursed lips were offering him a kiss.

"Denise, I said I have work."

"Okay." She pushed the last of the bar into her mouth, ran a slow finger around her lips and walked back up the aisle. At the door she paused, looked over her shoulder. "I think he wants to beat you up, Mr. Ross."

Before he could say anything she was out the door and gone. The urge to chase and strangle her propelled him around the counter until he stopped himself with a "Jesus!"

What in hell was going on, he wondered, wiping his brow with a palm. This place is going nuts. Efron, Cameron, now even the stupid kids. He snapped the candy wrapper from the floor and tossed it behind the counter, turned and stared at the entrance, daring her to return.

Who he saw was Carter Naughton, hands on his hips, a knowing expression on his face.

"Naughton, I want to talk to you!"

"Fuck you, teacher," Carter said. "I'll see you later."

A single step was enough to send the boy running, another before he was able to stop himself from panting, unclench his fists and wish for Peg to return. He had no idea what idiotic scheme the kids had in mind, but he didn't like the feeling that hinted he just might be helpless.

Frankie Adams sat hunched in a cardboard cave— empty cartons piled behind the drugstore, arranged into a private place where he could sit and smoke and think of ways he could get his sister away from Naughton so Carter would notice him for a change. It wasn't that he didn't know anything about women; those magazines Cart gave him told him all he had to know. And it wasn't that he was jealous, for God's sake, because Denise the Bitch was his sister, for God's sake. And she was *ugly,* for God's sake!

What it was, was that it just wasn't fair.

That's all there was to it—it just wasn't fair.

He did practically everything Cart told him, hardly ever wiseassed him, and he was still treated like shit. Was it his fault his mother wouldn't buy him the weights that would give him muscles? Was it his fault he was always broke because he had to turn over his paycheck every week to his old man? Allowance. Jesus H. Christ, he was sixteen years old and *still* getting an allowance. He drew on the cigarette from the pack he'd stolen from the store and let the smoke trail from his nostrils. He'd seen that in a movie, and he'd seen Cart do it once. He'd nearly choked to death before he'd mastered it, and now, who gave a damn?

He squirmed and hugged his shins, jammed his chin onto one knee. The ground beneath him was still damp from the rain, the cardboard walls sagging. Tonight, before he finished work, he'd have to crush them and stuff them in the dumpster. Of course, he might not have a job left by the time he finally showed up. But he couldn't go in there now. He'd seen Cart and his sister there, and later Mr. Ross had gone in. All those people, half of them thinking he was a sap and needed help, the other half thinking he was a sap and needing a swift kick in the ass.

It wasn't fair.

Nothing was fair.

Nobody was fair, except maybe Mrs. Fletcher. At least she let him have the keys, lock up and stuff like that, like he knew what he was doing. Once she'd let him fix the small generator in her backyard shed, the one she used when storms knocked out the electricity. He'd shown her how to store the kerosene, and she'd given him twenty dollars. Just like that. Twenty dollars.

His mother, for God's sake, still treated him like a baby even when she was sober. *Frankie, darling, don't forget your coat, it's chilly today. Frankie, darling, you need more than a T-shirt, it's chilly today. Frankie, finish your supper. Frankie, finish your breakfast. Oh, Frankie, why do you have to wear your hair that way when all the other little boys have nice haircuts?*

Little boys. Jesus . . . H. . . . Christ.

He scowled and dug his heel into the ground.

And the old man. Hell, he's nothing more than a janitor in school, and anyplace else he can find someone dumb enough to give him a job. What a jackass. Jesus.

He held the cigarette to his palm to see how close he could get before he had to pull away. Cart could put it right on the skin. Cart could flip one around into his mouth and stick it back out still smoking, and not burn his tongue. Cart could walk into the supermarket and tell his old man to give him some money and tell his old lady to shut up, and all they did was yell and give him the money just to get him away. Frankie had tried that once. He'd walked into the house and told his old man to give him ten dollars, and when his mother had started to babytalk him and grill him and ask what he wanted the money for, he'd told her to shut up. His old man had beaten him half to death.

His mother had given him the money when his old man wasn't looking, but he was still beaten half to death and could barely walk for a week.

Cart had laughed. Cart was always laughing at him, and he was getting tired of it. Then Cart told him today to get lost. Just like that—*get lost, shithead.* Just like that.

But damn it, he wasn't a shithead. He knew that. He wasn't as smart as Denise the Bitch, maybe, but he wasn't a shithead. Cart knew that. Somehow, he had to make sure Cart knew that. God, if Cart didn't pay attention to him anymore, he wouldn't have any friends left, because Mrs. Fletcher didn't count.

He sighed, crushed the cigarette under his heel, crawled through the opening he'd made and stood with his back to the wall. There was no one around. The sun was setting fast. He was ready to get inside and tell Mrs. Fletcher why he was late, when he heard footsteps on the graveled path beside the building. He ducked quickly behind the dumpster and held his breath, looked up and saw Mrs. Fletcher hurrying toward Ocean, cutting between the church and the library. He frowned and wondered who was watching the store. A moan. Muriel, that's who. Who else? Muriel North, who once told him out of the corner of her mouth when she thought no one was listening that he ought to be taken out in one of the boats and dropped over the side. Chum, fish bait, that's what she called him; bloody bits of dead fish to attract the sharks. Chum. The old bat, with her fingers so yellow from smoking she looked like someone from a kung fu movie, for Christ's sake.

Hell, even his mother didn't talk to him like that, even when she was drinking all that crap and shittin' up her liver like he'd seen one time in school, like what happened when people drank too much and all. One of these days, the first day she stopped babytalking him, he was going to smash all the bottles she hid in her closet. Or maybe he'd do it anyway, for Christmas.

Merry Christmas, Ma, you're sober again.

Hell.

Well, there was no sense going in the store now because all he'd get would be grief and a half. Muriel North was a goddamned expert at handing out the grief, and that was something he didn't need right now.

And Cart was gone with Denise the Bitch, and he didn't dare go home because he was supposed to be at work, and . . .

He fell back in sudden panic with a choked-off curse, hitting the wall hard when a small gull squawked loudly and landed in the browning grass a

109

few feet away. He stared at it a moment, rubbing his sore shoulder, watching it hunt boldly for edible garbage. It complained to itself as it found little more than a moldy orange rind, and Frankie was tempted to find a rock to put through its head to make people think the gull-killer was back. But before he could move, his eyes widened, his lips parted in a smile.

Gull. Bird. Tess Mayfair and her fancy birdbath in that garden behind the boarding house. Cart had tried a million times to steal it, and the old fart had nearly caught him. She was the only one on the island Cart was afraid of. Of course, he wasn't a coward. Anybody'd head the other way when she was running full tilt at you. God, she must weigh five hundred goddamn pounds.

But he wasn't afraid.

And if he could get that birdbath and bring it to Cart, by Jesus Cart'd listen to him then.

The creep. Who did he think he was, calling him a shithead?

He spat and sidled to the corner of the building, checked the street for traffic, and broke into an easy lope that took him behind the other stores, the theater, Naughton's Market. He was in the trees fifteen minutes later, running easily, dodging the low branches, once in a while taking a fallen log at a leap. He was grinning. And he didn't even care that the shadows seemed to follow.

TWO

The haze thickened, closing out the blue and softening the light to a faint shade of gold-gray. What leaves stubbornly remained on branches stirred restlessly, trembling; and those fallen to the gutter clustered close to the curb. The scent of last night's rain still clung to the air, but there was a stronger one now that made the growing slight breeze unpleasantly damp.

Peg held her jacket closed with one hand as she walked toward the setting sun, her free hand shading her eyes. Rather than go to the corner, she cut around the back of the drug store, hurrying to Ocean between the library and the church. A large Doberman chained to an iron stake near the sidewalk lunged at her, barking, snarling, and wagging its tail. She grinned and waved at it, and continued across the street, to the next, and the third, finally slowing on the pathway flanked with chainlink fencing. The house on her left belonged to the Adams, the one on her right to the librarian, Hattie Mills. Straight ahead was her own, and there was a man on the front walk waiting for her.

She moistened her lips nervously. Bob Cameron had called her only half an hour ago, asking if she would mind talking with him for a bit. When she asked why, he oddly declined to give her a reason except to say it had something to do with her late husband.

Then she told herself sternly to stop overreacting. It was probably nothing. It was the day, the Screamer. Almost every hour she had gone to the window to check the sky for thunderheads, the tingling along her arms the same sensation she experienced before a storm. Others felt it too, commenting as they paid their bills and left without delivering the usual ration of gossip.

It was the day, not Bob Cameron. It was probably some stupid way to get him her vote.

He waved as she approached, and she managed a polite smile. He was taller than she, burly and wide-mouthed, tanned so dark his wavy graying hair seemed almost as white as the suit he was wearing. She stepped around the hood of the car at the curb, had gone three steps beyond before she realized there was someone behind the wheel. She turned and frowned as Cameron touched her arm.

"Glad you could come, Peg." His voice was as smooth as the cologne he had on.

"I can't stay long," she told him. "Poor Colin is minding the store, and I don't want to go broke."

He smiled warmly and squeezed her elbow. "No problem. It won't take but a few minutes, I promise you."

Suddenly, she had a distressing feeling that he was about to declare himself and had called her away to get her free of Colin. It was foolish, she knew, but she couldn't shake it loose once it had taken hold, couldn't for the life of her remember if she'd ever given him even the slightest hint she might be interested at all. Good lord, how could she? After what had happened to Jim, how could she?

She tilted her head to place his face between her eyes and the sun. "Well?"

"I'd rather we do it inside."

She shrugged and pulled her keys from her pocket, had the knob in her hand when she heard the car door slam. Cameron was right behind her and eased her over the threshold.

"Bob?"

Immediately behind them two men followed, and Cameron steered her directly back to the kitchen.

"Damn it, Bob!" But softly. An annoyed glance over her shoulder.

He sat at the round table unbidden, and as she blinked in a combination of undefined fear and annoyance, the others took seats and stared at her openly. Suddenly she was outraged, and an order to leave was hard at her lips when the man on her left—incredibly thin, blond, with a jaw that came to a nearly-perfect honed point—introduced himself as Michael Lombard. His hands were folded primly on the table, his back was straight.

"Mrs. Fletcher, I'm terribly sorry for the intrusion and this apparent mystery," he said with an apologetic smile. "And you shouldn't blame Bob here for all this rush. It's my fault, I'm afraid."

"Yes," she said, and waited. She avoided looking at the other one. She didn't like him. He was much heavier, his features flat from nose to cheeks, his striking blue shirt open two buttons down to expose a chest of dark hair and a jagged gray scar that reached up toward the hollow of his neck.

"Mrs. Fletcher, I work in Trenton," Lombard explained, "and it's my job for the governor to see that what the politicos call the undesirables are shown the first highway to the border." He smiled self-consciously. "That sounds like something out of a western, I know, but it's what I do."

She sensed what was coming and turned to the sink. A milk glass left over from breakfast lay near the drain. She picked it up and filled it with hot water. "Yes, so what does this have to do with me?"

"Your husband, Mrs. Fletcher. We have reason to believe the man or men who killed him are back in New Jersey. In fact—"

She cut him off with a harsh gesture without turning around, put the glass down, and began filling the kettle and sugar bowl while her mind found its gears. Jim was

113

dead, and she had had all these years to bury the bitterness of both the impending divorce and the police's lack of success; all these years to put her life back on the track. Now, suddenly, like a tidal surge that flooded the beach without warning, this man from the capital was trying to bring it all back.

Amazed that her hands weren't trembling, she set the kettle on the stove, turned the burner on high, and kept her gaze on the flames curling up around the bottom. "Mr. Lombard," she said, her voice tight and direct. "I'm sorry if I seem callous or ungrateful, but I just don't care anymore."

There was a subtle shifting at the table. The second man coughed politely. "Mrs. Fletcher, we're only trying to warn you—"

"Against what?" she said sharply, spinning around so quickly that she caught Cameron's leering eye before it left the curve of her buttocks. "Against what?"

Lombard smiled—a professional smile, meaningless and quick. "Mrs. Fletcher, I understand how you must feel at this time, but you must also understand that we feel a certain—"

"Wait a minute," Cameron interrupted, one hand up and shaking. "Just a minute, please." He waited until she had reached for the squealing kettle, then rose quickly and helped her set the cups and saucers on the table. "Peg, these men are friends of mine, all right? They came here last night, and they want to be sure this guy, whoever it is, doesn't come back to Haven's End. I know you think it's impossible, and I know the police have been all over this place a hundred times, but you can't tell about these mob fellas, y'know? This guy, whoever he is, he might still have it in his head that Jim kept all his records here."

Peg gaped at him, and felt cold for the first time. "No," she said with a shake of her head. "No."

"Mrs. Fletcher," Lombard said quietly, soothingly, with a side glance to Cameron, "you know that and we know that, but *he* might not. And there's a good chance he'll try to contact you, perhaps try to lever you into revealing what he wants to know."

"But I don't know anything!" she said helplessly.

"Yes, yes," Cameron said, laying a hand on her shoulder and massaging it gently. She looked at him desperately, and he brought her to a chair. "I know, Peg, I know. It doesn't make any sense to ordinary people like you and me, but these gentlemen make their living at this. They know, Peg. They know how the criminal mind works."

She put her hands to her face and thought of Matt playing at the marina, Colin fumbling behind the counter, all the cartons of Jim's papers she had burned in the fireplace—thought of the not always peaceful years since the car had been reduced to black metal and black ash. And immediately the image of the automobile's destruction came to mind, she thought of Bob Cameron.

"Mrs. Fletcher, are you all right?" Solicitous, unctuous.

"Peg, can I get you anything?" Cameron, concerned.

Cameron. Would a man involved in her husband's violent death wait six full years before trying to discover if she were still hoarding incriminating evidence? Six years?

"Bob," she said, hands still covering her eyes, "I told you long ago I'd burned all Jim's things, what the police hadn't taken away. You know that." Her hands lowered and her eyes narrowed. She stared at Lombard and his companion. "Did he tell you that? Did he tell you I burned it all?"

"No," Lombard said after a long, annoyed silence.

Her gaze shifted to the second man, whose oversized hands were clasped as if in prayer. He shook his head.

"Who *are* you?" she asked softly. And without waiting for an answer she rose from her chair and backed to the sink. A glare to the doorway. "Bob, I don't want to talk to these gentlemen anymore. I'd appreciate your leaving."

Cameron didn't move for an interminable second. Then he heaved himself to his feet, the chair skidding away as he waited for the others to join him. "Peg, you're making a mistake here, believe me. A very big mistake. I . . . I don't want anything to happen that you'll regret later."

Her eyes widened in disbelief and her hands slapped on the table. "My God, are you threatening me, Robert Cameron, or just trying to scare me?"

He held up a fast palm. "Lord, no. I just want you to understand—"

"I understand nothing, and I've already asked you once to go. Now do it, please. I have a business to run and I've been away too long already."

Lombard shook his head once when Cameron, his face flushed, leaned forward to argue. Then he rose and nodded to her, reset the chair in its place and led the way out of the kitchen to the front door. After a brief hesitation he opened it, ushered Cameron through to the porch and turned to wait for his companion. Peg stayed in the hallway, watching, holding her breath, nearly bolting when the second man turned abruptly to face her.

"My name is Vincent," he said, looming above her and smiling so broadly she could see that his teeth were all black. "Theodore Vincent. You will remember it, please."

She couldn't help it—she nodded.

The door closed without a sound.

She stood a moment shivering in the hallway, trying to keep her legs from failing and her teeth from chattering, then she turned the bolt and peered through the glass pane in the door. The car was gone; the street was empty. Her tongue pushed into her cheek, and she made a soft growling sound before heading for the study.

In one of the cabinets under the bookshelves was a small bottle of brandy her mother had given her for Christmas two years ago. It had been tapped only once, when Colin had come over for Matt's last birthday. She held the fat bottle in her hand now, a glass on the desk, and she took a deep inhalation of the sharp aroma before pouring herself a drink. A sip, then, and she waited until the fear had been replaced by a slow-burning rage.

Her house. Her womb. Her . . . she scowled and looked for another word. Then she emptied the glass in a swallow, brushed back the tears that flooded her eyes, and went for the phone. Matt; she had to check on Matt. Damn Mrs. Wooster for being in Philadelphia! What the hell's a housekeeper for if not to be here when she's needed. Three times she fumbled with Alex Fox's number, and when no one answered at the first ring she fell into her armchair and bit down on her lower lip.

She thought she tasted blood.

The second ring, the third, and Alex finally answered.

Yes, he told her, Matt was in the yard with his own kids. No, he hadn't seen anyone around all day what with his finishing a paint job in the workshop and securing boats against the storm they'd probably get by morning. And could Matt stay for dinner, he's such a good kid and Amy and Tommy would love it.

The urge to refuse politely was killed when she heard the distant joyous shrieks of children playing outside. Matt would be all right. If anyone on the island was suspicious of strangers, it was Alex Fox. As young as she, but with an old man's distrust of anyone he hadn't known for at least twenty years. Sadly, sometimes it seemed as if that included his wife.

The moment she rang off, she was back in her jacket and out the front door. An apprehensive glance at the empty street, and a puzzled one toward Bridge Road where a great deal of traffic seemed to be heading for the ferry, and she hurried back to the store, for the first time in her life not liking the way the houses rose above her, not liking the columns that held them up, not liking the twilight permanently snared between the pilings.

She paused only once.

In the middle of Ocean Street something dark, something flickering, made her look down toward the school. It could have been a dog, a cat, even a low-darting bird. A shadow from the pines. Yet she could not shake the feeling that something or someone had been standing by the school, and when she had stopped it had fled.

Watching her. It was watching her.

The Doberman chained by the library started up its barking again, and again she greeted it with a smile and a wave, grateful this time for the distraction it provided. Friendly little beast, she thought sourly as she passed. It belonged to the librarian and usually lay on the grass, panting, watching, nudging the passing children for handouts and a scratching.

Today, however, it appeared to be reverting to the image of its breed—fierce, unpleasant, almost satanic. Though she tried, she couldn't remember the last time it had so much as even growled. If it didn't stop that noise, Hattie would be in trouble, if for no other reason than Reverend Otter was a stickler when it came to disturbances. He had once tried to have the school caution the students not to shout when they left for the day; his meditations were being disrupted, and God abhorred a poor sermon.

An image of the gangly minister standing on his porch and railing at the kids made her lips pull at the corners. She hadn't believed the story until she'd come to see Matt's teacher one day about his grades. And she hadn't made things better by laughing aloud.

Not exactly the reclusive widow, she thought as she reached the store and pushed inside. And if Colin gets his nerve up, a widow no longer.

He was at the back, leaning casually against the

118

register and reading a magazine. She had to rap her knuckles twice on the counter to get his attention.

"I want you to assassinate Bob Cameron," she said when he looked up to smile.

Matt liked Amy and Tommy Fox. They were in the same grade, and they both hated his teacher as much as he did. Of course, Mrs. Adams wasn't all that bad, except that she limped and her husband was a janitor who always chased them from the playground as soon as school was over. But her breath smelled funny, and no one was surprised last Monday when they all walkèd in and found a substitute at the desk.

Amy said she was dying from a rare disease that struck only teachers, and you got it from rotten fish. Tommy said she carried a bottle of whiskey in her purse and drank from it at the water fountain in front of Mr. Ross' room.

But the best thing about them was they didn't make fun of the pictures he drew, and Tommy knew almost as much about James Bond as Matt did.

They were kneeling now at the end of the marina's last dock, dive-bombing tiny fish with gravel from the drive. Matt liked the way the stones seemed to curve as soon as they hit the water. Once in a while he would turn and pitch a stone lightly toward the half dozen gulls sailing above them waiting for the trawler.

Amy, whose face was round and heavily freckled, was a carrot-top with green eyes and a stub for a nose. She stuck the tip of her tongue between her lips and stared thoughtfully at the mound of pebbles shimmering under the water. "I think there's a Viking buried under there. He's come all the way across the ocean and he died in a battle with the pirates who used to live here."

Tommy, his sister's twin save for the lack of flesh on his bones, shook his head. "Nope, that's a place, a hole where they put missiles to kill the Russians."

"There aren't no missles under the water," she told him with disdain."

"Are too."

"Nope. There's a Viking down there," and she turned to Matt for collaboration.

"It's a fortress," he said, dropping another gravel bomb. "A guy's in there and he builds super lasers and things to shoot down planes when they fly over the island." He pointed to the shallows at the dock's other end. "He wants to get a whole lot of them along here, see, so no one can get here unless he says so."

"That's silly. it's a Viking," she insisted, her face puffed and pouting.

"Can't be. Vikings are dead."

"I said he was buried there."

Tommy jabbed an elbow in her side. "The fish ate him last week."

"They can't. Vikings are too tough."

"How do you know that, smarty?" her brother demanded.

"I saw it on TV. They wear bearskins and metal shirts and horns on their head."

Matt giggled. Tommy sneered, grabbed a handful of the gravel and threw it in as hard as he could. The splash drove them all back from the edge, Amy scrambling to her feet and nearly pitching off the other side.

"I'm gonna tell Daddy," she said when her balance recovered.

"I'm gonna tell Daddy," Tommy echoed. "But if you tell Daddy and he tells Mommy," he shouted after her as she started to march toward shore, "we're not getting any ice cream tonight."

She hesitated, turned to retort and clamped a hand to her mouth.

Tommy looked to Matt who was studying the water, then looked up to the trees that grew close to the workshop. "Matt," he whispered suddenly. "Matt, look!"

Matt looked up, and saw Lilla coming toward them. The gulls began screaming.

She wore a long black dress splattered with dried mud and sand, with long ragged tears at the hem and across one shoulder. Her feet were bare. Her hair was tangled—like bristles, he thought—and laced with torn blades of grass, grayed by sand as if she'd rolled in it all night. Her eyes were hidden, but he felt her staring at him, saw her lips parted and her tongue running slowly over her teeth. One hand clutched at a stiff fold of the dress, the other lay flat against her stomach as she walked.

Amy instantly bolted for the house, her brother only a few yards behind her.

Lilla ignored them.

Matt could barely move. He rose slowly, seeing she could easily cut him off before he reached the safety of the lawn. She made no move to intercept his friends, only glided across the lawn until she reached the end of the dock. He swallowed, and his right hand brushed nervously against his pants. One by one, the gravel stones fell from his grip, bounced off the wood and dropped soundlessly into the water.

The gulls whirled and shrieked.

One of them swooped down at her, banked, and its wing brushed hard through her hair. She ignored it.

Matt looked up at the agitated birds, pulling his lips between his teeth and trying not to breathe too loudly. He wished Amy and Tommy would find their father and bring him out here; he wished his mother had told him to come right home after school.

A second gull dove and managed to jab at her shoulder, parting the black fabric to expose a line of pale flesh and a thinner line of running red.

She ignored it.

And they kept screaming.

Matt swallowed again and managed a weak, "Hello, Lilla."

He could almost see the shudder that rippled up from her feet to the vague bulge of her chest, the shudder that made her sweep back the hair to show him her eyes. They were dark, and they were pleading, and he found himself moving toward her. He didn't want to go. But if he could wait until he was only a foot or two from her, he could leap from the dock into the shallows and scramble up to the grass. By that time, Mr. Fox would be outside and yelling and Lilla would go away.

He couldn't make the jump.

He stopped close enough for her to reach out and touch his head lightly. Her hand was cold, as if she'd just come from winter.

The gulls swirled.

The haze deepened to clouds that promised another storm.

"Little Matt," she said then, and he frowned because in spite of her looks she sounded perfectly normal. He didn't understand. He knew what people who looked like this should sound like—deep voices that had echoes, with thunder all around them and lightning outside the window. But she sounded just like the old Lilla who gave him ice cream and laughed, who put extra cheese in his sandwiches and extra catsup on his hamburgers.

"Colin," she said, urgently now.

He could feel the passing wind of a diving gull at his back.

"I—"

She gripped his shoulders tightly and shook him. "Colin!"

He cried out softly and struggled, breaking one hand free and looking up to demand she leave him alone. What he saw made him shove at her chest in a sudden startled panic. She released him, and he backed away hastily.

Her eyes. They were white.

No color. Just white.

The back door slammed, and he heard Mr. Fox bellowing Lilla's name. She leaned down to him and said, "Colin!" turned and ran back into the trees.

Her feet were bare.

When he stepped off the dock, he could see the grass lightly stained with blood.

* * *

"Now what," said Garve Tabor, "would you like me to do, huh?"

The best answer Peg had was a helpless, weak, smiling shrug. Despite her anger, it hadn't been her idea to come here at all; Colin had insisted. As soon as she had finished her description of the meeting and he'd told her of his phone call, his eyes had gone dark. Wolf dark. His hands had become fists that pressed against the counter, and she could hear his heel tapping angrily on the floor. She wouldn't have minded so much if he had shouted or sworn, but he had done neither. He had only glared at his hands and taken several deep breaths as if preparing to scream. His control was unnerving. And when Muriel came in, he'd snatched up his coat and dragged Peg out the door.

"Well?" Garve said.

Peg only shrugged again.

The office was small. Two wooden desks side by side a few feet back from the entrance, a pair of ladder-back chairs she and Colin were using, gray metal file cabinets along the left-hand wall, a bulletin board on the right under which was a low table holding the dispatcher's radio unit. There was a single door in the rear wall leading to the three cells in back. A gun cabinet beside it, its glass front locked, the rifles and shotguns inside gleaming with new polish. Light came from four white-encased fluorescent tubes that ran half the width of the ceiling.

Tabor was behind his desk, leaning back, his hands clasped on his paunch. His tan shirt was open at the throat, his gun belt lying on the empty desk blotter.

Colin, who had shoved his chair against the wall by the bulletin board and stared blindly out the large front window, shook his head. Peg, directly in front of the chief, sighed.

"I don't know, Garve. It's—"

"Jesus," Colin said, "can't you run them out of town or something? My God, they actually threatened her!"

123

Tabor brushed at his forelock futilely and shook his head as if he were dealing with children. "I heard what you told me, Col, but if Peg is right, the threat—if there was one—"

"If . . . ?

"—was implied, and I'd be up to my butt in false arrest suits if I did anything now. It's a subjective thing, Col, Peg, and there's really nothing I can do."

"Talk to Cameron, then," she suggested.

"About what? His friends?" He waved her silent as he straightened and pushed a closed folder to one side on his blotter. Then he opened a side drawer and pulled out a handful of fountain pens, their caps long since missing. His chair swiveled around and he tossed one at the bulletin board. It stuck in the cork like an ungainly dart.

"I'll tell you something."

"Please," Colin said sourly, moving his chair aside when a second pen nearly pinned his ear to the wall.

"You were talking to Mike Lombard and Theo Vincent, right? Sweet fellas, both of them. Lombard has oil for a smile, and Vincent looks like he eats nothing but sugar."

Peg shifted impatiently, but was too fascinated by his errant marksmanship to say anything in protest.

When the last fountain pen skewered a wanted poster yellowed with age, Garve snorted and faced her.

"Peg, they're nasty, the both of them. I know it. I talked with them back when Jim was killed. But I can't ride them out of town because in the first place, I'm not Gary Cooper, as I told Colin last night; and in the second, there's no law against visiting someone in her home and passing on information. You chose to make what they said a threat, but Lombard is an expensive lawyer who would have me beachcombing in a week if he wanted to. And I'll tell you the truth, I wouldn't want anything but a smoking gun for evidence before I faced Theo Vincent."

"Jesus," Colin muttered in disgust.

Peg, however, saw the man's point and knew he was correct. And perhaps she'd been right all along; perhaps it was the mood the day had gotten itself into. She sighed noncommittally and rose from the chair. Colin muttered under his breath and raised his eyebrows in a shrug.

"You feel it, too," she said suddenly, without knowing why.

He nodded. "Yeah."

Garve looked astonished. "You talking about the weird that's come over this town?"

"Weird?" Peg said.

"That's what Annalee calls it."

"Annalee, huh?" Colin said, wide-eyed and innocent.

"Yes," Garve said. He reached for a pile of message slips and waved them briefly at the phone. "She says Doc's been working her tail off all afternoon. A million people coming in with complaints that don't exist, I got a million calls here from folks who've decided to go away for the weekend and would I keep an eye on the house. El's at the ferry now, as a matter of fact. The second fender-bender this afternoon. Lord, if they had water wings, they'd stick 'em on their bumpers and try to drive across, the jerks. Sterling's probably making a fortune." He glanced up at the round clock fixed over the door. "Four now. If this keeps up, we'll be the only ones left by sunset."

"The storm," Colin suggested. "You said there might be one of those Carolina somethings—"

"Screamers."

"Yeah. That could be it. And Gran, and . . . well, I guess a night on the town is just what they need."

"Sure," Garve grumbled as the telephone rang. He listened for a moment, looked heavenward for mercy, and muttered a few words Peg didn't hear. Then he dropped the receiver and spread his palms in the air. "I was waiting for it."

"What?" she asked.

"Reverend Otter. That goddamned Doberman's

been keeping him from his beauty nap. Jesus, if I've told Hattie once, I've told her a hundred times to keep that fool animal inside. God!"

Peg laughed, more from abrupt relief than from thinking the situation comic; as long as these two had felt what Garve had called the 'weird,' then it really was possible she'd overreacted to Cameron's visit. She nodded then when Colin reminded her of the promise of a ride, glad for the chance to be alone with him for a time. When they reached the door the phone rang, and Tabor swore. When they reached the sidewalk, a mud-spattered jeep braked loudly at the curb. Alex Fox was driving and Matt was huddled in the seat beside him.

As soon as Peg saw the dazed look on her son's face, her throat went dry and her skin turned cold. She rushed to his side and gathered him silently into her arms, looking to Fox as he climbed from his seat.

"Lilla," the red-haired man said. "She come out of the woods and scared the kids half to death."

She stroked the boy's cold cheeks, his rigid shoulders, brushed his dark hair away from his eyes. "Darling, are you all right?"

"She didn't touch him, I don't think," Fox said, standing at the curb as Garve came from the office. "I chased her off," he said to the chief, "but Jesus, Garve, God knows what she might've done. Damn, she's crazy!"

Colin stood beside her. "Matt, you okay?"

The boy nodded quickly several times.

"Did she say anything?"

He nodded again.

Peg cupped his chin with a palm and turned his head toward her. "What, darlin'? What did she say?"

"Colin," the boy whispered.

"I'm here, pal."

"No. She said 'Colin.' "

"Anything else?" Garve asked from over her shoulder.

"No."

126

Peg eased him from the jeep, a protective arm hard around his shoulders. "I'm going to take him home," she said tightly. "Then I want to talk to Lilla."

"I'll go with you," Colin said.

"Don't bother," she told him, and led Matt around the corner as she whispered to him gently, telling him it was all right and nobody was hurt and Lilla still feels bad about Gran and something like that sometimes makes people do strange things.

Matt pulled away from her. Slowly, not abruptly. He shoved his hands into his pockets and stared at the sidewalk, the curb, the sidewalk again. A pebble got in his way, and he kicked it aside. She looked back only once, faltering when she saw Colin storming around the corner of the hedge, heading for the Run. But damn it, what did he expect her to think? Does Lilla ask for help from someone who's known her all her life? Does she ask for Peg, who had held her when her parents died, and fought with Gran to let her go to college, and was more than a friend, practically a surrogate mother? No, of course not. She frightens Peg's only son to death—God knows why she picked on him of all people—and then she asks for Colin. Colin Ross the artist. Colin Ross the man she's only known for five years. Not Peg. Colin.

A year ago she had seen them on the beach, sitting there, watching the waves, Lilla talking, Colin listening, Lilla suddenly turning to kiss him on the cheek for whatever response he'd given. He'd laughed. She'd kissed him again, was on her feet and running. Peg, as with the first time she'd seen them, hadn't the nerve to confront him for an explanation. It was, of course, all very innocent. Lilla was only a child (seventeen, Peg, and hardly a child), and everyone knew she had a crush on the artist.

But Colin never said a word, and Lilla never said a word, and of course there was nothing to it, and she'd felt cheap for her inadvertent spying, and now here it was again and . . . she blinked once, slowly, and almost exclaimed aloud: My God, Peg Fletcher, you're actually jealous. You're so frightened for Matt you've made yourself jealous.

Good God, a hell of a thing.

"Mom, what's for supper?"

"Crow, my darlin'," she said wryly. Good Lord, jealous; I haven't felt that in years.

He grimaced and stuck out his tongue. "That's rotten."

"Yes," she said, impulsively hugging him. "Tell me all about it."

She followed his gaze as he looked at the sky. The storm clouds—white slashed with black and reaching for the blue—had drained off all the haze. And over the mainland the slowly-sinking sun glided broad golden beams to the tops of the trees. It was so perfect it was unnatural, and she wasn't surprised when Matt told her, "I don't like this day, Mom. It doesn't feel right, y'know?"

"Yes," she said quietly, "I know exactly what you mean."

At their front door he looked fearfully over his shoulder.

"It's all right," she assured him. "Lilla's not there."

He frowned, then nodded in silent contradiction.

Peg closed the door behind them, and made sure it was locked.

Frankie crouched behind a wall of red-thorned shrubs and scratched at a pimple breaking on his cheek. He frowned. He stared at the back of the boarding house and wondered if Mayfair was working in the kitchen, or sitting in the front room, or sitting on the porch talking to herself. The house was brown and three stories high, bay windows and additions everywhere you looked. There were dim lights here and there, and dazzling reflections from the sun lowering to the treetops. There were no cars in the driveway, but that didn't mean a thing; Mayfair didn't drive. And he figured there wasn't a car big enough to hold her.

If she were in the kitchen, he was dead, simple as that.

The birdbath was halfway between him and the back porch, and nothing but dead grass and weeds to hide him if she saw him.

Maybe, he thought, it would be a good idea to wait for dark. But if he waited for dark, Cart and Denise would be holed up in one of the empty motels, going at it on one of the beds, taking a little dope, laughing at nothing and calling him a shithead.

No. He had to do it now. He had to take the chance that the concrete bowl would lift off the pedestal easily and wouldn't be all that heavy to carry. Hell, if he did it right, he could roll it like a hoop.

He stared until his eyes watered, thinking about Denise and Carter and his mother and his old man, and he turned around twice when he heard the squirrels bounding through the leaves in the shadows behind him. After the second time, he realized he was losing his nerve.

Damn, he thought, double damnation.

Slowly, listening to his knees pop, he rose and licked at his lips. A deep breath filled his lungs. A palm rubbed his stomach in slow circles.

Okay, Frankie, he thought, in and out like a fuckin' rocket.

He eased around the brush.

And a hand grabbed his shoulder.

THREE

Colin shoved through the Clipper Run's door almost at a run and stood panting in the narrow foyer while he tried to catch his breath. There was silence, and from where he stood he could see no one at all. He was glad; it would give him a moment to try to calm down.

The restaurant's interior was constructed on two levels. The upper, straight in from the scrolled oak door and the cubbyhole of the check room, stretched along the right side of the building. A long, dark mahogany bar curved from one end to the other—brass footrailing, padded black leather handrail, black leather stools with high backs for unsteady drinkers, a huge mirror edged in daily-polished silver behind the artfully-stacked bottles. It was separated from the dining area by three broad, carpeted steps and a waist-high railing of lemon-waxed, hand-smoothed teak.

He moved in cautiously and grabbed the back of a stool, leaned on it heavily and brushed a hand through his hair.

The dining room held two hundred people at irregularly placed, small round tables, each with captain's chairs, white linen, red-chimneyed candles and a slender white vase with blossoms in season. In the room's center was a grand piano Alex Fox's wife played when she wasn't waiting tables; no jukebox, no taped music.

From the exposed-beam ceiling hung netting and intricate shark's-tooth mobiles. On the walnut-paneled walls were original oils and water colors of MacKay's clipper ships, Fulton's steamboats, whalers, Cape Cod trawlers, and a three-master in full sail at sunset flying a bold skull and crossbones.

There were no windows. What lighting there was came from bracketed brass lanterns on the wall and on the squared rough posts that supported the ceiling. Only a few of the wicks were burning; the restaurant was dim, and filled with static shadows.

On the far side of the bar were three doors. The last two led into the kitchen, and he could sense slow movement in there, a preparation for the dinner hour nearly upon them. The first, with a blank brass plaque in the center, led to Cameron's office. Colin stared at it, taking deep breaths, clenching and opening his hands, pulling once in a while at the bottom of his jacket.

It hadn't taken him long for his temper to snap again—the look on Peg's face, the muttering of Fox and Tabor behind him as they speculated on Lilla's problem—his lungs had filled and his eyes had narrowed and he had stalked away from the station without saying a word. He saw Peg and Matt on the next block, but he didn't call out. There was nothing to say. Peg feared for Matt, and Lilla had a crush on him, and he was so dense he'd never suspected Peg might be a little jealous. It was dumb, but it was there, but if it hadn't been for Cameron and his cronies she never would have reacted to the situation that way.

He took a step across the thick red carpet, and stopped again.

It had finally struck him that the room was empty.

He looked at his watch: It was early Friday evening, just after five, but no one was here.

And that was all wrong.

By now there should have been a dozen people at the bar, and a scattering of families and couples down at the tables. There should have bene visitors from the mainland, groups from the island, and Cameron watching it all from the maitre d's station. A sudden thought and he turned around, there was no one in the cloakroom. And when he turned back, Cameron was standing in his doorway.

"I kind of thought you'd show up sooner or later," the man said, not moving. A bright light from the office darkened his face.

"It was a lousy trick, Bob, sending those men to Peg like you did."

Cameron shook his head nervously. "It wasn't my idea, Colin." He moved into the room and pulled a cigarette from his jacket, lit it and threw the pack on the bar. "These men are big investors. They have to be sure everything's clear or they won't give Haven's End a good recommendation to their people."

"That's not what you told Peg." He walked forward slowly, unsure now what he was going to do. "She—"

"I know," Cameron said. "And what I said was true. They just happen to have other interests, that's all."

He nodded. "I see."

"No, I don't think—" He clamped his mouth shut and stared at the cigarette. There was a man in the doorway behind him. Colin squinted through the gloom and from Garve's and Peg's descriptions knew this must be the one called Theodore Vincent. But he looked bigger, and his teeth behind the pulled-back lips looked blacker than he'd imagined. Cameron started when Vincent mumbled something to him, stepped to intercept the man when he began moving around the bar. Vincent didn't look down; he moved Cameron aside with a casual brush of his hand.

"Now listen here," Cameron protested.

"He was," Mike Lombard said from the doorway.

Colin looked at the new man, at the extraordinary thinness, at the pointed jaw. Lombard nodded to him in greeting; Colin felt himself nodding back.

"Listen, Michael," Cameron began.

"Hush, Robert," the lawyer said.

132

Cameron hushed and looked away.

Vincent stood in front of Colin, looking down, not smiling now. "You're running against Mr. Cameron in the election," he said.

Colin backed up a step, the better to meet his gaze. He wasn't sure what was going on, what he'd said, but he could hear Cameron whispering harshly to Lombard. He glanced over, and saw the mainlander ignoring Cameron completely. Then a stiff finger jolted Colin's shoulder.

"I *said*, you're the man that's running against Mr. Cameron."

"Yes," he answered, frowning and clearing his throat.

"I heard of you, you know. You probably didn't think so, but I heard of you."

"That's . . . nice," he said.

"Cameron here told me you're famous or something. I said I knew that. I've seen your pictures. They're okay."

"I'm glad you like them," he said, wondering what in hell this was all about.

"I meet lots of famous people."

"Theodore," Lombard said, "Mr. Ross isn't interested in the celebrities you've known."

Vincent nodded without shifting his gaze from Colin's face. "You ever gamble, Ross?"

He shifted to one side. "Bob, what the hell is this?"

"I *said*, you ever gamble?"

"Bob!"

The finger again, and a sharp pain that made him grab for his shoulder. His frown deepened. It would have been nice, perhaps even poetic, if he could suddenly slam an iron fist into this huge man's jaw and watch him sail back against the wall, his eyes glazed and his teeth rattling. He would land on his feet, stagger drunkenly around a bit, then slink dejectedly into the office where he would collapse unconscious on the carpet, never once knowing the power that hit him.

It would have been nice; but Vincent was easily one hundred pounds heavier and five inches taller than he. Nice, but suicidal. And he hated the feeling of cowardice that chilled him.

"Theodore," said Lombard softly, "the man has a right to his own opinion, isn't that correct, Mr. Ross?"

"I would think so, but your friend obviously doesn't."

"I think," said Vincent, "I don't like the trouble you're causing."

"All right, Bob," he said, "I've had enough." He turned to leave, and a hand clamped on his upper arm and spun him around. His mouth opened, and his right hand fisted, but he only had time to blink once before he felt a fist slam sharply into his stomach.

Instantly, he folded his arms over his belt and dropped to his knees. The air in his lungs was gone; when he inhaled, nothing happened. There were tears in his eyes, and a spreading ache in his chest. When he inhaled, nothing happened, and the noise he made trying to breathe frightened him to gasping. He swayed, he heard voices, and when he inhaled a third time, nothing happened.

A hand gestured feebly for help; his mouth opened wider; motes of black winked in and out of his blurring vision. He tried to focus on the pattern of the carpeting, and he couldn't. He tried to keep himself from toppling, but he fell slowly, heavily, onto his side, legs curled up, one arm beneath his head.

Then his breath returned abruptly, and he rolled to his knees again and tried not to retch.

A hand patted his back, another took hold of his shoulder. Someone was asking if he were all right, if he wanted water, but all he could do was move his lips and make gagging noises like a man near drowning.

He sagged.

One moment every muscle in his body had been drawn tight and was quivering, the next he had to snap out a hand to keep himself from falling. His head lowered, weighted and aching, and he swallowed bile convulsively.

"Col, for God's sake, say something!"

He opened his mouth, and choked.

"Goddamn, I'll get a doctor."

Colin lifted a hand to stop him. When his vision cleared, he rocked back onto his heels and tilted his head to stare at the ceiling while his hands gripped his waist. He drew in a breath, and another, and allowed Cameron to help him to his feet. When he could see without tears, Cameron's face was gray beneath the tan. They were alone; Lombard and Vincent had left them alone.

"Colin?"

The light from the office turned the air sickly yellow.

"Colin, please."

"You're stupid," was all he could say before he shoved the man away and staggered to the door. He closed his eyes, one hand on the brass knob, breathed again, and was outside without Cameron responding.

It was almost sunset. The storm clouds were dark, and they left little room between them for twilight to prepare. The blue that remained was indigo and cobalt, yet there was nothing on the breeze that heralded rain.

The cooling air revived him. He moved stiffly to the sidewalk and winced when his belt buckle dug into his stomach. Instead of heading for Tabor, he walked straight to his home. He stumbled up to the door and almost sat on the threshold. Then he flung the door open, letting it slam against the wall.

"Stupid," he muttered, his mouth tasting like iron.

He closed the door behind him, didn't turn on a light.

In the bathroom he pulled his shirt from his trousers and stared at the bruise spreading over his abdomen. A fingertip brushed over it gingerly, and he drew in a hissing breath. He shook his head, chiding himself for not going to Garve and pressing charges against the

135

man; then he chided himself for thinking the man would be arrested. Oh, Garve would bring him in, of course, and both Lombard and Cameron would deny that anything had happened. Then later, much later, shadows would move and he had no doubt at all the next message sent wouldn't stop at a single punch.

He changed his shirt, put on his boots and jeans, found his denim jacket and stood in the living room, hesitant, wondering.

The Screaming Woman on the table watched him, unmoving.

This is stupid, he thought then; this is really and truly and unquestionably stupid. *He* was stupid. He and his white horse had run into the real world without knowing what had happened. Haven's End, for all its insulation, wasn't a paradise found in some romantic's dream; it was a large plot of land that attracted interests more powerful than any fishing industry. He was only a teacher, and a part-time one at that, and someone who dared commit dreams to a canvas. What chance did he have then against men like Michael Lombard?

He crossed the room and dusted the carving absently.

In a way, he was very much like Gran, he thought. He didn't care for the comparison, though much of it rang true.

A shudder began in his shoulders and traveled to his neck, made his head palsied for several too-long seconds. Then he spun around and strode quickly outside, slid into his car and drove to Atlantic Terrace. He knocked on the door; twice more, and it opened.

When he was inside, both he and Peg began talking at once, laughing by the time he'd crossed the threshold, holding hands without thinking when they walked into the front room. Matt was sprawled on the windowseat, and he was giggling when he saw them. Colin instantly tried to pull away, but Peg wouldn't let him.

Then he suggested the drive a third time, telling her

he was worried about Lilla; after all, her real home was only two doors down and there was no reason at all why she should stay out at the shack, especially since Gran's place would probably flatten in the Screamer. Peg had agreed without hesitation, and Matt was already charging for his coat and telling them the Foxs' invitation to dinner was still good. He had the door open long before they got there, giving them a mock bow from the waist and winking at his mother.

"You okay?" Colin asked, bending over at the threshold to examine the boy's eyes.

"Sure." Matt shrugged.

"She scared you, huh?"

"She's *weird!*"

"No, she's just . . . unsettled, Matt. It isn't easy for someone like her to lose what's left of her family." He crouched, his hands draped over his knees. "Eighteen may seem awfully old to you, pal, but believe me, it isn't."

"Eighteen isn't old," Matt said. "Thirty is."

"Thank you," he said, frowning and throwing a mock punch at his arm. "And your mother thanks you, too."

"Colin!"

He exaggerated a wince, winked once, and stood. Five minutes later they dropped him off at the marina, Alex Fox waiting by the door with a reassuring wave.

"Are you sure you're all right?" he said as he steered the car onto Neptune and headed slowly south toward the cliffs. The road was narrow and slightly humped in its center, the broken yellow lines fading nearly to gray. Though it wasn't really cold, he had his jacket zipped up to his chin.

"I was spooked, that's all," Peg said. Her hair was tied back in a ponytail, exposing her ears and the side of her pale neck. Her coat was red, her shirt a vivid plaid, and she was slumped in her seat so her knees rested against the dash. She turned her head toward him and smiled. "Really. Seeing Matt like that just scared me to death."

137

"Well, if you're sure."

She looked at him, almost laughing. "Yes, Mother Ross, I'm sure. I've been on edge all day. For that matter, it hasn't been a very pleasant week, either."

They rode past the drug store, a pair of clothing stores, the luncheonette, all on the right. The bench where Gran did many of his carvings was deserted, and Colin shook his head.

"It doesn't look right, does it?" he asked.

Peg glanced at the bench, and the thin oak sapling struggling beside it. "No."

They passed the chalet-shaped bank, the movie theater Bill Efron's brother ran, and Syd Naughton's market, all on the right. There were several cars in the parking lot, and he was tempted to stop when he saw Syd pushing several shopping carts toward the door, at the same time arguing loudly and with violent, one-handed gesticulations with three men who trailed behind him. They were in workclothes, fishermen just off their boats.

"No catch," Peg said when she saw him looking. "Soon as I got home I got a call from Ed Raines' wife complaining. All day, and they didn't catch a single damned fish."

"Why'd she call you?"

She twisted a stray hair around her finger. "She owes for a prescription. A pleasant way to spread gossip and tell me she can't pay me this week." She stared until the market fell behind them, was replaced by a gas station, three houses, and the forest. "Matt thanks you."

"For what?"

"For taking me out. I was was driving him crazy."

He grinned. "I was driving myself crazy." He slumped a little to ease the strain on his stomach, and saw Peg watching him with a concerned frown. "Exercising," he explained. "I lost my balance and fell into the kitchen table."

She looked straight ahead. "You're driving awfully slow."

"It's a lovely day."

"It was."

The clouds in twilight deepened the shadows on the road. He switched on the headlights. His stomach ached, and there was pressure in his chest that made him breathe through his mouth. He sniffed, rolled up his window and planted his elbow on the frame. He hummed, whistled a bit, sniffed a second time and was silent.

"What happened at Bob's?"

With his right hand on the steering wheel, and left raked into his hair, he shrugged. "We discussed his visit to you and his call to me."

She looked at him skeptically. "Discussed?"

"I met Lombard and Vincent, too."

Her mouth opened to say, "Oh, but nothing came out. She only looked out the window, at the trees and the underbrush and the midnight darkness beneath the boughs.

They drifted between the two motels, had gone only a hundred yards beyond when he pulled over to the side, turned off the ignition, and twisted around on the seat with one arm stretched across the back. Peg straightened, her hands in her lap.

"There was never anything between Lilla and me, Peg."

Her hands clasped, and she stared at them, nodding.

"Really."

"I believe you. I told you it was the day, that damned storm coming."

He tried to see through her, into her, find the paths that led to whatever created her thoughts and emotions and the laugh that made him smile even when he was sleeping. He had been frightened in the restaurant, just before he was struck, but the fear he knew now was something considerably more.

"You know," he said, "once, when I was in Massachusetts, there was this old man who lived down the street. He ran an antique shop for the tourists and for the college students who needed furniture for their dorms. He'd charge one price for the students and twice as much for the others. He—"

She looked at him suddenly, one corner of her mouth pulling back in a smile. "Is this one of your stories, Col?"

"Huh?"

"One of your stories," she said. "Every time you want to say something you think is important, you have to start off with a story of some kind. And every time," she added with a disarming smile, "it doesn't have a thing to do with whatever you're saying."

He leaned away slightly. "I do that?"

She nodded.

"All the time?"

She nodded again.

"I'll be damned."

She laughed soundlessly and lay a palm to his cheek, pulled the hand away and covered his on the seat's back. "Just tell me, Col. This once, just tell me."

His tongue swiped at his lips once, and his cheeks puffed with apprehension. "It's—"

"Just tell me."

He watched her for a long time, and she didn't look away. Then he tucked his chin toward his chest and took a deep breath. "I want to marry you, Peg. I mean, I want you to marry me. I mean, will you marry me is what I mean. I mean. Yes." He nodded once, sharply. "Yes, I want to marry you."

"Then it's mutual," she said.

"No joke," he said, his stomach suddenly feeling queasy and hollow.

"No joke, Colin."

He frowned. "But I've never said I loved you."

She slid toward him and laced her hands around the back of his neck. "Yes you have," she said quietly. "Every time I see you." She kissed him, and he sighed and wrapped his arms around her, kissed her gently and leaned his chin on her shoulder while he stared at the trees.

"This is . . . nice."

She said nothing.

"I mean, this is great! I mean—" He pulled away and looked at her, frowning until he saw the color slipping from her face. "Peg?" Her lips were quivering just enough for him to see, and her right hand was pushing hard at his shoulder. He turned. "What's . . ." His eyes widened.

Across the road was an elm whose branches had been shaped by the wind until they grew around the trunk, leaning away from the ocean. The bole was wide and gnarled, several knobs of roots thrust through the ground.

He saw a hand there, part of an arm, a dark shape beyond them stretched under the tree.

The hand was a dull red, and so were the leaves beneath it. Peg was out of the car before he could move, waiting by his door when he finally realized she was gone. They held hands as they crossed the tarmac, slowly, trying not to stare and staring just the same. At the opposite verge she stopped and pulled back, but Colin released her and kept going until he could see Warren Harcourt sprawled in the shadows.

A fly walked across the dead man's brow.

"Oh . . . Jesus," he whispered, and closed his eyes, too late. At the man's neck, over his coatfront, and staining the tops of his sandy bare feet . . . never in his life had Colin seen so much blood.

Tess Mayfair liked to cook. If she had her way, she'd stay in the yellow-and-copper kitchen from breakfast to dinner and do nothing but watch the blue flames on the stove reach under the pots to boil the water and brown the fries and crisp the potato skins and curl the bacon. All while the TV on the windowsill would play her favorite western.

These days, of course, there was precious little to do what with the summer people gone and Muriel North working nights at the drug store and no one else from town bothering to come out to see her. That left her alone. All alone. Alone enough to wish sometimes she

141

hadn't driven her third husband away five years ago because he was fooling around with a girl he'd met on the beach in July. And that's what she was. A girl. Thirty years younger than he, and there she was with her tanned little stomach and her tanned little legs and no chest to speak of and no brains, either, considering her choice.

It was damned embarrassing.

She'd seen him with her twice, suspected him more than that, and in a temper and snit on a Sunday afternoon she'd packed his bags and left them on the porch. Locked the door. Pulled down the shades. Listened to him bellow and plead and finally tell her what he thought of her and her westerns, while he staggered and stumbled down the flagstone walk to the street, staggered and stumbled along the pebbled verge until he was out of sight. Still yelling. Still cursing.

Five years gone, and the son of a bitch hadn't even sent her a postcard.

Crumb didn't even know what he was missing. Lord, she still had all her teeth, and her hair was still black without any fancy rinses, and her eyes were still bright and brown, and so what the hell if she was a little overweight.

She sniffed, and shook her head and plunged her hands back into the dishwater. A slow job tonight, just her own plates and coffee cup. As she stood at the sink she looked out at the garden through the gap in the yellow chintz curtains on the eye-level window. Next spring, she decided, she'd have to do a little weeding. Zinnias didn't grow this year, and those fool roses looked like hell. The wall of irises on the left she didn't need to touch at all; they were like her, independent and strong and too stubborn to die. The squirrels had dug up the tulip bulbs, though, all around the birdbath. Mums and tulips, she decided with a nod that rippled her three chins, mums and tulips against the birdbath.

She reached for a towel to dry her hands.

She reached for a cold roll she hadn't eaten at dinner.

142

She looked out the window again before heading in for the big TV in the living room, and saw the boy standing just in the trees.

A groan of exasperation, the dishcloth splashed back into the sink. Why, she wondered, didn't they ever learn? Every year it was the same thing. They didn't even bother to think of something new—wait until she had put a tape on the machine, or was watching a regular show, then sneak up the back and make a grab for the bowl on the concrete pedestal. They thought she couldn't hear them, but they didn't know she had ears that would put a prime fox to shame. They thought she couldn't run, but she grinned when she remembered the summer Cart Naughton had made it all the way to the birdbath, and she was out the door and down the steps before he could look up. Just a little luck and she would have had him, had his neck in her hands and his life popping out his eyes. But he ducked, and all she got was his black leather jacket.

The scream he gave when it tore off his back and dangled in her hand had her laughing for a week. She even tied it to the flagpole in front of the house and prayed he'd try to get it back. A lot of kids drove by and yelled, pointed, laughed when she beckoned with a sweet smile and a fist hidden behind her waist. But Naughton never came for it, and finally a storm ripped it free and blew it away.

So there he was again, and she sighed. On another day she would have welcomed the fun, but not tonight. Tonight she needed to rest because today had been worse than the hottest day in August—sweat bulging on her forehead, making her hair itch, had her looking out every window in the house hunting for the thunderheads she was sure were overhead. It wearied her. It made her think about starting that diet again, maybe even cutting down on her smoking.

She wasn't in the mood for this crap, not at all, not at all.

So she picked up the baseball bat she kept by the stove and she pulled open the door.

"Damn you," she shouted in her worst, fiercest voice.

The boy didn't move.

She leaned forward, peering, and the breeze took the hem of her print dress and snapped it at her legs, drew it tight across her massive chest, puffed the sleeves and gave her a chill. A brittle leaf bounced across the porch. Tentacles of ivy dropped from the gutter and wove at her, scratching the air and whispering to themselves.

"Beat it!" she shouted.

The boy didn't move.

The woods behind him were encased in black, a soft and shifting black that shaded up toward dark green. She could hear a gull wheeling overhead, and the faint sound of the ocean moving in with the tide. A step forward, she grabbed a roof post, held the bat on her shoulder and decided that this might be better than TV.

"Well, if you're gonna do it, do it," she said, pretending she didn't give a damn one way or the other.

The boy shifted, and she could finally see his freckled face, his curly brown hair, those skinny arms that could barely lift his trousers around his skinny waist.

"Oh Lord, Frankie," she said as she moved down to the lawn, "what are you tryin' to do, anyway?" She laughed then, loudly. "You think you can really lift that thing?" She pointed at the bowl with the bat. "You lift it, boy, you can have it."

She waited.

Frankie began walking toward her, and she matched him step for step. She was in Dodge City now, facing down the Adams Kid, and there was no way in hell he could win because she had all the townspeople with rifles hiding in the hotel and the saloon and in the general store. Tim McCoy was on the stable roof, Ken Maynard was in the post office, and over there behind that buckboard she had Bob Steele waiting.

She smiled.

The goddamned Adams Kid was going to get himself blown dead away.

144

When they were ten feet apart, the birdbath between them, she finally saw his eyes.

They were wide. And they were white.

No color. Just white.

She frowned. "Frankie, you on something?"

He reached for the bowl.

"Frankie, damn it, you answer me, boy. I ain't so old I can't give you a lickin' to learn you your manners."

He gripped the sculpted edges.

His eyes were white.

Her tongue brushed her lips. She didn't like the way he looked at her, no expression, no nothing. Maybe he was wearing one of them fancy contact lenses she read about in the *TV Guide*, that changes a person's eye color for the part he was playing.

He lifted the bowl.

Her palms were suddenly wet. The muscles in those skinny arms weren't even bulging, and he was holding the bowl as if it were paper.

"Frankie . . ." she said, backing away.

The wind snarled her hair in front of her face. She brushed at it impatiently, and when she could see again he was holding the bowl over his head.

Jesus Lord, she thought, he's going to throw it. The little prick's gonna throw it.

The bat dropped from her hand as she turned and started to run. Muscles or no muscles, she could outrun the little bastard any day of the week and twice on Sundays, and once she got to a phone she was going to call Garve and let him know that Frankie Adams was destroying private property. The little crumb was just like her husband—no respect for her and hers.

At the steps she turned, to be sure he wasn't following.

Frankie suddenly turned sideways and threw the concrete bowl like an oversized discus.

It came slow. It came fast. It may have hummed and it may have wobbled and it might have just missed her if she had ducked in time.

It struck her just below her breasts and smashed her through the door.

The small TV on the sill fell into the sink and shattered.

Frankie walked across the garden.

The wind didn't touch him, and his eyes were solid white.

FOUR

The wind came alive just after sunset, just as twilight had turned to autumn dusk.

Wally Sterling sat on a high, three-legged, peeling red stool in the ferry's cramped cabin jutting over the water from portside, center. Its octagonal walls were glass from waist to squared flat ceiling, the narrow panes pitted and smeared by salt spray and driven sand. The boat rocked gently, boards creaked, chains swayed. A gull pecked at a candy wrapper lying in the stern. Out of the chest-high sidewalls rose tall iron rods looped at the top and strung through with roping from which bleached plastic pennants hung, listless and dripping.

He stared as the last car reached the top of the slope, flared its red taillights and sped inland across Flocks. After it was gone, he shook his head and brushed a hand down over his yellow slicker, straightened his yellow nor'easter, sniffed and coughed loudly. The spoked wheel in his left hand was slick with sweat, and he slipped his palm around it absently, turning it once to make sure it still worked.

He was tired. That damned fool Screamer had these idiots pissin' in their pants they were so anxious to get away.

He groaned as he slipped off the stool and opened

the narrow door, sidled out and walked stiffly to the ferry's steel lip resting against its place on shore. He grabbed the hooked end of the rusted iron guard chain, drew it across the opening and snapped it back into its eye. A loud sigh just for the sound, and he pulled the slicker open, his hands reaching around to grip the small of his back. He stretched, rolling at the waist while he groaned loudly again, blinked rapidly, taking in deep breaths and blowing them out in short, sudden bursts.

He was God-almighty and lay-me-down-to-die tired. And he was thirsty enough to empty the bay, what with all that exhaust and crap lodged in his throat. He coughed, spat, and the oily, metallic taste made him grimace and swear and think fondly of the cheap brandy he kept in his shack.

As he stepped to the right he heard the noise.

At first he thought it was a damned fool oil truck barreling down the highway through the state forest. That's what it sounded like, by God, and he was in no mood to tell the dumb ass driver politely there was no way in God's hell he was going to put such a rig on his poor little boat. Jesus, the old girl barely made the last crossing she was so weary of all the loads.

He stepped over the chain and walked to shore, kicking aside gravel and spitting toward the water. Goddamned Screamer, sending all them idiots inland like they never saw one before and thought they'd be dead come morning. Fools. A little wind never hurt nobody if you was careful. Fools.

Then the noise changed.

Over the roaring, the rumbling, he heard a whispering and a whistling that brought to mind dreams he'd just as soon not remember; but he was curious enough at last to take the slope to the road, shaking his head and muttering to his fists and not looking up at all until he reached the flat.

And when he did, his one eye widened, his bristled chin dropped, and he half turned to run, though he knew he wouldn't make it.

It wasn't a truck, or a van, or a race car without mufflers.

It was the wind.

He could see it coming, though it was half a mile away. The woods closest to him didn't move at all, were dark and normal and holding shadows to their trunks. But straight down the road it was different—dust and leaves and branches and small stones were churning and spinning and dancing straight for him as if an invisible tidal wave were shoving them toward the beach. The stones he could see, and the branches and the dust, but the wind was without form. As far as he could tell it held to the road, and he could see it all coming, half a mile and closing. The trees on either side bent away, groaned away, some of the older ones nearly snapping in two, losing large boughs that bounced and pinwheeled into the woods, or slammed onto the tarmac and trapped leaves and dust and pebbles in their webs.

Wally only had time to throw himself down below the top of the slope and cover his head with his arms.

And it was on him.

Whispering and whistling, stabbing him in a hundred places, raising welts across his knuckles, stinging his neck and rattling against the slicker. His face turned toward the bay, and he could see the ferry lift and draw back, the moorlines creaking and straining. The water broke into whitecaps that swept toward the island, crashing high against the boulders that marked the opposite shore, spraying the trees and turning the air gray.

And just when he thought he was going to have to scream, just when he thought the air would be sucked clean from his lungs, it was gone.

Just like that it was gone.

One minute hell had been stamping hobnails and boulders all over his back, and the next it was as peaceful as it ever gets at night. Unsteadily, licking at his lips and being careful of his legs, he rose to his feet and stared at Haven's End. The wind was gone, and

149

the only thing that let him know he hadn't dreamt it was the blood he wiped from the backs of his hands, the only way he knew he wasn't part of the Screamer was the direction.

And if it wasn't the Screamer . . .

The ferry rocked, slower, slower.

The whitecaps vanished.

Behind him, the forest was as quiet as dawn.

Jesus *damn,* he thought, and raced for the pistol he'd put under the cot's mattress. Jesus God damn! He'd better get himself a gull soon, because this place wasn't healthy.

By the time the wind reached the ocean it was spent, and the debris it had carried had been dropped in the bay; the few outside to hear it thought it was thunder over the horizon. When it rushed past them, they ducked away and yanked up their collars, thinking for sure they'd be drenched in a moment and goddamn the weatherman who can't read his own charts. And when it was quiet, no rain or lightning, they shrugged and headed home, and wondered about their neighbors. Blaming it on the Screamer was for some too easy; that wasn't due until late the next day, plenty of time to board the windows, fetch the cat, and take the ferry out. No, there was something more, they thought. Folks were unaccountably nervous, but the leaving seemed over and the night was fairly calm despite the clouds overhead. Supper, then, and the news, and a quick change of clothes. After all, it was Friday, with half-priced beer at the Anchor Inn and quiet music at the Run, a new double feature at the theater and some TV before bed.

And only a few stopped to listen, with a nervous snap of their fingers.

The wind dropped to a breeze, and Lilla didn't know the difference.

She sat alone, cross-legged on the ground in front of

150

the shack, and didn't bother to count the minutes until the sea turned black. The waves flared white, between the clouds there were stars, and once in a while at the horizon she could see the multi-colored eyes of a slow-passing liner. She was still in her black dress, and loose around her shoulders was a faded blue woolen shawl; she drew it snugly over her chest and nuzzled her chin into the worn tufts that had never been trimmed.

She thought of nothing.

She rocked on her buttocks and didn't feel the sand. Her tangled hair stirred and she didn't feel the cool. She rocked, and she hummed, and when the night had gone full dark she wiped a bubble of saliva from the corner of her mouth.

She thought nothing, and that was fine.

The fog was with her, comforting and warm and sparkling like diamonds snared in a spider's web especially for her. It dazzled and it lulled, and though she could not reach out to touch it, it felt very strong. It protected her. It hid her. It trembled when there was danger and it floated when Gran was back.

As it floated now when she heard the shack's door rasping open behind her. It closed, and the web shuddered. Her nostrils flared at the acrid scent of spilled blood.

Blood; the web vibrated. Blood; the web parted. Blood and Warren Harcourt, and suddenly the fog was gone, the web torn, and she was running. Down to the beach where she stood at the brink of the climbing tide's foam and dared herself to walk in, walk in and keep on walking until she would either force herself to swim or choose to join her parents.

You told me they'd come back, Gran. You told me. You did.

A wave fanned in, pulled back, covering her feet with dark sand.

But Gran was angry now and wouldn't talk to her, not even in the fog. Not since that first time, after the funeral, after she'd found him and brought him back

151

and sung him the words that had brought her the blood.

He was supposed to have been grateful, and he was supposed to have been smiling. But she knew now he had lied to her, lied to his Lilla. He had lied, he was angry, and he wouldn't let her go.

She was frightened. She had spent the remainder of the night hiding in a cave just below the top of the cliffs, a cave not even Gran knew was her place to escape all the demons and ghosts. All day she had stayed there, until she thought she was safe. Then she had run to find someone to tell them Gran had come back.

She really hadn't wanted to scare the little boy but she knew him (forgot his name), and she knew he was Gran's favorite because he could do things with his hands, and she knew he was close to Colin, and she needed to talk to Colin now more than anything in the world. And when he hadn't come, the fog had come instead, and Colin (and the little boy with no name) was forgotten because the fog and the web and the diamonds were so pretty, and so warm, and the way it used to be when Gran loved her and held her and wouldn't let anyone do her harm.

She glanced furtively at the shack as if he'd somehow overheard her, and she was running again, veering sharply off the beach and scrambling over the dunes toward the houses. The big houses. The rich houses. Past their warm yellow lights and their warming shining cars and their warm pretty gardens bedded down for the winter. Past them and soon onto Neptune, past the darkened boarding house where her nostrils flared and she thought she smelled the blood.

It was easy, she told herself. If Colin wouldn't come to her, she would find him at home.

Because of all the people on the island, only he would understand when she told him about Gran.

Only he would understand why Gran had her singing.

She was halfway to the cottage when she felt Gran

slipping back to spin the web, ride the fog. Tugging, coaxing, urging her back. No, she thought, *no, I won't let you!* And she was startled when the tugging stopped and she was left alone to keep running. She knew then his strength wasn't as great as she'd believed. Despite the sacrifice of Warren Harcourt's blood—the only time Gran walked, so he could drink the blood himself—it would take him a long time to be what he wanted. Meanwhile she had a chance. She had a chance to warn Colin, who would warn Garve and the others.

Warn them. Warn them. Like someone she knew from history who warned all the people that the enemy was coming.

Warn them, she had to warn them—and she stumbled. *About what?*

A frown loosened sand caked to her forehead and her lips tasted salt when her tongue flicked out.

I have to warn . . .

About what, Lil? About what?

Concentration quivered her lips. *Warn them about Gran, about the singing, about the . . . rest.*

She slowed and shook her head to rid it of the fog. She slowed and looked up, and saw the stars between the clouds. They were pretty. They always used to be pretty, but now they were prettier than she'd ever seen them before. Winking at her like lovers she had stored in her dreams, not cold as in all the poems, but whitely warm and . . . pretty.

She slowed to a walk.

Pretty stars, lovers' stars, and her eyes darted from side to side because she knew she was going to the cottage where Colin lived and did his work, and if she took her time and thought hard she might remember why.

The reception room at Doc Montgomery's used to be the garage. Now it was paneled in pine, carpeted in soft gold, furnished with Audubon prints and up-to-date magazines, two beaten leather sofas and a handful of upholstered chairs. It smelled of lemon polish and recent cleaning. The five narrow windows had just that morning been washed.

Colin stood by the entrance, one hand on the door frame. He was frowning. The odd wind had battered through only five minutes before, and already he was wondering if it had been his imagination. A howling, and a whistling, and leaves slapped against the panes, and Peg, sitting on a sofa beside Garve, had nearly jumped into his arms. Now it was quiet. Dark, quiet, the radio on the end table switched off when they arrived.

Doc was in the examination room with Warren, Annalee assisting. Eliot was on his way to Flocks with a clear plastic bag containing Harcourt's wallet which Garve had found at his side.

Colin shivered against a cold that wouldn't leave his system, turned away from the window and leaned against the wall. Peg had driven back for the chief when Colin insisted on remaining behind, had returned in less than five minutes, but five minutes too long. He'd had a chance to look at Warren, at all that goddamned blood on his clothes and on the ground, and he'd had a chance to wonder who would want to kill a harmless alcoholic. Garve had asked the same question while he examined the corpse without touching it, wondering aloud about Cameron's friends, wondering aloud about Jim Fletcher and the enemies he had made. It was all speculation. No weapon was found, no footprints, no clues. Then Eliot had arrived with the patrol car, and Montgomery.

All the doc had said was, "It's too dark to do anything out here. Let's bring him back to my office."

A green plastic sack was zipped closed around him, and he was placed in the trunk and driven back.

While Montgomery played coroner, Garve asked the questions.

That was fifteen minutes ago, and now he was silent.

"I don't get it," Colin said at last, not liking the quiet. "I just don't get it."

154

Peg murmured helplessly, her hands winding and twisting in the folds of her lap. A strand of damp hair was slanted across her forehead.

Garve shoved himself to his feet and paced the width of the room, stared out at the night, closed the curtains and turned around. "Here," he said and he patted his stomach, "I know it was Theo Vincent. But . . ."

"But what?" Colin said impatiently.

"But where's the murder weapon, the proof, the evidence? Why would someone want to cut that poor dope's throat?"

"He knew something he shouldn't have," Peg suggested.

"Oh sure," he said sourly. "Sure."

"Well, hell, Garve," Colin said, "he walked all over the place all the time when he wasn't drinking. He could have heard things, known things—jeez, he even knew about Peg and me, I know I didn't tell him." He pushed away from the wall and sat next to Peg. "He might have heard them talking about . . . something, I don't know what."

"That's just it," Tabor said. "You don't know, and I don't know."

"So are you just going to forget it?"

The look was one of tolerant disgust. "Of course not. I'll go over and have a word with them, as soon as Doc's finished. But I'll tell you this, m'boy, I won't get what I want. They'll be surprised, y'see, and shocked, and they'll alibi each other until the tide turns and then some."

"It sounds to me like you're already giving up."

"No, just being realistic."

"What about the wallet?" Peg said. "Eliot's going all the way into—"

"Because there's a very small chance it just didn't fall out of his coat when he fell. There's a chance someone picked it out, and if they did there'll be fingerprints. Or maybe whoever did it picked it up, dropped it again when he heard someone coming. I

155

don't know," he said in irritation. "Christ, I wish I did."

The far door opened and Hugh Montgomery came out. He was small, sandy-haired, his over-sized glasses continually slipping down his nose. When he smiled there was a large gap between his two front teeth, a gap made larger by the handlebar mustache waxed and poking below his chin. His white coat was stained faint red, and he was drying his hands on a towel.

"Razor," he said. "One slice. Sometime this morning, I'd say shortly after midnight. Can't be sure, but I don't think I'm far wrong."

Tabor reached for his coat. "Anything else?"

"What else is there?"

"You're the doctor, you tell me."

Montgomery scowled, and pushed at his glasses. "There is nothing else."

"Suicide?" Peg asked in a small, trembling voice.

"Absolutely not." He gave her a quick smile. "You want the details?"

"Thank you, Hugh, no."

"I'll be back," the chief said, and left with a brusque nod.

The moment he left, Montgomery stripped off his coat and tossed it into the other room, made for the nearest chair and fell into it with a sigh. He took off his glasses and rubbed the bridge of his nose. "Brother," he said quietly. "Brother."

Colin wanted to leave, but he couldn't help thinking of the way he'd found Warren, and that the lawyer was lying dead on the other side of the wall just behind him. The thought held him, and he barely felt Peg's hand slip into his own and squeeze.

"They're going to get away with it, aren't they," he said.

"Who?"

"Lombard. Vincent."

Montgomery shook his head. "Now, you don't

156

know that, Colin, any more than Garve does. And if you want my opinion, I'd say you were wrong."

"Oh really?"

Hugh nodded. "Really. It serves them no purpose—"

"—unless Warren knew something he shouldn't."

"And it isn't their style." Then he looked deliberately at Peg. "I know what you're thinking, dear, but five years ago they were too far away from setting up the casinos, and they might have taken the chance. *If,* of course, these are the same men. But not this time. This time, if you'll excuse me, Colin, they're damned close to winning."

"I know," Colin said, shifting into the sofa's corner.

"So why screw up a good thing?"

"Because if Warren talked . . . about whatever . . . they'd lose for sure. And even Cameron's not stupid— if they lose this time it won't come up again."

Montgomery replaced his glasses, and whistled soundlessly through the gap in his teeth. "Colin, think about what you're saying here. Who would listen to him, really? Warren? *Our* Warren? A nice guy drunk, a self-pitying slob sober. If he walked up to you and said he knew something terrible was going on between Cameron and those men, would you believe him? Quite aside from the fact that it wouldn't surprise any of us, would you believe it if *Warren* told you?"

Colin wanted to say yes. Instead he waved away the question. Another thought floated briefly, and he looked at Montgomery. "I guess," he said, conceding the point. "But if they didn't do it, Hugh, then who the hell did?"

"Ask Garve. He's the chief around here."

"Yeah. Thanks."

A silence laced with apprehension.

"Are you finished?" Montgomery asked.

Colin nodded.

"Then may I suggest the two of you get the hell out of my office so I can chase Annalee around the table?

Go home, get a drink, I don't care, just go away. Okay?"

"I . . . okay," and Colin followed Peg to her feet, yelled a good-bye to Annalee and was outside, in the dark.

"Colin?"

"Yes?"

"You'll . . . stay?"

He nodded.

She leaned against him and he slipped an arm around her waist, thinking this was going to be a hell of a thing to tell their grandchildren. *On the night I proposed to your grandmother she had just said yes when suddenly we found a bloody corpse. We spent the rest of the night waiting for the island doctor to tell us he was razored, going home and turning on every light in the house because we thought there was a madman on the loose out there. A nut. A psycho.* A hell of a story.

He closed his eyes, then, and saw Warren bleeding. Not the dried blood on his coat, or the dried blood on the ground, but fresh blood, running blood, seeping from the black gash beneath his chin—like the blood that had seeped fresh from the gashes on his wrists. He shuddered, and Peg squeezed his arm.

"Changing your mind, sailor?" she said too brightly.

He remembered. "Listen, Peg," he said, reaching into his pocket and pulling out the keys to drop into her hand, "there's something I want to get from the house. You pick up Matt and I'll meet you there, okay?"

"Colin?"

He kissed her cheek softly. "Hey, it's all right, don't worry."

"But whoever killed—"

"It's all right," he insisted, already walking away. "You get Matt. I'll see you. Twenty minutes."

He averted his gaze to avoid her eyes, stuffed his hands in his pockets as he headed toward Bridge Road. At the corner Peg drove by and waved at him.

He waved back and turned right, hurrying now, Warren's death temporarily shunted aside while he considered what we'd done.

It was curious. He thought he'd feel elation, or release, or some Busby Berkeley extravaganza exploding into glorious showgirls and vibrant celebration around him. But there was nothing but an odd sense of fear. He'd made up his mind to stop stalling and propose, and he'd done it; Peg had accepted. Now it was too late to turn back (do you want to?) If he reneged, he couldn't stay on the island (do you want to?) If he told her he'd made a mistake, would he be able to look Matt in the eye again (do you?)

Christ, he thought, I'm really fucked up.

The first time, so long ago he might have read about it in a book, he had proposed because it was the thing to do, the high school sweetheart and the ivy-covered cottage thing to do in order to complete a life not yet begun and destined never to end. The second time it almost worked (and would have if she'd lived, he demanded to believe). This time was calculated. This time it was deliberate. No passion, no yearning, no 'doing the right thing.' And though he'd felt fine when he'd said it, now he wondered if he had said the right thing.

God*damn!*

He swerved off the sidewalk and almost ran through the trees, took the stairs to the porch and had his hand out for the latch before something odd finally registered. He stopped with a palm slapped against the frame, staring down as if someone had thrown up a glass wall.

The door was open.

He knew he had closed it this morning, but now it was open.

The living room was dark, the only light a pale shade of night slipping in from the side window. He entered cautiously, avoiding the plank that creaked like an alarm just over the threshold. Water dripped in the bathroom shower; the refrigerator in the kitchen coughed on and sputtered; the furniture waited just beyond the focus of his eyes, blending into the walls and bringing them closer. He could feel the bruise on his stomach, Warren's blood on his hands, the roof of the cottage adding weight to the dark.

He could smell it, then, and he could touch it, and he could hear it in the way his mouth opened to breathe the stale air—there was someone in here. Someone was waiting for him, hiding in the black.

Vincent, he thought in a swift and brief panic, and an instant denial as his shoulder hunched in anticipation of another attack. Not Vincent, it was too soon. Not Garve, not Peg, maybe Cart Naughton bound to keep the promise he'd made that afternoon.

No. No one like that.

But someone was in here, back in the shadows, waiting for him.

And suddenly a lamp was switched on and the black was gone.

He blinked wildly and ducked, one arm up and across his chest to protect himself from a blow that never came.

By the window, by the table, was Lilla. She was looking at the sculpture of *The Screaming Woman;* she didn't turn around.

"God," he said, one hand bracing himself against the top of the television while relief weakened his knees. "God, you scared me half to death."

"Me," she said quietly, tonelessly. A finger reached out to touch the woman's open mouth, probe the darkened mouth. "This is me." She looked over her shoulder, and he saw the wide eyes, the sand-dusted cheeks, and no smile at her lips. "Gran did this of me."

Only then did he notice she was still in her funeral dress, ragged and damp, one shoulder nearly gone. It had only been a day, but she seemed markedly thinner, almost emaciated, and her fingers snapped at the air as if galvanized in a lab. He shook his head with relief and walked over to the sofa.

"Lilla, you will never know how glad I am to see you." He dropped with a loud, laughing sigh, filled his cheeks and blew loudly before patting the cushion beside him once to bring her over. When she didn't move at a second or third invitation, he felt no annoyance. No matter how she was acting, it was enough she had finally left that miserable hovel. "Peg and I, we were on our way to see you when . . . well, no sense in going into details, Lil, but I have to tell you Warren Harcourt's dead and some kind of killer is walking around out there. We were afraid for you. We were going to take you home."

Her gaze returned to *The Screaming Woman*. "Home."

"It isn't right for you to be staying out there, you know that. It isn't healthy. I know there's no such thing as running water or anything, and I'll bet a year's salary you haven't eaten since yesterday."

"I'm not hungry. Gran is."

"Listen, Lil, we were also thinking about Cameron's shindig tomorrow and we kind of thought it might be really nice if you . . . what?" He cocked his head slightly as if he hadn't heard what she'd said, and again she fixed him over her shoulder. "What did you say?"

"Gran."

He nodded, not quite frowning. "Yes."

Her lower lip drew in between her teeth, and he felt as though he were being examined, tested, her eyes unblinking while she searched him for something.

"Lilla," he said quietly, still smiling, easing forward to rest his forearms on his knees, "Lilla, what's wrong?"

She shifted, and he saw dark red stains splattered across the front of the dress. "Gran," she said, her right hand out to caress the head of the sculpture.

Oh God, he thought.

Warren. And the blood. All that goddamned blood.

"Lilla." He swallowed, and hated himself for staring, for checking to see if she were carrying a weapon. "Lilla, Gran's dead."

"Yes."

"You can't do anything for him now."

"I know."

He took a shallow breath and prayed for Peg to walk in the door. "He loved you, you know. He loved you very much."

She sniffed. "He was my Gran."

It can't be, he thought. God, Lil, don't read my mind.

He opened a palm to her. "He was indeed, Lil, and I know he wouldn't want you"—and he pointed at her disarray—"like this. Not like this, not his Lilla. He'd want you back in the house on the Terrace where it's warm and you have food and where your friends can come and see you, help you." He almost rose, but her eyes didn't move. "Lilla—"

She faced him fully, suddenly, and her hands drew to fists that brushed at her legs in time to the words that pelted him like hail. "He's mad, Colin. He's very, very mad. You think he likes you, likes me, likes everyone here, and maybe he did. Maybe he thought this was a fine place to live a very long time ago. Maybe he thought it a good place because the old place didn't like him and made him leave. They said he was crazy, that he did things wrong. He didn't, Colin. He did things, but they weren't wrong. And when he came here he thought it all would be better. Maybe he thought it was. But he doesn't anymore. Not anymore. He says he could be the big man on the hill, Colin, but no one gave him the chance. Not there, not here. Now he doesn't like this place anymore. He don't like anyone anymore. He's mad, Colin. He's mad."

It didn't take him long to recognize the hysteria in her eyes, to see her lips begin to quiver. He was on his feet quickly and had his hands on her upper arms before she could move. The dress felt like dried paper.

162

Bits of sand and kelp and dead leaves soiled her hair, and there was an odor he could not define, one that wrinkled his nostrils and almost made him turn.

Gently. "Lilla . . . love . . . he's dead."

She nodded.

"You and I and all your friends, we were together last night. We saw Gran, and we saw you, and it's over, it's all over."

She nodded. "And Warren," she whispered.

"You knew?"

"I hear. I know."

"But how? How—"

She caught a sob in her throat, and he held her closely, absently stroking her back until he realized he was waiting for her to cry, until he realized the long black hair felt like rope when he touched it.

"Lilla?"

She wouldn't look up. "He's mad."

"Lilla, please."

Her forehead pressed against his chest, but her hands stayed at her sides. "He wanted to buy me things, you know. He wanted to be the man on the hill, and buy me pretty things. But he's mad now. He said to me, 'Child, they took it all when I had it and now I give it to them in the way they gave it to me.' "

A deep breath filled his lungs until he had closed his eyes once, hard. When he opened them his hand was brushing through her hair, and through the grains of sand like insects burrowing in her scalp. For a moment he couldn't think of anything to say. The funeral had obviously twisted her sense of time, and she was telling him now what Gran had said most likely on his deathbed. A rush of anger then, at the stupid old man who couldn't die in peace, couldn't leave his own family with a smile or a prayer.

"Lilla," he whispered, "you knew Gran better than anyone. You knew him, and he was bitter." A nod toward *The Screaming Woman*. "He made those things, and people, very important people came down to see them. You know that. You know that's true."

163

She nodded, once.

Outside the cottage, the stir of a wind.

"And you know he was offered a great deal of money for them. Even if he'd taken it all he wouldn't have been rich, but it would have been more than he'd ever seen in his life. I swear they weren't patronizing him, Lilla, and they weren't doing it for me. They saw something in his work that . . . I don't know. I don't know exactly what it was, but they saw it, and they wanted it, and Gran was too contrary to give them a chance.

"I swear to God, Lil, I don't know why he wouldn't cooperate. I guess because he'd grown used to being angry, and anything else was . . . kind of a threat to the way he was used to living. It's crazy, but it isn't unusual."

"He's mad." The words almost lost in the thickness of his jacket.

"He *was* mad," he corrected gently. "But he's gone now, Lil. He's gone, and you're not."

She shuddered.

The wind rattled leaves softly against the pane.

"You're not listening," she said finally.

His lips parted slightly, almost a smile. "I heard you, Lil. You said he was mad because he thought we didn't like him and we kept him from getting rich, from being the man on the hill."

"No."

He frowned and held her away, but she wouldn't look up.

"Then what?"

She shuddered again, and he stared at his hands to be sure they were still gripping her arms. For a moment he thought he'd taken hold of ice.

"Lilla, maybe we ought to see Doc Montgomery."

"No!" And she shoved him away, so unexpectedly hard his legs clipped the back of the cobbler's bench and spilled him onto the couch. She was backed into the corner now, out of reach of the lamp. "No! No! Why won't you *listen?*"

"Lilla!"

"No! Gran won't like it!"

And just as he made to rise, Peg came through the door.

"No!" Lilla shouted.

"Colin, what's—"

He looked to her, pleading, one hand gesturing toward the girl. "She was here when I got back, Peg. She keeps saying—"

The explosion made him duck, made Peg scream. A pine bough slammed suddenly through the window, knocking over the table and spilling the lamp and the driftwood woman onto the floor. Lilla yelled hysterically, and Colin shoved the bench aside as he went to hold her.

And stopped when Peg grabbed hold of his wrist.

The wind growled through the broken pane, the fallen lamp sputtered and went out. The room was black.

The Screaming Woman rocked on its base, slowly, staring up.

"Lilla," Peg said as if comforting a child.

"No!" she shrieked, and lifted her head as she raced for the door.

No one moved to stop her.

It's the light, Colin thought. It's the light. It's the light.

The wind caught a magazine and flipped over its pages.

When Lilla screamed and ran, her eyes turned dead white.

FIVE

Damn, Eliot thought, what am I going to tell Garve now? One simple, lousy job, and those jerks in Flocks screw him up. It's a murder case, for crying out loud, and there they go and try to tell him the fingerprint lifted from Harcourt's wallet belonged to Gran D'Grou.

Gran's fingerprint, my ass.

He had told them the old man was dead, and all they did was stare at him like he was crazy. Then they as much as called him a liar and told him to stop farting around, this wasn't a joke. Of course it ain't a joke, he'd said, but they insisted all the way out the god-damned door that either they were right, or he was more stupid than they thought.

Gran. A dead man leaving fingerprints on a wallet. Shit and damnation.

The only good thing about this will be when Garve gets on the horn and chews those bastards out, or calls the chief at home and raises holy hell. That'd really be something else to hear, really something else. They wouldn't be so damned snotty if *they'd* seen Warren there under that tree.

He almost braked then when the headlights began picking out islands and swirls of stones and twigs scattered over the state forest road, and when he switched on the floodlight on the dash and directed it at the twisted trees along the verge, he wondered how the hell he'd managed to miss the hurricane. That goddamn Screamer wasn't due until tomorrow.

Suddenly he felt uncomfortably warm.

The night was too black, the dashboard light too green, the whine and thump of the tires too loud by half. Without thinking he turned on the overhead red-and-blues, switched the beams to high and snapped on the radio. It didn't matter that all he heard was static; what mattered was the sound, and the light, and the feel of the wheel sweating beneath his hands.

A large branch clawed at the side of the car. A rock bleached gray jerked him to the right. The dark ahead refused to give ground, and by the time he reached the landing his shirt was soaking wet, his hair dripping sweat down the run of his back. He braked and stared at the low-wave water grayed by the headlights. He stared at the canted shack, willing Sterling to appear. He honked the horn. He stared at the ferry. He honked the horn again.

Sterling came out, one hand buried large in his peacoat pocket, the other gesturing at him to be silent for crying out loud, he weren't deaf and he weren't a goddamned servant that he had to jump like a freak just because a cop blowed his horn.

El didn't care what the old man thought. He drummed on the dash until the chain was pulled away. Then he drove the cruiser over the steel lip and onto the boat, stopping it dead center. Sterling hobbled into the cabin and coughed the engines into grinding. The ferry shuddered and rocked and slipped away from the shore.

At length, he could see the island. At length—and none too soon for his oddly jangled nerves—the engines reversed, and the bow dipped toward the bay. An adjustment to swing the lip and landing into line, and the ungainly boat coasted into place. Smooth, easy, so expertly done El didn't realize what had happened until Sterling crossed through the beams with the guard chain in his hand. El nodded and fired the ignition, hesitated a moment when he remembered what he had to do, then tore off the boat with a screech and stench of rubber.

Sterling watched him bump up to the road, spat disgustedly over the side and dragged the chain back. Ground fog drifted into the glaring light. He waited for a moment, thinking it would be just his luck tonight that another car would come screaming down to the landing just as he'd shoved off. Then he'd have to coax the ferry in again, unhook the chain, and pray the driver didn't dive off the far end.

He had had enough trouble as it was this weekend. Goddamned folks spooked at the storm, and he was going to have to spend practically all day tomorrow making sure the ferry was secure enough not to be dumped halfway across the goddamned state. Good God, when it all went friggin' wrong . . .

He spat again and wiped a rough sleeve over his chin, had half turned to head for the cabin when he thought he saw something moving, out there just beyond the reach of the floods. A dark thing, undefined, perhaps a tree shadow or a break in the fog. He frowned, and waited, his hand curling around the target pistol in his pocket. The margin of the floodlights' reach formed a white wall on the landing, and now that he took a good look he knew damned well someone was standing there. He would have called out, but that had been Stu's job. Little brother Stu was the friendly one, always hanging back and screwing up the schedule to be sure they weren't leaving anyone behind.

He sighed, startling himself with the sudden and brief touch of loneliness that brought an even briefer burning to his eyes.

Then he shook it off and frowned, stepped over the chain and peered into the light.

"Hey!" he called, in memory of Stu.

The figure moved closer, and he could see now it was a short man. Or a boy.

"My God," he whispered. "Stu? Stu?"

And he cursed soundly and viciously when he saw Frankie Adams walking arrogantly toward him. What the hell right did that damned kid have, fooling him like that? It wasn't nice. It was cruel. The dumb—

Frankie walked through the white wall, and Wally's eye widened. The front of the kid's shirt was covered with blood.

"Jesus, kid, you all right?" he said, hurrying off the boat and wondering what he was going to do now. Frankie looked like he'd been hit by a truck, for God's sake. Maybe that wind, he thought suddenly, A branch came down and clobbered him maybe.

"Kid, listen, didn't you see Nichols go by just now? You should've flagged him down. I ain't got no car, for Pete's sake. Listen, I'll—"

He stopped abruptly.

Frankie raised his head and opened his eyes.

"Oh my God," Wally said. "Oh my *God!*" And he yanked out the target pistol and started firing. The reports were echoed, confined within the reach of the light and slammed back.

Frankie's shirt rippled, but Frankie didn't stop.

With Harcourt tucked back into his plastic sack, and placed in the large refrigeration unit kept in the office basement, Hugh Montgomery decided it would be the gallant and prudent thing to do to walk Annalee home. She protested, as always, but this time he managed to override her by pointing out bluntly that whoever killed Warren might still be on the island. It may be only an isolated episode, but you never knew about the kinds of nuts running around the world these days. He was pleased when he realized she was relieved, and he even kept his hand on her elbow the entire way. With luck, Garve would have finished whatever it was he was doing, pass by and see them. He might get jealous. He might even stop and grab Annalee, throw her into the car and put an end to everyone's agony, for once and all time.

Fat chance, he thought then, pushing his glasses back up his nose.

Annalee, though a full head taller, stayed close to him until they reached her porch. Then, while he waited patiently, staring puzzledly across the street at the darkened police station, she fished her keys out of her purse and unlocked the door.

"You want some coffee?" she asked, and gave him a smile.

Beautiful. God, she was beautiful! There were times when he wanted nothing more than to bury his hands in all that lovely hair, bury his face between those uncommonly lovely breasts; but there were also times when he knew he'd win the state lottery and retire a millionaire.

"Thanks, no, Lee," he said. "Feels like fog coming in again, and I want to get back." He rubbed the back of his neck, and sighed shyly. "I'm tired, too."

"You going to be able to sleep?"

"You mean with Warren keeping me company?"

She nodded, looking over his head, across the street.

"I've done it before. It doesn't bother me. Besides, if I get the insomnia, I can always call Hattie and let her tell me all about Greek gods or Egyptian burial practices or the mythology of the Manitoba backcountry."

Annalee laughed quietly. "She does go on, I guess."

"The world's leading expert on—" He stopped, realized he didn't have her full attention. "Well, don't worry, anyway. If Hattie isn't home, I'll take a pill or something."

She nodded again, absently, and opened the door. "See you tomorrow morning."

"Sure thing," he said, and was alone on the porch.

The blinking amber light over the intersection, the night sound of the ocean tearing at the island, and the fog. The lamp just extinguished in Annalee's window, Warren on the table, and the fog outside his bedroom.

He shuddered the images away and decided maybe

170

home wasn't exactly where he should be right now. The idea of listening to Hattie Mills fill him in on the latest mythological gossip was absolutely more than he could bear tonight. He had just put his hand to the driftwood door of the Inn when he heard a speeding car. He turned and saw the patrol car, lights whirling, hit the intersection and squeal into a sharp turn to race down Neptune. He wasn't quick enough to see who was driving, but knew it was probably Nichols. Even in an earthquake Garve would take his time.

He shrugged and went in, blinked at the dim lighting from the lanterns on the rough walls, and took a stool at the corner of the deserted bar. A glance, and he frowned; he was the only one in the place. But he said nothing to the bartender, only ordered Bloody Marys to be served in formation—when one was half-finished there should be another one waiting.

There was, each one perfect, and he stared at his hands and thought of Annalee and her breasts.

An hour later his knuckles were slightly blurred.

Poor old Warren. What a jackass.

An hour after that he was trying to figure out why the glasses were so slippery.

Poor old Warren. Leave it to the lush to get his throat cut when guys like Carter Naughton walked around still alive.

He blinked at the vicious thought, and felt a chill that disturbed him. He wasn't drunk; he knew that. He knew, and the bartender knew, his capacity, and he was still four drinks away from being barely able to walk home. What he felt was a gentle, and not unpleasant, buzzing in his right ear, a hydrogen cloud in his head, and a tingling in his left foot. So why be so maudlin about a dumb drunken lawyer, and so damnably cold about a miserable teenaged kid?

He shrugged, and nibbled at the celery stick plucked from his glass. Such philosophical musings were best left to daylight.

The door opened then, and before he could turn around, Garve Tabor slammed onto the stool beside

171

him and ordered a triple bourbon. As Hugh watched, mouth agape, Tabor downed it in a swallow and ordered two more.

"Jesus," he said, "you want to slice up your liver?"

Garve looked at him and scowled. "I've had a bad night."

Hugh nodded, knowing exactly what bad nights were. "You wanna . . . do you want to talk about it?"

"Nope."

Two more glasses emptied, two more in line.

"You're gonna get drunk."

"Yup."

Hugh sniffed, and pulled at the ends of his mustache. "You shouldn't, y'know. You have duties to perform."

"I tried," Garve said. Two gone; two more. "Goddamn it, I tried."

He waited for an explanation, and when none came he sipped from his last drink and looked in the mirror rising behind the bottles opposite his seat. It was obvious the man needed something, and that something wasn't liquor. Garve was, in fact, very much like himself twenty years ago. He had practiced on the mainland, was successful (except with women), and didn't quite know what the hell was wrong with his life. Then a friend had called, and would Hugh mind covering his office while he was in Barbados? Hugh asked where, asked where again, and decided what the hell. He came, he saw, the island conquered and his friend gladly stayed away because Haven's End was no place to make a million.

Fate, perhaps, but Hugh never questioned it. If he was, as his father had put it just before he died, a rabbit afraid of a little hard living, then this was the perfect burrow for his soul.

Garve groaned, and his elbow slipped off the bar.

"My friend," Hugh said, "I'm going to write you a prescription."

Garve nodded slowly, as if his head were threatening to come loose.

"In fact, I'm even going to fill it for you."

Garve nodded again and glowered at his reflection.

Hugh gripped the leather edge of the bar and slipped himself off the stool. When he was positive the door wouldn't move away, he headed for it, heard Garve shout behind him and ignored him. Outside, he shivered, angled to his left and aimed straight for Annalee Covey's.

Five minutes later Garve realized he was alone. He squinted at the stool beside him, rubbed the heel of his right hand over his eyes, and squinted again. Son of a bitch, he thought, the doc's a magician. Wish to hell I could make myself disappear.

He hadn't been kidding about "one of those nights."

He'd found Lombard at Cameron's house out at the Estates and had come on like some simpleminded refugee from the worst episode of "Dragnet." Warren Harcourt's had his throat slit just down the road and all I want is the facts. Just the facts, mac, and don't give me no crap. And they hadn't. They'd sat there in that cushy living room at least as big as his own place, and offered him Glenlivet neat or on the rocks, and smiled and talked and just about got him down on his knees so they could pat his head and call him a good dog.

Well, maybe not that bad. Cameron had had the sense to be scared out of his mind. Lombard, however, was oily and smooth and quiet and maddening, and when neither of them admitted to knowing where Theo Vincent was, he'd actually lost his temper. Something inside burst like a stoppered pipe, filling him with a bile he could only get rid of by yelling. He reared up and read them his own version of the riot act and stormed out as if he'd just whipped them to within an inch of their miserable lives. The door had slammed behind him. He had driven away so recklessly fast he'd jounced over three curbs before he regained control.

And he knew as he headed back into town that he'd

173

made an absolute jackass of himself. After that speech to Colin and Peg in Hugh's office, after all he'd tried to teach Eliot about the difference between the law and justice and the tightrope between them, he'd forgotten himself.

"You're an Indian, Chief?" Lombard had asked, as casually as if he'd been wondering if it were dark outside. "No. No, I'm wrong, and I'm sorry. Part Indian, right? A grandmother, as I recall."

So carefully phrased, so gently put, and it sounded to Garve as if he'd just been called a half-breed.

That was when his temper went, and that was when he stormed out and roared into the Anchor Inn's parking lot and thundered into the bar and began drinking himself to death.

Suddenly a blast of damp, cold air washed over the bar. His untouched paper napkin fluttered, the collar of his shirt jumped to cover his neck. He lowered his glass slowly, turned, and stared a long moment at Annalee before he finally nodded.

"Hugh wants to give you a prescription," she said. She was wearing a plaid shirt open two buttons down and pulled out of her jeans, sandals on her bare feet, a cardigan cloaked over her shoulders.

"Hugh," he said, stifling a belch, "is a noisy twerp."

She sat and folded her arms on the bar. "You're drunk."

"Not yet, but I'm working on it." He raised a finger to signal the bartender, and she grabbed it, held it until he turned to face her. "Lee, I'm not . . ." He was going to say, *I'm not in the mood,* but the look of her, and the touch of her hand, stopped him. He shrugged with a lift of an eyebrow and lowered his hand; she did not let go.

"Where's Hugh?" he asked, trying not to let the smell of her hair penetrate the sharp odor of the bourbon.

"On his way home, I hope," she said, her hand

shifting from one finger to the whole hand. "A little wobbly, but I think he'll make it."

"He's a good man."

"You said he was a noisy twerp."

He grinned lopsidedly. "I speak with forked tongue."

"You drink another one of those and you won't be able to speak at all."

He managed a barking laugh, picked up his glass, emptied it, and slammed it onto the counter so hard he made himself wince. There was no taste to the liquor at all; he'd burned out his tongue, and the fire in his stomach was rapidly turning to acid.

Ten minutes passed while they stared at each other in the mirror. Garve licked his lips. Her eyes, that hair—damn, but she was making him nervous.

"Hugh said you had a bad night."

"Hugh talks too much."

"You, uh, want to talk?"

Yes, he thought, Lord, yes.

"No," he said. Then he smiled. "I don't . . . I don't think I can."

"Okay," she said. "Maybe later."

Later? he thought. Jesus Christ, Hugh, what did you say to her?

"C'mon," she said then, standing and taking his arm.

"What?"

She pulled him to his feet, and grabbed his waist when he discovered that someone had substituted rubber for his knees. It wasn't right, he thought as she lead him carefully to the door, I can walk, damn it. She doesn't have to carry me.

The door opened, and the fresh air smacked his cheeks, dried his throat. "Oh God," he groaned, "I think I'm dying."

"You're impossible, you know that, don't you," she said, guiding him across the parking lot toward her house.

"Where are we going?"

She looked at him sideways. "Are you really *that* drunk?"

He felt stupid and helpless, and was amazed to realize that he didn't mind at all. As long as she was there to hang on and keep him from falling, as long as she was *there,* period, he decided he would survive.

At the end of the parking lot he stumbled over a raised section of curbing, laughed self-consciously, and looked up to the small house. Fog had drifted in from the woods behind it, pooling in the yard, clinging to his face and pulling his skin tight. He stopped when they were halfway there, turned and stared at the street. The bourbon was numbing him, fuzzing his mind, but he still didn't like the way the street looked.

He thought he heard footsteps on the grass, beside the house, in the dark.

"Lee?"

She was hugging his arm now. "Yes," she said. "I know. C'mon, let's hurry."

They almost ran the last few steps to the porch, and he was grateful she had not locked the door, that the lightswitch was right at hand, that she did not stop but led him straight to the bedroom.

"Lee?"

"Garve," she said, pulling at his shirt while he sagged onto the bed. "Garve, don't worry. I'm here. It's all right."

He rubbed at his eyes, felt the mattress on his back, and knew that she was lying. Whoever was out there, *what*ever was out there, it wasn't all right at all. It wasn't all right.

Eliot decided to check on the Estates, to try to rid his system of its inexplicable nervousness—they *weren't* Gran's prints, damn it—and to see if anyone needed help boarding windows, loading cars. He nearly braked when he reached the Sunrise Motel and thought he saw a light behind one of the drawn curtains. The hell with it, he thought, speeding up again; if

176

Cart wanted to take himself some tail that was no concern of his. With luck the storm would blow the creep away.

Just beyond Mayfair's he swung left, wincing at the tires' high-pitched protest against the tarmac, slowing as he entered Dunecrest Estates. The homes began on his left, dark for the most part, a few lighted as they swung left with the road. He parked at the curve and switched off the ignition, and with a glance to his right remember that Lilla was supposedly still in Gran's shack.

He hesitated, then thought, why not. Save a crazy-with-grief girl and make yourself a hero. It was certainly better than scaring himself to death.

This print, patrolman, belongs to Gran D'Grou.

He shuddered and slid out of her car.

The sand was cold beneath his shoes, the sawgrass slapping harshly against his legs. The ocean grumbled, a giant turning in its sleep, and he slipped once, going down on one knee before he was able to right himself again.

"Hell."

He dusted off his trousers, slapped his palms together, and grunted when the sand flattened and hardened and he could see the shack, just barely, just black.

He stopped.

He should turn around right now and try to find Garve, to give him the information and take the temper tossed into his lap. Even while he stood here the chief was probably ringing his house, cussing a blue streak and hitching at his belt. He may not have called Flocks, but he knew El was due back, and he needed to know what they'd found on the card.

A disgusted grunt, and he started forward.

There was a light on in the shack. He could see it wavering in the cracks in the walls, see it leaking from beneath the poorly-hung front door. He glanced around and scratched at the side of his neck, looked around again and lifted his hand to knock.

177

The door swung open.

He stared at his fist, at the door, at the darkened room beyond and the light in the back—a red-gold light that refused to remain still. Firelight. Candlelight. And with it a faint stench that finally registered and pursed his lips. He swallowed.

"Lilla?" Softly, as though he would frighten her if he used his normal voice.

"Hey, Lil, it's Eliot."

A foot over the threshold cautiously, one hand out to grip the door's frame.

"Lil? Lilla, it's El Nichols."

The light.

A board creaked sharply when he stepped inside, and he was back on the sand in a single nervous jump. He gnawed on his lower lip, pulled at the side of his neck. This was stupid. He should walk right in, calling her name, and tell her he was going to take her back to her home. Simple as that.

But the front room was dark, and the light was red-gold.

And the stench made him think of damp open graves.

He listened then, shunting the sound of the ocean to one side, thinking he might have heard the sound of her weeping. A moment later he gave up; there was nothing. His imagination. The shack was empty, except for that damned light.

And the beach was empty, except for the footsteps behind him.

He wanted to spin around with his gun in his hand. The night, the storm, and Gran's fingerprints, had spooked him. Instead, he turned slowly, a smile waiting to spread in case it was Lilla.

There was a shadow in the trees.

He relaxed.

"Lilla, for God's sake."

The light flared behind him, rushed past him, and stretched his shadow along the sand until its tip reached the feet of the shadow in the trees. Instinctively, his hand cupped the butt of his revolver, his fingers automatically unsnapping the flap. At the same time he began to sidle toward the dunes.

The light carved a cavern out of the dark.

He was ready to call out, but the moment his lips parted he knew he would sound like a little boy scared of slimy creatures in the corner. He swallowed instead, looked at the shack, and continued to back away.

The shadow beneath the trees stepped into the red-gold.

On any other day in any other month he would have laughed and shook his head at his own foolishness. But tonight she stood there in the black mourning dress, her hair snaked across her face, her arms rigid at her sides. She said nothing, and she moved no closer, but the light flared again and Eliot bolted.

His shoes thumped on the hard sand, hissed on the soft, and he threw himself over the first dune and slid into the trough on the seat of his pants. He looked up. She was standing there, in her black mourning dress and her eyes opened wide. He gagged and ran on, up the next dune, down the slope and onto the road, nearly tripping over the curb he'd forgotten was there. He didn't stop until his arms thrust out and he slammed hard into the front of the patrol car, gasping, his fingers trying to take hold of the paint.

Jesus. Jesus.

His head lowered and his lungs worked and he kicked at a tire until the pain stopped him.

Jesus.

The hood was cool, and the touch calmed him, suddenly made him ashamed that some grief-crazy woman had terrified him into cowardice. It was stupid. *He* was stupid. There was no other word for it. Yet when he looked over his shoulder, his mouth wide, nearly wheezing, he couldn't bring himself to go back. Jesus. She must think him drunk out of his mind for running like that. It was that dumb shack, that's what it was—that godawful smell and that candlelight,

179

enough to spook even Garve. But he couldn't go back; he wanted to, but he just couldn't. Not with the shack, and the light, and her not saying a word.

"Goddamn fool," he muttered as he pushed away from the car and hitched at his belt. "Idiot. Jackass!"

He kicked the tire again as hard as he could, stepped toward the door, and paused when he saw the woman by the rear fender.

Oh, Christ, he thought wearily, I don't need this now.

"What is it?" he said, not bothering to be polite. "Somebody dig up your garden?" He shook his head and waved her away. "Why don't you call in the morning, okay? Call the office. It's late and I'm off duty, and if you don't mind, I'm going home to bed."

He opened the door without bothering to wait for an answer, sat behind the wheel and reached for the door's handle.

Tess Mayfair grabbed his elbow.

Behind them, in the Estates, the lights blurred in the fog.

"Hey!" he shouted, trying to jerk his arm free. "Jesus, Tess, that hurts!"

Tess pulled again, dragging him half out of the cruiser, his hip catching the wheel and burning. He swung at her with his free hand, but it was too awkward—he was pinned, and she didn't seem to care. Then she pulled again, hard, and Eliot screamed as he heard his shirt tearing at the shoulder, screamed once again when his arm tore from its socket.

"I suppose you realize that the last time something like this happened was when Claudette Colbert stretched a blanket across the room to stop Clark Gable."

Peg nodded, but didn't turn around; she was spreading sheets and covers over the sofa.

Colin leaned against the windowseat, arms folded across his chest. "I'll bet he didn't sleep all night."

She grunted.

"That's from *It Happened One Night,* you know."

She nodded and slapped the pillow against the arm-rest.

"Peg—"

"I know," she told him kindly as she sat on the center cushion. "I know." From a one-sided smile: "You could always take a cold shower."

"I could, but they're cold."

Then he gave her a martyr's sigh and pushed himself back until he was sitting cross-legged, his spine against the window. The panes were cool, and without turning he could feel the fog climbing from the lawn. At his side was a snifter of brandy Peg had poured for him earlier, after she had returned with Matt and had seen him to bed. They'd talked for quite a while, of his past and hers, of the casinos and the past season that had been one of the island's most successful.

They talked of everything except Lilla, Gran D'Grou, and Warren.

He watched her until she looked down at her hands. He watched the lamp's light shimmer off her blouse and catch fire in her hair, watched the play of her lips and the stretch of her neck. It was a curious feeling, to see her suddenly ill-at-ease. The sly remarks and the innuendos had vanished the instant they both realized what it was they had done.

"I love you," he said softly.

She looked up without raising her head. "I know. I love you, too." A quick smile, and a deep breath. "What are we going to do?"

"Get married, I guess."

"No," she said. "About Lilla."

He shrugged. "We'll have to tell Garve, and Hugh, and then . . . then I suppose someone will have to go out there and get her."

"Oh, hell."

"Yeah."

He took a long sip of the brandy, shuddered, and uncrossed his legs. At the same time, Peg rose and stood in front of him, waiting until his arms slipped around her waist. Then she lay her head against his chest.

"Her eyes."

"It was the light," he said, much too quickly.

He turned with her still in his arms and looked out the window. All the lights were burning in Hattie Mills' place, and a few were still on at the Adams'. He kissed her hair softly. "I'll bet Rose has seen everything that's happened over here."

Peg turned her head and saw the second-story window glowing, the shades up, the curtains tied to one side. "She'll tell Mitch, and he'll clean your room a hundred times Monday, hoping to get gossip for her."

They stood for a long moment, a quiet moment, feeling shirt against blouse, trousers against skirt, the idea that it all felt too right for them to move.

"Tomorrow," he whispered finally.

"Huh?"

"Tomorrow," he whispered louder. "Soon as we let Garve know what happened we'll pack a ton of crap food and tooth-eating soda and we'll go to the cliffs for a picnic."

"It's going to rain."

"Nope."

She leaned back and looked up, smiling. "You sure?"

He smiled back. "I have arranged it, m'dear. You and I and Matt are going to have a hell of a good day tomorrow. Besides, it seems to me we owe ourselves some sort of celebration."

She agreed with a wink, then frowned as she looked at him from the corner of her eye. "We have to announce it, you know."

"I suppose."

"In the paper?"

"With our pictures and everything?"

"Or," she said, "we could do it at the party tomorrow night."

He drew back his head and stared. "You wouldn't."

"Wouldn't I?"

"Jesus, you're terrible."

"Yeah. I know."

They kissed, softly and for a long time before she leaned back. Her hand reached out to cup his cheek, poke the tip of his chin. "God help me, I do love you."

"Yeah," he said softly. "Yeah."

They kissed again, and he could feel the warmth of her lips and the press of her breasts and the way her legs stirred against his. His palm stroked her back; her palm cupped his head. He pulled loose her skirt and scratched lightly along her spine to her shoulders. She shuddered, moved her head to lay it in the hollow beneath neck and shoulder.

"Don't," she said when his hand paused. "Please, Colin."

He kissed her hair, kissed her cheek, shifted so he could unhook her bra strap. She sighed, lips brushing his neck; she sighed, and stood far enough away for his hands to come around to the front. When they reached her breasts she sighed again and half-closed her eyes.

"Your hands are cold," she whispered without protesting.

"Cold hands, warm heart," he said, "to coin an old cliche."

She kissed him suddenly, hard, and looked to the sofa.

He nodded and kissed her back, and they had taken one step when they heard a noise on the staircase.

"Mom?" Sleepy, worried.

He almost told her to ignore the boy, almost turned himself to send Matt back to bed. Then, when she couldn't help a smile, he repeated his martyr's sigh and shook his head in defeat.

"It's all right," she called to Matt. "It's all right," she said to Colin. "I'll take that shower for you. Turn out the lights when you go to bed." And she was out of the room and up the stairs without looking back.

He waited for several minutes, standing there listening, then took a deep breath and let himself grin. A grin that banished Warren and Lilla and the fog and the

183

island. His doubts were gone as he turned from the window and headed for the couch. His fears for the time were smothered by a buoyant growing bubble that expanded in his chest and made him feel giddy, making him wish he were back at the cottage so he could throw his arms up and shout.

Boots and socks off, shirt and jeans laid across the coffee table, the blanket pulled to the hollow of his throat, his ankles propped on the armrest, his head on the pillow. He was going to have a stiff neck in the morning, but for the moment he didn't care. For the moment he would deal with murder and madness and shuffle them back to the bottom of the deck.

He reached up awkwardly and switched off the light.

The room settled into pale gray from the spray of the streetlamp.

There was a chill from the night that made him shiver once and draw the blanket higher. But he was warm, and he liked it, and he hoped Peg would let him be there when she told Matt the good news.

A slow exhalation to beckon sleep from the corners, and just as his eyes closed the streetlight went out.

PART THREE

October: Saturday

ONE

"Here," Colin said, shifting on Matt's bed and taking up a red pencil from the pile scattered over the quilted spread. "What you want to do, see, is give the bird not exact detail so much as the illusion of detail. If you want pictures, get out a camera, otherwise you . . ." He studied the sketch pad in his hands, cocked his head and put the pencil to work. Matt sat Indian-fashion on the mattress beside him, frowning just as intently, every so often leaning almost nose to paper to see what Colin had done to make the gull look as if it would realize where it was at any moment and break free into the room.

"It's the wrong color, of course, unless it has a sunburn."

Matt nodded.

"But what the hell, right?" He glanced up, then, and put a finger to his lips. "Sorry. I'm not supposed to talk like that in front of you."

"Yeah," the boy said solemnly. "I'm too young."

"Right."

Matt giggled and covered his mouth with a palm.

Colin yanked at his hair and handed him the pencil. "You try it. Nothing special, mind. Just . . ." He reached out and held the boy's wrist with thumb and two fingers, guiding it gently.

Matt's tongue poked between his lips. "You and Mom are getting married, aren't you?"

Colin leaned back, startled, suddenly realized he was on the edge of the bed and snapped out a hand to keep himself from falling. The mattress rippled, and Matt's pencil skittered across the paper.

"That was close," he said.

"Well, aren't you?"

The sheet was torn from the pad, crumbled, and tossed to the floor onto a shallow pile of other sheets similarly discarded. They had been there since breakfast two hours ago, Colin studying the pictures Matt had done outside school. He'd grown excited as he spotted the tempering of raw talent the boy seldom showed him in his homework, saw it in the eye for detail and the imagery that did not always match what a camera might capture. What was missing was guidance, formal work, and the only thing Colin was unable to give him—experience. Living. A growing that altered the consciousness that was reflected on the paper, on the canvas, in stone and marble. The boy was naive; with growth he might become a Romantic.

Matt looked up at him, large eyes unblinking.

Colin cleared his throat. "Well . . . it's crossed our minds, yes."

"Would you live here?"

He shrugged. "I don't know. I guess so."

Matt pulled the pad over his knees and began doodling birds, small dogs, and elaborately-trimmed, sleek cars. "Mom says I'm the man of the house, so I have to take care of her." A pause. "That's silly. I don't need a babysitter, but Mom's really the man of the house." He paused again, then giggled. "If Mom's the man of the house, you'll have to wear a dress."

"There aren't any my size," he said.

"I'll get one of hers for you."

"You try it, m'boy, and I'll shave that pointy head with a dull toothbrush."

Matt stared at the pad, pushed it away and slipped off the bed. Colin stood as soon as he could get his own legs untangled, watched as the boy headed for the doorway. When he turned, there was a brief, Peg-like decisive nod.

"I think . . . it's okay, Mr. Ross."

Colin smiled. "Thanks, Matt."

"My father's dead, you know."

He nodded.

"He was killed. In the car. The one that exploded."

"Yes. I know."

"You'll be my new father, then?"

His cheeks puffed, deflated, and he whistled softly. "I'll be your mother's husband, for sure, but I hope we'll still be friends. Anything else is up to you."

"Okay," Matt said, grinning suddenly. "C'mon, we're gonna be late."

The boy was gone before he could move, feet pounding on the stairs as he shouted for Colin to hurry. He whistled again, wondering at the way children always seemed to know more than they let on, more than they seemed to want anyone else to know. Then he looked around the room and tried to remember what his own room had been like. He certainly hadn't had a television set, but he seemed to recall an old Emerson radio his father had threatened to leave in the dump. It had loomed, a grilled walnut cabinet in the corner by his bed, and he'd listened to it at night, to the last of the serials and adventure shows before they were taken off in favor of what some claimed was music.

He smiled to himself wistfully. The perils of advancing middle-age—nostalgia for the good old days which were, if he remembered correctly, damnably boring.

A quick stride and he was at the window, looking out at the trees that formed an evergreen wall at the back of the small yard. The sky was overcast, though the morning was sun-bright. He hadn't been outside yet, but he suspected the air had finally regained its sharp touch of autumn. It would be cool at the cliffs. Peg, however, had said nothing about postponement, so he assumed the picnic would go off as planned.

189

Listen, she'd said to him quietly just before she'd left for work, *he knows. Don't ask how. He knows.*

As he walked toward the stairs he marveled again at the powers of children, and at the relief he felt that Matt seemed to accept him. Though Peg was positive there'd be no trouble, too many times he'd seen the trauma of remarriage visited on sons, on daughters, on the innocent bystanders of lives gone wrong. Matt, was special, though, and Colin suspected strongly that his work being displayed at the Whitney would be insignificant indeed to the day the boy first called him Dad.

"C'*mon.*"

Matt was already at the door, wicker basket in hand, shifting impatiently from one foot to the other. He sighed as Colin reached for his jacket, fumbling with a sleeve turned inside out. When he'd finally pulled it right, he grabbed the cuff and pumped it as though he were shaking a man's hand.

"What was that for?"

"Nothing," Colin said. "A superstition. It's supposed to keep your good luck from getting away." When he saw the frown, he pursed his lips and stroked his chin. "So. I guess you're not superstitious. Okay, then it was just an ancient prayer to the gods of sunny days."

Matt peered anxiously at the overcast weather. "I think they're sleeping. Do you believe in God, Mr. Ross? Mrs. Wooster—she's in Philadelphia, you know—she says God lives on a mountain in the sky. Is that true?"

They took the steps together and headed for his car.

"Well—"

He stopped with his hand on the door as someone called his name. He looked up and across the street, first at Hattie Mills' place, then to the right when he heard it again. It was Rose Adams standing on her porch, wrapped in a flowered silk bathrobe that glistened without the sun. Her long, graying hair was hastily coiled into a bun, and he could see a glint of red on her nails.

"Hey, Rose!" he called with a smile as Matt clambered into the car and pulled the door shut. He walked around the front, keeping the smile on when she hustled down the steps and crossed the lawn toward him. He held back his relief when she stopped at the far curb.

"Going on a picnic, Colin?"

"Yup," he said loudly, so she could hear him. Rose was slightly deaf, her own voice naturally loud and carrying.

"Thought so."

He looked up. "Not a great day, but it'll do."

"Could be worse. Could get that storm, but I doubt it. I really doubt it." She smiled but it was forced, and he could see the makeup pancaked on her puffed cheeks gleaming like suede worn too long. "Say, I wonder if you could do me a favor."

"If I can." He avoided looking at Matt. "What is it?"

Her hands, as puffed as her face, retreated into the robe's deep pockets. "It's my little boy." She shook her head sadly. "He didn't come home last night that I know of. I've been calling Garve all morning, but he must have better things to do with his time than chase after someone's lost child."

He guessed then she hadn't heard about Warren.

"Well, I—"

"Of course, Mitchell is hunting him now, but you know how he is. He'll have the child strapped to within an inch of his life if he catches him before I do. Mitchell," she said with a saint's forbearance, "has a temper when it comes to protecting his own."

"I can imagine," he said, the smile beginning to strain. "But I'll do—"

"I'd appreciate your keeping a sharp eye out, then," she continued. "Maybe, if you pass by, you could stop in at Garve's and leave him a note if he's not there."

191

He opened the door and hefted the basket into the back seat. "I'll do that, Rose."

The hands left her pockets and clasped at her waist. "Oh, thank you, Colin, you're a dear."

"I try, I try."

"And if you should see that . . . that Carter Naughton—"

"I'll ask around, Rose," he promised, and ducked behind the wheel, closed the door and rolled down the window. Matt was deliberately looking the other way, and he poked the boy with his forefinger before firing the ignition and sweeping the car into a U-turn that ended in front of Mrs. Adams. She leaned down and smiled expectantly.

"Open the window, Matt," he said, and poked the boy again.

"I've talked to Denise, of course," Rose said, the pancake at close range cracked and peeling, "but she's just like her father. She's loyal. Very loyal. Of course, if something happened to Frankie she'd tell me in a minute. That's why I'm not worried. She hasn't even gotten out of bed. But it's Saturday, and a day off, I always say, is a day well spent sleeping till noon."

Colin smiled and slowly lifted his foot from the brake.

"You tell Garve I'll be around later," she said, raising her voice as the car drifted from the curb. "Around one or so, if I can make it."

Colin nodded and lifted a hand to wave. When he checked the rearview mirror she was still there, silk bathrobe, red nails, distance smoothing the pancake and taking twenty years from her face.

"Tommy says she has liquor in her purse," Matt confided once they'd reached the corner. "Does she really?"

"I doubt that, Matthew," he said, not bothering to signal since there was no one behind him and no cars on Bridge Road. "She's just had a bad time of it lately."

"Tommy says she smells like gin!"

"Really? And how does Tommy know what gin smells like? His father doesn't drink and his mother's never at home."

"I don't know," Matt said, "but Tommy says so."

"Oh."

Two blocks later he braked slowly to a stop, staring at the Clipper Run.

"Gee!" Matt said, poking his head out the window.

Bob Cameron was standing at the entrance in soiled jeans and a workshirt open to the belt. His hair was dark with moisture, and around his forehead was tied a rolled blue bandana. A large truck was in the parking lot, and several teenaged boys were busily unloading cartons of foodstuffs. When Cameron looked toward the street, Colin started to move, but it was too late. The man was beckoning, and his hand was a fist.

"We're gonna be late," Matt said.

"This won't take long, pal," he said, turning off the engine and dropping the keys on the dash. "Hang on, I'll be right back."

He wanted to smile, or say something about this being the first time he'd ever seen Cameron out of a suit unless he was on the beach, but the look on the man's face precluded anything but a studied, concerned frown.

"What's up?" he asked as he reached the end of the hedge to meet him. "Your suppliers go on strike?" He recognized all the boys, each one a local.

"It's that goddamned Sterling," Cameron said angrily. "Went on one of his toots last night, left the goddamned ferry at the island landing. I was lucky Ed Raines was in the bay and heard the horn or I'd have shit for dinner tonight." His hands gripped his hips tightly and he spat at the street. "Son of a bitch oughta be locked up."

Colin almost laughed until he suddenly glanced down Bridge. "You mean there's no one to run the ferry?"

"Well, *I* can, so can a few others if it comes to it. We're not marooned if that's what you're thinking.

193

But it's the principal of the thing, Ross. Jesus Christ, you can't depend on anyone these days."

Cameron nodded sharply to punctuate the condemnation, then took Colin's elbow and drew him down the street, away from the unloading, away from the restaurant. When he stopped he dropped his hand, pulled a handkerchief from his pocket and mopped his face vigorously.

"Listen," he said then, his voice lowered, his gaze on the library next door. "Listen, Colin, about yesterday—"

Colin shook his head. "I don't—"

"Listen!"

He almost turned on his heel and headed back to the car, but the harsh voice didn't match the look he saw in the man's eyes. He waited, though he couldn't find a way to still the chill in his stomach.

"Those men, Lombard and Vincent, they're . . . damn it, Colin, I'm in trouble."

It took a moment, a long moment, before Colin said, "Yes. I think I tried to tell you that once."

"Yes," Cameron admitted. "But you still don't understand."

"I think I do. But this isn't the place for another one of our discussions, Bob. I've got Matt Fletcher in the car and we're—"

Cameron grabbed his arm, stared hard into his face. "Half the land back there in the woods belongs to me, you know that," he said quickly, softly. "That's where the casinos were going."

"Were?" Colin said.

"Oh, they still are, for sure, but now there's a catch. Lombard says I have to sell half of it to him or there isn't going to be a deal."

"I didn't think there was supposed to be a decision until after the election."

Cameron's eyes closed slowly, opened slowly, and he took his hand from Colin's arm. "Ross, this election doesn't mean a damned thing. Christ, haven't you realized that by now? Those men, and their fatcat buddies over in Trenton, up there in New York, and out in Las Vegas, they're going to have all the land they need and the legislation they need to put up the casinos whether I win or lose."

Colin stepped away. "You've known that all along?"

"I think so."

"You *think* so?"

Cameron's disgust turned on himself. "All right, all right, I kind of knew it, but I didn't think they meant it and I wanted to get a piece of the action myself, you know what I mean?" He inhaled deeply and craned his neck until the tendons grew stark against the tanned skin. When he spoke again, it was with a weariness born of fear too long suppressed. "It's all gone to hell, Col, and I don't know how to stop it."

"Great," he said. "That's just great."

"I thought you should know."

"Yeah."

"I didn't mean it should happen this way."

"Yeah."

They faced without seeing each other, until Cameron walked around Colin and started back up the street. Colin watched, then caught up. "Maybe we can do something." It was a gesture—not peace, but a truce. Cameron looked gratefully at him though his eyes were still wary. "Something, but I don't know what yet."

"Think fast, Colin," Cameron said urgently, lowering his voice as they neared the unloading. "Garve came to my place last night asking Lombard all sorts of questions. A shitty thing about Harcourt, you know?"

"I know."

They stopped.

"Lombard didn't say a thing. He was with me the whole time, I know he didn't leave."

Colin looked at him. "And the Hulk?"

195

Cameron licked his lips nervously, his gaze straying to Colin's midsection and back. "I don't know. I swear to God, I don't know."

He thought about Montgomery's explanations and Garve's doubts and Peg's worry that both men were wrong. "Okay," he said. "I don't know what I can do, but maybe by tonight."

"Sure," Cameron said, unconvinced but relieved. "And while you're at it, think of a way we can deep-six Sterling. The stupid drunken bastard. The way things are going today, that damned storm'll hit and I'll be stuck with four thousand bucks worth of god-damned bitty sandwiches."

Colin managed a smile, one that shrank to tight lips as he reached the car and got in.

"Well? Well?" Matt asked eagerly.

"Seems the gulls grabbed old Wally and took him to Florida," he said, pulling away from the restaurant.

"No kidding," Matt said, his eyes wide with astonishment until he realized he was being had. "Aw, Mr. Ross!"

"Don't take it so hard, pal. Wally was too heavy. They had to drop him in the bay."

Matt jabbed him hard in the ribs, and he laughed, more to release the tension than because the boy tickled. And by the time they were parked in front of the drug store, he was determined not to let this news spoil the rest of the day. It had been too long coming; Cameron was just going to have to wait.

"Are you mad or something?" Matt asked as they left the car and stood on the sidewalk. There were no pedestrians, and he could hear no sounds from the direction of the beach.

"No," he said absently.

"Okay."

He swept a finger down the length of his nose, then gave the boy a gentle shove. "You get your mother. I want to see if Chief Tabor is in."

Matt looked at him doubtfully, but dashed off quickly enough when he lifted his hand in a mock-

196

fisted threat. Then Colin hurried down to the station. The patrol car was at the curb, freshly washed and reflecting the overcast sky brightly. He noted it only in passing, but when he reached the open office door he hesitated. There was no one inside. It was quiet—no telephones ringing, no radio units crackling, the fluorescent ceiling light sputtering without sound. He called out, heard nothing, decided whoever was on duty had stepped out for lunch. He scribbled a note on scrap paper he found on Garve's desk, telling him about Frankie Adams, adding a postscript about Lombard and Vincent that was enigmatic enough, he hoped, to force Garve to seek him out. He was about to leave when he remembered his promise to Peg to tell Tabor about Lilla. He hesitated, uncertain, then took a second sheet and wrote another message. When he was finished he dropped the pen quickly and wiped his hands on his jeans. He gave a second glance around and returned to the car just as Peg and Matt were taking their seats.

Once behind the wheel he turned to her and kissed her cheek, looked to Matt in the back, and winked. The boy winked back, and they laughed, loudly, as he pulled out on Neptune after checking for traffic.

"You two are in an awfully good mood," she said, smiling.

"You don't know the half of it," he said.

"Mom, can I explore?" Matt said, folding his arms on the back of the seat and resting his chin hard on his wrist.

"You may not, young man."

"But *Mom!*"

Peg sighed, and Colin sensed a year-long argument destined never to be settled. "Not really a good idea, pal," he said quietly, realizing they were waiting for him to take sides.

"But Mr. Ross," Matt complained, sounding almost betrayed, "the caves are filled with gold?"

"Oh, really?"

"He found a coin in there last year," Peg said,

reaching up with her left hand to pat the boy's head. He ducked away, scowling. "I didn't let him go then, either."

"Jeez."

"Now, Matt . . ."

"Look," Colin said quickly, "why don't we just wait until we get there, okay? I think the tide's in anyway, but let's at least wait until we get there."

Matt was unsure if he'd won something or not. "Okay. Sure."

Peg, however, dropped her hand on his thigh, smiled at him and squeezed—hard enough to make him wince. He sped up, barely listening as he commented on the lack of kids waiting to get into the theater, and the empty parking lot in front of Naughton's Market. But by the time they had reached the Estates he realized he hadn't seen a single car on the road.

He slowed and looked over. "I left a note at Garve's," he said. "About—" and he tilted his head toward the road that led to the development and Gran's shack. "I didn't call Hugh, though. I forgot."

"It's all right," she said.

"Somebody sick?" Matt asked.

"Little pitchers and big ears," Colin muttered.

"What does that mean?"

He saw the boy's reflection in the rearview mirror, and shrugged. "Y'know, pal, all these years I've heard that and I don't have the faintest idea."

The road ended a half mile later. Colin turned the car around and shut off the engine.

The woods were noisy. The leaves and needles husked in a light breeze, the surf's roar threaded its way through the branches, and a flight of unseen crows were raucous near the cliffs.

They wasted little time leaving the car and heading for the narrow trail that led to the cliffs. Matt took the lead at a dead run, Peg followed, and Colin moved as quickly as he could with the basket in his left hand. He didn't mind being last. It gave him a chance to watch

Peg in her jeans, the way her plaid shirt pulled snug across her back. Her hair was in a ponytail and it swung with her hips, and when she glanced back over her shoulder and gave him a broad wink, he grinned as he realized she knew what he was doing.

Fifteen minutes after they left the car, the light changed. It was more a glow than sunshine, catching in slow motion the dust in the air. The greens were dull, the autumn reds sullen, and the shrubs off the trail cloaked themselves in pale shadow. He looked up several times as if expecting to see the clouds thickening to storm, looked behind him several more times as if expecting to see something. The crows were gone, the breeze dead, and the waves tearing at the cliffs made him think he was a soldier walking into a battle in a time that wasn't his.

The air grew damp, and the light sparkled with errant spray.

Matt was gone, but Peg hung back, waiting until she could walk beside him as best she could within the trail's confines. He shifted the basket and held her hand.

Their shoes snapped twigs and broke the spines of piles of dead leaves; their breathing matched the pulse of the surf.

The trees began shrinking and bending away from the ocean, the shrubs falling back, the ground turning to rock until they were out in the clear and the water swept ahead of them to a leftward curving horizon. The boulders were huge, were small, were brown lined with color, and what grass managed to break through the cracks in the ground was rough and sharp-edged and tipped with darkred thorns.

Matt stood in a gap between two child-sized rocks, his hands on his hips, and shaking his head. "It's in," he said, nodding toward the tide.

Colin lowered the basket and joined him, looked down, and told himself sternly he wasn't going to fall.

One hundred feet to the water, surging as if it were

trying to climb, splattering, scattering, turning dark to white while spumes of its thunder were caught by the wind and thrown up just short of lashing them.

They were standing at the top of a precarious pathway, one that switchbacked unevenly more than halfway down. Ledges littered with broken shells, weakly fluttering feathers, every so often the bones of a gull. At the bottom the rocks were smooth, but elsewhere they jutted and forced gashes in the waves, gashes in the air. The wind caught his hair and forced it back, exposing his forehead, made him clutch the throat of his jacket and close it around his neck.

Matt pleaded with a look.

"No way, pal, forget it. Even I know the tide's higher than usual. That storm's on its way, and you definitely are not going to be its first casualty."

"What's casualty?"

"It means your butt turns red when you don't do what you're told."

"Oh."

They stepped back reluctantly, Colin first and watching as Peg, protected from the wind by a broken wall of massive boulders, unpacked the basket. He started toward her to help, stopped when Matt tugged at his waist.

"Pal, I said no."

Matt pointed.

On the horizon, merged with the overcast that lowered darkly and began to churn, was the fog.

"She's singing," the boy said.

"What?" He knelt, facing away from the cliff's edge.

"Lilla," Matt told him. "She's singing."

"Now how do you know that, pal?"

"It happens every time, Mr. Ross. Didn't you know that? It does. Every time she sings the fog comes back."

"Enough of that," Peg scolded mildly, looking up from the food.

"Indeed." He took Matt's shoulders gently. "You know what coincidence is?"

The boy nodded.

"Well, that's what this is."

"Nope," Matt said. "It isn't . . . what you said."

The wind screamed like an angry flock of gulls.

The fog.

Colin took a deep breath and let it out slowly. "Look, Matt, I know you believe this, and I guess that's all right for now. But I'm starving to death, in case you hadn't noticed, and I would appreciate tabling all ghost stories until after I've had some of your mother's lousy cake."

"Well, I like that," she said with a scowl.

Colin shrugged and nudged her son forward, then groped for his shoulder when Tess Mayfair walked silently out of the trees.

Her dress was ragged, her chest and stomach partially exposed and covered with dried blood. A rib poked behind ragged flesh. Her hair was matted and her eyes were wide.

Peg saw her the moment Colin did and grabbed for Matt, shoved him behind her as she rose slowly from the blanket and backed toward the rocks.

"Jesus, Tess," Colin said with concern. "God almighty, what happened? Do you need help?"

Tess walked toward him, stumbling on the rough ground but not losing her balance.

"Tess?"

She stumbled again and lurched toward him, forcing him back, into the gap that opened on the path. He couldn't look back, couldn't look down, didn't hear Peg shouting as she raced for the basket. The wind snared him and he grabbed for a rock. Tess didn't stop, not even when Peg threw a large bottle of soda at her head.

"Tess!"

She filled the gap.

And she lunged.

Colin threw himself to one side desperately, his right foot slipping on the spray-dampened ground, bringing him to his knees as Tess toppled over the edge. Silently. Arms reaching. Turning head down just as she reached the first ledge.

Peg screamed and Colin shouted.

And the fog began to whisper up the face of the cliff.

TWO

Noon was barely past when the fog brought the night, and the Carolina storm brought the wind to give it motion.

Garve sat heavily on the edge of the bed and crushed out his cigarette in the pink seashell ash tray resting on the floor. He was naked, warm, and despite the flesh that had been softened by his years, there was still the definition of muscles less for show than for power. His sandy hair was tangled, he needed a shave, and his hands hung over his knees at the wrist.

"I gotta get to work, I guess."

"Why? There's a crime wave or something?"

He grinned in spite of himself, and relaxed when Annalee's hands gripped his shoulders and began a gentle kneading.

"God, that feels good."

"Sure it does. There's a considerable amount of tension stored in here."

"An expert speaking?"

"Damn straight."

He allowed himself a sigh, kept his eyes closed, and didn't want to know the time. He guessed it was close to ten, but he couldn't be sure. And he didn't much care, not now, at least. Eliot could handle things alone, anyway. Nichols was a good man, though Garve wished he wouldn't make it so obvious that he hungered for the boss's job.

"A penny," she said, leaning into his back and snaking her arms over his shoulders, her fingers lightly scratching the roll of his waist.

"I think I love you."

"Worth a dime at least."

He half turned, and tested the air for sarcasm, drew up his legs and turned the rest of the way, sitting cross-legged and staring. Not at her slightly sagging breasts or the enviable flat of her stomach or the tanned sheen of her thighs; he stared at her eyes, at the chocolate brown that watched him from behind a wisping screen of blonde hair, at the dark lashes, at the gentle laughter he saw there as she reached over to stroke his cheek.

It almost banished the throbbing that had settled behind his ears. "I feel like a jackass, you know," he said.

"Why? Because that son of a bitch made you lose your temper?"

"Yeah. I shouldn't have done it, Lee. It was stupid. If there was a case there, I've blown it."

Concern eased her smile. "Was there one?"

He shook his head. "I don't know. I honestly don't know."

Her sympathy almost made him angry, but she forestalled it by leaning over and kissing him, drawing back and examining him again.

"Do you know how old I am?" he asked when the silence grew too long.

She shook her head.

"I'll be fifty-one come January." He laughed once and looked at his hands covering his lap. "Fifty-one. That's more than half a damned century."

"You wear your age well."

Maybe he did, but this morning he felt twice that. It was the humiliation and the fact that he had lost control for the first time in years. Punks like Cart

Naughton were simple to intimidate, and so was Bob Cameron. But when he came up against the Man, against those who claimed real power—the kind Bob dreamed of—he proved himself a flop. Cow flop. Horseshit. A fifty-year-old cop who couldn't find a killer in a state prison.

"You're feeling sorry for yourself."

He nodded before he could stop himself.

"That's all right," she said, tossing her hair back over her shoulders. "If you say you made a mistake, then I believe you. If you say you made an ass of yourself, well . . . you made an ass of yourself."

"Thanks a heap, nurse."

"Hey, cop, it isn't the end of the world. Since when have you turned saint?" When he looked up, eyes narrow, she returned the look without flinching. "You're not perfect, Garve," she said softly. "And don't tell me you really, honestly, expected him to crumble the minute you looked at him cross-eyed."

His gaze dropped to her knees, to his knees. "I can always hope, right?"

She shoved him, nearly spilling him off the bed. "You're kidding, right?"

He almost flared, but a short laugh became a long one and he reached out for her, hugged her, moved their legs out of the way and lowered her to the mattress.

"What time is it?" he whispered into the hollow of her sweet-smelling shoulder.

"After one, probably."

He rose up sharply. "What?"

A handful of hair brought him down again. "It's after one and if you leave this house without making love to me at least once, Garve Tabor, I'll never speak to you again."

"Lee—"

"Garve!"

He pulled back to look at her, higher to see the headboard, higher still to see the window.

"Jesus Christ, look at all that fog!"

"I know," she said. Suddenly he was cold, and reached for the blanket to cover them both.

It didn't help.

Especially when he thought he heard Lilla singing.

There was just enough light to let them see the fog, to let them see the branches whip out of the gray to lash at their faces and snare around their legs, boil out of the hollows and cover their feet. Peg thought her lungs would overfill and finally explode, and she exhaled in a rush that made her dizzy.

Matt was ahead of her, Colin urging her on from behind, but she couldn't understand a single word he was saying. The sound was there, and the thud of his footsteps, and the crack of his swearing when he stumbled and nearly fell. But she couldn't understand a word.

And she could barely see a thing.

Matt was there, she knew he was there because she could see his hair swinging, and his arms pumping, and his thin legs blurring as he ran. She could also see Tess Mayfair, larger than she'd ever seemed to be in life, lurching out of the trees as if she were drunk, reaching for Colin, nearly pushing him into the sea, tripping over something and disappearing, just like that.

She was ashamed of herself. Instead of trying to help the poor woman she had screamed like an idiot, screamed louder when Colin went down and almost went over himself. It was Matt, whose excitement made him slap her hard on the back, who made her realize what was happening, made her lunge to her feet and dive for Colin's hand. She grabbed his wrist the instant she landed, the air crushed out of her, her eyes flooded with tears of pain. But she held on, her lips pulled back and every muscle in her body pulled taut as a wire. Colin grabbed her forearm with one hand, grabbed her elbow with another, grabbed her shoulder, and she didn't know he was standing until he helped her up.

"Wow, Mom!" Matt said. "Wow, you did it!"

Colin could say nothing. He only swallowed and told her everything with his eyes.

But the running was the worst part.

Worse than understanding that Colin had almost died, worse than accepting her own dare and looking over the edge—to see Tess sprawled on the ledge more than fifty feet below, to see the waves claw at her dress, toy with her legs, wash away the red that ran in streams from beneath her head.

"She was hurt," Colin said behind her, each word a gasping. "She must have had an accident out here in the trees."

She nodded and kept running.

"God!" he said. "I thought for a minute she wanted to push me over."

She did, Peg thought, and slowed nearly to a halt when she realized what had happened. Matt called her name and Colin urged her on, but none of it changed anything—Tess had been trying to kill him. Tess had wanted Colin dead, and only the man's slipping had saved his life when she attacked.

They broke out of the woods and scrambled into the car. It stalled once, stalled again, and she pushed at the dashboard until the engine caught. When Colin sped north on Neptune, she turned and looked at Matthew. He was in the corner behind her, a blanket wrapped around his shoulders, looking pale, lips white. Without a word she struggled over the back and sat beside him, embraced him and looked at Colin's head.

"Why?" she said.

"She was hurt," Colin answered, leaning forward to see through the fog on the road.

"No. Yes."

"What?"

"She was hurt, I could see that, but she wasn't looking for help."

There was a silence.

"Peg, listen—"

207

She looked down at Matt and stroked his damp hair. "You know what I'm saying."

"I sure as hell do, and it's ridiculous."

The fog was so thick Colin had to slow down, so much so she knew she could run to town faster. When they reached the boarding house, she stopped shaking long enough to squeeze Matt more tightly, pull the blanket across his chest, and shift so her right arm was still around his shoulders while she put her face as close to Colin's as she could.

"You saw her?"

He nodded, muttering at the fog. Five miles an hour was no way to get the police.

"I don't see how she was alive."

His head snapped up, and he glared at her in the rearview mirror. "Peg," he said, whispering, questioning, and cautioning in a name.

"I mean it," she said, lowering her voice. "You saw her, Colin. I don't see why she wasn't lying down. I saw *bone* sticking out, for God's sake! She looked like somebody went after her with an ax."

"Warren," was all he said.

She sat back and stared at the low ceiling, blinking rapidly, feeling her son beside her and wishing the man in front wasn't so goddamned stuck on reason.

A signpost reared out of the fog and Colin yanked on the wheel, apparently not realizing he was nearly off the road. Then he said, "Lilla."

"What?" she said sharply.

"Lilla. If that guy's still at work, Lilla's in danger."

He stopped, and she sat up. "What the hell are you doing, Colin?"

"We ought to at least bring her back with us to the station where she'll be safe."

"The hell with her," she said. "What about Matt? Are you going to leave us in the car with a maniac running loose while you go chasing after another nut? Over my dead body."

His shoulders squared, and she knew she ought to feel some manner of guilt about the way she'd spoken

208

about a friend. But as far as she was concerned, Lilla was beyond their help now. The young woman needed a professional, a doctor, and what they needed was some safe place where Tess Mayfair couldn't get them.

She waited, blinking in disbelief when Colin swerved the car onto Surf Court. A hand lifted to punch the back of his neck, a curse throttled in her throat when Matt squirmed to get closer to her. Then the car stopped, and Colin opened the door. The engine was still running. When she leaned over the seat, he bent down and smiled with a shrug.

"I can't do it, Peg. You take the car and get hold of Garve."

"And what about you?" she demanded.

"I'll get Lilla and bring her here." He waved behind him at the houses on the street. "There're some lights on. I'll take her to Bob's or Efron's. I'll call as soon as I get there."

"Colin, this is stupid."

"No," he said. "Maybe. Now hurry. I don't want this dumb fog to get any thicker."

There were a dozen reasons why he shouldn't go, and a dozen more why he should. While she was debating, he reached in and grabbed her hand, squeezed it, and closed the door. He walked quickly toward the beach, hopping onto the curbstone and following it until he reached the sand. The fog was much thinner there, and he didn't disappear until he was halfway up the first dune.

"Mom?"

She glared at the spot where Colin had been, then struggled into the driver's seat, looked around and jerked her head until Matt understood and followed. He kept the blanket. He watched as she snapped on the headlights and made an awkward U-turn.

"Mr. Ross?"

"He went to get Lilla," she said, her hands holding the wheel white-knuckled.

"Will he be hurt?"

"No," she said; told him, "No," again, softly, when

she saw the fear widen his eyes. "No, he'll be all right."

The fog scattered when they reached Neptune, and she craned to take a hard look at the sky. It was darker now, the Screamer closer. She suddenly wished strongly they'd had another name for the windstorm. She blinked—twilight on Haven's End before it was even two. She drove recklessly, not slowing when gray patches flared the car's lights back into her eyes.

Then she looked at her hands; they were trembling. She squeezed the wheel more tightly. When that didn't work she pushed a palm over her cheeks, shoved clawed fingers back through her hair. The car slowed when they reached Naughton's Market, slowed even more until they reached the intersection, and the amber light winked on the hood, turned the windshield gold, followed with sweeping shadows as she swung a tight circle and parked in front of the station. The lights were on, and she could see Garve at his desk.

"Mom?"

She couldn't move.

The next thing she had to do was turn off the engine, but she couldn't loosen her grip on the wheel.

"Mom!"

She swallowed, closed her eyes, and couldn't help a short scream when someone rapped the window next to her head.

Matt grabbed her arm and shook her, calling, until she made herself as stiff as she could, suddenly released the hold on her muscles and sagged back in the seat. She smiled weakly at Garve and didn't protest when he helped her out of the car and into the office, one hand at the small of her back and the other on her elbow while he listened gravely to Matt explain what had happened.

When she was seated, a cup of steaming coffee in her hands, she smiled again. "It's true," she told Tabor when he sought her confirmation. "It's true. She was . . . I honestly couldn't stop her, Garve. Before I could move she was . . . gone." Peg sipped, wincing at the hot liquid, shuddering at the chill that refused to leave her system. "She was hurt terribly even before she fell."

"Yeah!" Matt said excitedly, standing in front of the gunrack back by the cellblock door. His fear seemed gone, concern for his mother settled now that Garve was in charge. "Boy, it was just like you see in the movies! Her—"

"Matthew!" she shouted, coffee slopping into her lap.

He cringed and turned slowly, the protection he'd constructed gone with the name that struck his back like whip.

"It's all right," Tabor said. "Take it easy, the two of you, all right?" He dropped into his chair and clasped his hands at his stomach. "First thing is to call Hugh and let him know what happened. Then I'll take a ride out there and—" He stopped when she stared at him. "No, you won't have to go back."

Mutely, she accepted the paper napkins he handed her and daubed at the spill darkening her jeans. She felt terrible. Very few things bothered her more than losing control, and all control had left from the moment she'd seen Tess plunge off the cliff. A part of her reasoned the reaction was natural, part because she was thinking first of her son.

But she *had* lost control, and what kind of way was that to keep Matthew from harm?

Gingerly, she took another sip of coffee and smiled apologetically at her boy who was still by the gunrack watching her fearfully. By the time Tabor finished his call to Hugh, she felt somewhat better, and turned her smile to the chief when he queried her a with look.

"Okay, then," he said. But he didn't move. Instead, he dialed another number, waited, scowled, and slammed the receiver down. "Goddamn Nichols," he muttered.

"El's not here?" She looked around, realizing for the first time the deputy was missing. "But the car—"

"Yeah, I know. But it was here when I got back.

Washed like he was expecting to be in a parade. The car, but no Eliot. I've been calling his place for the past hour, but I can't get an answer and nobody I can raise has seen him. Jesus, he must be under a tree with Wally."

"Nobody . . ." She set the cup on the desk. "Garve, what's going on?"

He looked back at the boy, who was studying the shotguns and the rifle in the cabinet. Then he pulled his chair as close to the desk as he could, leaned forward on his forearms and rubbed his chin with a thumb. "Peg, I got to be honest, I haven't the faintest idea. Half the town leaves yesterday like the whole place was on fire, that's on account of the Screamer. But today . . . well, you're the first person I've seen since I got up. Except for Lee."

She passed on a comment that rose automatically; this wasn't the time to kid him about his lovelife.

"Maybe . . . maybe they're afraid the storm will hit sooner than after midnight. They might be too busy to answer."

"Oh, it will." He snapped a finger at a pink sheet of paper. "Got the word about five minutes ago. Damn fools at the National Weather place, they didn't want to make a mistake. It moved right out into the ocean, stopped, thought about it, and it's coming right back."

"Oh, God, the windows."

"Yeah, exactly. Between trying to get hold of Eliot, I've been calling everyone I can think of." He shook his head, and shrugged. "Hardly anyone left. This place is going to be a disaster if they don't come back soon."

She sighed, bit softly on her lower lip. "What was that about Wally?"

He looked disgusted. "Bob comes in a while back, bitching about Sterling leaving the ferry unattended. No sign of him, the ferry's at the island. Cameron had to bring over his supplies on his own." His expression was sour. "He was lucky he didn't end up in Chesapeake Bay the way he pilots that thing."

"Lilla," Matt said, so loudly they started, not realizing he had walked up behind the chief.

"What's this?" Tabor asked, half turning in his seat.

"Matt, I told you not—"

"Lilla, sir," Matt said when he didn't look away. "I told Mom and Mr. Ross about the fog, but they didn't believe me."

Peg kept her silence when Tabor lifted a hand to prevent an interruption, but she could not help an annoyed frown when Matt explained to the chief about the fog and Lilla's singing. She expected him to laugh, or to touch the boy's shoulder and nod to humor him. What she didn't expect was the thoughtful expression that blanked Tabor's eyes for the briefest of moments.

"Garve, you don't believe that."

"I heard her this morning, Peg."

"Yes, but—"

"I *told* you, Mom. And I'll bet the storm—"

"Matthew, please!"

Tabor rose, walked to the open door, and put a hand on the frame as a smoke gust of fog drifted down the street. "It's an odd day, Peg," he said. "That Screamer just turned around like someone yanked on its chain. It should be halfway to France by now. Halfway to France." He sniffed, scratched his head. "An odd day."

She rose and joined him, folding her arms under her breasts. "Odd, yes. But nothing more."

"Yeah. Sure."

"Honestly, Garve, you're going to scare the boy with talk like that. It's bad enough, what he saw. Don't make it worse."

He nodded an apology, and snatched his hat off the rack. "You staying?"

"I have to," and explained again about Colin's call.

"All right, then." He looked at Matt. "You're a deputy now, son, okay? You have to protect your mother and watch for the crooks while I ride out to the cliffs."

213

He looked stern, but she caught a wink as he waited for Matt's answer.

"Really?" the boy asked, "really?"

"Really. Your mother, she'll do the easy stuff like answering the phone for me. You have to do the rest. Think you can handle it?"

"Oh, boy!"

"Right." Another wink when she mouthed *thanks* as he passed her, a wave before he was in the patrol car and ghosting down the street. She stood at the door for over ten minutes, returning inside only when the fog suddenly thickened.

And from the woods across the way, she heard Lilla singing.

THREE

The wind had already routed the beachside vanguard of fog by the time Colin reached the top of the last dune. The light here was brighter than under the trees, clinging to a muted glow as the overcast broke apart to gather again in dizzying swirls and sweeps of high roiling black; the beach was gray, desolate, and covered with remnants of settling, quivering foam as the tide raced in thunder for the woods, retreated, held its breath, and charged again; what warmth remained had turned to a damp chill that penetrated his jacket as if it were gauze.

He squinted against the wind, entranced for a moment by the dark of the ocean, a black-ice depth that resembled the face and fury of a season not yet arrived. Deep winter storms were his favorite, when there were no bathers around to tempt the undertow and give the impression that the Atlantic was friendly—a nice place to cool off, a great place to frolic, a fine place to cultivate a smooth-sheened tan. In the cold, however, when the tourists were gone, the ocean gave up the sunlight masquerade and turned its true color—metallic and harshly beautiful, slashed through with white, rising in great swells not meant for surfing or diving—exposing the power that stalked behind the façade of a tranquil summer.

But it wasn't yet Thanksgiving, and the sea he watched was already December's.

He turned away quickly and headed across the flat toward the shack. There was no sense calling out; the wind would carry his voice clear to New York before Lilla would hear it. He grunted when he tripped over an exposed rock and nearly lost his balance, remembering the slow-motion fall of Tess Mayfair off the ledge.

She had tried to kill him.

He knew it, even though he'd denied it to Peg.

She had tried to kill him.

And worse Peg had not seen her as closely as he had. She had not seen the white edges of Tess' ragged wounds, the bleached look of her ribs smashed and stabbing through all that flesh, the complete lack of blood anywhere on her. And she had not seen the fact that Tess' eyes were pure white.

If Tess had been lying on the road in that condition, he would not have hesitated in pronouncing her dead.

Though he had said that Tess was probably attacked by the same person who had murdered Warren Harcourt, once away from the others he couldn't quite believe it. It had to have been an accident. A car accident, or something like that, something at the boarding house that maybe brought a portion of it down on her. Not a fire; they'd neither seen nor smelled smoke and there was no . . . he swallowed . . . there was no charring on Tess that he'd been able to see.

No; not assault this time, though that did not make his intention to get Lilla any less urgent. The wind out there was bringing the sea too damned close.

His hands hid in his pockets as he approached the shack, his mind forceably shifting away from the cliffs to the present. Garve, he thought, would take care of Tess' puzzle. Right now, he reminded himself again, he had his own task to do, and as he rounded the shack's corner he wondered if this was such a good idea after all.

216

But he chided himself half humorously when he reached the building and hesitated. Then, with a mental kick to his backside for giving in to the day and to Peg's case of nerves, he knocked, the door swung open slowly, and he reeled around and stumbled a dozen paces away, one shoulder up, an arm flung across his face. Gagging, retching, flailing with his free hand at the stench that enveloped him and burned through his nostrils.

"Jesus . . . *Christ!*"

He fumbled in his hip pocket for a handkerchief, found none, covered his nose and mouth with a palm, and, breathing through his mouth, stared incredulously at the shack. There was no light inside, and the light where he stood wasn't strong enough to penetrate. He glanced around the room as if he expected to find Lilla, and stepped forward slowly, almost sideways, watching the weathered building as though it were an old and angry lion waiting to spring.

The stench increased.

He gasped, rubbing at the tears that rose and swept to his cheeks.

Hoarsely: "Lilla!"

He was half bent over by the time he reached the door again.

"Lilla!"

She couldn't be in there, not with that smell.

"Lilla!"

It was so strong he was afraid that if he lit a match the entire island would explode.

"Lilla, it's me!"

He staggered over the threshold, leaning heavily against the jamb as he waited for his eyes to adjust to the light. In a far corner he saw a bundle, gray and water-stained. The shroud, he thought, and told himself he was wrong. The shroud held Gran, and that was under the ocean surface.

The flesh across his cheeks felt tight, close to shredding.

The door to the rear room was ajar, and he could see

shadows in there, shadows but nothing more. Maybe a bed, something else, something scattered over the floor. He tried to move forward, push himself away from the rough-plank wall, but his legs refused. The stench was a bludgeon now, a slow swinging club of rotting fruit and rotted meat and the carnage of a battlefield hours later in the sun.

He couldn't do it.

He threw himself out the door and fell, rolled, didn't stop rolling until he came up against the pines that separated the flat from the beach. A hand to the coarse bark, he pulled himself to his feet, and stood with head lowered while tears streamed and his throat burned. He gulped for air, blinked rapidly and brushed a forearm across his face. When he was ready he staggered toward the dunes, looking back only once and wondering what in hell the old man had had in there that could die so foully.

At the end of the first climb his legs gave out and he dropped to his knees, arms limp at his sides, the wind cold at his back. The ocean rose; he glanced over his shoulder and saw the nearest jetty already half covered, the waves breaking at the end of the beach now, and flattening the slatted dividing fence. Farther up, the waves had already begun to tease the grass at the forest's base.

He couldn't understand why the fog wasn't gone.

It was there, ahead of him, settling in low patches between the dunes, hovering about the peaks of the Estates' houses, in a thick unmoving wall at the end of the street. It wasn't possible, yet it stayed—gray, and shifting lazily, and totally oblivious to the wind.

His eyes squeezed shut and he rubbed them with his knuckles, took another long breath and pushed himself to his feet. This, he decided, was yet another island phenomenon Garve or Hugh would have to explain the next time he saw them. Curious, unsettling, but beside the point at the moment because he still had to find Lilla to warn her about the killer, and now about the storm.

218

He slid, and climbed, and found himself on Surf Court, hands on his hips while he shook off the dread and the memory of the stench. Most likely, he thought, Gran had had a pet, a stray dog or something, that had died and had not been buried. Or maybe it was food gone bad, or some of the old man's horrid incense he was forever burning while he worked. Whatever it was, it had finally driven Lilla away, and for that small favor he was grateful. What he had to do now was get to a phone and call Peg, as he'd promised, tell her what he found, then find a ride into town.

The wind clawed his hair down over his eyes, and the fog didn't move.

As his legs regained their strength, he walked more quickly, collar up, arms swinging, around the road's slight curve and into the Estates. He didn't bother to use the sidewalk; by the time he reached the first house he realized hardly anyone was there.

The yards were wide, the trees full and not quite as tall as a roof, the houses mostly cedar shake or fronted with false stone. On the left, most were surrounded by hedges fighting the salt air, and their windows were large and framed by tall shrubs. On the right, the windows were adequate, nothing more—these houses faced the sea and saved the views for the horizon. There were no streetlights, but more than half the drives were marked by tall gaslights that trembled in the wind. It was too soon for illumination, but it was apparent that most of the places were empty. They had the bleak air of desertion—no cars in the drive, no toys on the stoops, the panes reflecting nothing but the drapes closed behind. No sound. No movement. No evidence of pets.

As he walked, Colin suddenly imagined himself stalking Dodge City as the church bells tolled twelve. He could feel his arms tensing, could feel his legs going slightly stiff, could feel his heels hitting the tarmac deliberately hard. It was silly, and he gave into the fantasy for just a moment more, until he remem-

219

bered Tess Mayfair's passion for westerns and heroes and remembered the last time he had seen her alive.

And she *was* alive, he told himself sternly.

There could be no questions about it—she *was* alive.

He veered abruptly to his right and walked up the drive of an over-sized, two-story Dutch colonial, with brown shakes, and white trim, and a large gold station wagon parked in front of the closed garage door. The vast lawn was immaculate, expensively lush, and centered by a circular rose garden whose plants were protected by low white-wire fencing. There was burlap tied over the bushes now and wood chips piled on the earth around them. Evergreen shrubs masked the high foundation, the ground here sloping down and away from the house to keep water from collecting.

The stoop was bordered with a black wrought-iron railing, and he used it to pull himself up to the door. The draperies were drawn, the shades pulled down, and he looked again at the wagon before he rang the bell. The wind prevented him from hearing anything, and he pushed the lighted button again, just in case. Then he rechecked the neighborhood, whistling soundlessly, jerking his head now and then to shove the hair from his eyes. He rang the bell a third time. He looked to his right, down to the far end of the street and the woodland abutting, saw the fog crawling first from the trees and onto the tarmac, then boiling out and over the houses as if a fan had been turned on. He rang the bell a fourth time and looked away from the fog.

The shrubs scratched at the house. A torn page of newsprint scuttled around the corner of the house and caught against the wagon's front tire, fluttering, fighting, until it broke free and pinwheeled toward the gutter.

He knocked, loudly, insistently.

The fog settled and thinned, and touched the backs of his hands like the brush of a damp fern.

"Damn it, Bob, c'mon," he muttered. He stood back and looked up at all the windows he could see—

220

shades down, panes blank, not a sign of life or anything else.

He took one step down, changed his mind and returned to the door. His hand folded around the knob, and the door opened before he could turn it. He snatched the hand back and rubbed it against his jeans, his head forward to look into the carpeted foyer.

"Hey, Bob?"

No answer.

He stepped up, and in.

"Hey, Bob, it's Colin!"

After only a slight hesitation he closed the door behind him and unzipped his jacket. The house was warm, and close, as if it had been closed for a year. He cocked his head and listened, looked to the dining room on the right, the living room on the left, at the flight of stairs directly ahead. He'd been here several times before, knew the floorplan well, but something about the silence made him feel like a stranger.

"Silly; you're acting silly," he said as loudly as he dared, and hurried into the living room—dark Spanish oak, dark thick carpet, dark prints of game birds in dark frames on the white walls. A stack of newspapers in an armchair, a console television under the front window, bookshelves mostly empty. He headed for the telephone on the end table by the couch, snorting when he realized he was walking on tiptoe.

"The thief in the afternoon," he intoned dryly as he picked up the receiver, turning as he did to scan the room he was in again.

The dial tone was unnervingly loud, and he winced as he leaned over to punch Garve's number. He had three done when he saw the movement at the window.

"Bob?"

Stupid, he can't hear you.

He put the receiver back and walked to the television, put his hands on the polished top and leaned close to the pane. The fog had thickened in several patches on the street, hiding the house directly across the way. Through it he could see someone moving up the street as he had. He stared for a moment, then hurried to the door and flung it open.

The wind had died.

"Bob! Hey, Bob!"

He moved to the top step and took hold of the railing, one hand pushing his jacket back as it hooked into his hip pocket. A spiderweb of mist tangled over his face and he brushed at it impatiently, wishing Cameron would get a move on so he could make the call and get back to town.

"Bob, come—"

The fog puffed like woodsmoke and peeled away, and his hand suddenly tried to pull the railing from its mooring.

Theo Vincent staggered to a halt in the middle of the road, pivoting slowly until he saw Colin at the house. His suit jacket was missing, his white silk shirt shredded to the waist, and the legs of his pegged trousers were ragged and torn and stained with wet grass. Colin saw the pink-rimmed bone that used to be the man's left knee, saw the way the man's shoes were dark and gleaming.

"Vincent? My God," he said, thinking suddenly of Tess, "what the hell happened to you?"

Vincent only shuddered, his bald scalp glittering as the fog settled over him, curled up and settled again. A piece of his shirttail beckoned in the wind.

It had to have been a car accident, he thought as he started down the steps; Vincent driving, maybe, and veering off the road and somehow hitting Tess. It was a reasonable answer, one that provided solutions to even more questions. It was trauma, fear; something had sent her away from the scene, into the woods, to the cliffs where she had tried to get help and had only succeeded in dying. Vincent seemed less badly injured, though it had to be the anesthesia of shock that kept him walking on that leg.

Just as Colin reached the last step, the injured man moved to the lip of the drive and shuddered again, the tattered flaps of his shirt pulling away from his chest at the insistence of the wind. Then he looked up and blinked slowly, wiped a hand wearily over his eyes and down to touch gingerly at the wounds on his breast.

"Bastard," he said.

Colin stopped in mid-stride.

A groan rose curiously high-pitched, and Vincent glared at Colin. "You goddamned bastard."

"Now wait a minute," Colin said, his temper ready to flare before he reminded himself sternly that the man was seriously hurt and needed a doctor.

"Bastard," Vincent said a third time, his voice cracking to a sigh. "Couldn't fight like a man, huh?"

He frowned his confusion and started forward again. "Look, Vincent, I haven't the faintest idea what you're talking about. Now let me help you inside, and we'll call—"

The man's hands came up and doubled into fists. He swayed, shifted his weight, and a run of fresh blood began pooling at his foot. "Couldn't fight on your own, could you, bastard? Sent your little army out, right? Couldn't do it on your own." He raised his head, aimed his chin at Colin's chest. "Whose idea was it to get me, huh? Yours? Cameron's?"

"Get you?" he asked stupidly. "Get you? Are you saying you think . . . my God, you can't mean that." He vacillated between concern and righteous anger, wanting to strike him, wanting to hold him until the blood stopped flowing.

"I'll kill you," Vincent said, spitting blood at the grass.

"Somebody's already had a pretty good start on you," he said coldly. "Why don't you do us both a favor and let me get you inside so I can call the doctor."

Another groan, and one arm lowered slowly. "Jesus, Ross, it hurts."

And before Colin could reach him, he toppled. His knees remained locked, his hands stayed at his side, and his forehead struck the sidewalk with a soft, watery thud. Colin was at his side in a half dozen long

223

strides, kneeling, rolling the man over while whispering his name. Vincent's eyes were open, his face laced with blades of grass. Blood stained his teeth, and a bubble of red shimmered in one nostril.

"Vincent?"

The man blinked, snorted the blood from his nose, and took a long minute focusing.

"Vincent, where was the accident? Was Lombard with you? Is he hurt?"

"No accident, bastard," and he tried to lift a hand to grab for Colin's throat.

It was unpleasantly easy to brush the arm aside, and worse when a tear slid from the corner of the man's eye.

"I didn't send anyone after you," Colin said gently. "Now you have to tell me if your buddy was with you."

"Kid," Vincent said, the deep voice so soft Colin had to lean close to understand, and could smell the bittersweet phlegm that stained the man's breath. He tried to sit up; Colin easily forced him down. "Kid."

"A kid was with you? What kid?"

"You know."

His own hand fisted, and he took a deep breath. "Vincent, this is bullshit. I didn't send anyone after you, okay? You're only making it worse for yourself. You've got to lie still or something else will go wrong. And, Jesus, will you please tell me if Lombard was in the car too?"

"Kid."

Colin lost his patience. "Goddamn it, what kid are you talking about?"

Vincent sighed through a drooling of pink saliva. "You know him, bastard. The kid with the freckles."

His eyes widened. "What? Frankie Adams?"

"The kid, you bastard. Oh, *Jesus,* it hurts."

Colin stripped off his jacket, and bunched it into a pillow he eased under the man's head. He leaned back and was about to ask him what he meant by accusing

Frankie Adams, when he realized that Vincent's open eyes weren't seeing a thing.

"Oh . . . hell."

The ocean raised a cannonade high above the jetties.

He touched two fingers to the side of the man's neck, rocked back on his heels and looked over his shoulder. He knew he should have been shocked, or at least moved to some sort of decisive action, but he could only crouch there and watch the fog, half-expecting Lombard to come stumbling up the street after his friend. Then he realized that if Tess Mayfair and Vincent had survived the accident this long, Lombard might have too. He launched himself out of the crouch then and raced for the steps, banged through the door and grabbed the receiver.

He stared at the buttons, at the cradle, and stiffened as a surge of winter cold replaced all his blood. His teeth began to chatter. His hands began to tremble, first slowly, then violently, and he dropped onto the couch and closed his eyes until the delayed reaction had passed. The dial tone burred loudly. The molded plastic was ice in his palm. He shook his head once and hard,then tried to punch Tabor's number.

It took him four times before he finally got it right.

The line was busy, and he stared at the window while he counted to fifteen.

The telephone rang and Peg grabbed for it, juggled the receiver clumsily, laughed softly and self-consciously when she heart Matt giggling from his place by the door. She listened, then, and sighed with a martyred lift of her eyebrows. No, she told Hattie Mills, Chief Tabor wasn't here, but she really didn't think Reverend Otter was trying to kill her poor dog. She nodded. She grabbed the coiled cord in her right hand and squeezed it as tightly as she could. She nodded. She suggested that Hattie bring the dog inside the library where it wouldn't bother the minister, and regretted the mistake when she spent the next five minutes taking the brunt of a brusque lecture on civil liberties and the causes of the American, the French, and a dozen other revolutions whose purposes were to permit her to keep her aging dog where she damn well pleased. That in turn led to a survey of precedents for such actions leading all the way back to Saturn's revolt against the Titans. Peg agreed several times, making faces at Matt, and when she finally hung up she looked at the clock, then at her son who was closing the door against the wind.

The telephone rang, and Annalee answered it without much enthusiasm, her voice slipping automatically into a professionally concerned tone, nodding once, doodling a scaffold and hangman on a prescription pad, finally interrupting with a polite clearing of her throat to tell Rose Adams that she really didn't think Doctor Montgomery had the time to search for her son, but if she really felt it was affecting her health she should bundle herself up and walk on over. That tactical error cost her another few minutes listening to a lecture on the inalienable rights of a patient who was half crippled at best and couldn't see why the good doctor couldn't make house calls to a place less than three blocks away, for crying out loud. When she finally hung up she glanced at her watch, looked toward the empty examination room, dutifully logged the call, and closed her eyes to daydream about the coming night and the plans she had for Garve.

The phone rang in the restaurant, and nobody answered.

The phone rang in Cameron's living room, but it only rang twice. By the time Colin reached it from his place at the front door, there was no one on the line. He shook the receiver and threw it at the cradle, mouthed a half dozen curses when it bounced off to the floor. He was tempted to leave it there and teach it a lesson, but instead picked it up and slammed it back

226

into place. When it didn't ring again, he wished he were home so he could find something to throw.

He had tried three more times to raise the chief's office, the line infuriatingly engaged at each attempt. Unable to stop thinking about Lombard lying alone out there on the road, injured, perhaps fatally, he decided to wait until he could find out more about the accident. And what Frankie had to do with Theo Vincent's death.

He also couldn't shake the feeling that he had missed something important at Gran's shack. He didn't know why the idea had struck him, but once taken hold he couldn't pry it loose. For a moment he was convinced that bundle was indeed Gran's shroud and weight, that Lilla in her grief had retrieved her grandfather from the grave.

That, however, would have to wait until later.

He glared at the telephone, daring it to ring again, then strode to the door and had his hand on the knob when the pounding began.

A pounding so hard the knob jumped from his hand.

FOUR

"My God, there's a dead body out there!" Montgomery said as he pushed past Colin and rushed into the living room. "Right on the goddamned driveway." He snatched up the receiver and dialed, turned and took off his glasses. "Hello, Colin, what are you doing out here?"

Colin could only lift a hand and follow meekly, not wanting to admit that the diminutive physician had nearly scared him to death.

"Hell of a thing," Montgomery said with a sigh, one foot tapping impatiently as he waited for the connection. "Looks like he was run over by a truck. Did you see him?"

"I—"

"Lousy, I tell you. The island's gone lousy with corpses. The next time—hello?" He frowned. "Do I have the right number? I wanted Chief Tabor's office. Oh, hello, Peg. You working parttime for the Indian now?"

Colin hovered by the coffee table, forcing himself not to grab the receiver from the man's hand.

"Well, look, dear, I want to talk with Garve." He scowled. "Now that's a hell of a thing. I just left there, for crying out loud. Well, listen, when he gets in have him call me. I'm at Cameron's place, with Colin." He

228

laughed suddenly, sharply. "No, he's all right. There's been an accident, though. Some—no, Colin's just fine, he wasn't involved. You have Garve call me immediately, though, okay? Or that fool Nichols should he decide to go to work. Fine," and he hung up before Colin could tell him to hold on, to let him speak to Peg.

"Hell of a thing." He wandered to the Regency sideboard in the dining room, opened the lower panel and pulled out a bottle of Black Label. He held it up for Colin's approval, found glasses and poured them each a tall drink. Then he returned, sat on the sofa and pulled at his mustache.

"Wait a minute," Colin said, gesturing toward the door. "Are you going to leave him out there?"

"He's dead, m'boy. And I really don't fancy having him in here with us."

Colin stared. "Hugh, for crying out loud—"

"You saw him, I expect," the doctor said after downing half his liquor.

Colin explained briefly, and Montgomery shook his head again.

A fisted wind rattled the window frames, and the glasses on the sideboard shuddered.

"Beautiful," Hugh muttered. "Just beautiful. You tell Bob?"

"He must still be at the restaurant. I've been trying to get a line out of here for twenty minutes."

"Oh? I didn't have any trouble. You know what killed him?"

Colin hesitated, examining his glass. "He said something about Frankie Adams."

"Bullshit."

"I know, I know." He looked to the window and rubbed his hands on his trousers. "Listen, we should at least cover him up or something."

"Suit yourself, Col, but I'm not moving."

He vacillated between yelling and strangling the doctor, then marched into the foyer and up the stairs. On the second-floor landing he found a linen closet, grabbed a dark brown sheet from a tall rainbow pile, and hurried down again. At the door he glanced at Montgomery, who only raised his glass in a silent, almost mocking toast.

The wind was still intermittent, but stronger. The fog was gone, as far as he could tell, the temperature slowly dropping as the sky boiled with grays, blacks, slashes of ugly white. After a quick look at the other houses, he trotted to Vincent's body and lay the sheet over it, secured it at the four corners with rocks he pushed over from the garden. Then he scanned the road, the houses again; he saw nothing, heard nothing, and the scene bothered him so much he virtually ran back into the house.

Montgomery was refilling his glass. "You say this man told you it was Frankie Adams?"

"That's what he said," Colin repeated as he picked up his glass and dropped into an armchair near the door. "And as long as you're here, I ought to tell you about Tess, too." The doctor squinted one eye, and Colin recounted the aborted picnic, and the reason for his being in Cameron's house in the first place. After he finished, he emptied his glass and moved to the sideboard to pour himself another. The scotch warmed him falsely, but he didn't care; Dutch courage was something he thought he needed just now.

"Hysteria, I guess," Montgomery said, after a silence filled only by the increased howling of the wind.

"Whose?"

"Yours. Peg's. If Tess was as bad as you say she was—"

"Goddamn it, Hugh, I saw her! Matt practically went into shock, for God's sake."

"She couldn't have walked all that way from the boarding house. Even trauma wouldn't permit that, believe me. Damn," he added softly. "Tess was a bitch, but she doesn't deserve an end like that. Y'know, I wouldn't put it past Garve to try and pull her up on his own. The idiot." He sighed, took off the glasses and polished them on his sleeve. "Hell of a thing."

Colin heard the baseboard pipes begin to pop and clank as the furnace turned on, and a shattered cloud of leaves twisted past the window. "Hugh," he said, struggling for restraint, "it's bad about Tess, but I saw what I saw. Good lord, even Vincent—"

"—didn't have his innards exposed." He frowned then and rose, walked to the window and looked out at the street. "Y'know, I only came out here because Bill Efron was all hot about his wife coming down with the plague or something. The man's an old woman, you know that, don't you? The poor girl can't sneeze without him screaming for the experts to fly up from Atlanta. Soon as Lee got hold of me I drove out. She's all right, so I thought I'd drop in on Bob. Funny. I didn't see any signs of an accident."

"I told you what Vincent said," he muttered heatedly.

Montgomery turned and leaned back against the console. "Yes, and I told you it was bullshit. Little Frankie Adams against that monster? Even if there were more, I'd be inclined to doubt it very seriously."

"Maybe Cart was there, too."

Montgomery considered, and finally nodded once, a partial shrug. "Now Cart I could see, with a little help from his toadies. But there's no reason, Col. Why should they pick on this guy?" Then he peered at him closely. "Who *was* this man anyway? You knew him, I take it."

Again Colin found himself in the middle of an explanation, this one tinged by his distaste for the subject. The doctor didn't move from the window, sipping occasionally, grunting when Colin told him about the scene in the restaurant.

"Bob," he said finally, "hasn't the faintest idea where the high water mark is, you know. He could be in over his head and think he was still breathing. The jackass."

"You're sorry for him."

"I am. Believe it or not, I really am." He laughed silently. "I know what I sound like—he's a good boy, deep down, a good boy. But it's true, Col. He just forgets that Haven's End isn't the most important spot on earth. Big fish here would get lost in an aquarium anywhere else. From what you say, he's found that out, only too damned late."

"That doesn't change anything," Colin said coldly, looking to the telephone and hoping it would ring. Maybe, he thought, he ought to call Peg and reassure her. Maybe he ought to borrow someone's car and leave Hugh to wait for Garve. Efron; he was around and would probably lend him a car.

A look at his watch. It was just past three.

Montgomery saw the move. "Garve should have checked in by now."

"Maybe he went out to the cliffs when he couldn't get you."

"Yeah."

The room darkened slowly, as if a cloud had stalled over the roof. The shadows grew cold, and Montgomery wasted no time switching on a lamp. Then the cloud passed, but the gray light remained.

Montgomery began pacing.

Colin thought about Lilla and wondered where she was.

"Frankie Adams, huh?"

Colin nodded.

Montgomery snorted and returned to the window. "Jesus," he whispered. The glass came down hard on the top of the console. "Colin."

He rose carefully. "What?"

Montgomery lifted his chin.

Colin looked outside, at the trees bending, hissing away from the wind, at a flurry of leaves tumbling down the street, at the flapping sheet on the driveway where Vincent's body used to be.

The tiny lamp was covered with a dusty yellow plastic shade; the single chair was yellow plastic, the bedspread thrown to the floor a crinkling, floral yellow and red. There was the damp scent of sand and salt

232

rising from the sheets. The television was on—a western with the sound turned off, the picture flickering blue and rolling as the wind hummed through the antenna. The sliding glass door was opened just enough to let in the air, the yellow-and-red striped drapes pulled back halfway to frame the forest behind the motel.

A seashell ashtray was filled with cigarette butts, and a bottle of Wild Turkey lay empty on the thin green carpet.

Denise Adams was sitting cross-legged on the bed, her back against the paneled headboard. Her hair was wet and tangled, her cheeks flushed, and hr plaid shirt was unbuttoned and pulled out of her jeans. She was grinning at Cart Naughton, who was standing naked by the dresser, his back to the mirror. He was glaring at her, hands on his hips.

"You see somethin' funny?" he demanded, knowing full well what it was she found laughable.

She giggled. Her left hand rubbed lightly along the side of her neck, lowered until it was lying against the flat of her chest. She shrugged.

"It ain't funny, Denise."

The hand slipped lower until it covered her nipple. Then her fingers parted, and her tongue moistened her lips.

"Damn it, Denise!"

She rolled her shoulders until her shirt slipped to the mattress, then her right hand unsnapped the top of her jeans.

"Listen," he said, shaking his head in sudden confusion, "I don't know," and he kicked angrily at the liquor bottle, spinning it against the glass door. It turned crazily and slipped out onto the second story's building-long balcony. "I must be tired." He attempted a sly wink. "Last night, y'know?"

"Oh, sure," she said. "Last night. Yeah."

"I mean, Jesus, I ain't Superman, y'know." He was almost whining.

"Yup, I know that."

"Aw shit, Denise, gimme a break, will ya? Christ," and he grabbed a length of his hair and yanked, hard.

A thin coil of perspiration trickled out of her hair and down along her cheek. She shivered, but made no move to stop it, to wipe it away. It felt cool in the stifling room, felt tickling as it dropped from her chin onto her breasts. She looked down, smiled absently, and rubbed the salty moisture into her skin with her palm. Slowly. Half closing her eyes.

"Now that's sick, Denise!" Naughton exploded, but he didn't move to stop her, didn't look away. He was furious—at her for being such a bitch, and at himself for not being able to show her what he could do. The goddamned liquor; he shouldn't have tried to drink the whole bottle at once.

A bubble of nausea rose in his stomach and he swayed, turned and grabbed for the edge of the dresser, looked into the mirror and saw her sitting there, that dumb ass look on her face, touching herself like some kind of whore, staring at him from under those lashes. Teasing him. Mocking him.

"Denise," he said, dangerously calm.

The wind changed direction and something thumped on the balcony.

"Friggin' place is fallin' apart," he grumbled.

She ignored him. She pushed herself unsteadily to her feet, one hand holding the top of the headboard, and pulled her jeans down over her hips. A slow fall onto the pillows, and she rolled onto her back, kicking her legs until the jeans flew at Cart's chest. He snared them and flung them aside.

She rose to her knees and one by one fanned her fingers over her abdomen, pulling in her chin and pushing out her chest.

"Denise . . ." But hoarsely.

She began a slow bump and grind.

"I'll knuckle those damned eyes," he warned, silently cursing the dryness of his throat that made his voice crack.

She cupped her breasts and stuck out her tongue.

A shadow passed across the drapes.

Cart saw it just before it disappeared, and swore.

"What?"

"Someone's out there," he said, unconcerned for his nakedness as he strode to the sliding glass door, pushed it open and looked out, slapping at the drapes swirling around him. "Probably your goddamned brother trying to get his rocks off, the son of a bitch. Jesus, I hate him."

"He ain't that bad." She caressed her stomach, and wished Cart would stop playing games. He got her all hot and bothered and ready and slick and then . . . nothing. Nothing. Just like always, half the time, nothing.

Cart grunted.

"Well, who the hell is it?"

"No one," he said, and turned around to face her. "Could've been your old man, too. I wouldn't put it past him. I bet he watches when you take a shower, right?"

She thrust out her hips and flicked a thumb at a dark nipple, stared pointedly at his groin and pouted. "Ah, poor Cartie," she whispered. "Poor, poor Cartie." She crooked a finger and beckoned. "C'mere, Cartie. Maybe we oughta play."

"I don't like that stuff," he said, though not as strongly as he wanted.

She dropped to her hands and looked down at her hanging breasts. "Cartie?"

He took a step toward her, and she lifted her head, lowered herself slightly and raised her buttocks high. The dim yellow light glowed along the length of her back, and her breasts vanished in shadow. He took a deep breath and ordered himself forward. This was no time to fail; there was a repuation at stake if he wanted to keep walking.

Her mouth opened slightly. "Cartie, I'm hungry."

He felt a tingling in his groin. "I don't like that shit, Denise, you know that."

Her mouth opened wider. "Lollypop time, Cartie."

The tingling grew stronger.

"Jesus, Denise."

And the glass door shattered inward.

Denise screamed and scrambled frantically back across the bed, grabbing up the sheet to cover herself, unable to turn away as something flailing in the drapes finally shredded them over Cart and dumped him to the floor. He shouted angrily, and thrashed, finally pulled the material aside and pushed himself back against the bed. He was ready to kill whoever was fucking him around, but there was nothing he could do except gape when Frankie reached silently for his throat.

Denise stared in disbelief and shrieked her brother's name. He paused and looked up at her over the edge of the mattress, smiling through the dried blood that coated his pale face.

She gasped, froze, couldn't will herself to move until the thing that had been her brother reached for Carter once again. Then she flung the sheet aside, leapt from the bed and raced for the door, her hand too slick to hold the knob and turn it. She heard Cart begging, gagging, heard nothing else but the wind that tore into the room, scattering papers and sheets and rippling the bedspread as if a serpent were trapped beneath it. She prayed and grabbed the knob with both hands, finally got it to turn, and yanked the door open.

Again she cried Frankie's name, but she didn't turn around. Instead she sprinted down the hall toward the staircase, passed the fire station and skidded to a halt, her shoulder slamming into the wall as she spun around suddenly. There was a hose behind the glass, and a red-handled ax. She hesitated, then pulled the door open, grabbed the ax from its rack and started back to the room.

Cart wasn't screaming.

The wind pushed a sheet of motel notepaper into the hall.

She moved slowly, pushing her bare feet along the carpet until she reached the door.

236

Then a hand touched her shoulder and she whirled, holding the ax high and ready.

Her eyes opened, and a tear welled in one.

"Daddy?" she whimpered. "Daddy?"

Just before she screamed.

The wind died.

Nothing moved.

The only sound was the surf's roar as it slammed into the woods, the tide so high now the beach remained flooded.

A single gull drifted over the tops of the trees.

The patrol car was parked at the curb in front of Cameron's house, engine still running, its lights flaring. Montgomery and Tabor were standing near the hood, arguing heatedly though their voices were low. Colin couldn't hear a word they were saying, but he could guess. From the moment Garve had arrived and seen the liquor glasses, smelled their breath, he hadn't believed two words either had told him, especially when they searched the immediate area and found no trace of Vincent's body. The only thing that saved them was the blood on the grass and the blacktop; the only thing that kept the chief from driving off was Peg's and Matt's corroboration of Tess' condition.

As Montgomery had feared, Tabor had driven straight to the cliffs when he couldn't get hold of the doctor. He had found the picnic site, and had fought his way through the wind down to the first ledge along the path. There was no blood, no shards of bone, no strips of cloth. There was nothing to prove Tess Mayfair had landed there; she was gone.

In disgust, Colin had walked away from the argument. He stood leaning against the station wagon's tailgate, arms folded over his chest, legs crossed at the ankles. It was all too damned ridiculous, and he wanted to go home. He didn't give a damn about Vincent and he didn't care about Tess and it would be just fine with him if he could crawl into bed and pull

237

the sheets over his head and pretend it was Saturday morning, and he was going to see Peg.

He looked around and wondered where all the people were. It was a solemn and universal truth that neighborhoods were incapable of ignoring the police, especially when they were parked in front of that neighborhood's most prominent house. But there was no one. Not even Bill Efron—who could easily have seen everything from his front window—had bothered to come over to find out what the trouble was.

Like everything else today, that wasn't right at all.

He's mad, Lilla had said, *he's very, very mad.*

The gray bundle at the shack.

"Ridiculous," he muttered, trying with a violent shudder to banish the abrupt sensation that all of this was not a grim sequence of unpleasant coincidences. Then he looked over at the two men and saw them watching him, frowning slightly, either pity or sympathy twisting their lips. "Jesus."

He pushed away from the car and walked down the drive, trying to look everywhere but at Tabor, his neck muscles taut and lips pressed to a hard line as he willed someone, anyone, to come out of a house and head their way with a dozen morbid questions.

"The point is," he heard Garve say, "somebody stole the damned body. Lombard, most likely. Who the hell else?"

"There was no one out here," Montgomery insisted.

"You were watching the whole time?"

A silence.

"I thought so."

Colin shook his head and looked to his left, to the curve of the street as it headed inland toward Neptune. The wind had picked up again, still lifting over the houses and barely ruffling his hair.

And in the distance he could hear it—the namesake of the storm.

Screaming.

A faint and undulating wailing as the wind charged over the sea and dragged the dark clouds behind it.

He looked down at his windbreaker and saw it darkening in patches, then wiped a hand across the back of his neck, and it came away damp—the seaspray was thickening to a condition much like drizzle.

"Colin!"

He turned. Montgomery was standing at the patrol car, the passenger door open. Garve was rounding the hood to the driver's side, yanking down his hatbrim.

"Colin," Hugh said, "we're going with Garve to hunt for Tess and Vincent. C'mon."

Deputy Ross at your service, he thought sourly, and had taken a single step toward the cruiser when he saw Lilla. She was running up the street, had just reached the curve and was heading for the dunes. He called out, and pointed, and broke into a slow trot that increased to a sprint when she saw him, threw up one hand and veered sharply away. A car door slammed, another, and the engine turned over. He reached the corner and leapt the curb, nearly tripped on the dune's loose sand, scrambled on hands and feet to the top. Lilla was below him in the shallow trough; she'd fallen, her legs pumping hard to drive her up and away.

"Lil!"

She didn't look back, as he slid and ran down the slope at an angle to keep from stumbling. Shells skittered from under his feet; sawgrass lashed at his legs and stung his outstretched hands.

"Lilla!"

She was at the top of the second dune when he reached her, lunged forward and caught one ankle. She fell with a shriek and kicked out at his head. He ducked and backed to his knees, pulling at her, dragging her toward him until he was able to snare the other leg.

"Goddamn it, Lil!"

She broke away with a vicious kick at his arm,

rolled and scrambled feverishly until she was headed back toward the Estates. He followed with a curse, leapt and tackled her, heard her thump against the ground and groan at the impact. He knelt and shoved her to one side to grab for her waist, and she sat up awkwardly and lashed out with her fists. One cracked against his jaw and he blinked, momentarily stunned, though he managed not to release her. He dove on top of her, pinning her and rolling over until they almost returned down the slope. He yelled, and she answered, spittle flying from her mouth, her eyes so wide he thought they would split open. Once beneath him again her head whipped from side to side while he sat on her stomach and trapped her arms against the ground.

Then he looked up.

A wave hissed over the first dune and filled the trough with foam.

Lilla took advantage of the momentary distraction to buck him off his knees. He sprawled to one side, but instead of running away she lunged for his throat, her teeth snapping at his cheek, his neck, while he clawed his fingers into her hair and tried to force her away. She shrieked. A wave crest launched by the wind splattered them, drenched them. He jerked up his head and butted her. She tried to twist her wrists free, and butted him in turn, directly on the lips. His mouth filled with blood, and when he spat, her face was freckled.

Then Montgomery was on her back, yelling and unable to pull her off. Tabor appeared a moment later, and Colin couldn't see what he had done, but within the space of a gasp her mouth slackened and her eyes began to close. He shoved and Doc pulled, and she toppled to her side, unconscious, the fingers of one hand digging weakly in the sand.

"I . . . *God!*" he said, pushing himself to his hands and knees, spitting blood and discovering a loose tooth with his tongue. "God almighty."

Tabor said nothing. He lifted Lilla without effort and

cradled her in his arms, looked once at the sea spilling over the dune, and headed back for the car. Montgomery helped Colin to his feet and supported him as they returned, saying nothing directly, only muttering to himself.

They put her in the back seat with Hugh; Colin was in front, eyes closed, his head against the seatback. His mouth was numb, and he could feel the upper lip beginning to swell. He licked at it once, tasted his blood, grunted when Garve swung the car around and headed down for Neptune.

"She needs help," Hugh said quietly, gently.

"Yeah," Tabor said as if disgusted with himself.

"We can put her in one of the cells until we can get her to the mainland."

"All right."

"I'll get—damn, I left my bag at Efron's!"

The cruiser turned right onto Neptune and sped up. The wind shoved at it, faintly screaming.

It wasn't quite dark enough for the headlights to do any good.

Colin sighed loudly.

"You all right, Col?"

He tested his lips, his tongue, before he said, "Sure. Just banged up."

"Strong."

He sat up, half turned, and looked at the girl lying across Montgomery's lap. Except for the rise and fall of her chest, she could have been dead.

"I don't believe it," he said. "I don't believe it."

"She's crazy," Tabor said flatly, and winced.

"She's scared to death," he said.

"Of what, Gran's ghost?" Tabor said.

Just as Colin turned to answer yes, Tabor slammed on the brakes. Montgomery yelped, and Colin braced himself against the dashboard as the cruiser skewed wildly on the slick wet tarmac, spinning in a complete circle before it finally stopped.

Tess Mayfair was standing in the middle of the road.

Lilla groaned.

241

"Christ," Montgomery said, leaning across the seat and pushing up his glasses. "My God, look at her!"

She was less than six feet away from the hood, her dress nearly gone, her forehead indented and her nose bent harshly to one side. Her lips were smashed, her chest exposed and gaping, and when she started to walk forward Colin shoved as far back as he could, watching silently as Garve fumbled his revolver from its holster.

"It's . . . it's a miracle," Montgomery whispered. "She oughta be dead."

Tess reached the patrol car and stared at them. Suddenly the car began to rise. Colin yelled, and Hugh fell over Lilla. Tabor, without thinking, reached his left hand out the window and fired two shots. The first went wild, the second struck the massive woman in the hollow of the throat. Her head jerked but there was no blood from the wound. Tabor fired again, hitting her right shoulder. The dress tore, and bone chips flew, but the car kept on rising.

Then Colin slammed his left foot on the accelerator.

The cruiser shuddered, tires smoked and squealed, and as Tabor grabbed the steering wheel the vehicle slowly moved forward, toppling Mayfair out of sight. There was a sickening thump, a skewing sideways, and Garve stopped, trembling violently, ten yards away.

"You killed her," he said as Colin turned around. Garve was trembling.

All Colin said was, "Look."

Tess Mayfair was standing in the middle of the road.

FIVE

Matt was disappointed. He had ducked through the heavy door to the small cell block when his mother had answered the phone, expecting to find something far different. There were three cells ranged along the back, but none of them had straw matted on the floor, or red-eyed rats chittering in the dark corners, or thick cobwebs swinging gently from rotted beams on the ceiling. There was no rickety pallet, just an iron-rimmed cot bolted to the wall, with a thin mattress and pillow rolled up at rhe foot. There were no rusted chains hanging from the cinder-block walls, just a narrow shelf over the beds holding a handful of tattered paperbacks donated by the library. And there was no old man hanging by his wrists from rusty old shackles, his beard tangled and filthy and hanging down to his ragged trousers, his teeth old and yellow, his eyes dull and white. There wasn't anyone there at all.

It didn't smell, and it wasn't damp, and there were no signs of bullet holes or whip marks or even escape tunnels as far as he could tell.

He stood on tiptoe and tried to see through one of the high windows, though he knew that all he'd be able to spot would be the back of the Clipper Run's hedging around its parking lot. He supposed that anyone staying there would have to be content with a view of the

243

sky unless there was someone in there with him to hold him up for a look.

Then he heard his mother's voice, soft and urgent. He turned and looked through the door, saw her talking on the telephone again. She had her back to him, and he couldn't hear what she was saying. But that was all right; he didn't want to. It might be someone telling her more about Mrs. Mayfair. He didn't want to know more. He had seen enough.

When his mother laughed quietly, he turned back to the cells and walked to the last one on the left. He held onto the barred door with one hand and warned Billy Bonny again between huge chaws of tobacco that he'd better not try to escape. Twice in one day was plenty; the next time it happened, he wouldn't be responsible for what the townspeople did if they caught him. The Kid was somber and contrite, hung his head abjectly and nodded. Matt didn't believe him for a minute, but he moved to the center cell where he found Jesse trying manfully to grab hold of the window sill and haul himself up. Jump, grab, slip, fall—over and over and over again until Matt was laughing and pointing, and Jesse was whirling around with fire in his eyes, his hands slapping leather that was no longer there. Silly, Matt told him; you're just being silly. Jesse looked awfully mad, but there was nothing he could do except kick at the wall and swear eternal vengeance.

The last cell, opposite the door, was empty. Cole Younger had been in there before they took him away to hang him, and now it was waiting for its next resident to show.

"Matt?"

You guys just better watch it, he cautioned with a sneer, and went back to join his mother.

"What are you doing, deputy?" she said.

"Watching the bad guys, like Chief Tabor said I should."

"Okay. You're not getting into trouble?"

"No, Mom," he said, wondering how that was possible with nothing in there to break.

"Well, listen, I think we ought to—"

She stopped with a hand to her chin when the police cruiser came to a squealing, rocking halt at the curb, its front bumper less than an inch from the front of Colin's car. Peg was out of her chair and at the door before Matt could say anything; then he hastily stood to one side as Colin hurried in with Lilla cradled in his arms. Matt thought she was sleeping, maybe even dead, and paid no attention to his mother's low questions or Doc Montgomery's clipped responses. He watched Chief Tabor grab for the phone on his desk, watched as Colin opened the first cell and kicked the mattress flat. Lilla didn't move when laid her down, and Colin backed out in a hurry, slammed the door shut and forced the bolt home with the heel of his hand.

Matt reached out to touch him, pulled back and bit his lip. "Mr. Ross? Mr. Ross, is she all right?"

Colin leaned hard against the wall, knees bent, one hand on the boy's shoulder while the other brushed back through his hair. "I don't know. I hope so, pal."

He was a funny color, and sweat was pouring off him. Matt didn't know whether to put an arm around his waist or ask him a question or . . . or what. Then he heard his mother in the front office.

"Impossible," she declared firmly. "Absolutely impossible."

Colin closed his eyes.

Matt sidled around him and stood in the doorway.

There was a feeling in the room now that he didn't like at all.

Chief Tabor was sitting at his desk, Doc Montgomery standing at the window, and his mother was between them with her hands on her hips, looking from one man to the other with an expression he recognized all too well—*Matthew, the next time you tell me a story like that I'm going to tan your behind, you understand me?*

"Listen," Garve said, one hand lifted weakly from the blotter where he was trying to stand a pencil on

245

end. "Listen, you can say that all you want, Peg, but there were three of us there, and we saw what we saw."

"And *I* saw her go over that cliff," she insisted, eyes narrow and chin stubbornly set. "I *saw* her."

"I don't doubt that, believe me."

"But—"

Montgomery rapped his knuckles on the door frame. "A little order here, please," he said. "We aren't going to solve anything by arguing over what's inarguable."

"You're crazier than he is," she told him. "For God's sake, Hugh, you're a doctor!"

"That's right."

"Then—"

"Then nothing," he snapped, yanking off his glasses. He stared at them, blew on one lens, put them back on. His voice sounded hoarse. "She took a bullet in the throat, one in the shoulder, she was run over by the length of the car, and as God is my witness, Pegeen, she was standing up and moving the last time we saw her."

"Then for God's sake, why isn't anyone out there to help her?"

Neither man answered. Montgomery looked out at the street and pulled at his mustache while Tabor opened a desk drawer and took out another pencil.

"Garve? Garve, for Christ's sake!"

Matt didn't like the feeling at all. It was almost like the time they came and told him his father was dead, and he felt so bad because he couldn't bring himself to cry. He was supposed to, he knew that, but all he could think of was that there'd be no more beatings and no more lies and no more broken promises, and his mother wouldn't go to bed crying at night. It was almost like that—something unreal and not right, yet this time there was something more, something that almost had an odor to it, and it came from the two men who were trying not to look at his mother.

"All right," she said, temper and fearful confusion

making her voice thin and high, "Why don't I ask Colin, okay?"

"Ask," Montgomery said. "Ask away."

Matt jumped then when Colin walked past him into the room. He started to follow, but changed his mind immediately when he saw his mother's face shift from hope to disbelief.

"My God, not you too," she said.

"Peg," he said in the middle of a long sigh, "don't say another goddamned word until you hear me out. Just remember what you were thinking when we took off and went for Lilla."

Matt turned away. Colin was angry and trying very hard not to yell. He didn't want to hear that, so he returned to the cell block and leaned against the wall where Colin had stood. Looking at Lilla. Remembering how she'd come to him at Tommy Fox's place. He looked up, out the small wimdow, and saw the dim light and the wires trembling and the leaves flying by as if chased by the night.

"Hello, Little Matt."

She was sitting up, her hands in her lap, her bare feet close together. The dress was worse now than when he'd seen it the day before, and her hair was pressed so close to her scalp she looked almost bald. She looked terrible, but her eyes were all right.

"Hello," he answered softly. But he didn't dare move.

She tilted her head and raised a corner of her mouth in what might have been a smile. "They're doing a lot of yelling out there, aren't they?"

He shrugged. "I guess so." His hands were cold, and he could feel an icicle pricking the back of his neck.

"They're talking about me, you know."

He lifted a foot and pressed the heel to the wall in case he had to push off quick and run. "I guess." It was funny, though. She sounded just like the old Lilla now, not like the spooky Lilla who had come after him at the marina. It was funny. She even looked at him in

247

the same old way—nice, and friendly, like she was going to tell him a secret about the ice cream old Gran hand-cranked in the back. "Something happened, I guess."

"Yes." Then she straightened, and looked right at him. "And you know, don't you, Little Matt?"

"Oh, no," he said quickly. "No, I don't know anything."

"Oh, I bet you do. Maybe not everything, but I bet you know more than they do."

He was ready to deny it, to tell her she was crazy and he was going to get his mother; he was ready, but he said nothing because the way she studied him, the way she nodded and pointed at him once, made him realize that he'd been right. All along, he had been right.

It must have shown on his face because she seemed to relax abruptly. "I knew you were smart, Little Matt. I knew it all the time. Gran knew it too. He knows a lot of things like that."

Suddenly, without quite knowing why, Matt was excited. If she could do that, if she could talk to the fog and things, then she would be the first real witch he had ever known in his life. This wasn't like James Bond or anything like that; this was his home, and this was *real*. A hundred million questions stumbled over each other in their haste to get out, but he couldn't find the right words. All he could do was watch as she rose slowly from the cot and looked up at the window. Then she looked over her shoulder and gave him her beautiful ice-cream smile.

"Shall I sing you, Little Matt? Shall I teach you a song?"

He remembered lying under the covers and listening to the melody cloak the island and bring the fog.

Gran in the water. . . bodies in the ground . . . fishes and worms and holes in your stomach . . .

"Shall I?" she repeated. "Shall I, Little Matt?"

He nodded.

She began to hum, just loud enough for him to hear,

248

her hands clasped primly at her waist and her gaze so strong he couldn't look away. The old Lilla was gone; this was the new one, one he didn't know. He heard her, and he listened, and he saw a jumble of black-red images spinning madly down a dark corridor toward him, images that were mouths and lips and tongues and teeth, all of them humming and singing and asking him questions he didn't understand.

She hummed, and looked once more over her shoulder.

"Look, Little Matt. You should be proud."

He looked.

The fog was back.

"You should be proud that you know, and the others won't believe me."

Smoke clouds, fire clouds, rolling and tumbling and sailing silently past the station, smothering the town.

He wanted to say something, to ask her how she did it and could she teach him, but he was stopped just in time when Colin hurried into the cell block and grabbed his shoulder. "Come on, pal, I'm taking you and your mother—"

Matt pulled away, and pointed to the window.

Lilla was still singing.

Colin gaped.

Matt tried to hear the words.

The fog slipped through the bars in thick bands and gathered at her feet as if spilling from a cauldron. It pooled and thickened and extended an arm that braided slowly around her calves, her thighs, her waist, disappeared behind her back, and came over her right shoulder. The coil became a serpent that opened its black-red mouth and hissed a steaming wind in Colin's face.

"Jesus," he whispered.

A serpent's tongue of flaming amber licked at Lilla's face; a serpent's tongue of crimson reached out to the bars, and Colin flinched as if scalded.

Lilla's mouth moved, but it wasn't Lilla talking. "Jesus damn, Colin you got no imagination."

249

Matt's fascination snapped at the sound, and he shuddered. It wasn't interesting anymore, it wasn't fun or exciting—it was too close to the nightmares he'd had just before old Gran was lowered into the sea. He clamped his arms tightly around Colin's waist and pressed his face into his belt, trying to block the old man's voice slithering from the girl's mouth.

"No imagination, boy, you know that, don't you? A terrible shame it is, because it will kill you. No imagination will kill you as sure as I stand here."

A laugh, harshly soft and echoing from a tunnel.

Colin dropped a protective hand to hold Matt hard against him.

The voice deepened and grew harsh. "Oh, I got tricks, Colin. I got tricks plenty. One, two, three, four. I got plenty tricks, and you got no imagination, and that gonna kill you. It gonna kill you for sure."

Colin lifted a hand as if to strike at the voice, but the fog-serpent vanished at the beckoning of the wind, and the fog outside vanished as though it had never been.

Lilla strode to the cell door, took hold of the bars and began to push out. Colin hesitated only a moment before thrusting Matt aside and calling out for Garve as he leapt to the door to hold it. Lilla's face was blank; she was gone, nothing there but the dress and the features and the tangled bloodied hair. She pushed, and Colin's cheeks reddened as he hunched his shoulders and shoved back. Garve raced into the block and saw the struggle; he grabbed Matt by the collar, lifted and nearly threw him over the threshold. Matt heard his mother gasp, but he turned around to see.

"Damn!" Garve yelled, and Colin grunted with exertion.

Then, without warning, the bolt snapped and the iron hinges parted as if they were paper. Colin was thrown back against the wall, and the door was thrust to one side, pinning Garve against the bars. Lilla raced out and into the office, one hand snapping against the side of Matt's head and dropping him to the floor. There were lights, and a rushing like the sea, and as he pushed himself up he saw her dodging around the desks while Montgomery yelled, and his mother stood at the doorway with a chair held in front her as if she were warding off a lion.

Lilla shrieked.

Montgomery charged her.

Peg jabbed with the chair, and Lilla swerved to one side, folded her arms in front of her face and leapt through the window.

The plate glass bulged just as the launched herself from the floor, shattered before she reached it, scattered so when she landed she wouldn't lacerate her naked feet. She landed squarely, the momentum slamming her against Colin's car. A brief, too brief second to catch the air back in her lungs, and she spun to her left and raced around the corner. There were no cars. No lights on porches. No sign of the fog as the wind stopped playing with the island and began to gather itself to storm.

And as she ran she saw herself in a cell like the one she'd just escaped—a narrow dirty cell, with a single metal chair, and she was tied to it around the waist by a length of rusted chain. Her eyes were wide, her mouth opened in a single life-long scream, her hands tearing at her dress and hair, while someone beyond her vision slowly closed the cell door. She was screaming. Screaming like the wood-woman on top of Colin's table. Screaming. Mouth bleeding at the corners, nails gouging her chest, feet kicking at the chair legs because they were bolted to the floor.

She ran past the Clipper Run and the houses and the trees, not swerving at all until she came abreast of Colin's cottage.

Heedless of the sharp pebbles that dug into her soles, *something* nudged her into the center of the street and she followed the white line straight through the woodland until she came to the ferry.

She stopped, not breathing hard, barely sweating as she saw the box of wooden matches clutched in her hand. She stood, the wind sighing angrily in the pines, until the same force pushed her, and she walked down to the slanted deck. The chain was down. The door to the cabin was open and slamming back against its hinges. She looked until she found a small flaking pipe jutting through the floor and out the far side. Turning, she followed it under the deck as though the warped and unpainted wood could not block her vision, followed it to a round metal plate barely visible in one corner.

The ferry rocked, and the gulls overhead began to gather in an agitated white cloud.

The ferry rocked, and the bay raised its whitecaps, and the gulls swooped lower without uttering a sound.

The fingers of her left hand reached into a depression and took hold, pulled, pulled and turned until the scoured metal plate suddenly clattered free.

The stench of marine gas was blown away by the wind.

She lay the matchbox by her foot and tore a length of cloth from her dress, wound it tightly into a makeshift fuse, lowered it into the hole, and soaked it.

Then she returned to the cabin and sat on Wally's stool, her right hand reaching automatically for the red starter. She pushed it, the engine sputtered, coughed hoarsely, sputtered and caught. The ferry strained, her hand moved again, and the boat slipped away from the shoreline.

Rocking, bucking, while she held the wheel tightly.

Then she released the wheel and quickly tore off another length of dress, using it this time to tie the wheel into position. When it was clear the ferry was headed directly for the mainland dock, she left the cabin again and walked to the fuel tank.

She knelt again, picked up the fuse, this time leaning forward until her arm disappeared to the elbow, leaning back to pull the cloth out and lie it carefully on the deck. She started at it, and picked up the matches. She pushed the fuse until three inches of it slipped back into the hole. She opened the box.

She watched the mainland lurching toward her, staring as if she were able to judge the distance to an inch. And when the bottom began rising, the wind stopped, and she struck a match against the box.

She stood and dropped it on the end of the cloth.

It flared blue and sizzled, low timid flames that moved slowly while she turned and hurried back, not running, not looking around.

She reached the far side of the ferry and without pausing, walked off the edge. She didn't feel the water, nor the sudden loss of air. She began swimming automatically, and Wally Sterling's boat exploded.

There was a muffled *whomp* that raised the ferry half out of the water, a pillar of raw flame that rose first from the fuel tank, then pushed through the deck and separated the canted cabin from the hull. Flame and smoke billowed angrily into the gulls that still hovered overhead. Charred and flaming splinters of wood and metal showered into the bay, several pieces striking Lilla's head and back—and she didn't feel a thing.

The ferry burned and began sinking not six feet from the landing, and a black-faced gull killed by the explosion fell on the shack's roof, rolled off and landed on the gravel.

When Lilla sank beneath the whitecaps, there was nothing on the bay but the screaming of the wind.

Michael Lombard sat behind Cameron's desk and carefully patted stray renegades of blond hair back into place.

He looked up, then, at Cameron, who was sitting in a club chair, facing him and worrying his thumb nail with the edge of his teeth.

"He should have been back," Lombard said evenly.

"The wind, maybe," Cameron said, suddenly wishing the room had windows.

"Theo is a brave boy. He isn't afraid of the wind."

"I didn't mean that," Cameron said, irritated. "The wind is raising the tide, and I wouldn't be surprised if Neptune is already flooded in a few places."

"He has two legs, he can walk."

"It'll take longer."

Lombard checked the mariner's clock on the panel wall. "It's already after four-thirty, Robert. He's an hour overdue."

The silence was filled with an unspoken question.

"Maybe," Cameron said, "I should go look for him."

"All he had to do was talk to this man and apologize for hitting him. Then all he had to do was come back and tell us this man was going to drop out of this goddamned two-bit horseshit election so we can *get on with it!*" He punched at the blotter so hard Cameron winced. "Jesus Christ, this island is too much!"

Cameron was on his feet swiftly. "I'll go right—"

"The hell you will," Lombard said, straightening his tie unnecessarily, and rising. "I will. You," and he pointed at the telephone, "listen for that. Theo may have come across another problem we'll have to solve. He does that on occasion. He's not as stupid as he looks."

Cameron, uncertain whether or not he should smile, backed quickly out of the man's way and watched as he walked out the door. Then he scrambled around to his chair behind the desk, dropped into it and hoped that Ross had come up with a solution to this mess. If he hadn't, it was going to be one hell of a night.

Five minutes later he stopped trembling. He reached for the phone and began calling his people; there was a party tonight, and he needed every extra hand he could get. He only wished it was his idea, not Lombard's. The hard sell was dead; now the soft sell would begin.

Then he changed his mind and made a call to the mainland, to the home phone of his broker. By noon Monday, he wanted every share of Lombard's dummy concern out of his portfolio; he wanted nothing of the profits that would come with the casinos. That is, none of the profits that would come with rising stock. The land was something else again. No one could nail him

254

for owning a few acres that just happened to be slated for massive construction.

He smiled and leaned back. Then he reached for the phone again and realized with a start that the lines were dead.

Lombard stood at the restaurant door and listened to the wind. He'd never heard anything like it. He looked toward the office door, and considered going back and sending Cameron out. He looked over to the dining room and saw the shadows, and wasn't at all sure he wanted to stay here, either.

The muffled sound of an explosion decided him. He pushed open the door and hurried down the walk, turned in time to see the cruiser screaming toward the bay. A check of the sky over the trees showed him a faint rippling glow at the base of the clouds. Beautiful, he thought, just beautiful. This place I just do not believe. I was an ass for getting into this, I'll be an ass even if I get what I want. Now where the fuck did Theo go?

He hunched his shoulders against the wind before heading down the block, thinking he would cut across to the main drag between the rectory and the church. It wasn't the closest access, but he didn't like the looks of that wooded lot beside the police station. Too dark in there, and the idea of a church at his side was ironically comforting.

He snorted a laugh and left the sidewalk, aiming for the back of the supermarket. That's probably where Theo was anyway, one of his goddamn light snacks that would feed a goddamn army. If he wasn't there, then Cameron could get off his duff and do the searching himself. It was *cold* out here, for Christ's sake, too cold for October.

He jammed his hands in his pockets, kept his gaze on the ground until he heard a door open. He looked back over his shoulder and saw a tall man with wild white hair standing in the church's rear entrance. His clothes were disheveled, and his shirt was an odd color that looked as if it were shining. A quick shuffle through his memory for faces and names, and he stopped and turned.

"Reverend Otter," he said, "how good to see you again!"

Graham Otter tried to talk, but whatever he said sounded to Lombard like gargling.

"Reverend Otter, are you all right?"

The minister stumbled flat-footed down the steps, swayed with reaching hands before he fell face down. Lombard stared before running to the man's side. He knelt after a quick look around, and rolled him onto his back.

"Jesus, Mary, and Joseph."

Graham Otter had no throat.

He staggered to his feet and wiped his bloody hands over his suit jacket. He knew he would throw up if he didn't look somewhere else, but the sight of the minister lying face up to the storm fascinated him, held him, until he heard stumbling footsteps inside the church.

Christ, he thought, not liking how helpless he was suddenly feeling. Christ, where the hell is Theo when I need him?

"Hey!" he shouted, heading quickly for the steps. "Hey, in there, I need some help! The preacher's hurt!"

He took the three wide steps at a leap, and grabbed the frame to keep himself from plunging in when he saw the woman coming slowly toward him out of the dark.

"Miss North, right?" he snapped. "Look, your reverend's hurt bad out here and I need—"

He stopped when Muriel reached him, turned to run when he saw what was left of her face and what passed for a smile, screamed when her hands reached around his head, her thumbs unerringly slipping into his eyes.

Peg stood in the doorway while Garve and Hugh positioned a sheet of cardboard over the broken window. She hugged herself and watched the sky blacken,

256

turned and saw Matt sitting on Colin's lap, his eyes closed, his breathing regular.

Her eyebrow lifted in a question as she nodded.

Colin saw her and smiled, mouthed *he'll be just fine*.

Maybe where he hit his head, she thought, but what about inside?

Garve stood away from the window, half expecting the plywood to fall. When it didn't, he crossed to his desk, picked up the phone, dialed and scowled.

"Goddamned thing's out."

Suddenly the wind stopped, and Peg held her breath. Her eyes were half closed when she heard, faintly, the explosion. She looked to the others, and saw they'd heard it too.

"What?" Montgomery asked.

Garve swore and raced out to the car, was gone before anyone could choose to join him.

"I don't believe this," Peg said, more to herself than the others in the room. "I don't believe this."

No one answered her; Matt stirred in Colin's lap.

And before they were able to begin speculation, Tabor was back, his face red and his mouth set tight. "The ferry," he told them when he slapped his hat hard on his desk. "The goddamned ferry's gone."

"But why?" Montgomery asked, bewildered.

"It figures, doesn't it?"

"How?" Peg said.

"How else do you get off this island?"

No way else, she thought . . . except the fishing boats.

Garve saw her expression, and he grabbed for his hat again. "Yup. I think I'll make a quick run to talk to Alex. He must've heard the ferry go, too."

"Wait," Colin said, and Matt shifted in his arms.

"Look, Col—"

"No. Just listen a minute. You're going out there to warn Alex, right? Well, would you mind telling me what you're going to warn him about?"

The chief stammered a moment before saying, "Lilla, who else? She's obviously crazy, she probably killed Warren, and now she's doing things like that," and he gestured in the vague direction of the bay.

"You don't know for sure she did it."

"She was heading that way."

Colin squirmed to get more comfortable. "And what about Tess, Garve?"

No one said a thing.

"I think before you leave, we'd better decide exactly what it is we're really facing out there."

"You have an idea?"

He stroked Matt's hair, and Peg wanted to cry.

"Yeah. Yeah, I think I do. I didn't know before, but after what I saw and heard back there in the cell, I have a fair idea."

"If it has anything to do with ghosts," Garve said, half joking, half angry, "I don't want to hear it."

"Then don't listen, friend, because that's all I have."

Rose Adams sat in the living room and stared mournfully at the brown class register on her rolltop desk. So many names there, she thought as she brushed a finger over her own name embossed in gold on the flexible cover. So many names. She tried to run through each of her classes for the past ten years, a trick she'd learned from an older teacher long since gone, a trick that was supposed to help her remember the new students.

It had never worked, but whenever she was feeling depressed, whenever her family got too rambunctious and rebellious, she tried to remember every name she could. Like counting sheep, it would dull her mind to the demands it made on her.

Not today, however.

The wind was screaming something fierce outside the window, and Mitch hadn't returned from his search for baby Frankie, and Denise had somehow managed to sneak out of the house without her seeing. My God, when would they ever wake up and really appreciate all the things she did for them, all the sacrifices she'd made just so they could have clothes on their backs and food on the table. God knew, if she left it to Mitch they'd be on welfare by tomorrow.

Now here it was Saturday, and tonight—she looked at her watch and realized with a silent gasp it was less than four hours away—tonight at seven there was the big party at the Clipper Run. If they didn't get home soon, they wouldn't have time to make themselves presentable.

She sighed loudly, slapped her hands wearily against her thighs and pushed herself out of the chair. She was still in her bathrobe, but there'd been little incentive so far to get into a dress. With no one around to care how she looked, even on a weekend, why should she bother?

She looked to the sideboard, then, and the cabinet beneath. A drink, maybe. A fortification against the battles she knew would come when they returned. No, she thought with a decisive shake of her head and a deliberate glance away. It was too soon for that, and she hadn't clung to the wagon this far with Hugh's help to fall off now. Though God knew she needed a good toot now and then when Frankie started acting up and Denise refused to listen to her advice. My God, she'd say, I'm a *teacher*, don't you know that? A *teacher!* I *know* things. I know *life*, for God's sake!

But Frankie would only shrug and look sullen, and Denise would just smile and wiggle her ass out of the house.

Rose looked at her watch. Not time for the first drink yet, but what she should do is take a shower, be ready when Frankie or Mitch or Denise finally came home. That would show them. That would teach them a lesson, that planning in the home is just as important as planning in the classroom. She'd be all ready and sitting properly in the living room while they were all running around swearing and screaming and working up a sweat that would stain their good clothes.

259

Oh, God, she thought as she headed up the stairs, isn't it bad enough I got this sickness without having this family, too?

A hour later she wrapped a pink terrycloth towel around her and scuttled out of the bathroom, laughing to herself as she stumbled into the bedroom and switched on the vanity light. God, she loved that massage thing Mitch had installed at the beginning of the summer; it did things to her she thought were almost sinful.

A look at the gold watch placed carefully on the dresser, and she went to the closet to choose the dress she would wear. At the window, however, she stopped and looked out. She expected to see the fog that was giving her a case of nerves she didn't need.

What she saw was Mitch, Denise, and Frankie standing in the middle of the backyard.

She rapped a knuckle on the pane.

They looked up, one by one.

Thank God, she thought in relief and annoyance, and turned to hurry from the room when something about them made her look out again. It was Denise; she was naked, and there was a stick or something clinging her to shoulder. Oh, God, she prayed in furious resignation, what are they doing to me now? What if the neighbors . . . she clenched her fists until the spasm of rage subsided, then rushed to the stairs so she could give them all hell when they came in to explain.

The wind toppled a patio chair and tore a shingle from the roof.

She changed her mind and headed straight for the kitchen, where she could face them squarely, the queen of this damned house and they'd better not forget it.

Denise was the first to come through the door.

PART FOUR

October: Saturday

ONE

Twilight

Colin stood in the front of the boarded window, a lighted cigarette in his right hand, his left jammed into his hip pocket. Crushed butts littered the floor at his feet, and his hair was a slick tangle over his brow from constant tugging and violent shakes each time the enormity of what he was saying thrust itself home.

"We saw the signs of what was happening a hundred times." He stopped, changed his mind. "*I* saw them, but didn't know what I was looking for, so didn't know what I was seeing. But they were all there—Lilla's reluctance to have Gran buried in the usual way, her insistence that he was furious at us for imaginary evils. . . . I kept assuming her grief had mixed up her time sense. What else was I going to think?

"But at my place yesterday, just before Peg came over, Lilla was telling me straight out he'd not died at all, or he'd come back somehow, and he was out to get what he believed was his due. He was using some . . . some power of his to get what he thought we had cheated him out of.

"He was dead, and now he's back.

"Needless to say, I didn't believe a word. Power like that belongs in dreams and movies."

"It doesn't exist," Montgomery said simply. Seated at El's desk, he looked at Garve first, then at Peg and

Matt who were in a chair at the back of the room, Matt still asleep and sprawled in her lap.

"It *does* exist," Colin insisted without heat. "I don't know what's behind it, how it does what it does, but it damn well exists and Tess Mayfair's walking is the proof. What Garve and I saw there in the cell block was just icing on the cake.

"And now that I think about it, I'm sure that what I saw at the shack was Gran's shroud. After the funeral, after she was sure we were all in bed, Lilla went into the water and brought him out. She had to have done it, she must have—there was no one else to help her."

An hour had passed since he'd begun, speaking quickly, not giving himself a chance to think, and therefore backtracking several times. But the more he argued, the more he believed—and the horror of it was, he could see them believing as well.

And then he had offered what, for him, was the best argument outside any physical evidence: If he had been able to convince himself that the entire world had misunderstood him, had stacked deck and arrayed enemy against him to the extent that the only way he could win would be by ending it, why couldn't someone like Gran hate just as much? And it had been hate. Hatred for those fools who should have known, and didn't; hatred for those so-called friends who should have cared, and didn't. Colin had hated without understanding that his self-pity was blinding and the people he railed against were the very people trying to help him. His hatred had created a world beyond the real, and the only person who inhabited it was him.

Gran had hated the same way.

The difference had been in the final step.

Colin had slashed his wrists, and the pain had shocked him into the recognition of folly, into the realization that his so-called beliefs were false and falsely based. Gran, however, found himself dying and took a claw-hold on all those ancient beliefs and rituals he had brought from a home that had exiled him summarily. He took hold and refused to release them,

264

and in that refusal made them as tangible as the shack in which he was ending his life—his rage had shredded the fragile curtain between the supernatural and the present.

"The point is," Colin said—he paused and looked at Hugh—"the point is, we're not in our world anymore. We're in Gran's now. And for the moment he's calling all the shots." His expression was grim. "All bets are off now. The rules we used to know aren't the rules anymore."

"What about Lilla?" Garve asked, though he needed no convincing.

"I don't know. I wish I did, but I just don't know."

"She isn't Lilla anymore," Peg said quietly, and they turned as one to stare. "She's not. Not the Lilla we used to know, that is. Maybe not Lilla at all. She was when she tried to warn us, she was when she tried to talk with Matt at the marina. But not anymore. Something happened, and if that business in the cell is any indication, she's . . . not. Right now, I don't know any other way to put it.

"Matt was right all along, too," Peg continued. "It was the songs. The ones we heard every night. She must have been using something—spells, maybe, or whatever you call them—that Gran taught her, to . . . I don't know, to bring him back, do something more? But I do know I'm right. She's either been driven crazy by Gran's influence and is doing these things without knowing what she's doing, or she's totally possessed.

"But whatever it is, Lilla is lost to us. We can't go to her for explanations. She just can't help us anymore."

"She's right," Colin said, crushing one cigarette beneath his sole while lighting another. "And we don't know enough. If we're going to get out of this, we have to know more. Jesus, we've got to know these new rules."

"And we have to tell the others," Garve reminded him, and looked angrily at the dead telephone.

Hugh only shook his head sadly.

Colin strode to the desk and leaned over it, glaring. "What is wrong with you now, for God's sake?"

Hugh met his gaze with a glare of his own. "You're talking about Lilla being crazy, but have you been listening to yourself lately? Jesus Christ, Colin, I mean . . . really! Have you heard what you've been saying?"

He forced himself not to reach over and grab the doctor by the throat. "Look, Hugh, not one hour ago you were telling Peg about what happened with us and Tess. By God, you sure as hell believed then. What the hell happened?"

"Your so-called explanation," Montgomery said simply. "It's fantastic."

"Literally," Colin said. "You got a better one?"

"Give me time."

"Well, how much time do you think we have?"

The plywood shuddered, the venetian blinds on the outside clattering like musketfire.

Colin pointed toward the door. "The storm is starting to push in the tide. If we don't do something soon, we're going to be wading hip-deep in the damn ocean."

Hugh rubbed his eyes, pushed a hand across his lips. "You accept it all so easily."

"No," Colin assured him, "it isn't easy at all. But I don't have to meet more than one Tess Mayfair, or hear Lilla with Gran's voice, or see another demonstration like we did in the cell before I decide that evil isn't just another word in the dictionary. I'm a grown man, Hugh, but I'm scared shitless because there's a damn nightmare out there, and it ain't going away just because I say it isn't real."

The ceiling lights dimmed, grew bright again, and Garve stood and reached for his hat.

"Where are you going?" Hugh asked fearfully.

"If the phones don't work, I have to find out who's left in this place on my own, right? In the car."

"Crazy," the doctor whispered. He took hold of the ends of his handlebar mustache and begin to twist them, muttering to himself, sighing, jumping when something slammed into the plywood.

Garve left without a word, and Peg watched as he slid into the patrol car. He fussed with the sun visor, reached into the glove compartment, and stopped moving. She held her breath and waited, staring, until he left the car and returned to the office. He said nothing. He only threw a crumpled, soiled file card onto the desk. Colin frowned and smoothed it open.

"My God."

Peg looked a question.

"This is a fingerprint card, from Flocks." He looked to Garve. "Is this what El went for?"

Garve nodded.

"Well, what?" Hugh demanded. He snatched the card away instead of waiting for an answer, and examined it. "Jesus. It's Gran's fingerprints," he said to Peg. "It was Gran's fingerprints on Warren's wallet."

"That son of a bitchin' old man," Garve said intensely. "That goddamned old man." He set himself in front of Peg, and she could barely meet his gaze. Colin wanted to intervene, but he waited instead. "You were closer to that family than any of us," the chief said tonelessly. "Can you help? Did Lilla ever tell you anything about Gran?"

She shrugged weakly. "I don't know. Not much. He . . . he wasn't from Haiti or anyplace like that. He was from one of the smaller islands, the Caicos, I think they were. Lilla told me once they're somewhere north of Haiti." She pursed her lips. "Haiti. Lord, you don't suppose this has anything to do with voodoo or something like that? It couldn't, right? I mean, it just couldn't." No one responded. Her voice lowered. "He had to leave there in a hurry, as I understand. A big hurry."

"Yes," Colin said, looking toward the cells. "When Lilla came to the cottage, she said something about him having to leave where he was. She said he did things wrong, and claimed they weren't wrong at all."

267

"Maybe he was a dissident," she said, looking at Hugh to be sure he was listening. "Or a blasphemer, something terrible like that. Voodoo's a religion, you should know that, and every religion has a few grumblers who think it's being done all wrong. Gran might have been one of them, and when he came here and didn't get rich right away . . . well, it's just like you said, Col. He got angry for all the wrong reasons."

"Great," Garve said. "Then he's still alive."

"No," Colin contradicted. "At least I don't think so. But he's still around, and he's using Lilla to help him."

"But how?" The chief grabbed at his hat and holster. His frustration was running high. "Jesus Christ, how?"

"Hattie Mills," Peg said then.

Garve turned and frowned. "What?"

"Hattie Mills, Garve. Hattie, for heaven's sake. We need to know more, and maybe she can help us. Good Lord, we've all gotten enough lectures from her about this god and that beast and what all the hell else. If anybody knows something about what's going on, she certainly has to."

"I saw Tess shot," Doc said helplessly, more to himself than Colin. "Shot twice, run over, she fell over a cliff." Still leaning against the desk, he took off his glasses and lay them on the blotter. One finger pushed them around until he could poke at the front of the lenses. "She's dead."

"She is," Colin said gently.

"Then we can't kill her again, can we?" He looked up and blinked. "My God, Colin, do you hear what I'm saying? That Gran has hold of the dead, and he's making them—"

"I hear you. And I can hear me, too. Don't you think I'm wondering if *I've* lost my mind? But *I* know what hate can do to a man. I know."

Though no one said a word, there was no silence. The wind had taken their voices and set them screaming.

Garve strapped on his gunbelt and pulled a box of cartridges from a drawer. He shoved it awkwardly into his pants pocket, and unsnapped the holster's flap. A hitch at his belt and he started for the door. "I better get moving."

"The Run," Peg said then.

He paused, staring.

"If you do find anyone, have them go to the Clipper Run."

"Right," Colin agreed. "It's bigger than this place, and it has fewer windows. If it comes to that we can . . . we can hold out until the storm's over." He grabbed for his jacket and pulled it on. "I'll get Peg and Matt over there now, then Doc and I will see what Hattie can do for us."

Without asking permission, he went to the gun cabinet and pulled down a rifle, turned and looked at Hugh. The doctor pushed himself wearily to his feet and retrieved his glasses. He blew on the lenses, examined them, put them on. Then he stroked his mustache and looked around slowly. When he saw Colin waiting, he nodded, and Colin tossed him the weapon and a cartridge box. Then he turned around and took a shotgun for himself.

"It didn't work on Tess," Hugh whispered.

"Well, I'll be damned if I'm going to spit in her eye," Colin said, and put his arm around Peg's shoulder. Garve left a moment later, and Matthew roused himself from his protection. He glanced around sleepily, saw the guns, and cringed. Colin winked and explained where they were going, took his hand firmly and led him to the door. Peg followed Hugh, and closed the door behind them.

The street was still fairly dry, but a needled spray in the driven air clung to them as soon as they gathered on the sidewalk. The wind bent them over, made talking impossible, and the glow over the island had shifted from uncertain daylight to a faint and soiled gold-gray. They had just reached the corner when the amber traffic signal over the intersection snapped

269

loose from its guy wires and crashed to the blacktop in a scattering of glass and metal and a palsied whirl of colorless sparks. The wires lashed overhead, slapping against the road until they tangled against telephone poles, one curving until it fell into the Inn's parking lot to remain there, jumping.

Though the temperature hadn't dropped more than a few degrees, Colin clenched his teeth to keep them from chattering. He hoped Peg and the boy were getting some measure of strength from the pressure of his arm, the squeeze of his hand, but he was unable to find much of it for himself. Had this been a perfectly normal day, with a perfectly normal autumn sky, televisions and radios playing, kids shouting in backyards and the boats out at their trawling, he would have ordered Hugh to lock him up until he could be transported to a state hospital on the mainland for prolonged and extensive observation. But the wind that caused his ears to ache, the here-and-gone slap of his shoes on the pavement, and the continuing afterimage of the fog-serpent coiling around Lilla's legs and waist, made him as afraid as he had been on the day he had thought he was going to die.

And as far as he knew now, it had always been that way.

He squinted and urged them on, noting as he ran that all the streets were deserted, no cars were at the curbs, and unless he was mistaken there wasn't a single lamp burning in the entire village. He didn't want to think about how many had left safely, and how many remained behind to fall under Gran's vengeance.

The children in his classes—he bit his cheek hard to prevent himself from seeing them all like Tess Mayfair.

He glanced over his shoulder; the patrol car was heading for the marina, and ripples of muddy water coursed across the Inn's parking lot to lap at the raised curbing. They rounded the hedge and pounded up the walk to the Clipper Run's entrance. The banner under the eaves had torn free at one corner and it lashed at them as they slammed through and shut the door behind them. Hugh fumbled for a moment, thinking he could lock it, then gave up with a frustrated curse and followed the others out of the foyer.

The dining room was dark, silent, and the wind thankfully muffled to a vague memory of moaning. The office door was open, a light beyond, and they moved toward it cautiously, keeping close to the bar while they strained to hear beyond the rasp of their own breathing. Colin noticed immediately there were no signs of the party that was scheduled to begin in less than two hours—no bunting, no special cloths on the tables, no one dusting or cleaning or behind the bar preparing glasses. A gust punched at the roof, and a streamer of dust twisted down from the ceiling.

Peg pushed a reluctant Matt behind her when they reached the far end of the curved bar, and reached out to brush a finger across Colin's back as he neared the office threshold.

Then they were in the light, and Cameron was startled out of his seat as they scattered immediately and soundlessly to the nearest chairs. The indignant protest already halfway out of his mouth died when he saw the looks on their faces, the weapons in their hands, the fact that none of them had a spot of color on their cheeks despite the harsh wind. When Colin reached for the telephone, however, he said, "It doesn't work, and what's going on here? You guys hunting wild gulls or something?"

"El Nichols is missing," Colin said, ignoring the sarcasm and sitting heavily on the edge of the desk. "Your friend Vincent is dead and his body's gone, and Tess Mayfair is dead and she's walking around."

Cameron started to laugh, but when he heard how shrill he sounded he coughed himself silent and retook his seat. "You're going to have to do better than that, Ross. I'm not one of your kids, y'know. I don't believe in fairies. And what are you talking about, Vincent's dead? Lombard just went out to find him, for God's sake."

"If you don't like that, then try this—Gran D'Grou is doing his best to wipe out the island."

"As I recall," Cameron said, "the old fart's long dead and buried."

"Yeah. I know."

Before the man could answer, Colin walked over to Peg and kissed her on the cheek. "You going to be all right?"

"Yes," she said. Then smiled. "No, I don't think so."

"Good. I'll assume that means you won't try anything stupid while Hugh and I are gone."

"Not as stupid as you, going out there again."

"Would somebody mind explaining all this?" Cameron demanded.

"Mr. Ross?"

He knelt beside Matt, put a hand on his arm.

The boy's eyes were bloodshot, and his skin was cold. "Can I go with you? I know the library real well. I go there all the time."

"I'm sorry, pal, but you can't."

"Hey, Ross," Cameron said loudly, "would you *mind?*" He glared then as Montgomery walked over to his private bar, poured himself a glass of his best bourbon, drank it without taking a breath, and smacked his lips loudly. "Hey, damn it!"

Hugh pushed his glasses up, poured himself another and offered it to Cameron. Cameron glowered. "You better have a good reason for all this spy stuff and bullshit, pal. You hear me, Ross? You better have a good reason for this."

Colin ignored him. "Matt, you and your mother stay here with Mr. Cameron. You find out some way to lock that front door, check the back, the kitchen windows, things like that. You mustn't let anyone in here, you understand? No one but me or Doc or someone you're sure is . . . is all right."

Matt closed his eyes slowly, opened them again and attempted a smile. "Somebody who isn't dead, you mean." When Colin leaned back in surprise, the boy shrugged. "I wasn't always sleeping." Colin wanted to hug him, swallowed and did. The wind vanished for that moment, until he released the boy and stood again.

A jerk of his thumb over his shoulder toward Cameron. "Tell him, Peg," he said. "And for his sake, he'd better believe you by the time we get back."

He and Montgomery started for the door. With the knob in his hand he looked at Cameron, whose bewilderment had him gaping like a fish. "You have a gun, Bob?"

"A what?"

"Gun, stupid," Montgomery said. "The man asked if you have a gun."

"I . . . just a little . . ." He reached into his desk and pulled out a revolver. Montgomery considered, then tossed him the rifle. Cameron grabbed it and clutched it against his chest, staring at the barrel reaching up past his cheek. When Colin questioned him with a look, he said, "A bullet hole obviously doesn't do it, Col. That shotgun, though, might knock someone off his feet."

Colin nodded and led the way into the dining room. He stopped and poked his head back into the office long enough to tell Cameron to turn on all the lights; he didn't have to say it was to kill all the shadows.

Then Montgomery took Colin's arm and pushed him to the door. With his hand on the pushbar, Hugh blew a sigh and said, "I'm sorry."

"For what? For not believing the dead can walk? If you're sorry for that, you're as crazy as I am."

Montgomery's short laugh was more a forced wheezing; he ushered Colin through the door, followed and slammed it shut behind them.

The wind pummeled them sideways as they made their way to the sidewalk, slanted left and headed for the library. Colin was unnerved again by the emptiness of the town, the houses that should have at least had their porch lights on in this odd-colored dusk. At the end of the street the school reflected little but the winking on of the streetlights, and the flag on the pole was already shredding at the tip as it pointed the wind toward the bay and the mainland.

Hugh had hold of Colin's elbow as they turned into the library's walk. "I just want you to know I'm keeping an open mind," the doctor shouted.

"Good for you," Colin shouted back, and grinned as they ran up the wooden steps and paused on the porch, away from the main thrust of the storm. He shifted the shotgun from right hand to left and pushed through the glass double doors.

A single lamp was lighted on the rectangular check-out desk in the center of a foyer as wide as Colin's living room. A large room to their left, a larger one to their right, cluttered once with furniture and family, cluttered now with dark-metal shelves that measured the extent of the ten-foot ceilings. The aisles between were barely lighted by green-shaded bulbs hanging from the plaster on double-braided chains. Reading posters were neatly taped to the floral wallpaper, a straight chair and two benches along the entrance walls were piled with books and magazines. A stack of record albums lay on the carpeted floor beneath one of the benches.

"Hattie!" Colin yelled, peering past the desk to the staircase directly behind.

"Knew the guy who used to live here," Hugh said quietly as they moved deeper into the building. "Dumb bastard thought he'd get a leg or two up on heaven if he gave the town a library. He wouldn't spring for the money while he was alive so he willed this white elephant to the island, then hung around until he was at least ninety. Son of a bitch made napalm or something."

"Hattie!"

There was no echo, no resonance; the name struck a wall and died as if absorbed. The panes in the windows rattled like crystal.

274

"Place used to flood out every winter. That's why the biggest rooms are on the second floor. The guy didn't give a shit about what he kept down here. Had the gout, would you believe. The goddamned gout."

Colin wanted to tell him he wasn't interested right now in the library's history, but he needed the sound of the man's voice as he peered into the front rooms, squinting as though that would enable his vision to peel away the shadows that clung to the aisles and hid the titles of the books. Hattie wasn't answering, and if she already knew what was happening, he didn't blame her. What bothered him was the absence of the Doberman; that bloated guard dog should have been at their throats five minutes ago.

Montgomery pointed toward the stairs, then made a circling motion with his hand—Colin was to go up, he would finish looking around the first floor.

Colin nodded and brushed around the desk, stepped over a file folder lying open on the carpet, and took the stairs two at a time. The landing above was dark, the turn made slowly as he stared through the ornate balustrade at the huge single room that had been made of the upper floor.

Stacks, aisles, bookcarts, a door to his left of the landing that was Hattie's office, seldom used.

He kept the shotgun aimed straight ahead.

The wind screamed outside, living up to its name.

"Hattie, it's Colin Ross."

He heard Hugh downstairs, calling her name as well.

Shit, he thought, she can't be dead, for God's sake—and caught himself with a sour, mocking grin, wondering why it was that old ladies and children were automatically supposed to be exempt from the plagues of nightmares and the horrors of the real world. He stopped and warned himself sharply there was no difference in this case: The nightmare had taken strength from a madman who had his own rules, and it had supplanted the real. It had become the real. The dead were walking on Haven's End, and the only thing

275

he could do was find a way to destroy them. Thinking he was still dreaming was going to get him killed.

He tried Hattie's name once more and reached behind him to tug at the office door. It was locked, and a rap of his knuckles produced no response.

A muffled clattering from the ceiling made him swing the weapon up, listening until he was satisfied it was only a family of squirrels hiding from the storm.

Another tug at the office door before he crooked the shotgun in his arm and began checking the meticulously handlettered file cards taped to the end of each stack, looking for the area where he'd find the information he needed. When he failed to locate a mythology section—silently condemning Hattie for the peversity of her own system—he checked for the Caribbean. He found half a dozen books on Cuba, Haiti, the Lesser Antilles, and the rest, but nothing specific to what he needed; they were little more than tourist books.

Neither was there anything under voodoo or satanism; under religion only the vaguest, superficial references to the pantheon brought over from Africa, embellished and altered and intensified to suit the needs of the slaves who had little else for comfort. There were no volumes at all on the occult, and he was surprised; with Hattie's famed interest in the other world, this was a singular and puzzling lack.

He wandered up and down the aisles, squinting at titles, feeling time press in on him. His breathing was shallow, his patience on short tether, and twice he raised a helpless fist against the unfairness of it all.

Then, more by accident than design, he discovered a small section on magic. It was on a bottom shelf in the far corner, tucked under a curtainless window. He glanced out as he knelt, and saw the trees rippling away from the storm, saw telephone wires quivering, ans grabbed the dusty sill when he spotted lights in a house two blocks away. Atlantic Terrace, Peg's street. A cloud of mist obscured his vision for a moment, and he swiped at the pane impatiently until it passed. A moment later he was positive the lights were coming from the Adamses'.

Oh Christ, Rose, he thought, remembering the party and her intention to attend. For once in your life, woman, get someplace early.

Then he propped the shotgun against the sill, and pulled the books out one by one, flipping through them swiftly as he held them up to the fading daylight, checking indices and scowling as he realized every one dealt with stage magic. Two of them had been written to debunk the claims of charlatans and the ancients, and his silent laugh was bitter. They were so damned cocksure that science and sleight-of-hand provided all the damned answers.

He snorted in self-disgust at the attitude he'd taken—as though he had believed in spells since the day he'd been born. And maybe he had. Maybe he'd always been like Matt, but had somehow forgotten because grown-ups told him it was the right thing to do. Put aside fantasy and face up to the world. Put it aside because we've forgotten how to control it.

Kids, he thought, have more answers than we realize.

Which wasn't getting him anywhere at the moment, and he began angrily slamming the books back into place. Suddenly he frowned and cocked his head. He was positive he had heard someone coming up the stairs.

"Hugh?"

No answer.

"Hugh, you find anything?"

A prolonged creaking of careful weight on a stair.

He turned slowly, still kneeling, and pulled his weapon to him.

He was just beyond the reach of the overhead light's pale white fall, could barely mark the place where the landing swung around. The glow from downstairs wasn't strong enough to cast shadows, and though he could see through the balusters, an elephant could have made it all the way to the top before he recognized what it was.

Beneath the eaves the wind began to moan.

He rubbed a knuckle over his eyes and rose to a crouch, his throat abruptly filled with grit that made him want to cough and spit the obstruction out. He kept as close as he could to the right-hand stack, feeling the books give against his shoulder as he winced and passed through the exposure of the light. The floor was silent beneath his shoes, and it wasn't until he reached the end of the aisle that he realized the light was behind him and giving him form.

Too late. If he was being searched for, he was seen. The only thing he could do now was drop to one knee and bring the shotgun to his shoulder.

Shit, he thought; oh, Jesus, shit.

In less than a minute he saw a figure on the stairs. Moving. One step at a time. Wood shifting, and the banister groaning.

He moistened his lips with his tongue and swallowed to get rid of the sand. Slipping a finger around the trigger, he held the stock tightly against his side and rose with one hand bracing himself against the shelves. The figure reached the landing, and he held his breath, praying it wasn't someone he knew, realizing it was a vain wish since he knew everyone on the island, if only by sight. That he would have to do *something* against someone he once spoke with and laughed with and perhaps even kissed was a consideration he hadn't dared face. Until now. Until the figure stepped away from the railing and he tightened his finger around the trigger.

"Hugh?"

The frenzied scrabbling continued in the ceiling; a sash rattled in its frame.

"Goddamn it, Hugh, say something or I'm gonna have to shoot."

"I found the dog," Montgomery said, his voice deeper than usual. "Stuffed in a supply closet. Its head was torn off."

278

Colin staggered out of the aisle and sagged against the banister, lowered his gaze and saw the bloodstains on the man's shoes. He shuddered, looked up and was handed a small book.

The office door on the landing was open less than an inch.

"I found this downstairs," Hugh said, stabbing at it with a finger. "I flipped through it. I think it's what we need. I mean, I think it'll give us some clues if nothing else."

"Where the hell was it?" he said, opening the cover and trying to read as he moved toward the staircase.

The door.

"It was under Oceanography."

"What?"

Montgomery shrugged, "Ask Hattie. I haven't the slightest idea."

Colin held the book close to his face, to see more clearly a reproduction of a wood-carving that depicted a group of dark-faced people in tattered clothes kneeling in a woodland clearing, their faces averted as a tall, half-naked man walked toward them, his winding sheet in tatters around his waist and legs. His eyes were blank. There was a crow on his shoulder. Behind him was an open grave and a shattered, burning coffin.

The door opened wider, hinges silent, no light behind.

On the next page was a similar scene, except here the avid worshippers were intent on a feathered priest as he beheaded a black rooster, catching its blood in a shallow wooden bowl. The sketch was in black-and-white, but he could see the color just the same.

A shadow in the doorway.

A third picture, the feathered priest again, this time standing behind a kneeling man. In the priest's hand, a dagger he had apparently just drawn over his victim's throat. Blood spilled into a bowl. The priest was drinking from another bowl slopping over with blood.

Oh Christ, he thought—Warren. Warren was the sacrifice to give Gran the power.

Montgomery made a forced gagging sound amplified by the stairwell's narrow passage. "Great," he said as he took the first step down.

And Hattie Mills lunged from her office to grab for his throat.

Hugh whirled around in terror as Colin bellowed a warning and brought up the shotgun. The blast punched the librarian square in the side and propelled her into the wall. He pumped and fired again, and she flailed in a frenzied circle, falling out of sight into the room. Through the smoke he could see nothing but her shoeless feet at the threshold. They were kicking. She made no sound. Only the thump of her heels against the worn floorboard.

Ears ringing, nose wrinkled at the stench of gunpowder, he pressed his back against the stairwell and began to descend, one step at a time, the shotgun covering the open doorway and trembling so violently his fingers began to cramp as he tried to hold it steady.

When the first foot drew back, he knew she was trying to stand.

"That is the most fantastic and juvenile story I have ever heard in my life," Cameron said from behind his desk, his hands folded pompously on the blotter. "I cannot understand how you expect me to believe such a thing."

"Frankly, Robert," Peg said, "I don't give a shit."

Cameron held up a palm to show her he was trying. "Peg, for God's sake, I'm not calling you a liar, understand."

"It sure sounds like it to me."

"Well, I'm not. But surely you can understand my position. I mean, look at it from my point of view. The Three Musketeers come charging full-bore in here like you were chasing Dillinger or something, and you give me a lot of mysterious double-talk about Lombard and Vincent. Then two of you take off on some very mysterious mission, and then I have to sit here and listen to a story that's . . . well, honestly, I'm trying to be charitable, Peg, but Jesus, it's a crock of shit.''

She was sitting on the club chair directly opposite the desk, slumping wearily and knowing she hadn't done much at all to convey the urgency of their discovery. And she didn't blame him for scoffing. Despite the fact that she now insisted Tess had deliberately tried to kill Colin not five hours ago, she'd refused for hours afterward to take the final step. And when she had, she was weakened by a lethargy that frightened her as much as this nightmare; it was self-defeating, and it was dangerous, but she couldn't resist it. It wasn't comforting, but it was easier than leaping to her feet and screaming.

She also knew exactly what it meant—that she was sick and tired of fighting. Fighting with Jim until he died, fighting old-timers and the old-fashioned after his death to prove she could exist on her own without a husband to protect her, fighting her mother's suffocating sympathies, fighting to hide the fears of staying alone from Matthew when he worried, fighting Colin's reluctance to propose, fighting . . . all of it.

All of it, for years.

And just when it seemed as if the fighting was over, the rest of her life perhaps smoothed into some semblance of comfort, the world exploded. Nuclear wars she could understand; food riots and racism and the idiocies of politicians were standards she could depend on. But not this. Definitely not this. The dead had stayed dead until Lilla had started singing.

Lilla; she hated her. Peg felt her skin warming, her breathing erratic. Hated was precisely the word she wanted. It didn't matter that the girl had somehow been made a dupe of her grandfather, if Colin was right; it didn't matter at all. And it didn't matter that Lilla had been a dear friend for the whole of the girl's life. Lilla—and she had said it herself—wasn't Lilla anymore. She was someone else, and she was a monster. She was tearing down all Peg had worked for and was threatening the life of her child. Lilla who wasn't Lilla had started this horror; Lilla had perpetuated it; Lilla, by Christ, was going to pay.

"Peg, are you all right?"

"Leave her alone," Matt said sternly, standing behind the chair and taking hold of her shoulder. She lifted a hand to cover his, made a slow effort to tilt her head back and thank him with a wan smile.

"Boy," Cameron said to him sternly, "I don't think you should talk like that to me."

"Why? You're being stupid."

"Matthew!"

"Well, you are," Matt said, ignoring his mother and glaring at Cameron. "Lilla's a witch, and she's doing things to dead people. You should have seen her."

"That's ridiculous."

"He's right," she said. "If you'd seen her—"

"But I haven't, Peg, and that's the difference here, as I see it."

"And you won't believe me."

He leaned back in his chair, toyed with a pencil and looked to the ceiling. "How can I?"

"You went with Matt to lock this place up."

He shrugged. "I don't give a damn one way or the other. Doesn't look like anyone will be here tonight anyway. Goddamn storm."

"Jesus, Bob, it isn't the storm! I told you what Lilla did to the ferry. *Jesus!*"

"Jesus yourself," he snapped. He threw down the pencil, watched it bounce on the blotter and fall beneath the desk. "I've had enough of this bullshit. It's been very interesting, I assure you, but I have things to do, if you don't mind."

Her eyes widened. "You can't mean it. You're telling me to leave?"

"I have work, Pegeen. This doesn't run on its own, you know. Storm or no storm, crazies or no crazies, I have a business to run. If you don't mind."

"We're not going," Matt said with a sharp nod.

"Colin said we have to stay here. He's sending all the other people here, too."

"I heard, Matt, and I'll be glad to see them. *If* they ever come." He strained into the deskwell and retrieved the pencil, stared at the eraser for a moment before his shoulders sagged and his tan turned sallow. "It's a bitch, Peg. I thought Colin was going to help me."

"He's trying," she said tightly.

"I don't mean that," he said scornfully. "I mean about a hand to help me with Lombard and Vincent."

"Vincent's dead."

"So I heard."

"My God!" she said, rising, moving into an agitated pacing. "My God, are you calling Hugh Montgomery a liar too?"

When he didn't answer, she slapped at her thighs and headed out of the office. She stood for a moment in the dim light of the restaurant, her deep breaths a hissing. Then she grabbed the back of a bar stool and spun it around as hard as she could. The metal squealed softly; the bracketed lights on the dining room posts flickered pale gold. When Matt came out to join her, she hated Lilla even more.

"Mom, what about Amy and Tommy?"

"They'll be okay," she said automatically, putting a hand on his head, caressing his hair and not feeling a thing. "Chief Tabor's gone there, remember?"

"But what if he's too late?"

The fear in his voice was matched by the fear in his dark eyes, and she knelt beside him quickly, palmed his cheek, stroked his forehead. "You know Garve isn't going to let anything happen to them, Matt," she insisted gently. "He just isn't."

"But—"

"You'll have to trust me. Garve will bring the kids here as soon as he can."

His doubt was painful, and she looked away as she stood. But there was nothing else she could say. He knew what was happening, and he knew she was only trying to show him she was brave. And she wasn't. She wasn't brave at all. She was frightened to death and she was struggling to keep her bowels from letting go and if she didn't lose control in the next five minutes, it would be a goddamned miracle.

It would get a lot worse, however, if she just stood around like an idiot and thought about it. What she needed was something else to do, a way to pass the time quickly until Colin and the others returned.

What others?

Her eyes closed for a moment—another question for which she had no answers at all.

"Mom."

A slow breath; she looked down. The boy looked so *old;* he was too young to be so old.

Another reason to kill Lilla; she stiffened when she realized that was precisely what she meant.

"Mom, the door!"

She heard the pounding, then saw the brass bar trembling at the impact. Her knees locked and her legs would not move until she remembered Hugh and Colin, out there in the storm. But she wasn't about to open the door without a weapon. A frantic look, and she flipped up the bar panel, grabbed a bottle of vodka from a stack in front of the mirror, and paid no attention to the explosion of glass and liquor as the pyramid came down. Cameron seemed to leap into the office doorway, swearing when he saw the debris, striding furiously toward her as she moved into the foyer. Matt intercepted him with a vicious kick to the shins, and as he reached down to grab at the pain, the boy nudged him hard with one hip. He tottered, fell against the railing and had to grab it to keep from pitching over and landing on a table.

By that time Peg was at the door.

She held the bottle by its neck, knowing it was as heavy and as lethal as a brick, the movies notwithstanding.

The pounding continued, and she thought she heard

voices under the wind. She couldn't be sure. It could have been a wish; it could have been a memory.

"Mom!"

There was only one way to find out.

The brass bar was cold, almost burning. She grabbed it and pushed down, then she jumped back and held her breath against the wind's rush.

The door swung open suddenly, and the bottle was at her shoulder as Hugh and Colin stumbled in. The bottle fell, bounced, rolled out of the way. Matt cheered, and she embraced Colin fiercely, kissed him hard and let him virtually drag her down the two steps into the dining room while he talked about the book the doctor had found. She, in turn, railed against Cameron's callous disbelief, and Matt was demanding loudly to know what had happened.

It continued until, abruptly, there was a charged, unpleasant silence.

All the words were out and gone, the reunion complete. Colin dropped to the piano bench and opened the book in his lap.

"Ross," Cameron said, making the name a threat as he moved toward him, hands fisted. "Ross, I've had enough of this. You and these other nuts get the hell out!"

Montgomery turned to him and planted a fist in his stomach. Cameron's eyes widened, narrowed, and he fell into the nearest chair, legs splayed and hands cupped protectively over his waist.

"One more word," the doctor said, brandishing the bottle Peg had dropped, "and I'll smash this across your fucking nose."

Peg sat beside Colin and took the book gently from his hands. His fingers were trying to turn the pages, but they wouldn't work properly, and she could see his frustration building to a rage. A quick glance at the title, which meant nothing to her, and she flipped to the table of contents, then back to the index. Colin grunted and pointed.

As she searched for the proper chapter, she said, "Hattie?" without daring to look up.

"The dog's dead, Peg. Hattie is . . ." He swallowed. "I had to use that," and he pointed shakily at the shotgun lying by his feet.

She found what she was looking for and scanned it quickly, noting as she did how oddly detached she felt, as if she were researching a term paper or looking up something for Matt that puzzled him. But when she was finished, she realized that even Cameron was waiting for some sort of confirmation.

"Well?" Hugh asked, rubbing his palms together nervously.

"He wasn't a real priest," she said. "This calls them *houngans*. But he wasn't one of those."

"We know that," he said. "But real or not, he knows real stuff. Knowing Gran, and from what Lilla told us, he probably wasn't satisfied practicing his— what? magic?—in a village. He would want to strike out at the whites holding the island. And those on the other islands, too. He wanted power and he wanted gold. And they wouldn't let him subvert their religion. That's probably why they kicked his ass out."

"It says . . ." A look to Matt. He was standing at the back curve of the piano, elbows on the top, palms around his cheeks. *So old. So old.* He was watching in rapt fascination, the tip of his tongue pink at the corner of his mouth. The weariness was gone. If she didn't get this right, her son was going to die . . . was going to die and never be buried.

"It says you create a walking dead by stealing its soul. You hold it until it does what you want, and then you release it. The dead are allowed to rest and their souls are free to go wherever it is they believe souls go." A shuddering deep breath that passed like razors down her throat. "You get the souls at the moment of death."

"Yeah," Colin said numbly. "Yeah. Shit." He rubbed a thumb under his nose, raked his hand back through his hair. "He's got them all."

286

The others said nothing.

Colin nodded. "He's got them all. There's a picture in there, I think it means that the gulls were killed to provide Gran with blood to . . . I don't know, sustain him while he was in the water. Then Warren was killed to give him strength. He was a sacrifice, so he doesn't . . ." He hesitated, hating now the sure sound of his voice. "He doesn't walk, like the others. Then Gran uses the others to kill even more. And he has them now. He uses them, like he uses Lilla. He tells them where to go and what to do. They're his, and since they're dead—"

Peg dropped the book on the piano. "You can kill them by pouring salt in their mouths and sewing their lips shut. They rest, see, when the owner of their soul doesn't need them at the moment."

"You . . . *what?*" Hugh said, standing, turning in a circle, slapping a hand on a table and making Cameron jump. "You're . . . we can't! My God, Peg, we can't! We just *can't!*"

She wanted to object, but she knew he was right. They weren't simply talking about people they had lived with all their lives, people they had loved as well as hated, people who had touched them in one way or another. Quite aside from all that—and it was horrid enough—there were too many of them, uncountable at this point, and too strong. She couldn't see herself sitting on Tess Mayfair's chest while someone poured a box of Diamond down her throat and put a needle to that mouth. It was unthinkable. And she doubted that Gran had arranged for any of his slaves to rest until the entire island was taken over, and he at last had his control.

"Fire," Colin said, giving her a quick reassuring look as he pushed at the book. "Look, as long as we're talking about legends we might as well pull out all the stops, right? There's no sense holding back now, unless somebody still doesn't believe that what we have here is the supernatural."

No one said a word; Cameron shook his head.

287

"All right, then. Fire, silver bullets, crucifixes, all that other protection. Silver bullets we don't have, and I doubt a crucifix would do anything but make Gran laugh. But these creatures *are* corporeal, not like vampires or things like that. Burn their bodies and they can't hurt you."

"Impossible," Hugh objected without raising his voice. "We'd have to burn down the whole town, Col. And the storm won't help, either."

"You're all *crazy*," Cameron muttered, pushing Montgomery to one side and staggering to the bar.

"Then what are we going to do?" Colin asked calmly. "We can't wait for them to come to us. And they will come, you know. Maybe we can knock them off their feet and run like hell. But where? Another house? And how long do we keep going before they finally trap us?"

"Fucking goddamned crazy," Cameron declared, twisting open a bottle.

Peg closed her eyes and rubbed her forehead with her fingertips as hard as she could. She needed the pain to remind her this was real.

The wind slammed the restaurant; in the kitchen a pot fell.

Eliot Nichols felt nothing at all, heard nothing at all as he rose from a bed of sodden leaves in the woods and made his way through the underbrush toward the Anchor Inn. The wind was trapped in the boughs above him, the light like midnight beneath the dying autumn leaves. He came out of the trees behind Annalee's cottage, paused for a moment, then changed direction and headed for the back door.

It was unlocked.

He went in.

There was no need to turn on a light.

Rose sat up without a sound, her blood-spattered legs tangled in a kitchen chair. She kicked it clumsily, used the table to haul herself to her feet. She paid no attention to the tatters of her bloodied housecoat, or the straggles of her hair, or the purple-yellow bruises that formed a necklace around her throat. She walked into the living room, waited, turned and headed for the front door.

Her family walked behind her.

They were swayed by the wind as they left the porch, then walked down the street toward the woods, toward the last house.

An ax was still embedded in Denise's shoulder.

There was no blood.

Carter Naughton knocked on Bill Efron's door, slammed it in with a forearm when nobody answered. Efron was on the staircase when Carter looked up, and smiled.

At the Haven's End landing of the Sterling Brothers Ferry, Lilla D'Grou walked out of the water.

"The boats!" Peg exclaimed suddenly, smiling for the first time in what seemed like years. "We've forgotten about the boats. My God, think! All we have to do is take one of the boats from the marina! Lord, we could be safe on the mainland before we know it."

"In this weather?" Hugh said skeptically.

"You'd rather die?" she countered.

"Hold it," Colin said, a hand on her wrist. "Hold it just a minute and think, you two. Sure we can get off, like Peg says, but then what? We hike into Flocks and go to the police? Tell the police, 'Hey, fellas, we have a problem out there on Haven's End, see, and we're going to need a few dozen of you to help us kill off a few dozen dead people.' " He lifted a hand, drummed it on the keyboard lid.

"We can try," Hugh said.

"We can get ourselves locked up, too."

She hated him, then, for trying to steal her escape.

"And we can't just run away either," he continued as though he regretted it. "This salt thing that Peg

289

said, I'll bet that'll keep them away from the water, but sooner or later someone else will come out here, and . . ."

She hugged herself and rocked on the bench. "You're saying we can't leave until we do something about them."

"I'm saying . . . yes. Yes, that's exactly what I'm saying."

She looked at him steadily for a long, unpleasant moment, then rose and began wandering among the tables.

"Besides," Colin added, "how can we leave our friends here like this?"

She hated him even more; it just wasn't fair, making her feel guilty about creatures like that.

"Lilla," Hugh suggested. "If we get hold of Lilla, maybe she can help us. Maybe there's some way we can get her away from whatever influence Gran has on her." He stopped when he realized they were looking at him. "I . . . I've been thinking. I mean, it seems to me that Gran is able to do more than control her, take hold of her mind, as someone said before. I think—oh, God, listen to me—I think it more likely he's *in* in her mind. All that business about the salt water seems to keep him from walking around or we would have seen him before this. He would want to take care of us himself, right?"

They watched, and Peg swallowed a sudden bubble of bile.

"So he has Lil. Literally. She isn't Lil anymore, she's Gran, and that's the way he does it. So if we can get her, try to get through to the part of her that's maybe still the real her, maybe we . . . well, what the hell, it's worth a try, isn't it?"

"Uh-uh!" Matt said with an emphatic shake of his head.

She turned abruptly, her mouth open and the tip of one finger pressed against her lower lip. Matt. All this time she'd been talking about destroying a horror as if she were planning strategy for a high school football

290

game, and her son had been standing there quietly, listening. Feeling God knows what, and she had ignored him completely.

She felt the tears and blinked them away angrily. Then she heard Colin say, "Why not, pal?" as if Matt were an adult with an equal voice in destruction. She ran to him and pulled him away from the piano.

"Leave him alone!" she said, shoving him behind her. "He's a boy! Leave him alone!"

"But, Mom!"

"Matthew Fletcher, don't you say one more word!"

"But Mom, you said that the guy has the souls, and the people stay dead when the souls go back, and if Gran has the souls then why chase Lilla?"

"Matthew, damn it," and she slapped him, once, hard, refusing to release him when he rocked away from the blow. He whimpered and yanked angrily at her arm, and she raised her hand to slap him again when Colin snapped her name, and she froze. She saw her son cringing, saw Hugh staring down at his shoes, saw Cameron grinning at her from behind a tall glass of scotch. Her hand burned. She pulled the boy roughly against her and held his face against her chest, stroked his hair desperately and waited for Colin to save her.

He said nothing.

"I'm sorry," she whispered. "Matt, I'm so sorry."

"You're right again," Colin said, and Matt turned to stare. "We can't do any of the things we've been talking about, but by God, we can get Gran. And I know where he is."

"The fish ate him," the boy protested.

"No, I don't think so." He explained quickly about his attempt to get into the shack to find Lilla, about the light he saw and the stench that drove him back. And what he thought was the deadweight in the front room. "He's in there. I'd bet on it. I bet Lil went back out after the funeral and got his body. It's the only explanation, because she isn't a witch."

"Yes she is," Matt said. Peg wanted an explanation, but Colin was already up and talking, and before she knew it she was using her hands to dry her son's tears while at the same time listening to what Colin was saying.

Gran. All the time it was Gran, and now she knew she wasn't going to die.

"Burn the damned thing," she heard herself say when Colin paused for a moment. He looked at her, and she blinked in surprise at the sound of her own voice. "Burn the shack, and you'll burn his body. It's too wet for just brush or a match. We need something flammable." She was talking too fast, and she didn't like what she was hearing. "We need something that will burn in a high wind. Gasoline! But the gas station's closed, do you know how to get into the pumps?" No one did. "The generator, then. I have spare fuel in back of the house. A couple of gallons."

"Enough, I should think," Hugh said.

"Jesus, you are all fucking off your nuts!" Cameron yelled, drinking now straight out of the bottle, wiping his mouth with the sleeve of his jacket. He looked at his watch and unsuccessfully smothered a belch behind his hand. "You know it's after six-thirty? I had a hell of a great party starting here in half an hour and you guys are talking about burning down a dead man's fucking shack. Jesus!"

They ignored him, and he waved the bottle as if he were batting away pesky flies.

Colin grabbed the shotgun and followed Hugh to the front, Peg and Matt trailing apprehensively. Before the door opened, she suggested one of them get to the police station and try to contact Garve on the patrol car radio, let him know what they'd learned and what they were going to do. Though she held her breath when Hugh said he'd do it, Colin vetoed the idea as she'd known he would the moment she'd said it. It would mean splitting them up, and though it seemed it was easy to outrun the dead, there was no sense now in taking any chances, not when they were so close to ending it.

"You wait here," he said, "and I'll get my car. When I get back we'll get the kerosene, then Gran."

"What if the road's flooded?" Hugh asked. "The tide's already probably covered the beach."

"Then we'll walk, Doc, we'll walk."

And he was gone before Peg had a chance to say good-bye.

It was quiet.

The chill of the stormwind vanished as soon as they turned back toward the bar. Cameron, his satin tie unknotted and his jacket thrown over a stool, lifted a glass to them in a giggling toast. Hugh took an angry step toward him; Peg grabbed his arm and stopped him with a look. Matt moved quickly toward the far side of the room, giving the muttering Cameron as much berth as he could.

Cameron leaned over the bar then and stared at the floor with a soulful shake of his head. "Brother, this is a crock. Hey, who's gonna pay for this mess, huh? Hey, Pegeen, who's gonna pay for all this liquor?" He sat back heavily. "Christ, the place smells like a distillery."

Someone knocked on the door.

Montgomery turned to answer, but Cameron was at him before he could take a step. "My place," he said, voice and face surly. "My goddamned place, you two-bit, sawed-off quack. It's my place, and I'll let them in."

"Yeah, you do that," Hugh told him, looked to Peg and shook his head.

"Goddamn party's gonna start in a minute and I ain't even ready. Jesus. Hundreds of people, and all that beautiful booze gone. Jesus, what a mess." He pressed down on the bar to get himself on his feet. "You're gonna pay for all that booze, Peg, I swear to God. That stuff costs a fortune, even wholesale." He pointed stiffly at Matt. "And that stupid kid attacked me, goddamn it!"

He opened the door, turned away from the wind.

"Well, Jesus Christ," he said with a sneer, "where in hell have you been, you jackass? Hey, Peg, I thought you told me this dumb ass was dead."

He screamed when Theo Vincent took hold of his neck and lifted him off the floor.

He screamed when Vincent walked him to the coat-room and bent him over the lower door.

He jabbed a thumb in Vincent's eye, and Vincent snapped Cameron's spine.

Peg was already running. She grabbed Matt's upper arm and dragged him through the kitchen doors, Montgomery close behind after grabbing the rifle from Cameron's office. They ran down an aisle flanked by warming ovens and grills, butcher's blocks and sinks made of stainless steel; pots quivered on hooks over counters and stoves, ladles and cleavers and long knives caught the faint light and glittered. The floor was white tile, and their heels snapped like burning logs.

They rounded a corner and raced past two cold-storage rooms and a gaping pantry, hit the side door without slowing and burst outside, almost screaming. She paused and gathered Matt into her arms, sidestepping Montgomery who couldn't slow down in time. He skidded into the hedge, barely stayed on his feet. Then they darted toward the corner of the deserted parking lot, where the high hedge had been worn away by kids cutting through from Neptune.

They emerged behind the police station, ran right beside the wooded lot.

They did not check the shadows; Peg saw the street-lights burning brighter now. It was night.

Hugh was first to the sidewalk, and he grabbed hold of the building's edge and swung himself around to a slipping, falling halt. Colin's car was at the curb, the office door open.

"Where . . . ?" Peg gasped as she looked up and down the street. "It's only a block, Hugh. How could it take him so long to get here?"

She followed her son and Montgomery into the

office, did an aboutface and stood on the threshold. The water was spilling over the opposite curb now as the tide reached in from the beach, flooding the gutters and pooling around the storm drains. She could almost imagine she saw waves spraying high in the trees.

"Colin?" she whispered.

"He's not here, Peg," Hugh said, coming up behind her. "I don't know where the hell he is."

TWO

Dusk

Colin ran hunched over and turned against the wind, his free hand up to shield his eyes from the pellets of dust and slices of leaves that clouded past him every few feet. When he managed a look across the street he noticed there was still very little apparent damage to the houses he could see, aside from the occasional porch plant dashed to the ground, chairs tipped over, a dead branch or two littering the yards. He suspected then that the storm's strongest weapon was its numbing monotony. It blew steadily, without gusting, not near hurricane force but powerful enough to make normal movement difficult. And there was always the banshee screaming—through the trees rapidly stripped of their foliage, across the rooftops, humming high-pitched and tremulous in the bouncing telephone wires. The sound was enough to alert madness, and he wouldn't be surprised if that's exactly what threatened to happen after twenty-four hours: tempers disintegrating, arguments sparked and fanned by impatience, children banished unreasonably to their rooms, and more than one family wishing they hadn't thought it such a lark to remain behind and taunt the weather.

Assuming this was nothing more than a storm.

As he rounded the corner and headed for the police station, he swerved widely to avoid any indentation in the hedgewall that might hide the dead, not caring if he was being overcautious; anything less and he knew he'd be gone. And just as he reached the first window of the cell block, he saw the patrol car sitting in the middle of the intersection. Its headlights were on, and Garve was leaning out the window, beckoning urgently. Colin jumped the curb and splashed through the shallow running water, ducked around the hood and clambered inside.

"I gotta show you something," the chief said, not waiting for agreement but moving the cruiser off. Colin looked through the rear window to be sure his car was still at the curb, then shifted and explained what he and the others had come up with in the library. Even now, after accepting it, he detected a hint of disbelief in his own voice. It was someone else talking; he was back in his studio, working on Peg's portrait.

"Yeah," Garve said. "Yeah, and I thought of something else. All those folks who left on Friday? That weird we had all day? Bet it was him doing that. Far as I can see, the people who took off didn't mean a shit to Gran one way or the other. The only ones that stuck back are the ones he wanted. Col, as far as I can tell, there isn't anyone left but us. Not anyone alive, that is."

Colin considered this for a moment, and thought *why not?* It made about as much sense as anything else around here. But he did not like the idea that a man dead and unburied should be manipulating him as if he were little more than . . . he sniffed, wiped his palm over the shotgun's stock and refused to think the rest.

Then the blacktop on Neptune ran out and they were crunching loudly over gravel, the trees thickening for a hundred close yards before giving way to the expanse of the marina. When Garve pointed over the wheel, Colin gripped the edge of the dashboard and groaned.

The boats. Most were gone, and those still at their moorings had been wind-driven either onto the grassy shore or dashed hard against the docks. A few had burned. Every sailboat he could see was turned keel up.

"The storm?" he asked hoarsely, hopelessly.

"I thought so until I checked, and I doubt it now. I think at least half of them were untied or had their lines cut through. Took the binoculars and checked the mainland, what I could see of it. Spotted Ed Raines' trawler beached there, a couple of others. Lilla, probably. Gran isn't stupid."

He turned his gaze to the large open workbarn, and the house.

"No one," Garve told him, not needing a question. "The place is empty. I don't recall him leaving, but there's a few windows busted and I can't tell if they were broken into or just broken."

"Nothing left?" he asked dejectedly.

"I didn't say that." Tabor nodded toward the rocky shore just west of the house. "I found a small lifeboat that hadn't been bashed up. Dragged it into the trees. I think it's from the trawler."

"Then we *can* get off."

"Yeah. Eventually."

He eased the car forward to the end of the gravel, turned over the lawn and started to back up. The water was running high, white-foamed, regularly sloshing over the docks and leaving froth behind. As Colin watched, more numbed than dismayed, a small red speedboat was rammed repeatedly into a larger, sleek cabin cruiser; from the damage done to both hulls, he knew it must have been going on for hours. Then the two separated with a lurch, and the speedboat began to sink, submerging as far as its remaining mooring line would permit; the cabin cruiser listed sharply, the canvas awning over its flying bridge snapping at the air and tearing itself to writhing ribbons.

"This end of the island always floods first," Garve said as he maneuvered the car back toward town. "Lower, see. I just hope Alex and Sue were able to get the kids—"

298

He broke off when Colin turned away from the docks, gagged and pointed up the road.

Someone was standing in the middle of the gravel, and there were two others behind him.

It was Eliot, and his left arm was missing, the tattered ends of his uniform's shoulder curled away to expose bone and red-gray flesh. The others were Amy and Tommy Fox, Amy in jeans and a torn shirt, Tommy in a bathing suit, lacerations redly marking his thin chest.

Garve made a sound almost like sobbing; Colin looked for a way for the car to go around, but the trees were too close on the left, and the house too close on the right. If they were going to get back to the police station, they'd have to run the deputy and the children down.

"I . . . *can't*," the chief said, strangling the steering wheel.

"C'mon, Grave," he urged almost tearfully. "Jesus, C'*mon*."

Tabor rolled down the window and stuck out his head. "God damn you, Eliot! God damn you!"

Colin grabbed for his shoulder, threw himself back when a shadow appeared through the mist on the driver's side. Tabor yelped and closed the window, wiping tears from his face as the shadow began thumping on the door. He cringed away, fumbling for his revolver. Colin didn't know whether to try to shoot through the windshield or scream at the chief to get moving. Then Nichols approached the hood and began rocking the car violently while the children came to Colin's side and pounded their fists against the window.

They said nothing.

They stared, and the only sound was the rhythmic creaking of the car and the staccato crack of small knuckles.

He yelled and tried to bring the shotgun up, but Tabor was frantically trying to clear off his seatbelt, his elbow and hand slamming Colin in the ribs. He yelled even louder when the mist cleared for a moment and he saw Susan Fox struggling with the handle. He thought she was yelling back until he realized that her jaw had been broken and she couldn't close her mouth; neither could she swallow, and water ran freely over her teeth and bruised lip.

El slammed his palms on the hood.

Amy and Tommy had rocks now and had turned the window to spider webbing.

"Out!" Colin said, slapping Garve's shoulder. He gripped his weapon tightly, squirmed until his feet were in position against the door. When Tabor jabbed a finger into his shoulder signaling he was ready, Colin reached forward awkwardly, pulled up the lock button and at the same time kicked out viciously. The children fell away and back without a sound, and he was out and running, Tabor scrambling right behind him.

They raced past the front of the house—the front door was battered open, canted on one hinge—swerved to avoid the brick wishing well, and plunged directly into the woods without looking back. The patrol car's horn began to blare, and the siren shrieked madly over the voice of the Screamer.

In the trees they were caught in a maelstrom of hornets as the windstorm wrenched the remaining leaves from their places and propelled them between the boles. Edges stung and slashed, twigs jabbed for their eyes and lanced their cheeks and necks, hollows and depressions filled in rapidly and caused them more than once to go down on one knee because they thought they were on solid ground. Then Garve snared Colin's arm and began guiding him roughly to the left, and he could see through the bare branches the fractured outlines of houses.

Peg, he thought, for God's sake wait.

The wind screamed, and he wanted to scream back.

They lashed and kneed their way through a low wall of shrubs, flailed and stumbled out over the low curbing onto Ocean Avenue directly in front of Hugh

Montgomery's house. The street was deserted, an automobile midway up the long block tipped over on its side.

Colin's lungs burned, his throat was coarsely dry, and a pinprick of pain centered and spread through his left ankle. He gulped for air and raised his face to the sky, cornered his second wind and was about to move on, when Garve spotted the open office door. The chief slowed, apprehensive and indecisive, trotting several paces backward to check the forest behind them before he cut to his left and sprinted up the driveway. Colin shouted at him angrily and followed with a fruitless curse, slowing as Tabor stopped at the door and peered inside.

Neither could see anything but the wind-torn reception area, the open door to the examination room at the end of the short paneled hallway. This black-leather table had been overturned, a medicine cabinet and mirror smashed on top of it. Plastic vials rolled without pattern across the linoleum, and a wide arm of gauze bandage fluttered weakly against the baseboard.

They listened, and heard nothing.

Tabor moved forward cautiously, Colin impatiently behind. In the passageway they saw, passed, and returned to a narrow closet door battered but unbroken. Garve motioned him away from it, took the other side and lifted a hand. Hesitated. Moistened his lips and slammed a fist against the hinge. They dropped instantly to the floor when a shot was fired through the wood and a framed print of a pheasant in flight shattered on the opposite wall.

"No!" Garve shouted when another shot was fired. "Jesus, it's us!"

The brass knob turned slowly, and Colin aimed at the crack as the door opened in tiny fits and jerks. A moment later Annalee stumbled out, her eyes glittering tears, her cheeks streaked with dried blood. Garve took her instantly, embraced her, and guided her gently into the reception room to sit her down on the couch. Her long hair was damp and matted dark, her nurse's uniform torn at the seams under her arms and across her shoulders. Colin stood guard at the entrance. Garve held her upper arms until her trembling ceased, and he was able to fill her in on most of what had happened.

She doubted none of it. A flare of startled disbelief was extinguished when Colin corroborated in silence.

"They . . . came here," she said, the words more like sobbing. "God, they came, three or four of them. I thought Amy had hurt herself and I almost . . . then she threw a lamp at me and Tommy tried to rip off my uniform and they were so damned strong . . . the closet . . . I ran through the house but none of the phones were working, so I came back and hid in the closet. I couldn't go outside. Nichols was out there, down by the sidewalk."

"It's all right now, Lee, you're with us," Garve said, his gentle tone belied by the lowering of his brow. "You want some water?"

"God, no! I need . . . I need . . ." Her teeth clattered, her hands began to jump, and Tabor gathered her to his chest and rocked her for several minutes, stroking her hair and looking at Colin. Though he was anxious to get back, Colin smiled quickly, looked outside and finally said, "Zombies."

"What?"

"I said they're zombies."

Garve shuddered. "For a minute there I thought you said they were vampires."

"What's the difference?" he said in resignation. "What's the goddamned difference?" It was a Saturday matinee come alive, and there was no difference at all. He let a heartbeat pass before he added, "We have to get going, Garve. Peg and the boy are waiting for us at the restaurant."

Annalee insisted she was all right when Garve protested the rush, and they huddled at the door for the length of a scream before they plunged outside and began to hurry down the sidewalk. Lee's bravado notwithstanding, they could neither run nor trot; a fast

302

walk was all the storm and her nerves would permit them until they finally reached the corner and looked over to the Clipper Run.

Bridge Road was an inch or more deep in sea water along its gutters, and he estimated only an hour of two more before the storm drains were filled to overflowing. It was bad enough that the daylight had virtually slipped out of the air; there were only the streetlights now, rocking on their bases, their light blurring to a flat haze that barely reached the ground.

They crossed and made for the entrance, a step away from running when Colin slapped Garve's chest.

The door was open.

"Shit," he whispered. "Oh *shit!*"

When he eased up the walk he could see Cameron's body lying over the cloakroom door. The wind had puffed one trouser leg, and was rippling the other. His shoes had fallen off.

Despite his own warning to the others, the sight of the dead man smothered all caution. He charged into the restaurant calling Peg and Matt, paused only long enough to see that the dining room was empty before checking the office to find that empty as well. He staggered against the door frame and took several deep breaths, refusing to believe that Gran had somehow trapped them, unsure what to do if that had in fact happened.

A hand grabbed his shoulder.

He turned with a soundless shout, and Garve slapped the shotgun's barrel away from his face.

"Out the back," Tabor said, and pushed through the kitchen doors. Colin followed, incredibly and frighteningly tired, his vision softened and his reflexes too slow as he walked through the maze of white counters and mirrored appliances and out the side exit, not realizing until the wind revived them that Annalee had been holding his hand. She lay an arm around his shoulder and kept him in Tabor's wake, releasing him only when they reached the hedgebreak and pushed through.

303

Then he was running again, around the corner of the police station and hurtling through the door—but the office was empty.

"Peg! Matt!"

He had turned to tell the others they had missed them again, heard someone call his name, back in the cell block. He dropped the shotgun an Nichols' desk and ran, took hold of the doorjamb to stop him when he saw the trio sitting in the middle cell.

"It seemed," Peg said, "the safest place."

Hugh grinned.

Matt reached through the bars, groping for his hand.

They arranged themselves in the front office as comfortably as they could, most of them choosing a way to see through the front door's pane, to watch the leaves streak by in tricolor armies, to charge the building and scrape at the plywood. The water still fell over the curbing, the drains still swallowed, but high tide was less than four hours away, and unless the storm abated soon they wouldn't even be able to use the cars.

Then Annalee said, "They know where we are," and there was an uneasy stirring, a shifting. Colin put a hand to his forehead and rubbed. But it was true; Gran in whatever forms he could take to direct his revenge was evidently able to ferret them out, and Colin couldn't help wondering again if they weren't being herded. He wouldn't put it past the old man. Enemies taken one by one was perhaps a more satisfying situation; but enemies taken in a group was ill-guided justice delivered in exultation.

The idea should have depressed him, sent him back to the despair he'd felt when he had understood what the dead sought. Yet it didn't. The more he considered it the more a buoyancy filled his chest like a slow-rising bubble. It excited him, revitalized him—Gran in a hurry might just mean Gran against a deadline, that whatever he had done to reassure his return was something less than permanent. A day. Two days. Certainly not more. He tucked his chin toward his chest and stared at the floor, at the damp footprints drying to shadows, and he wondered further if Gran in his hatred had failed to reckon on Lilla's last attempts to warn them, or had underestimated their acceptance of something usually left to campfire stories and films of the thirties.

It was possible.

It had to be possible or they had no chance at all.

When he had assembled it, reordered it, and put it to the rest, there were no serious objections.

"You're surely not suggesting we wait him out," Hugh said grimly. "You're not, are you, Colin?"

"No. Not a bit."

"Just so I know."

"Why not?" Peg asked, though there was no contradiction in the question.

"Doubt," he said. "As long as there's doubt we don't dare take the chance."

She agreed, and began dusting at her knees. "There's something else," she said.

They waited.

"Suppose . . . suppose we're wrong and he doesn't have this deadline we've assumed. Suppose he can go on unless we take care of him." Her hands drifted up to her lap, still dusting. "Then if they get to the mainland—"

"Yes," Colin interrupted when he saw the look on Matt's face.

"Then I suggest we stop speculating and get on with it," Hugh said, standing. "We should take both cars, though, in case one conks out. Gran's place is fairly high on the slope, as I recall, so we shouldn't have trouble with the tide. Not yet."

"The ladies," Garve said then, looking to Matt to include him as well. "I don't think they should come with us."

"No," Annalee and Peg protested together.

"Right," Colin said. "The last time we split up we nearly had a disaster. Better we should do it in a group."

"In a mob," Hugh said sourly. When Colin looked at him, surprised, the doctor raised a shoulder. "A mob, right? That's what we are. The peasants charging the windmill at the end of *Frankenstein*, burn the sucker down and scatter the ashes." Then he grinned. "Always wanted to be a peasant. Not for life, you understand, but just for a while."

"Well, peasant," Colin said in relief, "let's get the torches and move out."

No one, however, hurried for the door. They were subdued, pleased that Hugh had regained his humor, less than pleased they had to confront a specter they'd once thought themselves incapable of accepting. Their expressions were the same: anxious, angry, let's be done with it so I can wake up and scream.

Peg smoothed Matthew's hair and kissed him on the cheek, not caring when he squirmed and protested with a quiet, "Mom." Colin filled his trouser pockets with shells, made sure both Peg and Hugh were given the other shotguns; Garve took a rifle, Annalee the same. When Matt complained he was the only one without a weapon, Tabor, without asking the boy's mother, handed him a revolver and pointed to the safety. Matt held it gingerly, his expression solemn as it dwarfed his small grip, then tucked it into his waistband and took his mother's hand to lead her to Colin's car. Hugh and his nurse rode with the chief.

The windshield fogged over the moment Colin turned on the ignition, Matt in the middle switched on the defroster. When the glass cleared he turned on the wipers, and it was the only sound they heard as they pulled away from the curb.

They made only one stop, at the Fletcher house to take the red cans of kerosene from the shed in the backyard and put them in Tabor's trunk. They worked without a sound, none wanting to look at the empty house around them.

306

Then they were back on the road, heading south out of town.

The headlights sparkled as the mist fell out of the dark.

The water sweeping across the road rose whitely against the tires.

"Mom," Matt said as they passed the gas station and headed into the woods, "what about Lilla?"

She refused to answer; Colin saw her hands tighten on the barrel.

"What about her, pal?" he said into the silence. "She isn't dead, is she?"

"No."

"Then shouldn't we try to save her, too?"

"No!" Peg said, scarcely parting her lips.

"If she's alive—"

"Matt," Colin said quickly, "when we do what we have to at Gran's, we'll see. Right now, though, there's nothing left of the Lilla we used to know. You saw that when we had her before. I think . . . I think that her trying to help us did something to her mind. That part of it we knew is long gone, I'm afraid."

"There's doctors for that, though," he persisted. "She talked to me in the jail. I mean, she really talked to me. She called me Little Matt, just like always."

He heard the boy's anguish, and felt his mother's rage. "Matt, for what we've all been through today, there are no doctors at all. And none for Lilla, either."

"It isn't fair," he pouted. "It isn't fair. I never met a real witch before. It isn't fair."

"She deserves to die," Peg said heatedly. Defiance pulled at her lips when she turned to look at Colin. "Well, she does! She started all this, and it won't end until she's dead."

"That's Gran, Peg," he said calmly. "That's Gran. Lilla never has been anything more than a dupe."

"What's a dupe?" Matt said.

"A dupe is a fool who believes someone who's lying," his mother said, staring hard out the side window. "Gran wasn't lying, and Lilla knew it."

307

Colin opened his mouth to disagree, changed his mind and concentrated on his driving. Peg's hostility bothered him a great deal, though he thought he understood why. And he was guiltily pleased that Matt had voiced what he'd been thinking himself. It was entirely possible that Lilla's retreat would be reversed when Gran was taken care of, and he didn't think it right they abandon her when all was done.

The wind shoved the car hard to the right, and his wrists were beginning to ache with the effort to keep the wheels straight.

Slow, he ordered when he felt the car's acceleration. Slow, you jackass, or you'll take out a tree.

Matt cleared his throat.

A rock thumped under a tire and they all held their breath.

The windshield wipers seemed louder, more final.

"Oh," Peg said as they passed between the twin motels.

He looked, and nearly braked. On the side of the road was Carter Naughton, walking. The headlights paled him, took him out of the dark until the car was abreast. He did not turn his head; he staggered sideways, righted, and kept on walking.

Twenty yards later they passed Tess Mayfair; on the left side Mitch and Rose Adams.

Pebbles rattled against the undercarriage, and a dead leaf plastered itself against Colin's window.

Denise was with her brother fifty yards along; the ax was gone from her shoulder, the naked bone stark and obscenely clean in the passing light.

"What are you *doing*?" Peg whispered, and he started, not realizing he'd taken his foot off the pedal.

Alex Fox, in his best suit.

Susan behind him.

The patrol car's horn blared, and he gasped while Peg grabbed for Matthew. The horn blared again. None of the dead looked around or slowed.

There was still sufficient light to outline the treetops, to give black substance to the swift-sailing clouds.

Muriel North beside Reverend Otter, whose head rocked on what little muscle had been left at his dying.

The temperature in the car rose until Colin cranked down his window an inch or two, no more. The wind was cut to a breeze, and it cooled him though the air itself was warm.

Hattie Mills, her blouse shredded and her black skirt in ribbons down her right side. Colin refused to watch her, though he felt Peg's gaze shift to see his reaction.

"They're gonna see Gran," Matt said matter-of-factly. His thumb rubbed over the rough butt of his gun.

Bill Efron, his vest open and his thick white hair spotted with mud.

Michael Lombard, carrying Bob Cameron.

Theo Vincent, dragging a bar stool in each hand.

Matt knelt on the seat and stared intently out the rear window. "Gee," he said softly. "Gee."

"Goddamn it, Matthew!" Peg exploded. She grabbed the back of his neck and forced him to turn around. "This isn't a game! This isn't a goddamned game!" Spittle bubbled in the corners of her mouth and she wiped it away with a darting, rigid finger.

"I know that," Matt said, jerking his head to shake his mother's hand away. "I know that."

Amy and Tommy Fox walked the center line. Colin slowed and drifted around them. Water from the tires eddied around their ankles and up over their shoes. Tommy carried a rock; Amy's hands were empty.

They passed no one else, and when he could no longer see the children in the rearview mirror he pulled over slightly and rolled the window down the rest of the way. He waved the patrol car alongside, and waited for Annalee to bring hers down too.

"Matt thinks they're going to Gran's," he shouted over the storm.

The others nodded. Hugh leaned forward, green-faced, his glasses blind. "Less time than we thought."

"Yeah."

"Maybe we should—"

Colin didn't hear the rest. Tabor suddenly accelerated as the island began to rise and the road lost its
shallow river. He sounded the horn twice, twice more,
and Colin followed closely despite his struggling with
the wind. The wheels shimmied, and he gritted his
teeth. Spray from the cruiser nearly blinded him until
he backed off. Matt leaned forward eagerly, biting his
lower lip until his mother ordered him into the back.
He did not argue. He clambered over the seat and
folded his arms on the rear shelf, watching for signs
the dead were in pursuit.

Too fast, Colin thought as he fought to keep the car
on the road, we're going too damned—

Suddenly the patrol car's brake lights flared, and it
began to slide inexorably to the right, sharply to the
left, finally skewed into a complete turn while still
moving forward. Peg shouted wordlessly as Colin
swerved to avoid the skidding vehicle, puzzled when
he saw streaks of black on the tarmac. Then his own
car lost its traction. He grunted, ignored Peg's warning
when he saw the pair of downed trees stretched across
the road. Tabor was unable to avoid the storm-born
deadfall, and Colin heard the ripping of metal as the
cruiser slammed broadside into the first trunk.

He spun the wheel desperately, touching the brake
pedal lightly as he found himself helplessly caught in a
spin. Then the right front wheel held and they were
jolted past the uprooted trees, branches scratching and
screeching like nails along the side. Peg smothered a
scream behind her hands. Matt instantly dropped to
the floorboard and covered his head with his arms.
The car jounced over the shoulder, and Colin threw up
his hands as they plowed through the picket fence at
the boarding house lawn.

Slats flew up and to the side, speared one headlight,
cracked against the doors.

The brakes locked, and they skidded across the
muddy lawn.

"Down!" he shouted, and threw himself to one side,
grabbing Peg as he did and forcing her beneath him.

The car slammed into the latice-work beneath the front porch, struck a brick-and-concrete post and shoved it two feet off its base before momentum was spent and the porch collapsed around them. Colin was thrown up and back, and when the automobile stopped, his forehead struck the dash. He groaned and fought for breath. He felt his heart racing, saw slashes of red, of white, of deep midnight black scale at him like knives. He closed his eyes, but the knives kept coming and he couldn't decide if he should call out or swallow what tasted like blood in his mouth.

There was something sticky and wet on his chin, something prodding his back, something trying to tell him he wasn't alone.

He tried to sit up, had no idea where he was or how he was trapped.

He tasted salt, he tasted blood, and he thought he heard Matt crying before the red and the white gave way to the black, and the last thing he heard was the wind hissing through broken glass.

Matt hurt.

The back of his neck, the length of his spine, the side of his left arm stung and throbbed, and for a terrifying moment he thought his father had come back to beat him for being bad. There were funny colors in his head for several unnerving seconds, then funny sounds in his ears until he uncoiled stiffly and sat up with a sigh. He could see nothing over the back of the seat, and when he looked to the rear window he saw a criss-cross of splintered wood, a waterfall of dust. Metal creaked, and something thumped onto the trunk. A soft hissing. A faint dripping. A startling rain of planks, as more of the porch flooring broke loose and gave way.

Gritting his teeth and swallowing acid that filled his mouth, he pressed a palm against the seat and pushed himself up. His lips quivered, and his eyes filled with tears not caused just by the pain. Colin was lying half under the steering wheel like a doll discarded in anger;

his mother was still sitting up, her head tilted to one side, her cheek on her shoulder. Blood on the dashboard. Blood on her shirt. Colin's face was red and shining like sweat.

He couldn't tell if they were breathing.

The keys in the ignition clinked like dead wind chimes.

He reached for his mother's shoulder and shook it, tenderly, not wanting to hurt her any more than she was. He whispered her name, he whispered Colin's, and he cried. Then he scolded himself for wasting time. They were unconscious and couldn't hear him. He would have to get out and fetch Chief Tabor to help.

He reached over the seat and pulled back the door handle, pushed and whimpered when the door didn't budge.

The car wobbled as if it were balanced on a stick.

He sniffed and wiped a sleeve under his nose.

He wished the tiny back windows could be rolled down so he could slip out.

He tried the door again, and knew he couldn't do it from the angle he was using. Gingerly, then, sucking in air loudly, he climbed into the front, crying out softly when his mother slipped sideways and her right hand fell onto Colin's bloodied hair. He tried not to look at them, tried not to compare them to the way he had seen Tess Mayfair.

They're not breathing.

Yes they are! Yes they are!

He put his shoulder to the door and pushed with all his might, filling his cheeks, tightening his stomach; he felt the door give.

Another shove and a kick, and a spattering of dust covered his head.

Again, and again, until there was just enough space for him to slide out of the car.

"Hang on, Mom," he said, swallowing and wanting desperately to give her a hug. "Hang on. I'll be back. Hang on, please. Please!"

312

Still crying and not caring, he squirmed out and made his way on hands and knees to the rear bumper. He could see the outside. There was a large gap between two sections of flooring, and he hurried as fast as he dared through it, fell over a length of railing and landed down on the wet grass.

He sobbed, and scrambled to his feet. The pain was still there but he put it away in a mind place that let him stagger to the gap where the car had gone through the fence. He couldn't see over the deadfall, but he could see the cruiser's lights shining into the woods on the other side.

There was nothing to hear no matter how hard he tried.

A deep breath for courage, and he took a step forward, reined in when he saw Amy Fox walking into the light with her brother.

He started to call them, and then he remembered.

He looked down at his shoes and saw earthworms swarming over the sidewalk and the curb, driven out of the ground by the influx of water.

Amy's head began to swivel in his direction.

His hand went to his waist, and he looked down when he couldn't find the butt of his revolver. It was gone. It had fallen out in the accident, and Amy's head was still turning. He whirled around and raced wildly back toward the car, veered and climbed nimbly onto the sagging porch, through the open front door and threw himself against the wall of the entry hall. He watched. He waited. They'll find you, he thought, and staggered deeper into the house, saw a door under the staircase, pulled it open and fell inside. It closed by itself. It was dark and it was warm. He hurt so much he wanted to scream.

He listened, then. Listened for Amy and Tommy wanting him to play. He prayed his mother and Colin would stay in the car. Amy and Tommy would find them if they didn't. Then the pain came again; the dark began to spin, the funny lights returned, and he slumped over to the floor.

313

Worms and fish of a hundred different colors, slipping between his fingers as he tried to stop them from eating and nibbling their way through his stomach; worms with horns, and fish with fangs instead of teeth, gnawing on his arms and chewing on his legs and spinning away from screams no one heard but himself; worms and fish and ugly white things that burrowed and tunneled and popped out through his chest with dark grinning faces that looked just like Gran.

A colorless corridor swarming with sea gulls; a colorless hallway flooded by the sea; a room, his room, filled to the windowsill with gleaming black kelp whose fronds groped for him when he tried vainly to raise the sash, lashed at him when he tried vainly to push through to the door, snagged his elbows and neck when he took out his penknife and tried to stab them away.

Worms, and fish, and the sea water rising, and no sign of his mother and no sign of Colin, and the light beginning to fade and he was afraid of the dark because it talked to him nicely, and whispered to him sweetly, and filled swiftly with fog that drew away, and glowed, and twisted into a serpent that opened its red mouth and swallowed him without a sound, sucked him into a place where he saw a dim light, a dimming light, a curiously dim light that . . .

. . . made him wince and groan when he blinked his eyes and sat up. Disorientation had him staring at nothing until he remembered Amy Fox, the trees, and the car. Then there were *things* in the closet with him, touching his head and face, groping for his throat. He thrashed and yelled, reached up to bat them away until his hand closed on one and he realized with a gasping it was only a coat sleeve.

He whimpered and lowered his head, sobbed and swallowed air until the shaking stopped. Then he prodded his chest and legs to be sure he was still in one piece and the worms and fish hadn't gotten him. He reached up for the latch, but the door wouldn't open. He stood and pulled frantically, calling out once for someone to hear him, stopped when he thought it might be Tommy who would. He pulled again, shook his head at his mistake, and pushed, kicked at the base until the door swung out and he was propelled by his momentum into the opposite wall. He made his way to the door.

The weakened porch roof had sagged, and he couldn't see most of the floor, but Amy was gone and so was her brother.

A strand of mist spiraled up from the lawn.

Mom!

Less frantic now, but no less hurried, he inched along the front of the house until he reached the steps, jumped and scrambled around to the place where the automobile had plowed under and stopped.

"Mom! Mr. Ross!"

He couldn't see through the rear window, and he didn't want to go under there again; the wood was dangling spikes into the dark and something moaned in the shadows every time the wind strengthened.

He climbed across the slippery debris, balancing himself, almost holding his breath. "Mom!" he said as he wrenched at the door and prepared to pull her out. "Mom, I'm—"

She was gone. Mr. Ross was gone. There was blood on the seat; the keys were still in the ignition. He leaned in to check the back; there was nothing there, either. He couldn't even see the gun the police chief had lent him.

He backed out painfully, backed all the way to the lawn where he sat on the grass and stared mutely at the house. He was too late. He just knew it. He had run away from Amy and Tommy, had let his mother down, had let Colin down, and now they were with *them*.

Now they were with Gran.

And he was all alone.

"Mom," he whispered.

The worms, and the fish, and the dark calling sweetly . . .

The wind reached out of the blackening sky and

315

shoved his hair into his eyes. He brushed it away angrily and swayed to his feet.

Gone. Captured, he was certain.

He had wanted to help them, had wanted to save them, and he hadn't done anything but run away and hide.

Numbly, not even sure if he were still in pain, he shuffled across the lawn. After a moment he took hold of a loose slat from the ruined fence, yanked it free effortlessly, and held it at his waist. It probably wouldn't help, but it would be better than nothing. He felt tears, then, and let them fall for several seconds before wiping them away with his sleeve and heading for the deadfall.

The patrol car was still there.

There was no one inside.

The chief, then, and Doctor Montgomery, and his tall, pretty nurse. They were gone. They were all gone. And he was alone.

They were going to Gran's shack, to burn it, he remembered. Maybe he could burn it instead. Maybe he could take that dead old man by the throat and toss him back into the water where he came from. Maybe he could save the world from Gran turning it into *things*.

Maybe.

And maybe he could do nothing. He had no matches and no fuel and the wind was so strong that even if he did he probably wouldn't make it.

Besides, there was still Amy and Tommy, still his mother and Colin. And he didn't want to see them the way they had to be now.

Damn Gran and Lilla for—

He turned abruptly, as if he'd heard someone behind him.

Lilla! His eyes shifted from side to side while he chewed on a corner of his mouth.

Lilla. No matter what anyone said, she was still alive even if she was crazy, and maybe between the two of them they could get off the island and bring

316

back help for his mother. She probably wasn't really dead anyway, right? She and Colin were probably just under some kind of spell, and Lilla was a witch so she would know the right words to bring everyone back.

And there was that boat the chief talked about, the one he saved at the marina.

He started to walk toward the end of the road.

It might work. It would work. Lilla was his friend from the days before all the dying, and she remembered him enough to look for him at Amy's, right? She didn't hurt him then, right? Even if Gran was inside her—though he didn't know how—she wouldn't hurt him because he had been Gran's favorite, they were going to be kings. So she was really his friend. She knew he was her friend, too, like at the jail when she showed him how to bring on the fog.

And if they could get that boat and go for the police . . .

He began to run.

Lilla. Crazy Lilla.

He swallowed and promised his mother he'd be back before she knew it, back with the right words and the right way to move his hands and the right everything and before she knew it she wouldn't have to walk that way anymore or do what Gran said or be hurt or anything. He promised her as he sprinted off the tarmac onto the path that led to the cliffs.

He knew where Lilla was.

He wasn't the only one who liked to crawl around in the caves and hunt for buried treasure and look for pirate bones all left in little piles; he'd seen her there a lot, and if she was afraid of Gran like Colin said she was, then it was the perfect place to hide. The other *things* couldn't get her there, because look what happened to old, fat Tessie Mayfair when she tried to get Colin. Fell right off. She fell right off and took forever to get back.

Though he didn't know why, he knew it had something to do with the salt in the water.

He ran over the spongy ground, swinging the picket

sword back and forth ahead of him, ducking when a spray of leaves whispered and sliced past his face, jumping over dead branches tossed to the ground by the wind. It was dark in here, but not as dark as it would be when night finally came. Dark, but not as dark as the day before when all the leaves were on the trees.

And there were darker shapes deeper in the woods that paced him and ran ahead of him. He wasn't sure who they were, or if it was only his imagination, and purpose gave way to panic as he tried to lengthen his stride.

His chest hurt. His left arm hurt. There was a stinging inside his head that wouldn't go away, and a roaring in one ear that made him dizzy.

He didn't dare stop. He had to stop. Just for a minute, it wouldn't take long, just for a minute so he could catch his breath and start all over.

He slowed, gulping and holding his right side, bending over, coughing, and spitting dryly on the ground.

Then he straightened and reminded himself what he had to do.

He ran hard, heard a thrashing, ran as hard as he could, and came around the last turn before the trees fell away.

Eliot Nichols stood in the path, watching.

Matt slipped and skidded to a stop just before he ran into the deputy, holding out the makeshift sword and slashing it back and forth while he looked desperately around him.

Nichols moved toward him, empty shirt sleeve flapping like a broken wing, face pale, eyes dead white.

"Go away," Matt said huskily, not wanting to leave the path in case there were others out there waiting. "Go away, you son of a bitch."

Eliot reached out, his hand streaked with dried mud and blood.

Matt shouted as loudly as he could and threw the picket at Nichols' head. It struck the deputy flat on the mouth and snapped his head back as if he'd been shot.

Matt bolted off the path, batted away the brush, took a moss-covered log in a leap and landed still running. He didn't look back; there were too many things trying to snare him and trip him and pull him down into the mud, too many dark places where he knew he heard voices telling him to join them.

He swerved around a boulder, ducked under a branch, and tripped over something he couldn't see at his feet.

He yelled as he fell, turned as he hit the ground and found himself crouched on the flat above the cliffs.

He was alone.

Above him the Screamer was ripping apart the clouds, allowing him just enough light to see the ocean below—white, and gray, and a belligerent, swirling black. The wind shrieked and the Atlantic bellowed; the clouds tore themselves to writhing shreds and the waves sideswiped the cliff face on their way to the mainland.

Harsh stinging spray drenched him instantly, and he blinked away the water as he crawled to the spot from which he knew he could climb down. He looked over the edge. The tide was in and high; another twenty feet and the most persistent waves would ride over the top. He licked his lips and tasted salt. If Lilla was down there, then there was only one place she could be. If she'd climbed any lower she would have drowned by now.

He willed her to be alive.

He willed her not to be as crazy as they thought.

He wiped his hands on his shirt and lowered himself over the edge.

The rock was slippery and dark, almost green, and the worn spots on the steep pathway were filled with trembling water.

His ears ached from the waves that slammed the rock below him.

His chest ached, and his knees. When he reached the first ledge he dropped against the rock face and covered his eyes with his hands.

The cave was less than six feet away.

All he had to do was get up and move over, climb over a low mound of smooth stone and he'd be there.

That was all, and he didn't want to do it.

"Mom," he whispered, "Mom. Mom."

If Lilla wasn't there, then his Mom was really dead.

A wave hunched and surged without breaking, sliding off the cliff face and falling back into its trough.

He grunted, not sure if the water on his face was from the ocean or his tears, and staggered to his feet. The wind shoved him back down. He cried out as he began a slow slide toward the edge, clawed at the rough path until he felt the sliding stop. He wanted to be back in school; he wanted to be in his room watching James Bond and Christopher Lee; he wanted to be in Colin's studio, looking at all the paintings Colin said were no good but he was keeping them around just to keep his ego down. He didn't know what ego was, but if Colin said that was important then he guessed it had to be. He wanted to be up top again. He wanted . . .

He sobbed, and crawled, and made it to the mound that rose as high as his head. He reached up and gripped the top, pulled himself to his knees and with a shout threw himself over.

He fell only two feet, slid two feet more under the cave's ragged overhang. The mouth was only four feet across, but the cave itself dug twenty feet into the island, the roof lifting enough so that someone like him could stand.

He sat up, pulled his legs under him and knelt.

"Lilla?"

He frowned as he tried to listen for an answer, peering into the dark to see if he could spot her.

"Lilla?"

He cupped his hands around his mouth and called her name again before he took a deep breath and moved deeper inside.

There was no light at all now.

At his back, the ocean.

The cave widened, and the battle sound of the surf was so loud it was almost silent.

Halfway to the back he began to cry.

She was gone. He was wrong, and she wasn't here. There was nothing on the ground that he could see, no candles, no lanterns, no flashlights. She wasn't here, and he had wasted all this time for nothing.

He dropped to his knees heavily.

Not here. Lilla wasn't here.

His mother and Colin were dead.

He drew up his legs and folded his arms around his calves, pushed his chin to his knee and let the tears come. He didn't care if he sounded like a baby. He didn't care.

"Aw, nuts," he sobbed. "Nuts. Goddamn."

Then he looked up and saw the shadow in the cave.

It was outlined by the last of the day's light, and it was moving toward him. Slowly. Without a sound. Its hands at its side, its head lowered.

He couldn't pull away; he was as far back against the wall as he could go, and he was so awfully tired that all he could do was shake his head. If there were words to stop the shadow he would have said them, but Lilla had all the words and he was just a kid and now he was going to be just like his mother.

The figure stopped.

It knelt before him.

It leaned close so he could see it.

"Hello, Little Matt," said Lilla with a smile, in a voice he wasn't sure was actually her own. "I sent the wind away. Can I play with you now?"

THREE

Night

Colin could think of nothing to say, and for a moment wished he'd been killed in the accident. As it was, he felt as though a great mass of living tissue had been scooped out of his chest and replaced with cold lead. A thin line of acid scorched across his forehead, and he stifled a groan. Peg didn't need that; she was beside him now, weeping silently as they followed Garve toward the dunes.

Ah, Matt, he thought, then pushed the thought away. There was neither sense in, nor time for, dwelling on the boy now. It was too late. He and Peg had regained consciousness at the same time, had seen the open car door and realized within seconds that the boy was missing. It had taken them a while to dig themselves out, a while longer in a frantic search of the yard and house before Peg had stopped dead in her tracks, turned to him and said, "Gran." Nothing more was needed. The boy had gotten out, and had been caught.

Colin stumbled over nothing and Peg took his arm, smiled at him grimly and pulled at him until they'd caught up with the others. Garve and Hugh were carrying the cans of kerosene taken from the cruiser's trunk; Lee held the shotguns. They'd been at the car when he and Peg finally reached it, using the first-aid kit from the glove compartment to bind their minor injuries. Lee's ankle, however, had been twisted, and she favored it with an awkward limp.

"I think my head's gonna fall off," he said quietly, gingerly putting a finger to the bulky bandage hastily cross-taped to his forehead. "God."

The side of Peg's neck was swathed, and she kept plucking at her shirt as if she were trying to pull off the blood. "I'm going to light it myself," she said tonelessly. "I'm going to burn that fucking old man my own goddamed self."

He shivered, not entirely from the chilled air, and took the fuel can from Tabor's hand to relieve him. The chief nodded his thanks, took a weapon from Lee and walked with her in front. Hugh was silent. His glasses were broken, the lenses smeared and shattered, yet he wore them anyway and couldn't stop reaching up to push them back into place.

"They'll be waiting for us," Garve said as they neared the bend in the road. Several of the streetlights were out, but there was still enough light from one on the corner for them to see the first dune. Tidal water from the yards poured into the street, swept over their shoes, surged now and again midway up their shins. "I don't know. I think they'll be waiting."

Of course they'll be waiting, Colin thought in sudden anger. What the hell did he expect them to do? Keep right on strolling into the goddamn ocean? Of course they were waiting—because Gran willed it.

The wind coasted directly into his eyes and he kept his head averted to keep his vision clear. He saw shadows beyond the curbing, shadows behind him, but he was too numb, too enraged to pay them close heed. Out of a whole town already cut down to a handful by the storm, there were only five of them left; out of a whole town, five to kill the dead.

Lee thrust a warning arm out, and they stopped at the road's bend—the Estates on their left, the dunes straight ahead, and Gran's shack in the darkness, off to the right.

At the top of the first dune stood Alex Fox, his blue

323

suit jacket flapping, part of his neck missing. Susan was beside him, her mouth grotesquely sagging.

Lee pumped a shell into the chamber at the same time Garve did, but no one moved.

"He's watching," Peg said, pushing her way to the front. "The son of a bitch is watching us."

Hugh took off his glasses and threw them away.

A window shattered explosively somewhere to their left.

Just before the last of the light had seeped from the sky they'd seen the clouds parting, disintegrating; there were no stars and there was no moon. Colin looked down at his empty hands and cursed. "Flashlights," he said in disgust. "We left the damned flashlight in the cars."

"No problem," Garve said without looking around. "Hugh and I'll get some from . . ." and he pointed toward the Estates.

"And leave us here alone?" Lee asked, astonished.

"Somebody's gotta watch them," the chief answered, using the shotgun for a pointer. "They're not going to stay there forever. Someone has to keep an eye out."

Alex swayed in the wind; Susan's skirt rolled and flared around her legs.

"Then go, for God's sake," Colin snapped, shoving at Tabor's shoulder. The two men broke into a run toward the nearest house, and Lee dropped back to stand beside Peg. Alex turned his head slightly; Susan stared whitely.

"Shoot them," Peg said flatly to Lee behind him. "Shoot the bastards."

"Peg," Colin said. "Peg."

"Shut up," she said. "Shut the hell *up*."

He saw her face then and didn't recognize her; the soft lines had creased, the eyes had turned to green stone, and despite the scratches and bruises that laced and splotched across her cheeks there was a colorless mask drawn from forehead to chin. Peg had lost herself when she'd lost her only child.

Lee was murmuring something calming to her then, but he couldn't hear it. The wind. The wind, and Alex Fox, and Matt out there somewhere walking around like a demonic puppet. And everything he'd worked for since he'd first come to Haven's End gone and done because of an old man's selfish hatred.

He began to breathe deeply.

Susan Fox stared at him.

The wind began to die.

At first he thought it was his imagination, that it was the blast of the night ocean against the flooded beach drowning out the storm. But when he looked up, looked around, he knew he was right. The storm was finally passing over.

He filled his lungs and held them full, held them full until he thought he would topple. Then he glared at the house where Garve and Hugh had vanished, glared toward the dark where Gran was waiting, and grabbed the shotgun from Lee's hands.

"Hey!"

He started for the curb, shrugging off her grasping hands, not bothering to look when he heard Peg say something sharply to her and heard a slap—hand against flesh, and Lee quietly moaning. He kept his gaze on Alex, stepped onto the sand and began a slow climb. The wind-blown spray had hardened the sand enough to prevent him from slipping, and when he was halfway up he stopped and raised the shotgun.

He could hear the sea water churning in the hollow between the two dunes.

Salt, he remembered saying, would keep these creatures on the island. The salt in the water.

Susan took a step down, Alex right beside her.

Peg called out a warning, and Tabor shouted angrily from a distance.

A flashlight beam took Susan in her face. Colin swallowed at the torn flesh, the gaping mouth, the blank dead eyes, and he pulled the trigger, then pumped in another round before the blast had lost its lightning. Susan toppled back, arms pinwheeling vainly until she fell over and he heard the muffled splash.

Alex moved more quickly, and Colin had to fire twice before the man was kicked into the water.

Tabor clamped his shoulder and spun him around. "What the hell good is that gonna do, goddamn it?"

Colin explained.

They climbed the rest of the way cautiously, waving the others behind. Sawgrass hummed. The wind died even more.

At the top, Garve directed the flash into the trough. Alex was floating face down and slowly turning; Susan's left hand poked out of the foam, dug into the sand.

"Son of a bitch," Garve whispered, grinning. "Son of a holy shit bitch!" And he turned and beckoned, his grin so wide Colin thought the chief would split his cheeks. But Colin felt the same—that finally they'd been able to do something, to win. So he grinned in return when Garve shook his hand enthusiastically, clapped his back, and stabbed the flashlight at the bodies for the others to see. Hugh nodded as he pulled at his drooping mustache, allowing himself a weak smile when Lee impulsively threw her arms around him.

Peg only stared.

"It's a start," Colin told her.

"Yes," she said, and made a sharp right turn.

The euphoria was brief, and the rest were soon on her heels, not stopping until the dune began to rise toward the flatland, the trees, and the shack hiding in the dark. Then Garve pushed his way to the front again, holding the flash in one hand, his gun in the other. Colin stayed beside him; Peg reluctantly followed.

They walked until the dunes were behind them and they were at the edge of Gran's clearing. The shack was thirty yards ahead, the beach fifty feet to their left hidden under foaming water. It was as if they had stepped onto an island.

Then Montgomery turned on his broad-beam flashlight and put a hand over his mouth.

They were there, over a dozen, ranged in a ragged line in front of the shack. All but El Nichols.

When the light struck their faces, their eyes glittered white.

"We'll never make it," Hugh said.

"Well, they can't run, for God's sake," Colin said heatedly. "And the spray, the . . . the salt spray, it must be slowing them down."

"There's too many," Hugh insisted, helplessly shaking his head. "There's too many. We'll be killed."

A few of them took a tentative step forward.

"Look," Colin said urgently, "there's no time to argue. They know we're here, and they can still follow us to some limited degree. Garve, you and Lee go to the left, over by the water there, and draw as many as you can toward you. Stick to the edge of the flat, and if you have to, jump in the water. They won't follow. Hugh, you and Peg go right. Same thing."

"And you?" Peg said. Her voice was cold.

"The first chance I get I'm going to get as close as I can and throw the cans against the shack. Someone, I don't give a damn who, shoot the hell out of them. The shack burns, Gran goes up in smoke, and . . ."He looked down, looked up. "And then we bury our friends."

Cart Naughton and Rose Adams began to walk.

"How do you know Gran's even in there?" Hugh said. "God, he could be anywhere!"

"My . . . Lord . . . how . . ." Colin could say nothing more. The goddamned fool had more questions than a seance, and he wished the idiot would either shut up or take off. But Hugh repeated the question, and he damned himself for not having an answer—because there was none. He didn't know. And realized he would have to be sure.

327

"No," Peg said, the cold gone for a moment, the mourning rage temporarily in abeyance. "No, I won't let you."

Frankie Adams picked up a rock, handed it to his father and picked up another.

"No time," he said. He gave the gun to Peg and hefted up the cans. "No time."

Thankfully, no one looked at him as though he were a hero. He didn't think he could stand that, not after having let Matthew down at the end. Besides, he was terrified. Standing here in the wind, listening to the surf dig itself a new coastline, watching animated corpses shuffling toward him, he was terrified; if someone didn't do something soon he knew he was going to run away. It was as simple as that—he was going to break and run.

"Lee," Garve said. He took her elbow and began moving. She shrugged him off, picked up a handful of stones and began heaving them toward Hattie Mills and Amy Fox. Immediately, several of them turned to follow. Peg pushed Hugh ahead of her, pushed again until his hands held rocks and he was following Lee's example.

Silently.

Not even the virtue of ragged, heavy breathing.

The rocks landed on the ground, landed on a chest, and there was no sound at all except the scream of the dying wind.

Colin eased along behind Hugh and Peg, watching, feeling the heavy cans pull at his throbbing shoulders, but not caring because it was going to work. A gap was opening, and as long as Peg and Hugh kept on drawing them to the right, it wouldn't be long before he could—

Lee shrieked, mournful, enraged, and he whirled to see her sprawled on the ground while Garve wrestled with Cart Naughton. He shouted, dropped the fuel cans and started to run, but Hugh put a foot into the back of one knee and drove him to the ground. Helplessly, then, sprawled not thirty feet from his friend, he watched as Garve lifted the dead boy off the sand,

328

turned sharply and had the body dangling over his head. Lee shouted from her position on the ground, and Garve yelled as he tossed Cart into the sea.

Then, breathing heavily, he turned to help Lee, and Graham Otter fell onto Tabor's back and buckled him to the ground. He screamed as the minister's hands tore at his throat, screamed while he tried to kick himself over onto his back. Lee scrambled out of the way, shrieking, crying, picking up her fallen weapon and slamming the stock into Otter's forehead once, and once again, screaming obscenities when nothing happened, sobbing as she turned the weapon around to fire pointblank into the dead man's skull.

Otter flew to one side, and Lee was on her knees, cradling Tabor's head in her lap.

Colin had no idea how much time had passed, certainly not more than a few seconds, before Garve opened his eyes with a slow fluttering. Even before Lee staggered back, shaking her head in denial, he knew what color they would be when Tabor looked up.

Peg took Colin's arm and pulled him to his feet.

Hugh flapped his arms in helpless rage. "Ah, Garve," he said again and again. "Ah, Garve, goddamn it."

Lee backed to the water's edge before she looked down at the shotgun still in one hand. Garve didn't move once he'd gotten to his feet. She braced the stock against her hip and aimed the barrel at his chest.

Colin despaired, looked around and saw Hattie Mills making for their position. With a vague gesture and a wordless moan, he picked up the cans again, to wait for his chance.

He refused to look over to see what Garve was doing.

And when a lane was finally opened, when Frankie broke into a quick shambling that made Hugh fire once, he ran.

Half crouching because of the weight he carried, he dodged an awkward swinging turn by Denise, veered clumsily around a pile of stones, and winced when someone else pulled a trigger, the flash like lightning that illuminated the shack's dingy wall. Another blast, and a fourth, and he was at the front door, his shoulder to it, and over the threshold before he could stop.

Garve. Shit, Garve, I'm sorry.

The stench surged and surrounded him.

He gagged and dropped the cans.

The stench—a fog of rotting flesh and defecation— brought him instantly to his knees. He opened his mouth to breathe while he forced his arms to stop their trembling. Then he saw the shimmering light oddly confined to the back room.

Jesus damn, Colin, Jesus damn.

Matthew, he thought, Matthew—God, I love you.

He lurched against the wall and staggered forward until he fell against the door frame.

Hello, Colin.

The headboard of Gran's bed was shoved against the rear wall, blocked on three sides by candles of varying sizes almost burned down to the floor. At least a hundred, he estimated—white, red, black here and there, all of them glowing an unearthly shade of orange that made him think suddenly of a pumpkin glowing at Halloween. Near his feet on the floor were the littered bodies of at least two dozen gulls and squirrels, and the head of the Doberman with its fangs exposed and its eyes winking green.

None of the light reached the ceiling; all of it was directed at the bed, and Gran D'Grou—he sat with his back to the wall, his legs crossed, his hands folded in his lap. He was naked.

Colin, you be in a hurry to die?

He thought he heard footsteps behind him, heard a shotgun explode in the dark.

Gran was facing him, and Colin had no doubt at all that the old man was dead. His body was shriveled, and there was sand and seaweed clinging to his skin. His mouth was closed.

Jesus, Colin, you are stupid tonight.

And his eyes were wide open.

Look around, Colin, and see what my Lilla give me tonight.

He heard the steps clearly now, and despite a silent command he looked over his shoulder.

A small boy in the doorway, with a huge rock in his hand.

The shotgun.

Peg shouting, Lee screaming.

The boy.

My favorite.

Colin felt it all leave—the hope, the rage, the compulsion to fight back. It slipped out of him and stained the floor; it burned his stomach and loosened his bowels; it made his fingers stiff, and he dropped the can at his feet.

The boy raised his arm.

I think, Colin, he wants you to stay here with me. I told you I had tricks. You never listen. Too bad.

"Matthew?" Colin whispered, unable to move. "Matt?"

The rock struck his shoulder and spun him around, spiraled him to the floor.

The boy lifted his other arm.

"Pal," Colin said.

Jesus damn, Colin. Jesus damn.

Peg called his name, and the wind fluttered the candles.

The boy aimed.

Colin blinked and the can came into focus.

And the rage returned; the artist, the teacher, the would-be father, the lover, gone. He grabbed the can and fumbled off the cap, whirled around and held it over his head.

Colin!

The rock struck him sharply between the shoulders, he grunted, and tossed the can as he pitched forward. It arched over the bed and landed against the wall

331

above Gran's head. It bounced into the dead man's lap, the kerosene spilled onto the nearest candle and flared. Before Colin was able to get back to his knees, the bed and the body and the room were a torch.

He screamed as the flames caught at his jeans; he whirled and ran, grabbing the boy by one arm and dragging him out of the shack as the walls caught, the roof caught, and there was light on the water rippling and rising; he ran, burning, screaming, toward the pines until he looked down at his burden and saw Tommy Fox.

He shoved the boy away, pushed Hugh aside when the doctor tried to stop him, and fell-stumbled-dove into the tide.

The second can exploded, and he saw Pegeen weeping.

There were hands on his arms, dragging him out of the water, pulling off his pants. Hugh nodded when Peg asked if he would be all right. Lee stood over him, and when he grinned they hauled him to his feet so he could give Peg a hug, a quick kiss, and hold her hand. There was no celebration. The joy he felt was dashed when he saw Garve lying with his head in the shadows. When they finally began to stagger from the burning shack, the sprawled bodies of the rest of their friends lay on the sand, mangled, torn, faces up to the night sky, their eyes finally closed.

He had little sense of time left. They were on the flat, on the dune, then on the street and heading back for the cruiser. Someone, he thought it might be Hugh, was talking about salvaging one of the boats at the marina and using it to get back to the mainland. The sea was too high, Lee (he thought) argued, and Mont-gomery hushed her with an uncharacteristic curse.

Garve found a boat, he thought, but couldn't say it. Garve found a boat.

He was tired. He knew he shouldn't be leaning on Peg so heavily, but he was so God-almighty tired that if anything that looked like a bed came within a mile of him he was going to use it and sleep without dreams for the rest of his life.

The fire cast their shadows.

At the patrol car Peg balked at getting in.

Colin knew what she was thinking.

When none of the others moved to help, he took Hugh's long flashlight and walked with her around the deadfall, turning the beam on the path their car had taken into the yard. They spent an hour searching through the rubble, through the rooms, this time opening closets and poking under tables. They spent an hour, and they found nothing. And when they came outside again, Peg had lost the armor she'd forged from her revenge.

At the sidewalk she stopped.

"I . . . we can't go until we find him," she said.

"In the morning," he said. "We'll never find him tonight."

"I won't go."

"You don't have to."

"Hugh said—"

"Hugh says a lot of things. And if he insists, well, there's more than one boat, you know." He put an arm around her waist, held her close. "We'll find him. I promise."

She seemed ready to agree, then shook herself and stared at him. "No. You go if you want. I can't. I just can't."

He touched a hand to her shoulder, nodded *it's all right*, and they walked toward the edge of the woods, toward the path to the cliffs. The trees still whipsawed in the dying storm, the flashlight's beam was coated with spray that had it glittering, fogging, picking out things moving where nothing moved at all.

They stopped at the edge of the path, and he licked at his lips. The way ahead was dark, filled with the growl of the sea climbing the rocks. Peg took his arm; they left the road behind.

"Peg," he whispered, wanting to tell her how fruitless this was. But she tightened her grip to silence him,

333

and he stared ahead, trying to see beyond the reach of the light, swinging it side to side, hunting for a telltale break in the undergrowth.

Five minutes and he was freezing.

Five more and she stumbled, nearly knocking them both down.

He sensed her resolve weakening, yet she pulled him on gently until they reached a widening of the path and saw the body ahead.

"Oh my God," she murmured.

The flashlight poked closer, and the body elongated.

"It's El," he said flatly.

Peg looked away, a cheek against his shoulder, and he had a hand out when he felt her stiffen and clutch him fiercely. He turned quickly, and saw the figure in the middle of the road, the shadow waiting for them in the middle of the path.

It was then he realized he hadn't brought a weapon.

Like a man with a torch fending off a jungle beast, he thrust the flashlight ahead of him, jabbing at the figure as it staggered toward them. Peg whimpered, was ready to bolt and run, when suddenly the light caught the figure's face.

"Matthew!" Peg screamed, and ran to take him in her arms.

His hair was matted in cords over his face, his clothes torn and drenched, but as far as Colin could tell, the boy wasn't injured.

A brief pain in his chest then when Peg cradled and lifted Matt, rocking him while she held him and tried to clean him off at the same time; another draining when he realized that finally it was over. He waited until the boy noticed him as well, and in a three-way joyous spate of talking, yelling, laughing, explaining, he heard something that made him hush them all with a sharp wave.

"What?" he said, taking the boy by the shoulder.

"I said," Matt told him as if he should have known, "I went to find Lilla and make her give you and Mom back. And she did! She really and truly did!"

"Lilla," Peg said dully.

Matt's eyes widened in excitement, in relief. "Yes, honest, Mom! She was in the cave. I went there and she was there. I was real scared at first because she was acting all funny, but then I told her what I wanted and she said okay, and then . . . then . . ." The boy's face darkened, and suddenly he was crying.

Peg carried him back to the car, Colin trailing and swinging the flashlight. As he watched them climb into the back seat, heard Peg's joyous laughter and Hugh's brisk professional manner, he shook his head and walked around to stand next to Lee.

"Lilla," he said.

"Should we look for her?"

"I'm tempted," he answered.

"Colin, no. I'll tell you the truth—I don't know what the hell it was we've just been through, and I don't think I want to know. Ever. Lilla, as far as I'm concerned, can rot alone in this hell."

He hated himself, but he nodded. "I only said I was tempted. I have no intention of finding her. I don't care what Matt says. She could have killed him out there, no matter what she was like after Gran was . . . taken care of."

"Good," she said. "Good."

He took the driver's seat, Lee beside him and holding his arm tightly. A false start and the engine caught, and he drove as fast as he could back toward the village.

As they passed the gas station, Hugh leaned over the back.

"It's done, right?"

"Damn right," Lee said.

"You're sure?"

"Hugh," Colin said, "why don't you shut up?"

"I was referring to Lilla," Montgomery said before slipping back to his seat.

"Yes," he said, and turned to look out the window. "I know."

They passed Naughton's Market, the theater, the bank, the luncheonette.

"Hope you can run a boat," Lee said with a forced laugh as they drove toward the marina.

"I can," Matt volunteered. And when Peg hushed him with a mock scowl and Colin began to laugh, he crossed his arms over his chest and pushed himself into the corner. "Well, I can," he insisted grumpily. "Gee. Nuts. Goddamn."

EPILOGUE

December: After

Twilight.

Silence.

The snow little more than flurries that looped and twirled over the bay's restless waters. A solitary gull coasted, wheeled away; the breeze faded with the light, gusted briefly and set the forest to trembling.

Colin stood behind the nail keg, a booted foot atop it, one gloved hand holding the binoculars while the other flattened the yellow wool cap closer around his ears. He imagined himself encased in a block of clear ice, a contemporary natural sculpture to be discovered by some astonished wanderer who would admire the realism and doubt the medium, and by the first light of Easter he would be a puddle on the landing.

He wanted to laugh, but the effort was too great.

A glance at his watch.

Three hours, not one minute of it passing quickly. It never had, not since he'd started. Every time he took position he remembered, and in remembering could not ignore a single moment. Three hours to relive a weekend no sane man should have survived.

And he'd wondered about that, fretted over it, examined it, and could not yet find an answer.

Sane. He didn't know anymore if he were indeed in his right mind. There were times when he truly believed he had retained his equilibrium, and times when he felt himself constantly, helplessly falling in maddening slow motion, with nothing below him but a pit filled with dead white eyes.

It certainly hadn't been sane that last day on the island, or the day after.

They returned to Peg's house and made the best of a night when no one could sleep. Hugh sat with Lee on the sofa, an arm around her shoulders while she spent the night weeping; Peg took Matt to bed with her, frowning when Colin stood in the doorway hoping to become a part of their waiting. When it didn't happen, he understood—too much had gone on, too many people had died, this wasn't the time for a walk into the sunset.

So he went to the study, sat at the desk and stared at the wall. He didn't know if he slept; perhaps he dozed off. But the next thing he knew, he and Hugh were at Gran's shack, sitting in his car, looking away from the damage the nightcrabs had started.

"We can't bury them all," Hugh said.

"No."

"You see, the police will want to know what happened, and all those graves . . ."

"Yes. I know."

The wind lifted tatters of clothing, strands of reddened hair; the sea had withdrawn to expose a beach as smooth as it must have been before the island had its people.

"And what about Lilla?"

"If Matt's right and she stayed down there in the cave . . ."

Then she was dead, drowned. No sense in hunting despite the fact that he could not imagine her gone with the others. She knew about Gran and knew what the old man had taught her, even after her mind had finally hidden itself in madness. If she were still alive, she was dangerous, more than anyone would ever believe.

"What'll we tell the police?"

"The storm is out," Hugh said immediately, taking away his one decent solution. "It was never that strong, and they'd never go for it." He turned. "Colin, there has to be a disaster here. It has to be storm-related, but it can't be the storm."

The wind blew steadily. It was a breeze in contrast to the Screamer of the night before, but a wind nevertheless, and even as he rechecked the island he didn't know who had the idea first, who seconded it, who decided they wouldn't tell the others. But it started with the market—a fire that fed on the cartons and boxes, ceiling and walls, was curiously dull in the dull morning air as it sparked to the church, which torched the library, which turned trees to matches and caught the building Peg's drug store was in.

A house was started.

The Anchor Inn, where they assumed investigators would notice the wires from the traffic light fallen during the night.

A second house, just to be sure, and the wind did the rest.

Without a word, using gestures only, they drove back to Gran's shack and piled as many bodies as they could into the trunk, into the back seat. The Adamses they returned to their own house; Hattie went to the library; Tess to her front yard under the wreck of Colin's car.

Hours transporting the dead to their temporary graves.

Then they wrapped Garve in a sheet and rowed him out beyond the jetty. Colin remembered the night on the beach, just before Gran's funeral, and knew at least that Garve wouldn't be alone.

The body sank without floating.

The fire spread, filling the island with the sound of wood crackling, of windows breaking, of tree trunks steaming as the sap boiled and expanded.

Then they found the boat Garve had hidden, rowed

through the smoke to the mainland, and watched the light for almost an hour before they began the long walk into Flocks.

A block outside town Lee shook her head. "I'm not going in there," she said. "They'll stare. The questions . . ."

It took the rest of the day to reach the other side, check into a motel with the money they pooled. They slept. They heard the news on the radio—electrical fires and the Screamer. A number of questions and the promise of investigations. They heard the cars filled with families who had fled on Thursday, and more filled with sightseers passing on the highway.

On the third day Hugh displayed a credit card. "This," he said, "is going to get me away from this goddamned morgue."

"What about Lilla?" he wanted to know.

"She's dead," he said simply. And he hitchhiked to the next town, rented a car, and returned for Lee. There were no good-byes, no tears. They checked out and drove west as fast as Hugh dared.

That night he and Peg sat in his room while Matt slept on the lumpy double bed.

"We have to do something," she said quietly. "We can't stay here forever."

She was pale, her hair without highlights, and she plucked endlessly at her shirtfront. "I'm taking Matt to my mother's for a while," she said in a rush. "I called her as soon as the news hit." She wouldn't look at him. "I had to. I couldn't let her think I was dead."

"Sure, of course." But why didn't you tell me?

She did look then. "I want you to come with us," she said. "I really do. But I can't let you just now." She shook her head. "These things are supposed to bring people closer together."

"Disasters do," he said. "I'm not sure about nightmares."

"I don't dream."

"Neither do I."

"Don't be mad."

"I won't be. This isn't like a plane crash, or a flood, or something like that. I'm . . . I'm trying to figure out how I feel, and I don't know. But, Peg, I *can't* go. Not until I'm sure."

"That's stupid," she said angrily. "It's done, for God's sake. It's done and I want to get away."

"Then do take the boy to your mother's," he said reasonably. "Take him, and I'll keep in touch."

They rose, embraced and kissed, and he still loved her. But he didn't try to change her mind. He only helped her get on a bus, watched as she climbed aboard and disappeared into the polarized dark. Matt stood beside him, holding his hand.

"You aren't going to forget me?"

"Hey, pal, you want me to shave your head?"

He smiled, of a sort. "You won't stay very long, will you? Mom's real sad you won't come. Me, too. I thought we were gonna be a family now." He frowned his puzzlement. "You gotta stay?"

"Just till I'm sure, pal, just till I'm sure."

Peg called to him softly as the bus's engine belched exhaust.

"Then listen," Matt said, pulling on his arm until he was kneeling beside him. They hugged, and Colin kissed his cheek, hugged him again. "Listen, I think everybody wasn't right about Lilla. She didn't let them get me. She really didn't."

"I know, I know." He stood. "You practice your drawing now, you hear? You be sure your grandmother lets you practice."

"I'll draw Lilla."

"A tree, the gulls, but I don't think your mother would appreciate a picture of Lilla now."

He pouted. "Nobody listened to me," he said almost angrily. "I kept saying she was a witch, but nobody listened."

They'd been over this ground a dozen times already, and Colin had exhausted himself trying to make the boy see that just because she befriended him didn't make her a saint. But he'd been too put upon by the other kids, for his art and his looks, and it wasn't surprising that he grabbed affection where he could.

"Time, pal," he said instead, and helped the boy up the steps.

And the following day Colin was gone as well, driving in a rented car toward Maine, not very far each day, less as each day passed, until as last he couldn't stand not knowing and returned to the motel.

From gossip and papers he learned of the inquiries, the few unanswered questions no one seemed to care about since the island wasn't a place people worried about for long. There had been funerals for the few bodies found in the burned houses and along the shore of the bay. And those who had left before, left again because rumor had it the island was haunted. Flocks laughed, albeit uneasily; fire and wind was better than anything resembling magic.

Lee and Hugh returned two weeks later. They walked into his room, he embraced Lee and shook Hugh's hand, and they said nothing because there was nothing to say.

The watch began on Christmas Eve.

Peg and Matt returned the day after Christmas, and there were smiles and laughter and an exchange of simple presents. He rode each day to the landing and watched the island turn to winter.

Three hours.

He lowered the binoculars and let himself sigh as loudly as he could, as though at last the nightmare were expelled from his lungs. No boats had gone there, no sign of life, nothing at all.

He supposed it was a form of therapy, and he didn't mind that it had taken so long. Tonight he was going to treat them all to the best dinner he could afford, and they would sleep without lights, and tomorrow they would leave this damned place behind.

He dragged the nail keg back to the shed, and after a

moment's thought buried the gull by the threshold. Then he returned to his spot and looked at the place where he'd thought he'd found a home, and understood—he hoped—that his home was at the motel with Peg.

What the hell, he thought, grinning; started over once, I can start over again.

He turned, then, and saw Matt standing at the top of the slope.

He didn't know whether to scold or laugh . . . laughed when the boy raced into his arms, hugged him and held his hand.

"We couldn't wait," he said eagerly. "We couldn't wait!"

Colin crouched and faced the water, and Matt stood behind him with his chin on the man's shoulder, his arms around Colin's chest. He felt tears in his eyes, and felt so damned fine he wanted to shout.

"There," he said, pointing to Haven's End, "is where you and I met, pal, and that's the way we should remember it."

"Are we going to live somewhere else?"

"What do you think about New England?"

"Is it pretty? Does it have an ocean?"

"Yes, yes, and there are mountains and lots of deer and moose and bear and raccoons, and it's going to be just . . . just great."

"You'll paint again!" Matt said excitedly.

"You can bet on it."

"The kids . . ."

Colin reached up and cupped the back of the boy's head. "I won't let them make fun of you, Matt. You do just what you always do, and I'll be there to help you." Then he rose, stretched and imagined the others waiting, just over the rise. God, it'll be great to be human again.

"You and me, we'll take care of Mom, too."

He lifted the binoculars; one last check before the end.

"And I'll take care of you."

He closed his eyes tightly, opened them, blinked and watched the island through the snow.

"I miss Lilla," Matt said forlornly. "She was my friend."

"I know, pal. I know."

He had to wipe flakes from the lenses with his gloves, and the view was slightly blurred.

"Can I look?"

One last sweep of the dead island, and he slipped the strap from around his neck, handed the binoculars to the boy and put a hand on his shoulder. "Not too long," he said. "Your mother's waiting for us, remember?"

Matt nodded, and looked, and when he'd had enough he took Colin's hand and they walked back to the road. Peg was standing by the car, Hugh and Lee inside grinning. Colin waved, felt a surge and broke into a run.

Matt followed more slowly, stopping once. Turning around. Wondering if Colin had seen Lilla standing in the trees. Standing and smiling, her lips moving in silent singing. If he had, it didn't matter. Lilla was *his* friend now, and some day he'd be big enough to come back here on his own.

Some day he would ask her to teach him her songs.